BIRDS OF A
FEATHER

BIRDS OF A FEATHER

A Jack Taggart Mystery

Don Easton

DUNDURN
TORONTO

Editor: Shannon Whibbs
Design: Courtney Horner
Printer: Marquis

Library and Archives Canada Cataloguing in Publication

Easton, Don
    Birds of a feather / Don Easton.

(A Jack Taggart mystery)
Issued also in electronic formats.
ISBN 978-1-4597-0219-6

    I. Title. II. Series: Easton, Don. Jack Taggart mystery.

PS8609.A78B57 2012   C813'.6   C2011-908008-7

1   2   3   4   5   16   15   14   13   12

  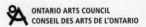

We acknowledge the support of the **Canada Council for the Arts** and the **Ontario Arts Council** for our publishing program. We also acknowledge the financial support of the **Government of Canada** through the **Canada Book Fund** and **Livres Canada Books**, and the **Government of Ontario** through the **Ontario Book Publishing Tax Credit** and the **Ontario Media Development Corporation**.

Care has been taken to trace the ownership of copyright material used in this book. The author and the publisher welcome any information enabling them to rectify any references or credits in subsequent editions.

J. Kirk Howard, President

Printed and bound in Canada.
www.dundurn.com

Dundurn	Gazelle Book Services Limited	Dundurn
3 Church Street, Suite 500	White Cross Mills	2250 Military Road
Toronto, Ontario, Canada	High Town, Lancaster, England	Tonawanda, NY
M5E 1M2	LA1 4XS	U.S.A. 14150

In memory of Jose Refugio Rubalcava

chapter one

It was three o'clock in the morning when Special Agent Greg Patton of the United States Customs Service in El Paso, Texas, dropped off his partner at his house. Forty-five minutes later, he arrived home to his own bed.

Even then, Patton couldn't fall asleep right away. His adrenalin hadn't settled from the night's activities. He and his partner had crawled over a fence into a backyard to peer through a window to catch a glimpse of some drug traffickers, only to discover a vicious dog sleeping under a back porch, which awoke and chased them back over the fence.

Would the drug traffickers suspect it was law enforcement agents whose shadows disappeared into the night? Perhaps they would think it was only a couple of the many countless thieves who preferred the cover of darkness.... Another hour passed before Patton fell into a restless sleep.

Patton's neighbours in the quiet suburb of El Paso, Texas, considered him to be a good neighbour. He was quick to lend a hand and was a man who always had a smile on his face. They knew he worked for customs, but he never wore a uniform. By his ever-changing appearance, from beards to short hair and back to long, they knew his work was likely dangerous.

El Paso is situated directly across the border from Ciudad Juarez, Mexico. Ciudad Juarez, or simply Juarez, as the locals refer to it, is renowned as a hotbed of illegal activity. Drug smuggling by warring drug cartels vying for supremacy over the narco dollar have resulted in a daily body count comprised of criminals and non-criminals alike.

El Paso had become a major point of entry for cocaine smuggled into the United States. Originating in South America, the cocaine was turned over to Mexican drug lords for continued distribution north, including Canada. Along with the drug smuggling came a host of other criminal ventures, such as contract murders of law enforcement officers, gun-running, and human smuggling, to name but a few.

The fact was that Patton's work was more than dangerous. It was dangerous to the extreme. He worked out of a secret office on a joint task force that included agents from the Federal Bureau of Investigation; the U.S. Drug Enforcement Administration; Alcohol, Tobacco Firearms, and Explosives; as well as special agents from the U.S. Customs Service.

There was a good reason why their office location was secret, as were their frequent excursions across the border into Mexico. One U.S. DEA investigator, Special Agent Enrique S. Camarena*, who had been assigned to work in Mexico, was kidnapped and tortured for two days before his eventual murder. A Mexican pilot who

---

* The DEA investigation into the torture and murder of Special Agent Enrique S. Camarena was the most in depth and longest-running investigation in DEA history.

had helped him locate a large marijuana grow operation was also murdered.

The subsequent DEA investigation discovered that the murders were orchestrated with the complicity of the brother to the then Mexican president. It was also learned a doctor had been utilized to keep Camarena alive and conscious to endure his torture for as long as possible before dying.

Corruption of the Mexican government, military, judiciary, and law enforcement agencies had reached a new high. One poll estimated 97 percent of policemen in Mexico were corrupt. Despite the high risk, Greg Patton and his partner, Special Agent John Adams, made frequent trips across the border. Today would be Patton's last trip.

It was noon when Patton awoke, showered, put on his jockey shorts, and padded barefoot into the kitchen to the smell of fresh coffee and bacon. Becky smiled affectionately and he kissed her and gave her a warm embrace.

Stepping back, he gestured to Billy and Samantha, who were yelling and chasing each other in the backyard with a garden hose. "Isn't today Friday?" he asked.

"Yes, but school is out this week. They only have to go in if they are writing exams."

"I see."

"Sorry, I knew you were late coming in. I tried to keep them quiet for as long as I could, but —"

"It's okay," he smiled, while giving Becky a pat on her backside. "It was time to get up, anyway. I have to go back to work in an hour. Have they had lunch yet? It would be nice to eat together before I go."

It was an hour later when Patton started the Honda Civic and backed out of his driveway, pausing only to wave at his family before heading off. His car, which was dented and scraped, did not look like it belonged to a law enforcement agency. In fact, it used to belong to a drug trafficker, but U.S. law allowed forfeiture of seizures by authorities to be used by the law enforcement agencies who seized them. It allowed for a large assortment of covert vehicles to be used by the investigators. The only downside was there was not a budget to go along with each vehicle to keep it properly maintained and repaired.

Normally Patton would have been required to drop the car off at the office for the night, but due to the late circumstances … and the fact the Honda Civic wasn't exactly a prized car in the office, he had driven it home.

He realized he was slightly ahead of schedule to pick up Adams and decided to take a slight detour and drive past the house with the dog. There was little doubt it was being used by drug runners. Intermittent surveillance had shown up to a dozen different muscle cars with jacked-up rear ends and custom-built hood exhausts parked in the driveway. *Low-life punks, but who controls them?*

Most of the cars had Mexican plates, which made it difficult to identify who was driving. Any inquiries to Mexican authorities would either return as being plates owned by someone else, or, if the dealers were connected to a drug cartel, then the cartel would be notified of the investigator's interest. Often it was only through the use of surveillance, photographs, and facial recognition that the framework of the drug cartels was identified.

Patton's excitement grew as he drove past the house. Parked in the driveway was a new Mercedes. It was painted emerald green with dark tinted windows. Tinted windows were common in the area to help keep the heat out, but it also made it difficult to identify who was driving. Patton slowed as he went past. It had a Mexican plate, but it was still worth copying down.

He then drove to the end of the block and parked where he could still see the Mercedes, but wondered if he should risk leaving to go get Adams. Would it still be there when they returned? The decision was made for him when the car backed out of the driveway and headed off in the opposite direction.

Patton followed, trying to keep his distance. Unlike in Hollywood movies, a one-car surveillance seldom went undetected. Today, however, the Mercedes ventured out onto a well-travelled road where the presence of other cars gave him cover. Soon he found himself on the Bridge of the Americas, crossing over into Juarez. His was the second car behind the Mercedes and he was glad the Mexican customs agent treated him like the others, with a lackadaisical wave of his hand to allow him entry.

The afternoon traffic in Juarez was heavy. It slowed the Mercedes while continuing to provide other cars for cover. The only disadvantage was the possibility of being left behind at a red light.

When the Mercedes stopped at a red light, three car lengths in front of him, Patton took the opportunity to call Adams. Unfortunately, like most people on surveillance, his attention was focused on who he was following ... and not on who might be following him.

Adams picked up when Patton rang and he quickly updated his partner on the situation. Adams wasn't overly concerned his partner was in Juarez. They were short-staffed and often ventured into Mexico alone. Sometimes it was even safer. One man in a car looked a lot less like a police officer than two men did. Especially two men who were in their thirties, physically fit, and not looking or acting like gawking tourists who had left their brains at home.

There was something else that marked them as law enforcement officers, although neither was aware of it. They both dressed casually and believed their infrequent shaving routine made them less conspicuous. Perhaps it did, but neither man was a trained undercover operative. Like most officers with police training, they portrayed a degree of self-confidence. Coupled with a strong Alpha-male attitude, it tended to make them stand out for who they really were.

It was one of the first lessons Adams would later learn when he worked with such an operative. There are times to act aggressive and times not to. Instinctively knowing when to do which could be a matter of life or death.

"Okay, we're moving again and he's turned down a side street," said Patton. "I'll call you back when I'm done and let you know when I can pick you up."

"Sounds good. Don't take any —"

"Shit, looks like I got company," said Patton, his voice going up an octave. "A black-and-white tucked in behind me and one of their crew cab pickups is coming up alongside. The cop driving is really giving me the hairy eyeball."

"Forget the Mercedes and get the hell out of there!" urged Adams.

"You don't have to tell — fuck!"

Adams heard the sound of crunching metal and Patton's high-pitched yell. "I got rammed into a row of parked cars! I ... I —"

"Don't stop!" screamed Adams. "Step on it! Get outta there and run for the border!"

"Can't! I'm blocked in!" came the frantic reply. "Fuck, here they come. They got their automatics out!"

"Don't hang up! Can you get one of their plates?"

In response, all Adams heard was the sounds of men shouting, followed by breaking glass and Patton screaming in pain before the phone went dead.

chapter two

On Friday afternoon in Chilliwack, British Columbia, Jack Taggart rose from his chair in the front row of the high school auditorium and clapped when Marcie finished giving her valedictorian speech. Beside him, Natasha, holding their seven-month-old baby, Michael, also rose. On his other side, Jack's sister, Liz, and his brother-in-law, Ben, also stood, clapping loudly.

Jack was proud of Marcie. She was still only seventeen years old, but was graduating from grade twelve with top honours.

Marcie had not had an easy life. Jack was a trained undercover operative for the Royal Canadian Mounted Police who was assigned to an Intelligence Unit targeting organized crime. Marcie was twelve years old when Jack rescued her from a life of drugs and prostitution. Half the credit to her success, he believed, went to Liz and Ben, who officially adopted her at that time.

The other half went to Marcie. She was intuitive, intelligent, and a hard worker. Her plans were to go to university and become a child-protection worker. Not an easy job, but one she had her heart set on. She was a caring person and, given her challenging background, he knew she would make a good one.

Jack thought she gave an excellent speech, but could see there was something else on her mind. Part way through her delivery, some late arrivals came into the gymnasium. He saw the optimistic look on her face, followed by disappointment as she continued to talk.

She's worried and it's not stage fright. Someone didn't show up...

As the audience sat back down, he locked eyes with Marcie. She was smiling, but he could tell it was not sincere. Jack quit smiling at her and raised one eyebrow. *What's up?*

Marcie's smile disappeared. She gave him a slight nod.

During a break in the ceremonies, Marcie took him aside and the words spilled out of her.

"My friend ... Lily, she's not here tonight!" said Marcie.

"Who is Lily?"

"I told you. She's my friend. Lily Rae. She should have been here! We were supposed to graduate together!"

"Maybe her car broke down or something."

"No! You don't understand. I haven't seen her for over two weeks."

"Have you called her home? What about her parents or family?" asked Jack.

"She only has her mom. She never knew her father and doesn't have any brothers or sisters. Her mom called me this morning. She hasn't seen her, either. Lily told her she was going away with her boyfriend for a couple of days, but that was a week ago. Her mom tried to call her on her cell, but turns out Lily had left it at home."

"Intentionally?"

"I don't think so. Since meeting this guy she is always forgetting stuff. I mentioned it to her once and she just got all dreamy-eyed and said I would also be that way when I fell in love. Both her mom and me figured she would be back before today. She was really excited about the graduation. We had made plans to be together tonight. Well, sort of."

"Sort of?"

"Lily and I had a fight a month ago," confessed Marcie. "We haven't talked to each other since. Still, I thought we would make up tonight and be friends again."

"What was the fight about?"

"It was my fault." Marcie sighed. "I should have kept my yap shut. I told her I didn't like her new boyfriend. She said I was jealous because I don't have a boyfriend. I said no way. I don't trust the guy. There's somethin' not right about him. I think he's a player."

"A player? As in dealing dope or into gangs?"

"Well … I'm not sure. She only met him about three months ago. His name is Earl Porter. He's like, thirty years old. She told me they're in love. I met him a couple of times when he picked her up at school. He drives a black Mustang convertible and comes across as a real charmer. Real slick. Lily mentioned he likes to gamble and throw money around. That's when I told her I didn't trust him."

"Sounds like Lily should know better."

"She said he's rich because his parents died in a car accident and he got a lot of insurance money. Maybe he did. I don't know."

"Is Lily into the dope scene or hanging out with gangsters?"

"No way." Marcie shook her head vehemently. "She wouldn't have been my friend if she was. She's really straight. Doesn't even smoke pot."

"What? Do you?"

"Hell no! Come on, Uncle Jack! Are you kidding? After what I've been through I won't even take a sip of wine because I'm scared I'll end up back on the spike. I like to be in control of my body and my mind."

"So why is Lily hanging around some guy who is a dozen years older? He sounds like a loser."

"The thing is, Lily will believe anything a guy tells her if he gives her a little attention."

"A lot of teenage girls are like that," Jack remarked.

"Yeah, but I think she's more needy than most. The only real family she has is her mom. Even that is not good. Her mom was in a car accident four years ago and has been in a wheelchair ever since."

"Sounds like Lily has had to grow up fast."

"Yeah, it hasn't been easy on either of them. Her mom is in chronic pain. Lily told me she thinks her mom is addicted to prescription drugs. Since the accident, Lily has been more of a mother to her mom than her mom has been to her. Don't get me wrong, her mom's a real nice lady, but, well, you know, sometimes life sucks." Marcie shrugged.

"Does Lily have any history of running away from home?"

Marcie frowned. "Yeah, about two years ago, but even then she came back after a couple of days."

"Where did she go then?" Jack asked.

"She spent two nights sleeping in someone's barn. I didn't know her then, but I think she was stressed out over looking after her mom all the time and going to school. The two of them had a fight over what she wanted to wear to school. Lily told me she was really embarrassed about it and would never do it again."

"Maybe she did run away again," mused Jack.

"No way. This is different." Marcie shook her head again, her mouth set in a grim line. "There's something wrong. She should have been here tonight. Even if she is still angry with me, this grad was a big deal for her. She talked a lot about it."

"What's her mom doing about it?"

"She was upset when she called me and said she was going to report her missing. But I'm worried. The police will hear she ran away before … you know how that goes. I bet they don't exactly bust their asses looking for her. I was hoping you could check out her boyfriend or something."

Jack nodded. "I'll look into it. Does she have her own car?"

"No. I was always giving her a ride until she met Earl."

"Is there anything else?"

Marcie took a picture out of her purse and handed it to Jack. "This is her. I scanned it and printed it on my computer so I don't need it back. Thought maybe you might need it if … if … like if there was an unidentified body in a morgue or —"

"You're jumping to conclusions," said Jack, looking at the picture of a pretty girl with long red hair. "Does she always wear that gold stud earring?"

"The earrings change, but she always wears a pendant. You can't see it in the picture because of her blouse, but she never takes it off. It's a little silver frog with ruby-red eyes to match her hair." A small smile crossed Marcie's face and she added, "Sometimes I would tease her and call her froggy …" Marcie looked at Jack and quickly added, "But not in front of anyone! It wasn't being mean. I just —"

"It's okay. Sounds to me like you're still her friend … and friends sometimes have arguments," said Jack reassuringly. "Bet she gets over it. In the meantime, I'll check out Porter and see what he has to say."

"I don't even have his number. Neither does Lily's mom."

"Don't worry. I'll find him. I bet she shows up, too. Maybe they eloped or something."

"Yeah, I hope so."

"Give me a couple of days and I'll get back to you, but if you hear from her, let me know right away."

"I will."

"Now ... I want you to enjoy yourself," said Jack with mock sternness. "Go out tonight and have fun. You've earned it."

Greg Patton lay with his face mashed into the floor mat behind the driver's seat of the Mexican police crew-cab truck. His gun, badge, and wallet had been taken from him before he was propelled into the vehicle. One policeman pinned him to the floor with a knee on his back. Patton felt the muzzle of a pistol digging into the base of his skull. He remained still and hoped the gun wasn't cocked to prevent an accidental discharge as the truck sped through the streets.

When they arrived at their destination, Patton was dragged out of the truck and brought into a small police station. For a moment, being in a station gave him some hope. *Better than being made to kneel before a shallow grave in the desert ...*

Even when six officers shoved and manhandled him into an empty cellblock in the rear of the station, he was still hopeful. *Perhaps they plan to lock me up for a while. Put the fear of god into me before letting me go ...*

Patton was more concerned when he was forced to strip completely naked. *Okay, guys, you've humiliated me. Yeah I've got a small dick. Everyone have a good laugh and then let me go ...*

What followed wasn't laughter. It was the faces of determined, angry men as they handcuffed him spread-eagled to the bars of a cell. Next, a pail of water doused his naked body.

Patton looked at the face of a man who approached him with an electric cattle prod and closed his eyes.

Briefly, he thought of Enrique Camarena and the horror he endured before he died.

"Special Agent Patton of the big American customs, how are you?" asked a voice with a heavy Spanish accent.

Patton opened his eyes and saw a man in a police captain's uniform smiling at him.

"What do you want?" asked Patton.

The captain gave a curt nod and the man with the cattle prod stepped forward. For a moment, Patton felt like someone had used a sledge hammer to drive his nuts up into his stomach. His head jerked back, hitting the bars and his jaw snapped shut, biting his tongue, before emitting a bloody scream.

"What I want, Special American Agent Patton, is to kill you in the most painful way possible. But ... before you die, there are some things we want to know. Things like what are the names of the people you work with? Their addresses ... what cars they drive. The names of their wives and children. The names of your wife and children. What schools they attend."

chapter three

John Adams sprung into action as soon as Patton's phone went dead. His first call was to notify his office. Did they have any investigators in Juarez at the moment? It turned out that four FBI agents from the downtown office were in one car returning from interviewing a jail warden at a Mexican prison. They were still in Juarez and would cover off one of the main routes through the city in the hopes of spotting the kidnappers.

Adams ruefully thought about the four agents travelling together for safety reasons. He and Patton often took a chance on going it alone. Now it was coming back to bite them in the ass. His next move was to yell for his wife, Yolanda, who was outside watering plants on their deck.

Yolanda was born in Mexico, but her father was a chemical engineer and they immigrated to the United States when she was a teenager. There was a happy innocence about her face that Adams adored. She had a certain look and smile like she was waiting for him to crack his next joke. That look vanished when Adams said, "I need you to call your lover. Make it urgent."

Adams was going to tell her they had grabbed Patton on the other side, but decided not to. The four of them were good friends and he was concerned the stress would show in her voice. He would tell her after.

It wasn't the first time Yolanda had called this man. John had explained to her that the phone calls were likely being monitored. Any suspicion on the part of those listening would have a deadly impact on the man she was calling ... and perhaps on her husband, as well.

Police Commander Jose Refugio Rubalcava sat behind the large wooden desk in his office. The desk was scarred up and had more than one bullet hole in it. At one time it had been varnished, but most of that had long since disappeared, leaving it to absorb a variety of stains.

Leaning against the wall behind him and within easy reach were an assortment of loaded shotguns, rifles, and automatic weapons. On the top of his desk were four pistols. Theoretically, the weapons were for him to sign out to his men. In reality, Rubalcava often wondered if he would be able to grab them in time to save himself from his men.

Rubalcava had ample cause to be worried. He was trying to be an honest cop. A very dangerous thing to be in Juarez, considering his six predecessors had all been murdered at the same desk he was sitting at. Rubalcava knew that many, if not all the murders, had been committed by policemen who still worked at his station.*

The choice given his predecessors was simple: *plata o plomo* — silver or lead. Six had bravely chosen not to accept the bribes. Their bravery had done nothing to

---

* As shocking and unbelievable as it may seem, nothing in this paragraph is fiction.

thwart the ever-increasing control the drug cartels were spreading across Mexico and North America.

Rubalcava was trying a different approach. On occasion he knew he had to accept the silver to stay alive ... or at least appear to keep the money. Local charities had done well from his kindness.

Rubalcava's position did not demand that he wear a uniform, so he tended to dress casually with grey slacks and a short-sleeved shirt open at the neck. Today his shirt was a light charcoal colour that matched his hair. His wife said it made him look handsome.

Rubalcava knew better. At one time he was considered handsome, but the constant worry had caused him to look much older than he really was. His hair was prematurely greying and deep crevices cut through the dark sacks of skin below his eyes. His eyes once held sparkle and were quick to smile, but in the last few years they had found little to smile about.

From the outer office, Rubalcava heard a ripple of excited, gleeful whispers spread amongst his men. Something was going on, but he decided to ignore it. He knew he was not completely trusted. Rumours persisted that he talked to the Americans too much.

Police commanders were in a position where it was expected that they might talk to the Americans on occasion. The drug lords actually welcomed it as a way of finding out what the Americans were up to. The information Rubalcava obtained for the cartels, however, was usually insignificant or too long after the fact to be of benefit. When confronted about this, Rubalcava said perhaps the Americans did not trust him, either.

There was another small commotion in the outer office and he decided to take a look. This time the voices were not whispers. One of his men, Detective Sanchez, had given the secretary a gift. She had always ignored his advances before, but appeared delighted with the small silver frog pendant dangling from a chain. The frog's red eyes matched her lipstick.

Rubalcava forced a smile and tried to look pleased with the happy atmosphere. *I wonder who was robbed or killed in order for him to give that gift?* He saw Sanchez eyeing him and their eyes met briefly. Sanchez smirked and turned his attention back to the secretary. *He knows what I am thinking ...*

Sanchez was protected by a drug cartel headed by Rafael Aguilar Guajardo. It was the top drug cartel in the region, although their supremacy was being hotly contested by the rival Sinaloa cartel.

The Sinaloa cartel was originally based out of the Mexican states of Baja, Sinaloa, Durango, Sonora, and Chihuahua, but had expanded operations and as of late had been encroaching on territory long held by the Guajardo cartel. At the present time, the Guajardo cartel still remained firmly in control of most of Juarez and Sanchez knew he had nothing to fear from his commander.

Rubalcava casually scanned the office again. *The excitement and whispers I heard earlier are not over a stolen pendant. Something else has happened ...* His thoughts were interrupted when his telephone rang and he went back to his office to answer it.

He immediately recognized the sexy voice asking to meet him again. Her husband had stepped out. They only had a few minutes of precious time before he would return. Rubalcava agreed and hung up the phone. *I wonder what John Adams's wife really looks like ...*

chapter four

It was late Friday afternoon when Jack arrived home and called the RCMP Telecommunications Centre to check Earl Porter's name on the Canadian Police Information Centre's computer. The CPIC query did not show any criminal record, but a notation did come back to say he was of interest to the Vancouver RCMP Drug Section.

Jack's next call was to Sammy in Drug Section.

"Porter, yeah, he used to be of interest to us," replied Sammy. "Not now, somebody must have forgotten to remove him from CPIC."

"What's the scoop?" asked Jack.

"Two years ago, Porter came up as a close associate of a guy who was our main target in an undercover operation. A fellow named Clive Slater."

"What's the story on Slater?"

"He's a real pompous ass who likes to throw his money around in the night-club circuit. He drives a red Ferrari 430 F1 Spider and tries to act like he is a mafia don or something. We had a snitch who told us Porter and Slater were involved in coke in a big way."

"Do you still have the snitch?"

"No. Last I heard the snitch is in jail in Ontario," said Sammy. "He wasn't deemed to be all that reliable, anyway. He was one of those types of guys who just suspects something, but then relays it as fact."

"How did your investigation end up?" asked Jack.

"Well, at the time we did some checking and it turned out Porter and Slater had business connections in Ciudad Juarez, Mexico. Porter owned a company that made tourist trinkets and Slater was involved in a fruit company. We had our liaison officer out of Mexico City make some inquiries for us. According to the Mexican police, the companies are legit, but the LO said the police are so corrupt down there that you have to take everything they tell you with a grain of salt."

"Sounds like the companies might be used for laundering money," said Jack.

"Could be, but neither of them have ever been caught with any coke."

"Maybe they're the financiers?"

"There's always that possibility," Sammy agreed. "We tried to snare them both in a UC operation, but Slater was too smart. Our undercover operator spent three months befriending him. Then he was with Slater in a nightclub one night and Slater, being the asshole he is, laughed and said he appreciated the RCMP buying him all these drinks."

"Who was the operator?"

"Ken Hales, out of Calgary."

"I've worked with him. He's a hell of a good operator," Jack commented.

"Yeah, I know."

"Maybe the Mexicans tipped Slater off after the LO made inquiries."

"Possibly."

"No problem then if I take a look at Porter and perhaps Slater?" asked Jack.

"Fill your boots," replied Sammy. "Neither are on our target list. Like I said, someone forgot to remove them from CPIC. We've had to reprioritize. Known gang members who are killing each other off are our number-one concern."

Adams crossed the Bridge of the Americas and was waved through customs. He had not bothered to go to the office and get a car, instead opting to use his own car. Time was of the essence. He had little hope that his office, currently going through channels with the American ambassador in Mexico City, would have any luck in getting Patton back alive.

The four FBI agents had agreed to stay in Juarez to assist ... providing assistance was still possible. That hope lay in the person Adams was going to meet.

Adams cursed and glanced at his watch. The minutes were ticking past and he accelerated along cluttered narrow streets to get to one particular back alley.

chapter five

Rubalcava saw the questioning glances of his men as he hurried to leave the office. As a commander, he was normally at his desk all day, except for three o'clock in the afternoon, when he went to pick his children up from school. Picking them up was more than a safety issue. Seeing the bright happy faces of his two sons gave him hope. Hope that someday the future of the Mexican people would also brighten. He had sworn he would do what he could to make that possible.

"Commander?" the secretary asked, while glancing at her watch. "It is only two o'clock."

"I know. I have to meet an old friend," he replied.

Like Adams, Rubalcava drove at high speed with a constant eye in his rear-view mirror. Even though he was satisfied he wasn't being followed, he still parked his car two blocks away from his destination. From there he cautiously made his way toward the alley on foot, while still taking the time to dart into a couple of shops along the way to see who might enter behind him.

Rubalcava knew if he were seen secretly meeting a gringo there would be serious questions. If the gringo was identified as a U.S. Customs agent, he knew any lie he could come up with would likely not be accepted and would result in his execution. He also knew Adams realized the danger. *What has happened?*

Adams sat low in his seat as he slowly drove down the alley in his white Celica. His windshield was tinted, making it difficult for people to see in, but the other windows were clear. There were few gringos in this part of the city, but it was also an area not known to be of interest to the cartels. Rubalcava stepped out from an alcove and Adams unlocked the passenger door.

"*Amigo,*" said Rubalcava with a worried smile on his face as he got in the car. "It is always good to see you." As usual, Rubalcava made no comment about the extreme risk in which Adams had placed him and instead treated their meeting like a friend who was happy to see him.

Adams didn't take the time to exchange niceties. The words tumbled out of him as if he were an auctioneer.

Rubalcava's face darkened. "This house, with the Mercedes that your partner followed. Which cartel did they belong to? Guajardo or Sinaloa?"

"I don't know. We were still trying to find out. An anonymous phone call complained of lots of men coming and going at all hours of the day and night. Lots of souped-up cars being driven by Mexicans who look like gangsters. Greg and I spent the last couple of nights trying to identify who they were."

"I do not have much that could help you if it was the Sinaloa cartel, but if it was the Guajardo ... it could explain why some men in my office were whispering and smiling about something an hour ago."

Adams checked his watch. "It was an hour and twenty-five minutes ago when Greg was grabbed. Maybe they heard the news. It fits. Would Rafael Guajardo be directly involved? If we locate him —"

"No, he would not risk being involved. Besides, Guajardo has been meeting some other drug lords in Cancun this last week. He has not returned yet and may not even know about it. The two jackals he left in charge, Vicente Carrillo Fuentes or his brother, Amado Carrillo Fuentes, could have okayed and planned the kidnapping on their own. Even then, they would have turned it over to someone else to complete. Do you know what colour the Mercedes is?"

"Green. Why?"

"Now it is coming together in my mind. Below the Carrillo Fuentes brothers, there are three lower bosses, who also happen to be brothers. One of them, a big fat man by the name of Chico, drives a green Mercedes. Chico controls much of the prostitution and collects money from the pimps who work for him. He often goes into El Paso to collect money from pimps who operate out of some strip bar. The Red something."

"The Red Poker Saloon?" asked Adams.

"Yes, that is it. You know the place?"

"I've been there. It's full of pimps, drug dealers, bikers, you get the picture. Does Chico control a particular police station here in Juarez?"

"Not him, directly ... but of course the Guajardo cartel controls many," replied Rubalcava.

"Do you think the police who grabbed Greg would take him back to their station?"

"Possibly. If they don't intend to keep him alive long they might take him there. If they plan on torturing him over a period of a few days they would take him to some place more remote. Probably outside the city."

Adams winced. "What police station would you suspect the most?"

"If he was taken to a police station, I think it would be one of two. Both are small and in outlying areas. The captains in both stations, along with their men, are firmly in the pockets of the Guajardo cartel."

"I've got a map of Juarez in the glove box. Dig it out and show me where the stations are."

Rubalcava spoke as he unfolded the map. "The first station is on the northwest side of the city. The police at that station specialize in kidnapping people for ransom. I believe there are about two-dozen policemen who work out of that office."

"So they are experienced at snatching people," noted Adams. "Sounds like it could be them."

"Perhaps ... although they do not use marked police vehicles when they kidnap. The captain there is very short with a pockmarked face."

"He'll have more than pockmarks on his face if he is responsible," said Adams tersely, patting the Heckler & Koch P2000 semi-automatic pistol tucked in the holster on his belt.

"The other station is on the southeast side," continued Rubalcava. "I believe there are about seventeen officers who work out of that station."

"If we find him, will you get any heat over how we knew where he was?"

"Nothing I can't handle. Lots of policemen will know about it. Any one of them may have talked."

"Thanks, my friend," said Adams.

"I am sorry I cannot help you further."

"I already have backup on this side of the border. Four FBI agents."

"That is not many."

"It's not like we have the time ... or the authority. I don't even know how far these FBI guys will go. They're feds. I can't count on them to break the rules."

"Then I wish you luck. If you find him and somehow rescue him, do not use the border crossings going back. They will be waiting for you."

"Thanks. If we manage to retrieve him, I know several places the illegals use. We'll use one of them."

"Now you must hurry. If he is at one of the stations and is still alive, he will not be for long."

"Let's hope he is only being held to inconvenience him," offered Adams.

"No, my friend," replied Rubalcava sadly, giving Adams's shoulder a sympathetic squeeze. "If that was simply the case, the men in my office would not even have been told ... let alone be as pleased as they are."

Adams called the four FBI agents. One of them, Antonio, was of Mexican heritage and suggested if he took off his suit jacket and tie, he might be able to blend in enough to do some close-up reconnaissance. The decision of what to do was given to Adams, as Patton was his partner.

The FBI agents were still in the heart of Juarez and with the amount of traffic it would take them about an hour to check out the police station in the southeast. Adams was about forty-five minutes away from the northwest station and an hour and a half away from the southeast station. He decided to send the four FBI agents to the southeast station while he headed in the opposite direction.

During the forty-five-minute drive, Adams thought of what he would do if he believed his partner was inside. Adams had been trained by the United States military as a Special Forces commando and was an expert marksman with a variety of weapons. His talent in that regard was still used. He was a reservist and was occasionally called upon for brief missions.

Adams's plan was simple. *If Greg is there I'll bust in and take him out ... the Mexicans are lousy shots, anyway ...*

When Adams arrived, he drove past the station and saw it had its front door propped open. People casually visited with one another near the entrance while citizens were coming and going out of the building.

He's not here!

Adams gritted his jaw, determined to fight back the tears of frustration as he spun his car around and raced back across the city to the southeast section.

Antonio walked down the block toward the southeast police station, his eyes taking in the situation all the while. A woman ahead of him tried to open the front door of the station and found it was locked. She peered in through the window, then quickly stepped back and hurried off down the sidewalk.

When Antonio reached the station he knew why the woman had left in a rush. From within the station he heard the terrified scream of a man in agony pleading for his life ... in English.

Antonio hurried back to the car to report his findings. Adams was still over an hour away and three hours had passed since Patton was captured. The four FBI agents decided not to wait. They also knew what they were about to do was illegal and could cost them their jobs ... if they lived to have a job.

Antonio returned and pounded on the door of the police station with his fists. A voice from within told him to go away and come back later. Antonio persisted and yelled that his wife had been raped. Again, he was told to come back later. Antonio continued to pound and when his fist cracked the glass, a policeman cursed and came with a billy club in his hand and jerked the door open.

Antonio's response was to stick his gun in the policeman's face while putting one finger to his lips as a signal not to talk. The other three agents rushed past Antonio toward a doorway leading into the holding-cell area. Before they could make it, another policeman appeared in the doorway and yelled to warn the others.

Pandemonium broke out as the agents raced inside. Three of the six policemen in the holding-cell area had time to fumble their pistols out of their holsters, but hesitated to shoot when they saw that the agents had already taken specific aim at them.

A barrage of screaming ensued before the Mexican policemen backed up a little, leaving Patton hanging like a naked wet rag doll on the side of the cell.

Patton was left where he was until the seventh policeman was ushered into the holding area by Antonio. Antonio and another agent used their own keys to remove the handcuffs from Patton, whose legs buckled beneath him as he was laid on the floor.

Antonio ran out to retrieve the car while the other three agents remained with their weapons pointed at the policemen. The sound of screeching tires announced Antonio's return, seconds before he ran back inside.

There was more yelling amongst the agents and the Mexicans, who were still pointing their weapons at each other. The agents tried to order the Mexicans into the cell, but they refused. Finally, one of the agents grabbed Patton's pants off the floor, and, along with another agent, lifted the injured man by the shoulders and dragged him out of the room.

"The first person to follow us outside will be shot," warned Antonio, as he and the remaining agent slowly backed out.

From the front door of the police station, Patton uttered his first words. "The notebook!" he blubbered. "Get the notebook!"

His comments were ignored as he was rushed from the station and tossed into the car.

Seconds later, the squealing of tires told the Mexican policemen it was safe and they ran out onto the street.

By then, the agents had already turned a corner and sped out of sight.

Adams received a call a minute later. Jubilation was slightly tempered. They knew every policeman in the city would be made aware of their escape. Trumped-up charges would follow. Charges that would be hard to refute once you were dead.

"They'll have machine-gun nests set up at every crossing," warned Adams. "When you get close to the border, you'll have to ditch the car and go on foot. I'll show you where."

One hour later, the four FBI agents, carrying Patton, staggered back into the United States.*

Patton was rushed to the University Medical Center Hospital in El Paso. He was hysterical, incoherent, and crying. He wanted to tell them something, but kept breaking down before he could get the words out. He was sedated and drifted out of consciousness.

Over the weekend, Patton was still listed as being in shock and only his wife was allowed in to see him. It would be Monday morning before he had recovered enough to be debriefed.

---

* The four FBI agents were never officially recognized for their act of heroism. Instead, they received disciplinary action for acting on their own and not going through official channels. They were allowed to keep their jobs, but were immediately transferred to separate regions across the United States.

chapter six

Early Saturday morning found Jack Taggart slowly
cruising through an upscale neighbourhood in Vancouver.
He had obtained Earl Porter's address, which was a
penthouse condo on Beach Avenue, overlooking the False
Creek marina. Besides his Mustang, the Motor Vehicle
Branch also listed Porter as owning a silver pickup truck.

The apartment building was monitored with
closed-circuit television cameras and had a secure
underground parking lot, but Jack simply bided his
time and gained entry by quickly walking through the
garage door after a car had entered. A quick look for
Porter's vehicles resulted in locating his convertible
Mustang, but the pickup truck was gone. From the
layer of pockmarked dust on the Mustang, Jack knew
Porter hadn't driven it for over a week since the last
rainfall.

On Sunday night, Jack returned to the condo and
saw that the lights to the penthouse were not on. He
pushed the intercom regardless, ready to pretend it was a
mistake, but there was no response.

On Monday morning at ten o'clock, Jack was scheduled to testify at the trial of several Satans Wrath motorcycle gang members who had been charged with conspiracy to traffic in cocaine. Jack, as an undercover operative with the RCMP Intelligence Unit, normally avoided going to court. He was, however, considered an expert when it came to organized crime and Satans Wrath in particular. He had well-documented evidence Satans Wrath was a criminal empire that had successfully clawed and murdered its way to become an international organized-crime syndicate.

The club had chapters in dozens of countries and was involved in almost every criminal venture a person could think of, including murder, extortion, drug trafficking, prostitution, bribery, theft, and loan-sharking. The crown was hoping to prove gangsterism charges under some relatively new sections of the Criminal Code.

It was only nine o'clock and Jack decided he had time before court to make another quick visit to Porter's condo. His timing was perfect. As he drove up to the condo, he saw Porter's silver pickup truck entering the garage.

Jack called Connie Crane, who was a veteran homicide investigator with the RCMP and assigned to the Integrated Homicide Investigation Team. Jack had worked with her on past investigations and although Connie had often voiced her objections to Jack's style of policing, he still highly respected her.

Jack quickly filled Connie in on what Marcie had told him about Lily Rae and what he had discovered about Porter from Drug Section.

"He's home now, CC. How long will it take you to interview him? Half an hour is all I'm asking."

"I do homicides, not missing persons."

"Yeah, like all the missing persons who showed up at the pig farm."

"That's a low blow, Jack, even for you. You know how awful I feel about that case."

"Sorry ... I know you're dedicated ... and overworked. We all are."

"Why me?"

"Next to a polygraph operator, you're the best person I know at sniffing out a liar."

"Thanks, I think I smell one now over the phone. Why don't you do it?" Connie asked.

"If you do it and think he's done something to her, then I'll try a UC approach. I don't want him knowing who I really am."

"Christ ... yeah, okay. I'll do it."

"Thanks, CC. I owe you one," said Jack.

"Hey, with you involved, I should be happy I'm not coming over to look at a body. Are you going to wait until I get there?"

"Can't. I have to be in Supreme Court at ten."

"What? You really do go to court sometimes?" said Connie sarcastically. "I never knew you to actually arrest someone. I thought when you were done with the bad guys you handed them over to the coroner."

Jack chuckled. "Don't give me too much credit. This isn't for anyone I busted. I have to give expert testimony and tell a judge that Satans Wrath really are a criminal group operating in concert with each other."

"Everyone knows about Satans Wrath. Tell the judge to read a newspaper."

"The prosecutor thinks I'll be done by eleven."

"You never know how long an interview will take. I'll call you or leave a message as soon as I've talked to him."

Jack gave his evidence and was off the stand by eleven. He had not heard back from CC yet and as he was the last witness, he decided to sit in the courtroom and listen to the summations by the Crown and the defence lawyers. The courtroom was almost empty, with the exception of a couple of wives and girlfriends. The defence lawyers knew it wouldn't help their cause to show their solidarity by having it packed full of bikers.

The only club member who did show up to watch was dressed in a suit and tie and looked like the wealthy businessman he was. Damien was the national president of the club and he and Jack knew each other well. Too well, in both their opinions.

The judge was about to render a decision when Connie stuck her head inside the courtroom and motioned for Jack to come out into the hallway.

"You got time to talk?" she asked.

"Yes, we're about done here. I think the judge has to get back to Disneyland."

"Where's your sidekick?"

"I'm flying solo these days. Laura's on holidays. Gone for three weeks. So how did it go with Porter?"

"I talked to him. To start with, he is paranoid as hell. Something has him scared. I had to hold my badge up to the camera at the front door before he let me in. He even locked the door once I was inside."

"What about Lily Rae?"

"No sign of her. I asked when he had last seen her and he wouldn't give me a straight answer. It was more like he wanted to know whatever I knew. Things like, 'What makes you think I would know where she is?' or, 'If something happened to her, I had nothing to do with it.'"

"The bastard."

"He's really insolent ... kind of got my goat. I tell ya, he's one guy I'd feel almost justified in smacking around. In the end, he said he dumped her over a week ago and didn't know where she was."

"Maybe he did and she got embarrassed or something and ran away. Marcie said she had run away before."

"Not a chance. That son of a bitch has done something to her."

"You absolutely certain?" asked Jack.

"One hundred percent. You should have seen his face. A kid in kindergarten could have seen he was lying. I think we should get our ducks in a row. Maybe check his phone records and talk to his neighbours. Find out if anyone heard any fights or anything and then bring him in and really question him. If he doesn't lawyer up, I bet I could get him to crack within an hour."

"How did you leave it with him?"

"I remained noncommittal because I wanted to talk to you first. I didn't want to freak him out any worse than he is and get him to thinking he should call a lawyer. I gave him my card and told him to give me a call if he heard from her or remembered something."

"I doubt you'll get much in the way of phone records. If he and his buddy Clive Slater are dealing coke, they'll be changing cellphones faster than you change your panties. I think you —"

Jack stopped talking as Damien exited the courtroom and walked over to them.

"Good day, Corporal Taggart," said Damien with a smile. "Hope you have a pleasant afternoon. I know I will," he added, before walking away.

"What was that all about?" asked Connie.

"He was letting me know the judge didn't accept my evidence."

"What? You're kidding! Everyone knows Satans Wrath's history of murder and dope dealing. How could a judge even consider the idea that they're not in it as a criminal venture?"

Jack shrugged and said, "Your guess is probably about as good as mine. Maybe the new law wasn't worded to the judge's liking. Or it could be one of a number of other things. The judge could be scared, obtuse, bought off, or has a utopian belief that any potential violation of civil rights outweighs the need to protect society as a whole. Take your pick."

"You don't seem all that upset," noted Connie.

Jack shrugged and said, "I've lost all faith in the justice system. Nothing surprises me anymore."

Connie studied Jack for a moment. *Of course you don't believe in the justice system. Explains why you completely ignore it a lot of the time. You prefer to send people directly to the morgue ...*

"Now, back to Porter," continued Jack. "Do your thing first. Get your ducks in a row and bring him in for proper questioning."

"Sounds good. Hopefully he doesn't lawyer up."

Jack's face remained impassive, hiding what he was thinking. *For his sake, he better hope he talks to you. Otherwise I'll get him to talk my way ...*

chapter seven

In El Paso, the sun had barely cracked the eastern horizon Monday morning when Adams went to the hospital. Becky was at her husband's bedside when he arrived, but when she saw Adams, she quickly got up and met him at the door.

"Becky, I'm so sorry," said Adams. "How's he doing?"

"Awful, but he wants to talk to you. He spent most of yesterday under sedation, but when he was awake, he kept asking for you."

"The doctors said to let him get some rest and give him time to settle down before debriefing him."

"I know."

"I don't know what to say. I'm just glad we got him back."

"What is there to say?" she replied bitterly. "Except that it's over. We're done with this shit," she added defiantly. "I can't take it anymore. As soon as he's out of here he's putting in his papers to resign ... and don't you try to talk him out of it," she added, vehemently.

"I won't," replied Adams softly. "I don't blame him. I expected he would quit. Anybody would."

Becky studied his face, wondering if he was telling the truth and said, "I'll wait out here, but keep it short. He can barely hold it together enough to say more than a sentence or two without breaking down."

Adams nodded and walked into the room. Patton propped himself up on the bed. His eyes were watery and one was bruised and swollen, leaving only a slit to peer out of.

"How ya doin', partner?" asked Adams. "Hanging in there? I'd have brought you a bottle of Jack Daniel's, but the stores aren't open yet. Figured it would be better than whatever prescription shit they're feedin' ya in here."

"I'm not good, John," admitted Patton. "I'm … I'm finished. I'm quitting. It's my idea as much as Becky's."

"I know, she told me," replied Adams, sitting down. "Don't blame you a bit. Yesterday Yolanda and I talked about it, too … and we don't have any kids."

Talk between Adams and Yolanda of quitting was a lie, but it was a lie Adams felt his partner needed to hear. The truth was that Adams was too enraged to quit. He wanted to get even. He wanted justice.

"There's something else. I, I really screwed up," Patton said, covering his face with his hands to try and stifle a sob.

"You didn't screw up. We're always working alone over there. They set you up and wanted you to follow the Mercedes. It was a proper ambush. It could have happened to me as easily as it did to you."

"It's not that," cried Patton. "I really screwed up. I told them."

"Told them what? What are you talking about?"

"They wanted the names of everyone I worked with. I told them. I didn't want to, but I did."

"Fuck 'em. Let them come after us. I hope they do."

"No ... it's not that. They wanted home addresses. The names of our wives and kids. Some of it I tried to make up. Giving fake names, but I had lost it. There was a lot of yelling and screaming. I was scared. I might have given them some real names, too. Or maybe I only think I did.... Every time I go to sleep it's like I'm there again. I can't tell my nightmares apart from what I really did say."

"Hell, I bet hardly any of them spoke English. They won't remember or know what —"

"No, the captain spoke good English. He was writing down what I was saying in a notebook. Then he would smile at me as he flipped the pages back and ask some of the same questions over again. They caught me lying a couple of times."

"Those fucking bastards," fumed Adams.

"I tried to invent new names, but now I'm not sure what I told them. I know I gave them some of the guys' real names because I figured they probably knew the names of guys who had been here for years. I even gave them yours. Not your real address, but your name. I'm sorry."

"Don't be sorry. We're flesh and blood. There is only so much any of us can take."

"But our families, John. My God, our families ..."

"You were gutsy to be throwing out whatever phony names you did. I can only imagine what the pain would have been like. Most men would have spilled their guts immediately. Did they ask about our office? Do they know where it is?"

"No, they never asked. I don't think it occurred to them that we wouldn't be working out of the downtown office. Which reminds me. What about the four guys who rescued me? Who were they?"

"FBI agents from the downtown office. I had never met them before, either. Pretty stand-up guys ... for FBI agents. Acted almost like real cops."

Adams's attempt to get Patton to smile failed.

"I never even thanked them," he said sombrely.

"I think they would have understood. Under the circumstances, I suspect you had other stuff on your mind."

"I think I had lost my mind at that point."

"I'll get ahold of them. I know they'll want to come and see how you're doing."

"Thanks."

"The green Mercedes that set you up ... I'm sure they've already switched plates. There aren't too many green Mercedes around, but was there anything besides the colour to identify it?"

"It did have a small white scrape in the fender behind the right rear tire. Why? You don't plan on going back to that house, do you? They'll have cleared out —"

"I think I already know who owns it. I talked to my friend and he said a guy in the Guajardo cartel by the name of Chico drives a green Mercedes. Chico is an under-boss to the Carrillo Fuentes brothers. He said Chico comes to El Paso regularly to collect money from the pimps who work for him and that he meets them at the Red Poker."

"So they might have used him to bait the trap at the house we were working on."

"Yeah ... and maybe to check out the addresses you threw at them." Adams stood up and added, "Get some rest, Greg. I'll be by to see you later."

"What are you going to do?"

"What do you think?"

"Don't, John. It ain't worth it."

"Yeah, you're probably right. Don't worry, I won't do anything stupid."

Adams felt more sickened and more enraged as he drove back to his office. He didn't feel any better after telling his boss, Weber, along with the other three bosses in the office what Patton went through and the questions that were asked.

Adams felt the four bosses shared the same attitude that was summed up by Davidson, who was the senior officer of the FBI contingent in their office.

Davidson shrugged his shoulders and said, "Well, not much we can do about it. I'm sure Washington will protest."

"Protest!" stammered Adams. "If we don't have the backbone to retaliate after this, none of our families will be safe."

"There will be no retaliation," said Weber, sharply. "We are not like them. It is what separates the good guys from the bad."

Adams glared at Weber. "You didn't see Greg's face. What they've done to him ... they broke him. He'll never be the same."

Weber sighed. "I know he's been through a lot. So have you. You're angry. We all are. I want you to take a week off. Go home to your wife."

An hour later, Adams left the office ... but he didn't go home. He opted instead to go to the Red Poker Saloon.

chapter eight

Earl Porter heard the light knock on his door. It had only been twenty minutes since the policewoman had left. He picked up her card from his coffee table and looked at it. *Corporal Connie Crane*. The knock came again.

"Who is it?" he yelled.

The quiet, but persistent knock continued.

Porter cautiously made his way to the door and looked through the peephole. What he saw was a young girl dressed in a Girl Guide uniform. He breathed a sigh of relief, unlocked the door, and opened it.

Two men burst inside. One pointed a pistol at him while the other brandished a hunting knife. The man with the knife mockingly said, "We have something to discuss, Señor Porter."

Connie Crane and Jack Taggart were walking out of the courthouse together when Connie received a call on her cellphone. Jack saw the shocked look on her face as she listened.

"I was just there," she said. "Less than two hours ago ... I was interviewing him over a missing person ... his girlfriend ... Lily Rae."

Connie paused and stared at Jack suspiciously and added, "Jack Taggart from Intelligence asked me to talk to him. Before this morning, I had never heard of the guy. I'm with Taggart now ... not a problem, we'll both be there." After Connie hung up, she stood quietly staring at Jack.

"What's up?" asked Jack.

"What's up? You mean you're going to stand here and tell me you don't know?"

"If I knew, I wouldn't be asking. Why are you looking at me like that? What's going on?"

"That was Wilson from VPD Homicide. After I left Porter's this morning, a maid went in to water plants because she thought he was still out of town. She found him tied and gagged to a kitchen chair ... with his throat slit."

"What the hell? I had nothing to do with it. I was in court. You know that. I'm trying to find Lily Rae. I didn't want the guy who could tell us where she is, getting murdered. Think about it."

Connie paused for a moment, biting her lip as she pondered the situation before replying, "Yeah, okay, I believe you.

"You should."

"Shit, don't blame me for being suspicious. It's not like you don't have a long history for doing things you shouldn't ... and don't give me that act surprised, show concern, deny, deny, deny routine. There have been far too many bodies turning up around you and far too many coincidences."

"So ... how's it feel with the shoe on the other foot?"

"What do you mean?"

"Well ... you know I'm going to have to be truthful when I talk to Wilson. You were the last person to see him alive. You then came to see me and appeared angry. As I recall, you even made some comment about feeling justified smacking him around. Jesus, CC. Why did you do it? You must have known you would get caught."

"What the fuck? Jack! I didn't! It was just a coincidence that —"

"A coincidence?" Jack grinned. "Where have I heard that word before?"

Connie scowled at Jack. "You prick. Quit screwing with me."

Connie and Jack arrived at the condo building and a uniformed member of the Vancouver Police Department opened the lobby door to let them in. Minutes later, Detective Wilson came out in the hallway to talk to them outside of Porter's penthouse.

Jack told Wilson what had prompted his interest in Porter, as well as Drug Section's past interest in Porter and his associate, Clive Slater.

"Business interests in Mexico," mused Wilson. "We already ran the footage on the apartment security cameras. The cameras show two men sneaking in through the underground garage this morning. They both look dark and I was thinking they were Aboriginal, but now that I think of it, they do look Mexican. One looked up at the cameras. I expected him then to try and hide his face. It was the opposite. The asshole sneered into the camera and laughed."

"He sneered and laughed?" said Jack, incredulously.

"We don't have sound, but you can tell he did. His sneer is one I won't forget, either."

"Let's nickname him El Burla," said Jack.

"Al who?" asked Wilson.

"El Burla. The Spanish word for sneer is *burla*."

"Sounds good," replied Wilson.

"You've got their faces, then?" noted Connie.

"El Burla for sure. Stocky, black hair covering the tops of his ears, and a very flat and wide nose. He acted like he thought he was invincible. As if he thought we couldn't touch him. I'll love showing a jury the camera footage once we catch him. The other guy's image isn't quite as clear. I'll have to see if we can enhance it."

"Porter was really paranoid when I came to see him," said Connie. "Now it makes sense. He knew somebody was after him. The thing is, he wouldn't open the door, even for me, until I held my badge up to the peephole."

"The door isn't damaged, so maybe he trusted whoever he let in," noted Wilson.

"Are you going to grab Clive Slater for questioning?" asked Jack.

"Definitely." Wilson looked at Connie. "Maybe you and I should work together. You for the missing girlfriend and me for her boyfriend's homicide."

"Sounds good to me," replied Connie. "Let's hope it doesn't turn into a double homicide." She looked at Jack. "Anything to add?"

Jack shook his head. "Not now. You two do your thing, but keep me apprised. I'm willing to help out with a UC approach if it is warranted. Maybe on Slater or whoever else surfaces."

"You said a UC was tried on Slater before," said Connie. "It didn't work."

"There are different approaches or styles to UC work," replied Jack.

"Yeah, go figure," said Connie. "And please, tell me, what would your style —" Connie quit talking as Jack walked past her a short distance down the hallway and gingerly picked up a small piece of cardboard.

"What is it?" asked Wilson.

"A cut-out picture of a Girl Guide," said Jack. "Explains why Porter opened his door."

"It does?" asked Wilson. He looked at Connie and she shrugged.

Moments later, both Wilson and Connie took turns peeking through the peephole in Porter's door while Jack remained in the hall holding the picture up close to the peephole.

"I'd have sworn it was a real kid standing in the hall," muttered Connie.

Wilson went to Clive Slater's apartment and found he wasn't home, so he stuck a business card in his door. A couple of hours later, Wilson received a call from a lawyer by the name of Jenkins who said he was representing Slater and asked what it was about. Wilson told him and Jenkins said he would call back. Minutes later, Jenkins called again and said Slater had agreed to meet Wilson as long as Jenkins was present. Wilson tried to set up an appointment immediately, but Jenkins said his calendar was full. Eventually the lawyer agreed to meet at Wilson's office the following afternoon at three o'clock.

Connie called Jack to let him know.

"Four hours after a murder and he's already law-yered up without Wilson even talking to him?" Jack was incredulous.

"Yeah, how about that."

"You can bet his hands are dirty, too," muttered Jack.

"Sounds like it. With his lawyer, I doubt Wilson will get much, but who knows. Wilson does have a good rep for being sharp. I'm going down there tomorrow when he interviews him."

"You going to interview him, too?"

"Not until I hear what he says to Wilson. Later, if need be, we can use Lily Rae as another excuse for me to interview him. Wilson might touch on her disappearance because they would expect us to know she was Porter's girlfriend, but we will likely hold back on any serious questioning in her regard until later. Maybe catch him without a lawyer. I'll be down at VPD to confer with Wilson if he feels the need. Would be good if we could reach you, as well."

"I'll be available on my cell," replied Jack. "Tonight, if you don't have any objections, I'm going to drive out and tell Marcie that Porter was murdered."

"Not a problem."

"What about Lily Rae's mother?" asked Jack. "She should be told, too."

"Go ahead. Saves me from telling her. Let me know if she says anything that will help. Also, if Lily uses a computer at home, I'd like to get it. Same for anything else you see that might help."

"Will do ... and tell Wilson good luck."

"Don't get your hopes up. With the lawyer there, I bet it will be a short interview."

"I'm sure you're right," agreed Jack before hanging up. He brooded for a moment as he formulated a plan on how to get Slater to talk.

Slater won't think it's a short interview when I talk to him. In fact, I bet he will remember it for the rest of his life ...

chapter nine

On Monday night, Jack and Natasha, with Mikey in an infant car seat in the back seat, drove out to Liz and Ben's farm in Chilliwack. Jack hadn't told them he was coming, as he wanted to be with Marcie and console her if need be, when he updated her on the investigation.

When they arrived, Ben, Liz, and Marcie came out of the house to meet them.

"What a nice surprise," said Ben. "What brings you out here?"

"Have you eaten?" asked Liz.

"We already ate, but thanks," replied Natasha.

"What about you, Mikey? Want me to throw on a steak or something?" Ben joked.

"Think we better wait until he grows teeth," suggested Natasha.

Jack saw the worried look on Marcie's face as she looked at him. He shook his head and said, "No sign of her yet, but I want to talk to you."

While the others went inside, Jack walked with Marcie down the long driveway as he told her about the murder and that Porter had been suspected of being involved with cocaine trafficking.

"Oh, no," cried Marcie. "I knew it! I knew something was wrong. Lily ... you think ... what? What do you think happened to her?"

"I know it doesn't look good, but there is still no sign of her. Whoever murdered Porter didn't try to hide his body. The fact we haven't found Lily yet could be a good sign."

"But where could she be?"

"I don't know. Maybe tied and gagged and in the trunk of some car. Porter may have ripped off some dope dealers. Maybe she was taken as a hostage to get him to return the drugs or something."

"But now that they've killed him ..."

"I know it doesn't look good, but don't give up hope."

"So what's going to happen?

"VPD Homicide have arranged an interview with one of Porter's associates tomorrow afternoon to see if they can come up with some leads. The guy is also suspected of being involved with cocaine trafficking. I'm sure he knows something."

"Why are they waiting until tomorrow? Talk to him now," urged Marcie.

"He lawyered up. That was the soonest the lawyer would agree to."

"What if he clams up?" asked Marcie, sounding panicked. "What then?"

"Then I'll do my thing."

"Oh ... I see," she replied, calming down. They took a couple of steps in silence as Marcie thought about it before adding, "Guess he better hope he talks to the cops tomorrow."

Jack frowned. Marcie was a smart kid. She had picked up a lot about certain things over the years. Things he wished she knew nothing about.

Marcie saw his face and said, "Sorry. That was stupid of me. I mean, you know, I meant you would do your undercover stuff or whatever."

"Yes, I know what you meant. Do you think Lily's mother is home? I would like to meet her and update her, as well."

"They only live about fifteen minutes away by car. Want me to take you there?"

"Yes, but we'll take my car. Save your gas money for university."

Jack pulled up to a small, single-level ranch-style house and parked. The home had a ramp leading up alongside the stairs to the front door. A flower garden bordered the front of the house and there was a small cedar wishing well in the front yard beside an apple tree. The home was being well cared for, with the exception that the lawn was in dire need of cutting and a few weeds had sprung up in the flower beds.

Marcie rang the doorbell. She saw Jack looking at the flower beds and said, "Lily always looked after that stuff."

Jack was introduced to Eva Rae and quickly told her he had nothing new on Lily's whereabouts, but there was something he thought she should know.

Eva looked up at him from her wheelchair with a face that expressed relief she wasn't being informed of her daughter's death, but at the same time, disappointment there was not good news. She invited them into the living room and Jack watched as she manipulated the toggle stick on her wheelchair with one hand. Her other hand was crippled and she held it close to her body.

Once seated, Eva offered them a beverage. Both Jack and Marcie declined.

Jack updated Eva on the investigation and Jack could see the shock on her face when she learned about Porter's murder.

"You knew!" exclaimed Eva, looking at Marcie. "You tried to warn her he was no good. She told me you two had a fight ... that you were jealous, but ... Oh, God," she cried, raising her hand to her mouth as the tears ran down her cheek.

"I should have tried harder," said Marcie. "I'm sorry. I —"

"No, don't you be sorry," sobbed Eva. "I thought he was no good, too. He was so much older ... I should have talked to her, but I was afraid." She looked at Jack. "I was afraid I would drive her away. When she said she was going away with him for a couple of days, I didn't like it ... especially when she wouldn't tell me where. I was upset, but she's almost a grown woman ... I was afraid to say anything about it."

"Any thoughts or guesses where she might have gone?" asked Jack.

"I had a hunch they were eloping to Vegas to get married. I think she wanted it to be a surprise. I'm only guessing."

"Sounds reasonable," said Jack, watching as Eva manoeuvred her chair beside him and grabbed his hand.

"She is all I have," said Eva, emphatically. She bit her lip for a moment before adding, "She is my only reason for living."

"Hindsight is twenty-twenty," said Jack, giving her hand a squeeze. "Sometimes kids need to find things out on their own ... but don't give up hope. We are exploring avenues to come up with a lead. I am confident one of Earl's associates will know something to help us with our investigation."

"Promise me you will do everything you can to find her," said Eva, staring intently at Jack's face.

"I promise," replied Jack. "You have my word on it."

Eva nodded solemnly. "Thank you," she said, letting her hand slip from his.

"One more thing," said Jack. "If Lily has a computer, I would like to take it. It might identify someone else for us to interview."

"She has one in her bedroom," replied Eva, still fighting to regain her composure. "Go ahead and take it. I've already gone through the rest of her stuff. I didn't find anything, but you're welcome to look and take whatever you need."

Eva led Jack to Lily's bedroom and Marcie followed. As Jack unhooked the computer, he glanced around the room. It was immaculate and consisted of a single bed that was made up and had a stuffed green frog on the pillow. Pictures on a dresser showed happy times with Lily and her mother.

One picture in particular caught Jack's attention and he didn't understand why. It was a portrait of Lily's face. Her features looked soft and he thought there was a certain wide-eyed innocence about her. *Forced at such a young age to look after her only parent ... her life can't be easy, yet she looks serene.*

As Jack carried the computer out of the room, he looked back at the picture again. Something about Lily's eyes fixated him. *It's like she's trying to reach out from the grave for me to help her.* He felt his stomach knot as an intense feeling of dread overtook his mind. *Something very, very bad has happened to her ...*

chapter ten

Early Tuesday afternoon in El Paso, Texas, a green Mercedes pulled into the parking lot of the Red Poker Saloon.

Adams sat upright from behind the steering wheel of his Celica and focused his binoculars. He caught a glimpse of the small, white scrape over the right rear fender of the Mercedes as it turned into a parking stall.

He immediately started his car and sped through the parking lot, stopping behind the Mercedes as Chico was walking away from his car.

Adams leaped from his car and yelled, "Hey, Chico!"

Chico turned and said, "Do I know you?"

"You're about to!" replied Adams, flashing his badge with one hand while pointing a pistol at Chico's head. "Immigration! Put your hands on the hood of your car!"

Chico slowly obeyed, but as Adams approached him, three men pulled up in another car and stopped nose-to-nose with Adams's car. The driver had his window down and yelled Chico's name. Chico kept his hands on the hood of the car, but yelled back.

"No talking, asshole!" ordered Adams, while putting his badge away and taking out his handcuffs.

"I just told them you were with Immigration," explained Chico. "There is a mistake. I am not an illegal. I have my green card."

The three men got out of their car so Adams pointed his pistol in their direction and said, "You guys want to be next? Back off!"

The three men stopped, but stood where they were and whispered amongst themselves as Adams searched Chico and removed a loaded pistol from his waistband.

"I have a permit to carry a concealed handgun," said Chico.

"I'm sure you do," replied Adams. "Your three friends probably do, too, so tell them if they come any closer I will shoot them."

Chico yelled over to the three men and they all looked at each other and took a couple of steps back as Adams handcuffed Chico's hands behind his back. He then grabbed the man by the arm and herded him over to his Celica and placed him in the back seat and did up the seatbelt.

"You do not even ask to see my green card?" sputtered Chico.

"Not interested in your fucking green card or your gun permit."

"So if you are not arresting me for being an illegal," Chico stared at Adams. "You are, you are…"

"That's right, asshole. Greg Patton was my partner!"

Chico yelled in Spanish at the three men as Adams slammed the door and returned to the driver's seat where he put the car in reverse and backed up to the end of the row to turn around. The three men scrambled back in their car and sped toward them, but came to a screeching stop when Adams lowered his window and pointed his pistol at the driver. Seconds later, he was out of the lot and speeding away.

"You can prove nothing," said Chico, when Adams stopped at a red light.

Their eyes met in his rear-view mirror and Adams said, "You were the bait car the other morning. You knew a Mercedes would attract our attention. You waited until my partner came by and then set him up to follow you."

"The other morning?" said Chico sarcastically. "I do remember some car behind me. I think the Mexican police thought he was up to no good and stopped him for questioning. That is all I know. You can prove nothing with me."

"I know what you did."

Chico smiled and said, "Knowing and proving, *señor*, are very different matters."

"I am not interested in proving it, Chico. Pay attention to where I am turning. We are going out into the desert."

Chico uttered a laugh from the back seat.

"Something funny, Chico?" asked Adam.

Chico sneered at him and said, "You can't touch me. I told my men who you are. If anything happens ... there are witnesses who can identify you."

"They're probably pimps and dope dealers. Who is going to believe them?"

"There were other cars in the lot. Other witnesses. I know you saw them. So did I."

"I don't give a fuck," replied Adams. "You are going to give your bosses a message."

"What bosses?"

"All of them. Including your top boss ... Rafael Guajardo."

"Rafael Guajardo? I have never even spoken with Señor Guajardo. I have nothing to do with him ... although I know him to be a respected businessman and someone who people look up to and admire."

"Yeah, you probably are too much of a peon to talk to him. Perhaps you only deal with the Carrillo Fuentes brothers. It doesn't matter. Guajardo will get the message."

"And what message am I supposed to tell them?" asked Chico scornfully. "That you don't like what happened?"

"There will be no need for you to say anything," replied Adams.

Adams drove for an hour out into the desert. By then, Chico had long since stopped laughing.

chapter eleven

On Tuesday afternoon in Vancouver, Detective Wilson was sitting with Corporal Connie Crane in a small office within the Vancouver Police Department when Wilson received a call saying Mr. Jenkins and a Clive Slater had arrived to see him.

Connie glanced at her watch. "Twelve minutes late."

"Yeah, the games people play," Wilson replied. "Maybe it empowers Jenkins," he added, grinning to himself as he shuffled to his feet and picked up a file from his desk. He glanced at Connie and said, "Well, time to get on with the show."

"Good luck."

Wilson was cordial as he directed Jenkins and Slater to an interview room. "Either of you like a coffee?" he asked, as they entered the room.

Both men declined, so once everyone was seated, Wilson took out his notebook and started asking some basic questions as to how well Slater knew Porter, along with where he was when Porter was murdered.

Wilson's appearance in the interview room gave the impression that he was barely interested in the commentary Slater was giving him. He jotted down a few notes, but acted like someone who was bored with his job and was only filling out the proper paperwork to complete a bureaucratic process.

After a few questions, Wilson stifled a yawn and then smiled apologetically at Slater and Mr. Jenkins. Wilson's appearance cleverly disguised the fact that his eyes and ears took in everything. It was not only Slater's manicured hands, expensive watch, jade bracelet, and tailored clothes that caught his eye, nor the just specific choice of words spoken by both Slater and his lawyer that caught his attention. Wilson was a trained professional who was acutely aware of the body language that both Jenkins and Slater displayed with every question asked and with every lull in the conversation.

"As you can now see," said Jenkins, "from what my client has told you, he has a good alibi for where he was two days ago when the murder took place. It should be easy for you to check out."

"We are not looking at you for the murder," replied Wilson, with a quizzical glance at Slater. "I am surprised you felt the need to bring Mr. Jenkins with you. I don't understand why you would be so nervous. Is there a reason you thought we might be looking at you as the culprit?"

"Nervous?" smiled Slater, shaking his head as he leaned back and crossed his legs. "I can assure you I am not the nervous type. However, having been the focus of attention of an undercover police operative two years ago, I thought it prudent to be cautious."

"An undercover police operative?" replied Wilson. "I am afraid I know nothing about that."

"Perhaps you don't, but if you had done your homework and checked with your brethren in the RCMP, they would have told you."

"Why were the RCMP after you?"

"My client does not know the reason," said Jenkins. "Anything he would have to say on the matter would be sheer speculation. From what I understand, their investigation revealed there was no wrong-doing on the part of Mr. Slater."

"I'm not opposed to speculation at this point," said Wilson.

"Well, I am," replied Jenkins tersely. "It can lead to all sorts of conjecture and false —"

"It's okay, Jenkins," interrupted Slater smugly, before looking at Wilson. "My guess is some of the people I had casually met at various nightclubs may have been involved in some illegal activity. The RCMP, being rather overzealous, and likely poorly equipped on a cerebral level, jumped to the wrong conclusion and thought I was involved."

"What illegal activities are we talking about?"

"I swear, I have no idea. You would have to ask them."

Wilson's face remained impassive. He had been lied to by hundreds of suspects over the years. He knew he had just been lied to again. "Well, the reason I asked you to come here was to help us. We understood Earl Porter was your friend. I presume you would want to help us catch who killed your friend?"

"My friend?" replied Slater, while touching his fingers to his chest and glancing open-mouthed at Jenkins for effect.

The theatrics were not lost on Wilson, but his face showed no sign he knew he was being misled.

"I would hardly say that man was my friend," continued Slater. "He was simply more of an associate than a friend. He was someone I bumped into occasionally on the nightclub circuit."

"I see. Do you know if he had any enemies?"

"Obviously he must have had one, don't you think so, Detective?" replied Slater with a smirk. "Under the circumstances, I would hardly think it was a random robbery."

"Any idea who this enemy could be?"

"If I knew, don't you think I would have come forward immediately without being summoned? I mean, why would I have waited until now?"

Wilson stared silently at Slater. *He is fishing for information. He wants to know what we know.* Wilson flipped through a couple of pages in the file as if looking for something. He read silently for a moment and nodded his head slowly. It gave an ambiguous impression.

Slater saw the nod and wondered, *Is he agreeing that I wouldn't have waited ... or is he nodding because he knows why I didn't come in immediately?*

Wilson caught the nervous glance Slater gave Jenkins before continuing. "Can you think of a reason why someone would kill him?"

"Who knows why? Life can be a crapshoot. Shit happens. Maybe he rolled the dice one too many times," replied Slater with a shrug.

"Watch it," cautioned Jenkins, putting his hand on Slater's arm. "Do not speculate beyond the questions put to you."

"Speculate on what?" asked Wilson. *Slater's comment may have been innocuous, but Jenkins's reaction says there is more to it ...*

"Nothing. Simply an expression," said Slater. "I know he hung around with a lot of different groups of people. Do you have any clues that could help me make a more informed hypothesis?"

"Nothing I can share at this time," replied Wilson.

"I see," said Slater, glancing at his watch. "Are we done, then? Tuesdays and Saturdays I have squash lessons to go to down at The Racquet Club. I'm billed for the time ... so if I miss it, will you compensate me?"

"Uh, no," said Wilson.

"I thought not," replied Slater, smiling.

"I am almost finished," said Wilson. "I want to ask you about a young woman by the name of Lily Rae."

Slater hesitated. "Am I supposed to know her?"

"Oh?" replied Wilson, looking surprised as he searched through some more papers in the file in front of him. "You say you don't?" he added as he paused to skim a report before looking up to await Slater's reply.

"Oh, hang on," said Slater. "Is that one of his girlfriends? Maybe I did meet her. I can't remember for sure. He goes through girls like candy."

"When was the last time you saw her?"

"I don't remember. Must have been weeks ago, maybe longer," said Slater, who was sharply aware that Wilson looked at the report again, only this time he used his index finger to point something out to himself. "She might have been someone he brought to my place once," Slater hastened to add. "I swear, I really don't know anything about her. Sorry."

"Yes, over to your place," said Wilson as though he was already aware of it. "You knew Porter more than from just bumping into him at nightclubs. Isn't that right?"

"Hang on," said Jenkins. "Just because someone invites someone home from a nightclub hardly means they're good friends. What evidence do you have to make you think they were good friends? Or that my client could reasonably be expected to even remember Miss Rae?"

"I'm sorry, but I am only asking questions as a matter of routine to try and find out everyone the victim associated with," replied Wilson.

"We hardly have the time to sit here all day while you randomly cast your net in the water for information," said Jenkins. "My client has been more than co-operative and I would suggest that unless you have something more concrete to ask, you should consider this interview over."

"If I could please ask you to wait another couple of minutes," said Wilson. "I would like to confer with someone."

"You have already wasted enough of our time," said Jenkins, getting to his feet.

"It's in regard to Mr. Slater's comment about whether I could share some of our findings to see if he could make a more informed hypothesis. I see no reason not to share it with him, but I wouldn't want to do it without permission from my boss."

Slater anxiously leaned forward in his chair and grabbed Jenkins by the sleeve of his suit jacket. "We've got time," he said, before looking at Wilson. "If I'm a few minutes late for the squash lesson, it'll be okay."

Jack received a call from Connie, who got right to the point. "I'm still at VPD. Slater showed up with a lawyer and Wilson just stepped out of the interview room to talk to me. Slater is lying and definitely knows something about the murder. He's like a textbook example of a liar. Psychologically distancing himself from Porter, using fake body language ... everything."

"What about Lily Rae?"

"Wilson touched on her just enough to know Slater is lying about her, too. He definitely knows something."

"The bastard. Any idea if she is still alive?"

"Can't tell, but it's been a couple of days since Porter was killed. I would think if she was still alive, she would have surfaced by now.

"Is Slater still there?"

"Yeah, but unless you can think of anything, we're going to cut him loose. He's bitching about having to go to a squash lesson."

"A squash lesson? Do you know where?"

"Said he has one every Tuesday and Saturday down at The Racquet Club. Why?"

"I could meet him through the squash club. Do a UC. That last UC operative was probably playing the nice guy. We've got a missing girl. Maybe it's time to stop being nice."

"Damn it, Jack. What are you going to do? Pull his fingernails out with a set of pliers?" Connie paused for a moment and then added, "Which is probably the only way we'd get this son of a bitch to talk."

"I appreciate your suggestion."

"I am not suggesting that!" Connie groaned.

"I know. Chill out. Tell me what you plan on doing to find Lily."

"There's not a lot left I can do at this point. Nobody knows where she is. Her boyfriend is murdered. From how Porter acted and what he said to me before he was killed, I suspect she's dead, too. Probably by the same people. The only real lead we have is Slater and he sure as hell won't talk. I think we'll have to put Lily on the back burner and see if Wilson can come up with the killers."

"The guys who swaggered in and nailed Porter weren't camera-shy. I'm betting they're back in Mexico. Good luck finding them," said Jack.

"Yeah, well, Porter's murder is Wilson's case."

"Lily Rae was reported missing out of Chilliwack. That makes her our jurisdiction."

"She's probably dead," said Connie gloomily.

"Yeah, so then you've got a homicide to investigate. What are you going to do?"

"I've still got her friends to track down and interview. I also have her computer you got for me, but so far it doesn't look promising."

"If you and Wilson have already written Slater off, why not let me take a crack at him."

"What, with the pliers?"

"What if I could get him to talk without physically hurting him? Just by doing a UC and maybe acting like a tough guy. Getting him to open up to me."

"Without hurting him? What would you do?"

"Whatever I thought was necessary. Mental pressure."

"Mental pressure? If you even raise your voice at a person to gain a confession, most judges will rule whatever the person says is inadmissible in court. Not to mention that Slater is pretty self-assured. Even if you started screaming at him, I don't see him as the type to break down and talk."

"I'm not talking about getting him to say something to incriminate himself. I'm talking about getting him to say something to help us find Lily. We know it wasn't him who murdered Porter. I want to find out who did."

"I know, but what if Slater is implicated?" Connie asked. "What if he murdered Lily? If you do something a judge says will throw justice into disrepute, then Slater will walk away from any charges we might —"

"What if Lily's not dead? Maybe she was taken hostage to put pressure on Porter for whatever he did. Maybe he ripped off their stash or something. The bad guys might have left her tied and gagged in the trunk of some car. They sure as hell didn't worry about hiding Porter's body. The fact Lily's body hasn't turned up should give us hope."

"Trust you to think of that scenario. You sure know how to keep me awake all night."

"Let's hope Lily is still awake. Come on, CC. I'm not even thinking of hurting Slater physically. Like I said, more of a tough guy image combined with a little intimidation."

"You think that would get him to talk? I get the feeling he isn't easily intimidated."

"The important thing to do is find Lily. I think he will talk."

Connie paused as she thought about it. "Nothing physical?"

"Nothing physical ... but, uh, I suspect whatever he says wouldn't be admissible in court."

"What you're saying all sounds pretty innocent ... but I know you. There's no way I'm going to okay this on my own. I'll talk it over with Wilson but even if he agrees, I'm still going to run it past a prosecutor. Hopefully one who doesn't know you."

"Make it soon. If she's alive, she may not be for long."

Connie sighed. "Okay, I'll get on it right away, but it's late in the day now and tomorrow's Canada Day. Bet I don't get an answer from a prosecutor before Thursday."

"Let me know. In the meantime, I'll try to think of an angle to get to Slater."

Jack grimaced as he hung up. He had a plan brewing in his mind as soon as he heard Slater had obtained a lawyer ... but knew it was a plan that if known, would never be approved.

chapter twelve

On Thursday in El Paso, Texas, it was eleven o'clock in the morning when Special Agent Adams awoke to the sound of Yolanda opening the bedroom curtains. She had been up for an hour and was already dressed.

"Christ, close those," muttered Adams. "The sun feels like someone hit me between the eyes with a hatchet."

"Serves you right," replied Yolanda, leaving the curtains open.

"How much did we drink last night?"

"How much did *you* drink is more like it. Come on, get dressed. It's almost lunchtime."

Half an hour later, Adams wandered into the kitchen and opened the refrigerator. Yolanda looked up from the table at the sound of a can of Budweiser being opened.

"After last night I thought you would have had enough. What's this? The hair of the dog?"

Adams nodded and took three gulps out of the can before sitting down.

"Want to talk about it?" asked Yolanda.

"What's more to say," replied Adams, taking another gulp of beer, more as an excuse to avoid eye contact than to drink. "We got a gun tucked away in every room of the house. Don't go out without taking the one in your purse. Always keep an eye in the rear-view and the doors locked."

"It's not that. I understand why we are on high alert, but …"

"But what?" snapped Adams, yanking a kitchen chair out to sit down. "What is it?"

"That's what I'm asking you. These last two days you've hardly said a word to me. Even last night when I drank with you, I may as well have been drinking alone. I know you. There's something going on you haven't told me."

"Can you blame me for being a little upset over what happened to Greg?" said Adams angrily. "He was my partner for Christ's sake!"

"Don't give me that," she replied in annoyance. "There's something else going on. I've watched you when you've been recalled to go out on special ops with the military. I've seen you when you and Greg were in the thick of things. Things I knew to be secret and things I've never asked about. But something has changed. These last couple of days you've hardly spoken." Yolanda's face softened and she leaned forward and put her hand on his and said, "I'm worried about you. I don't want anything to happen to you."

Adams lowered his voice, but his response was terse. "This is different. The bad guys crossed the line with Greg. They had to be sent a message."

"Had? What kind of message?" she asked, gripping his hand tight.

Adams stared at the Budweiser and didn't respond.

"What have you done?" cried Yolanda.

Adams looked at her and said solemnly, "Nothing I feel guilty about, so quit worrying."

Yolanda stood up and stared at Adams for a moment, before shaking her head in exasperation and walking out of the room.

Adams stared after her. He wanted to tell her how much he loved her. That he would do anything to protect her.

His cellphone rang. It was his boss.

"Get in here immediately," seethed Weber.

"I thought you gave me a week off," replied Adams.

"No time to be funny … you stupid, dumb fucker. You really did it this time. Davidson and a DA are going to interview you. They decided to leave me out of it to show impartiality because I know you. What a laugh that is. After what you did, I don't know you at all and I don't want to."

Adams hung up. He slowly finished the beer and left without saying goodbye to Yolanda. He was afraid to. He knew he would break down if he did.

District Attorney Norman White waited in Davidson's office for Adams to arrive.

"How long have you known John Adams?" asked White, grimacing as he took a sip of coffee. *Not exactly Starbucks …*

Davidson leaned back in his chair, clasping his hands behind his head.

"I was transferred in here five months ago to head the FBI contingent in the office. I met him then for the first time."

"What kind of officer is he?"

"Well, he comes under the direct command of Weber, but this is a small enough office that we all know each other to some degree. I consider Adams to be a loose cannon. Not one to follow rules, particularly. Surprising for a guy trained with the Special Forces ... they usually follow orders to a T. Adams and his partner ... or ex-partner now, were always working on their own and taking unnecessary risks."

"Did they get any positive results in their investigations?" White asked.

Davidson sat forward in his chair, momentarily drumming his fingers on his desk before replying. "Yes, I would have to admit they did," he replied. "Adams was good at developing confidential sources. It gave him an advantage."

"Does he have lots of friends in the office?"

"No. I would say none. He is more of a loner type."

"What about Greg Patton? Isn't he close to him?"

Davidson shrugged. "I think the type of high-risk work Adams does, combined with his pattern of continually ignoring policy, necessitated that he trust his partner. I'm sure the two men are close, but other than Patton, Adams pretty much sticks to himself."

"I was wondering if he might have already confided to someone about what he does."

"Maybe his wife, I don't know. With the psychological mess Patton is in right now, I doubt he would even tell him."

"I can't make Adams's wife testify against him, regardless."

"How do you want to play it when he comes in?"

"No doubt he acted out of a blind rage, but now he has to realize he did what he did in broad daylight and in front of numerous witnesses. He'll know he's caught. We'll be polite, but lay our cards on the table. We can even sympathize with him a little for what prompted his rage."

"What do you think he's looking at for jail time?"

"With his co-operation, an understanding judge

might go along with a twenty-four- to twenty-eight-year sentence."

Davidson shook his head sadly. "He'll have to spend it in solitary."

"It was his choice to do what he did." White took another sip of coffee and made a face. "God, this stuff is awful."

"He may demand a lawyer ... or even arrive with one."

"Possible, but I doubt it. In my experience, law-enforcement types who have crossed the line feel so guilty they are actually relieved to confess. You know him, so sit close and play the role of a sympathizer. I'll tell him I can make a submission to a judge for an agreed sentence. Once he admits it, I'll step out while you officially give him his rights and record a full confession. I'll bet you a dinner he doesn't request a lawyer."

Adams arrived and nodded silently as Davidson introduced him to Norman White. The three men sat down, with White behind the desk while Davidson sat beside Adams, his chair arranged at a right angle to face him.

"Mr. Davidson is present because he is with the FBI, and your own boss with Customs, could be viewed as lacking impartiality," said White.

"So I heard," replied Adams. "Mind telling me what this is all about?"

"You were seen, John," said Davidson, softly. "Two days ago at the Red Poker."

"I was seen?"

"Three of Chico's guys were right there," said Davidson.

"Not only by those three men," added White, "but by independent witnesses in two other cars who saw you cuff him and put him in your own car before absconding with him."

"So I picked him up. What's the big deal?" replied Adams.

"His body was found yesterday," said White. "Shot with his own gun."

"Barely even off the road," added Davidson. "It was like you wanted it to be found."

"If he was murdered, I'm not responsible," stated Adams firmly.

"Look, John, we know you're a Special Forces operative who sometimes goes on secret missions," said Davidson, "but this obviously wasn't one of them. Nobody is going to come forward and say you were authorized."

"Authorized to do what?" replied Adams. "I told you, I didn't murder him."

"John," said Davidson, "you've been caught red-handed. I know you know that. It's time now to make the best out of a bad situation." Davidson leaned forward, giving Adams a friendly squeeze on his shoulder and added, "It's time to come clean, John. Let's try and work through this together." Davidson then leaned back in his chair, giving Adams a sympathetic smile and a nod of encouragement.

After a moment of silence, White said, "I think, basically, you're a good man. You know what you did was wrong. Deep down inside you wanted to get caught. It's why you left the body on the side of the road. What we're doing is giving you a chance to tell your side of it. Explain what happened to your partner so a judge will get the full picture and realize the extent of the atrocity that triggered you to do what you did. Then I can make a submission for an agreed length of incarceration."

"Let's talk about it, John," added Davidson, giving Adams another sympathetic pat on the shoulder.

Adams sighed and said, "Okay, I'll tell you what happened. I did pick Chico up at the Red Poker."

"And then you drove him out into the desert," noted White.

"Yes. I wanted to scare him. Make him think I was going to kill him if he didn't talk. I wanted to find out who ordered Greg's kidnapping."

"You already knew it was the Guajardo cartel," said Davidson.

"Yes, but Guajardo himself was meeting with other cartel bosses in Cancun at the time. He may not have even known about it. He left the Carrillo Fuentes brothers in charge, but there is no evidence they ordered it. I was hoping to scare Chico into giving me the truth."

"And then what happened?" asked White softly. "Tell me how it went wrong."

Adams sighed. "Yes, it did go wrong," he admitted. "Chico laughed at me. The asshole never did say who ordered it. He never believed I was going to kill him."

"But by him laughing … naturally it would have infuriated you," said Davidson.

"It would anybody," agreed White.

"I'll say I was infuriated," said Adams bitterly. "I was angry at myself."

"Angry at yourself … for what he made you do to him?" asked White.

"No. I didn't do anything to him. I was angry I hadn't realized some of his guys had followed us out into the desert."

"What are you talking about?" asked White, glancing questioningly at Davidson.

"From the Red Poker, I guess. I presume it was his guys. When Chico was laughing at me and saying I wouldn't kill him, I asked how he could be so sure. He told me to look out the back window of my car. It was hard to see because the sun was in my eyes, but I could make out a car parked down the road from where I was parked."

"What did you do then?" asked White, well aware that Davidson was shaking his head.

"What could I do?" replied Adams. "I was pissed off at myself for not realizing I had been followed. Chico was demanding I let him out of the car immediately, so I did. I knew he probably had a gun permit so I threw his gun as far into the desert as I could and drove away. Last I saw of him he was walking over to get it. I don't know what happened after that."

"So you actually expect me to believe you being there was simply a coincidence with him being murdered by someone else?" said Davidson, while fighting to control his anger.

"Could be a coincidence, or maybe they thought he ratted and killed him for talking to me. Another scenario is he was collecting money from pimps in El Paso. I only took his gun. I didn't bother with his wallet so I don't know how much cash he had. The guys who followed us out there might have decided to use the opportunity to rob him."

"No way that happened!" yelled Davidson. "You were in a fit of rage over what they did to your partner and you took him out into the desert and murdered him. Admit it!"

"I'll admit I was outraged," Adams replied calmly. "I have also offered you alternative possibilities to what you had thought happened. If you are going to question me any further, then I want an attorney present."

Davidson and White watched Adams stalk out of the office.

"He's guilty as sin," said Davidson. "I don't believe his story of a second car one bit."

"I agree with you, but it would sure leave doubt in a jury's mind. We would never get a conviction."

"Then we'll get more evidence. There is no way we can let him get away with it."

White sat forward with his elbow on the desk and stroked his chin a moment, before asking, "Is he known to be a hard drinker?"

"Not particularly," replied Davidson.

"I could smell the booze on him as soon as he walked in," noted White. "He's under enormous pressure right now."

"Good point. I bet he cracks soon," replied Davidson. "All good cops who fuck up eventually do. Their conscience gets to them."

"Time to find out what makes him tick and figure out what the best plan of attack will be," said White. "I would think a full psychological profile is in order."

"I'll get hold of the criminal profilers."

"With what has happened, do you expect him to be transferred?"

"Without his confession, it puts his agency in an embarrassing position. If they transfer him it will imply to the Mexicans he is being relocated to protect him. They may think we are condoning what he did."

"But if he isn't moved, the cartel may kill him," noted White.

"That would save everyone a lot of embarrassment," replied Davidson evenly.

chapter thirteen

It was Thursday afternoon when Corporal Connie Crane called Jack to say she had met with a Crown prosecutor.

"Here it is in a nutshell," said Connie. "If a judge thinks you have used too much intimidation, then whatever Slater may tell you would be inadmissible against him at any criminal proceedings. However, if what you are told assists us in investigating other players, then you might be able to go after them. Of course, if that happened, we still couldn't enter any of Slater's admissions."

"What about calling him as a witness if he knows something? Threaten him with perjury if he doesn't tell the truth."

"You wouldn't be able to enter evidence to prove he was lying. If you tried, a judge might say it puts justice into disrepute and toss the whole case."

"So we can use Slater as a stepping stone, but even if he incriminates himself we still have to send him on his way with a get out of jail free card."

"I think you got it."

"Want me to go for it?"

"Yeah, we've got nothing else. Wilson's in agreement. Both of us think he knows something about her disappearance, but we don't think he is a hands-on kind of guy. If you think you can pull off some tough-guy scenario to get him to talk, go for it."

"I'll let you know how it goes. It may take a couple of days."

"That's good to hear."

"Why?"

"Because if you were using pliers it wouldn't take that long."

An hour after talking with Connie, Jack visited The Racquet Club. After a quick tour, he accepted an offer of a free pass used as a promotion to entice people to buy a membership. He was glad to see the customers used padlocks to secure their storage lockers. His ability to pick locks would make that step of his undercover plan easy.

The hardest job would be finding a remote spot and digging a grave that wouldn't be discovered. For that, he found a construction site where the workers got weekends off.

On Friday afternoon, Jack called Sammy in Drug Section. "Hey, are you still hiding that ugly face of yours with a beard?" asked Jack.

"I only have a goatee now. What's up, Jack?"

"A goatee is good. Need a small favour for a quick UC."

"Yeah? How quick? Last time I agreed to do something for you, I ended up sitting in a bar so you could burn me to get the bad guys to trust you."

"That worked well."

"For you, yeah. Me, I could have been shot."

"Never took you for a whiner."

"A whiner? Up yours!" Sammy chuckled. "What do you need?"

"I need you to stand on a sidewalk and phone me when some guy arrives and asks for me. I'll know when he's arriving so you'll only have to be there for a few minutes."

"Sounds easy enough. Beats being in a doper bar like last time. When do you want to do it?"

"Tomorrow around supper time."

"Tomorrow's Saturday ... yeah, okay. Where at?"

"Do you know where the west-side chapter clubhouse for Satans Wrath is?"

"Oh, fuck ..."

chapter fourteen

On Saturday morning, Jack awoke to the sound of Natasha singing to Mikey. She was lying on her back in bed beside him, but holding the baby up above her chest with her hands around his waist. Her voice was soft and sweet.

"Michael Edward Taggart ... you're our little boy. Michael Edward Taggart, you're our pride and joy. Michael Edward Taggart, you're such a little clown. Michael Edward Taggart, you're fun to have around!" With this last comment she stretched her arms high and pretended to let Mikey drop.

Mikey's bright eyes, coupled with his smile and bubbly giggle, begged for more.

Jack smiled to himself as he lay there. *Life can be so good.*

It was a special moment locked in time. One that would later come back to haunt Jack at the most dire moment of his life.

"He's a very happy kid," said Jack, as Natasha lay Mikey on her chest.

"Do you think so?" asked Natasha, turning to stare at Jack.

"Are you kidding? Look at him. He's always giggling. Look at his eyes. So full of life."

"I am looking. I think he just fell asleep."

Natasha made a pretext of looking at Mikey and said, "Probably because he's bored."

"Bored? He's not even seven months old."

Natasha smiled at Jack and said, "He needs a baby sister or baby brother to play with."

"It has only been a couple of weeks since we started trying. All in good time."

"Boy, are you slow this morning. Don't you know when I'm giving you a nudge?" she said, before kissing Jack on the side of his neck.

Jack scrambled out of bed, gently picked up Mikey and raced down the hall to place him in his crib.

"I take it that was enough of a nudge," Natasha said, laughing as Jack ran back into their bedroom.

"You want to see a nudge? I'll show you a nudge," he replied, leaping back into bed.

Later that afternoon Natasha saw a hard look come over Jack's face moments before he slipped on a black Harley Davidson T-shirt and left for work. She knew he was psychologically preparing himself for a role of some sort, but she didn't like it. He didn't look like the man she married and it scared her.

It was five o'clock when Slater walked out of The Racquet Club and got in his car. Ten minutes later, he received a call on his cellphone.

"Yeah, is this Clive Slater?" asked Jack.

"Who wants to know?" replied Slater.

"The guy who found his wallet."

"What? ... Jesus! I didn't even know it was missing."

"I found it in the dressing room at The Racquet Club. They gave me your number. Looks like you got about eight hundred bucks in it, along with your credit cards."

"I'm not far away. I'll be right there."

"Oh, I didn't realize you had just left. I'm already in my car and am late for a meeting. Guess I could have left it at the club, but I'm not the trusting type so they gave me your number. My name's Jack. I'll give ya the address of where I'll be if ya want to slide by and pick it up. Otherwise, maybe in a couple of days we can get together."

"No, no. God, no. I need it. I'll come right away. Thanks a million."

Forty minutes later, Slater's sense of relief at being able to retrieve his wallet was replaced by a feeling of dread as he arrived at the address he was given. A high chain-link fence protected a yard full of Harley Davidsons. Keep Out signs, security cameras, coupled with a well-known logo and an emblazoned sign reading SATANS WRATH told him he was in dangerous territory.

Slater slowed his car to a crawl as he drove by. A menacing-looking man with a goatee was strolling toward him up the sidewalk, but stopped when he saw Slater and stood with his arms folded across his chest glaring at him. Slater lowered his window and said, "Excuse me, uh, sir. Do you know if there is a guy by the name of Jack around?"

"Yeah," replied Sammy. "He said someone was coming by. Hang on. I'll put a call in."

Slater stopped his car on the street and listened as Sammy used his cellphone.

"This is the guard at the north side," said Sammy. "Tell Jack there is some guy here to see him." Sammy paused a moment and said, "Yeah, I'll tell him," he added, before hanging up. Sammy looked at Slater. "Go down the block, take your first left and find a place to park and wait in your car. He'll be out in a minute."

Slater breathed a sigh of relief. The last thing he wanted to do was go inside the compound, or worse yet, inside the clubhouse.

Sammy waited until Slater had turned the corner before hustling off in the opposite direction, all too aware that the hum of moving security cameras told him it was time to leave.

Moments later, Slater saw Jack approach and tap on his passenger window while holding his wallet up for him to see. Slater lowered the window.

"Unlock the door," said Jack. "There is something we need to discuss."

"Of course." *He wants a reward*, thought Slater, unlocking the door.

Jack got in and handed him his wallet. Slater quickly flipped it open and smiled when he saw that his money and credit cards were all there.

"Thanks a bunch," Slater said. "You're a great guy to be returning it, especially with all this money. Most guys wouldn't. Let me give you a reward for all your trouble," he added, fishing a hundred-dollar bill from his wallet.

"Fuck that," said Jack gruffly. "I don't need your money. Besides, I'm not really that great. I actually stole your wallet."

"What? Why? Oh, you're joking," replied Slater, giving a nervous smile.

"Does this look like a fuckin' joke?" replied Jack, flipping open his jacket to reveal a pistol stuck in the front of his pants. "I did it to get you down here. Easier than taking you away from The Racquet Club."

"But why?" stammered Slater as Jack put his hand on the pistol's handgrip. "I haven't done anything to you guys. I'm not even in any gangs or anything. Whoever you're after … you've got the wrong guy!"

"No, we know we got the right guy, so shut up and listen. I know you're a businessman, so let me try to put it into words you'll understand. We distribute a product. You're competition. You must have heard of a hostile takeover. Consider this it."

"What product? I don't understand!" cried Slater.

"A very white product," said Jack, putting his thumbnail up to his nose and pretending to snort.

"I have no idea what you're talking about," said Slater.

Jack sighed and said, "Okay, I can see you're not stupid. That's good. Now I want you to take me for a little drive. I've got something to show you. It could actually save your life. You don't want to end up like your buddy Earl."

"That was you guys!" exclaimed Slater.

"Who the fuck did you think it was?"

"T-O's guys," blurted Slater. "I mean, I don't know."

"Who the fuck is T-O?"

"Oh, fuck …"

"I'm not asking you again," yelled Jack. "Who the fuck is T-O?"

"Nobody I've met," Slater hastened to say. "Just someone Earl owed money to."

"Well, it wasn't us who whacked Earl. We were going to offer him the same deal as you."

"A deal? What deal? I don't understand. If Earl was involved with you guys or something, I didn't know anything about it. I'm just a businessman. I don't —"

"Yeah, I know. Like I said, we're businessmen, too. So start driving. I've got something to show you to convince you we know a little more than you think."

"Can't you just tell me? I mean —"

"It's something you need to experience and see to believe. Don't worry, if we were going to kill you, you would already be dead and this class-act set of wheels you got would already be on a freighter bound for Russia."

chapter fifteen

The sun was going down and elongated shadows from the trees cast darkened silhouettes over mounds of dirt gouged out of a forest on the side of a mountain. For now, only the pits in the earth marked where the cement would be poured to make basements for a new residential pocket of homes.

It wasn't the cold that caused Slater to shake as he parked beside the construction trailer.

"Get out," ordered Jack. "What I got to show you is on the other side of the trailer."

"I don't like this," whined Slater. "I feel really uncomfortable. Can't we talk in the car?"

"Uncomfortable? See how uncomfortable you feel after a bullet rips through your kidneys!" roared Jack, pulling out his pistol.

Slater automatically lurched back, pressing himself so hard against the driver's door it looked like he was moulded into it. His eyes closed and his face crinkled, expecting to be shot.

"Jesus, fuck! Stop acting like that," said Jack. "If I wanted you dead, I'd shoot you now. I only want to talk to you. We've got a business proposition for you. Hand me the keys, too. I don't want you trying to fuck off and leave me here."

Slater opened his eyes and tried to calm himself as he fumbled the keys out of the ignition. As soon as he did, Jack snatched them out of his hand and said, "Now get out! I'm not tellin' ya again!"

Slater got out of the car and tried to convince himself Jack only wanted to talk to him, but his fear increased dramatically when, a few minutes later, he found himself with Jack looking down at a dug-out basement.

"Climb down," ordered Jack. "What I got to show you is alongside those footings on the far side."

Slater squinted into the darkness, but all he could see were wooden frames filled with rebar left in preparation to pour cement. A nudge from the barrel of a pistol in his back convinced him not to argue. Once they had descended into the pit, Jack prodded Slater over to a waist-deep, grave-sized hole dug in the ground and said, "Get in!"

"You are going to kill me! You said you weren't!" cried Slater.

"Yeah, I know," said Jack, shoving Slater into the hole.

Slater landed on his feet with his arms draped over the far side of the grave. He spun around and pleaded, "Please, don't. If you want money, I can get —"

"Sorry I lied about not killing you," said Jack. "I've been known to do that sometimes. I know it's a terrible habit, but I thought it was easier than dragging you."

"Please ... don't ..."

"Fuck, I knew it," said Jack, "look at that. "Will you look at that?"

"What?" cried Slater.

"How tall are you?"

"What? I'm —"

"This hole ain't nearly deep enough. I told the guys to dig it deeper. Jesus fuck, why is it if you want something done right, you've always gotta do it yourself?"

"Please! Listen to me. I can get my hands on a lot of money. Don't kill me."

Jack reached for a shovel stuck in the mound of dirt dug from the grave and tossed it into the hole beside Slater. "Tell ya what. You dig the hole deeper for me and then I promise to make it quick and clean. You won't feel a thing. Otherwise I'll gut shoot you and let you crawl around for half an hour while I dig. Then if ya haven't already bled out, I'll bury ya alive."

"Oh, God, no!" cried Slater.

"Is it a deal?" asked Jack, trying to sound hopeful.

"Please, don't!"

"Start digging. I'm going to talk to you about something. Maybe how you answer might make me change my mind."

Slater picked up the shovel and started to dig. He believed he was going to die and there was nothing he could do about it. All hope was gone and his brain was going numb and shutting down to protect him from the horror he faced.

Jack's cellphone rang. The call display told him it was Natasha. He could have ignored the call, but decided Slater needed more convincing and knew every minute the scenario dragged on would seem like an eternity to Slater.

"I'm going to take this call, don't move," ordered Jack.

Slater's foot was poised in the air over the shovel and he literally did not move.

"Hi, what's up?" asked Jack, stepping back to ensure Slater could not overhear his wife's voice.

"Did I catch you at a bad time?" asked Natasha.

"No, it's not a bad time. I'm just standing around waiting for a guy."

"I was just phoning to talk. I think Mikey is getting a cold. I might put the vaporizer in his room for tonight."

"Did you say you want me to vaporize him or not?" asked Jack, knowing Slater could hear. "The phone keeps cutting out. If I lose your call I guess I'll just do it."

"No, I said I would do it," said Natasha.

"Hello? Hello? Are you there?"

"Yes, I'm here, Jack. I can hear you fine."

"Oh ... I can hear you now."

"Your voice sounds funny ... is somebody there listening?"

"You got it."

"I see. Can you give me any idea when you're coming home?"

"I've still got a big pile of work to shovel through, but it shouldn't take long."

"With you, I don't know if you mean that figuratively or literally," replied Natasha.

Jack smiled to himself. He and Natasha had been through a lot together. More than a husband should ever ask of his wife.

As Jack talked, he stared at the man in the hole in front of him. He knew Slater did not need further convincing. He had gone into a catonic state. His foot was still poised in the air over the shovel.

Paralyzed by fear was something Jack thought was only an expression. It wasn't. Slater stood as rigid as a mannequin. *I wonder how he can do that without falling over?* He spoke a moment longer to Natasha and then hung up.

"Okay," said Jack, turning his attention to Slater. "Where were we? Oh, yeah, I was going to tell you whether or not you live is entirely up to you. Like I said, we have a proposition for you. If you want to go into business with us, everything will work out great. If you don't, well, I think you get the picture. Where you're standing is the experience I said you needed to have. Talking about it isn't the same. Don't you agree?"

Slater gawked up at him, but didn't reply.

"You listening to me?" yelled Jack.

Slater nodded and slowly put his foot down.

"You can start by telling me all about your organization," said Jack.

"It's not really mine," Slater heard himself say. "It's the Mexicans. I only work for them." He thought his voice sounded far away and wondered if he was having an out-of-body experience. *Am I already dead?* "T-O is the real boss," he heard his voice say. It was as if his words were coming out independently of his brain. "Earl and I run the money back," his voice continued.

"Back where?"

"To El Paso. T-O's guys come across the border from Juarez and take it from there."

"And the coke?" asked Jack.

"Earl and I never had anything to do with that. We were to stay clear of the coke and strictly handle the money. T-O likes to keep it separate."

"And who is T-O?"

Slater worked up the courage and nervously looked down at his feet, then gave a sigh of relief and started to cry.

"Why the fuck are you looking in the bottom of the hole? Don't even think about trying to whack me with that shovel!"

"I wasn't … I was afraid … I thought I might see my body laying there."

"What the fuck? How could your body be laying there? You're standing! Are you stoned?"

"No, I just —"

"Shut the fuck up and tell me who T-O is!"

"I've never met him!" he cried.

"Quit your fuckin' bawlin'! It pisses me off!" Jack waited a moment for Slater to regain his composure. "Tell me how you know T-O."

Slater wiped his face with his sleeve. "I met the guys who work for him. I've heard one of them mention his name whenever he calls him. I can tell T-O's the boss by how respectful the guy sounds when he talks to him."

"And how did you meet his guys?"

"Some of T-O's other guys approached Earl and me at a nightclub in Vancouver. At first we thought they were bullshitting about paying us to make trips, but then they offered us half the cash up front for the first delivery."

"And you think T-O whacked Earl?"

"Yes, well, his guys did."

"His guys from Canada?"

"No, I know they were sending a couple guys up from Mexico. Professionals."

Professionals? thought Jack. *Professionals don't sneer into the cameras. More likely they were expendables ...*

"They didn't want to risk drawing any attention to the guys who are already settled in Canada," continued Slater.

"So they whacked their own mule," noted Jack. "What did he do, steal their money?"

"Not intentionally. Earl has ... had a gambling problem. While he was waiting in El Paso for T-O's guys to show up, he hit some casino, lost his own money, and dipped into theirs."

El Paso! Please don't tell me the asshole took Lily to El Paso ...

"Things went from bad to worse and he ended up losing most of it," continued Slater.

"So then what, he just came back to Canada?"

"Not right away. He switched motels and then went back to the casino hoping to make a million out of about twenty grand. He lost that and then called me from the casino in a panic. When I was on the line with him, one of T-O's guys called me, as well. I put Earl on hold and well, you know, I had to look after myself."

"What the fuck do you mean?"

"I know better than to fuck with the Mexicans. I told Earl to go back to his motel and everything would be okay, that I would help him straighten it out. I then told T-O's guys where Earl was and what motel he was staying at with his girlfriend."

His girlfriend ... he did take her there. Jack resisted the urge to jump in the hole and take out his frustration by choking Slater around the neck and shaking him the way a pit bull shakes a rat. He knew if he was to play his role properly, he would have to pretend he was not particularly interested in any girlfriend Porter would have had. "Was this motel right at the casino?" Jack asked, trying to sound nonchalant.

"No, I don't think so. I can't remember the name of it."

"So you ratted out your friend ... you're a real stand-up kind of guy."

"I had no choice. If they ever found out I lied to them, I'd be dead, too. I knew Earl was already a dead man ... whether he knew it or not. Guess he figured it out when he drove into the motel parking lot and spotted T-O's guys waiting for him. He spun a donut and fucked off back to Canada."

"What about his girlfriend?"

"Oh, I'm sure T-O's guys killed her, too."

You're probably right ... "Didn't want to leave any loose ends."

"Yeah, for sure."

Was Lily as straight as Marcie thought she was? "Guess nobody told her if you fly with the crows, you should expect to get shot."

"Well ... she didn't really know what was going on. Earl had given her some bullshit story they were going to Texas to party with some business associates and then stop in Vegas on the way home and get married."

Aw crap ... the poor kid. "He was going to marry her?"

"He told me it was the only way he could get in her pants. I don't think he planned on being married long."

"Sounds like a great guy," said Jack, bitterly. "Wish I had gotten to know him on a personal level."

"Well, he couldn't risk going to the cops or they might have busted him for being a runner."

"So you sold out Earl and his girlfriend both," said Jack, eyeballing Slater's throat while subconsciously tightening the muscles in his fingers.

"It's not my fault. I had no choice. I feel bad about it, but a guy has to look after himself."

"Yeah, for sure. Now start digging again."

"What! I thought we had a deal?"

"Shut the fuck up and dig."

"Please let me talk. I could make you rich. I'm supposed to make a trip down there within the next two weeks. You can take the cash. I'll say I was robbed. Beat me up or something ..."

"Oh, believe me, tearing you to pieces does appeal to me," replied Jack. He took a deep breath, slowly exhaled and said, "How much cash we talkin'?"

"I don't know, but I'm sure it's over a million."

"What do ya mean, ya don't know? You're the one who delivers it."

"Besides my car, I have a pickup truck they gave me. The paperwork makes it look like I bought the truck in the States, but it didn't cost me a dime. In it is a secret hiding spot. If you adjust the knobs on the dash a certain way, a hydraulic system raises a fake deck up in the back of the truck."

"So the truck has a duplicate deck in the back ... a fake one over top of the original one?"

"Yes, exactly. I haul a minimum of a million with each trip. Sometimes more. I've never had the nerve to count it all myself, but I've seen them unload it at the trailer."

"At the trailer?"

"Before, in El Paso, we used to have to drive the money way to hell and gone out into the desert to some mobile trailer where they would unload it. I don't think they use it anymore. On this last trip they told Earl to stay at some motel outside of El Paso and call them. Then T-O's guys were to come and take him and the truck to someplace in Juarez."

"When do they put the money into your truck?"

"The day before I go, one of T-O's guys borrows it from me for a couple of hours and then brings it back. My job is to drive it down to El Paso. I get paid forty grand a trip. I'm supposed to go in another week or two. I haven't been told an exact date yet."

"Sounds interesting. Keep digging while I try to decide what to do."

Slater dug for another couple of minutes before Jack cooled off enough to stop enjoying the vengeance and get back to the task at hand. "Okay, I was just fucking with you. I wanted to make sure you got the point to never fuck with me. Climb out of there and refill the hole."

Slater started to weep. "Really?"

"Yeah, really. I got some things to tell you, but I don't have all night, so hurry up." Jack reached out his hand and Slater took it to help himself climb out.

Jack waited as Slater, who had discovered new energy, quickly started to refill the hole. "First thing I'm going to tell you," said Jack, "is never tell anyone ... and I mean *anyone*, about tonight."

"I won't. Just ... thank you for not killing me."

"Yeah, I've always thought of myself as a good guy, although some might disagree." Jack remained quiet until Slater had refilled the hole and said, "*¿Habla usted español?*"

"What? No. Just *gracias*."

"For a guy who hangs out with Mexicans, you really are a dumb fuck. The Spanish word for uncle is *tio*. It sounds like T-O. The guy you were listening to was talking to his uncle."

"I didn't know that."

"For now, we will still call him Tio ... but I want to meet him in person. You need to arrange it."

"Why? I mean ... after tonight, I don't want anything to do with this business. I'm quitting. You guys don't need to look at me as competition anymore."

"We don't give a rat's ass about you. This is about Tio. We want to go into business with him. Once you introduce him to me, you can jump off a bridge for all I care, but until then, you better do what we want. We know the Mexicans have been sellin' coke on the streets cheaper than ours. That means they're getting it at a way cheaper price than we've been getting from the fuckin' Colombians. Get word to Tio we handle about three or four ton a year. That should spark his interest."

"Okay, sure, I'll contact one of his guys and let him know."

Jack had a major concern. He knew permission to go to Ciudad Juarez, Mexico, would never be approved because the police there were too corrupt and it would be deemed too dangerous. He would have to try and convince Tio to come to the U.S.

"There is one other thing Tio needs to know," said Jack. "I was in Mexico about a year ago and got into a little shit and used a chair to lay a beating on a couple of Federales who tried to arrest me. I think one guy was hurt real bad. I don't know how the situation stands for me there now. Tell Tio I want to meet him on the U.S. side of the border." Jack felt it was a lame excuse, but at the moment he couldn't think of anything better.

Jack, carrying the shovel, returned with Slater to the car where they continued to talk some more. Jack also had him go over the details again. His purpose was not only to ensure he had been given the correct information, but it was to give Slater a chance to calm down before driving.

Jack also used the opportunity to impress upon Slater the need for secrecy and told him that even with other members of Satans Wrath, it was still on a need-to-know basis.

It was midnight when Jack had Slater drive him back and park a block away from the Satans Wrath clubhouse.

"Here is good," said Jack. "I don't want you ever coming here again. The cops monitor our clubhouse a lot. I don't want them, or anyone else knowing we're connected. It will be safer for everyone in the long run."

"What about the cellphone number you gave me? Is it cool?"

"I don't trust any phone. If you call me, simply say you're interested in a game of squash and we can meet at The Racquet Club."

"Okay."

"How long do you think it will be before you hear back from Tio?"

"I don't know. I'll call my contact tomorrow morning. After that I'll have to wait. It might only take a few minutes for them to pass it on to Tio, or maybe it could take a couple of days. I've never spoken to Tio. I just know he's the big boss. I have no control over him."

"Understood, but make sure Tio knows we are his equals. I won't deal with some peon over this matter."

"Oh, I'm sure he'll know that. Everybody in the world knows about you guys."

Jack thought about asking Slater who his contact in Canada was, along with the names of his contacts in El Paso, but he knew to push for more information now might raise suspicion. *All in good time …*

"I expect you to get on it immediately."

"I will, but, uh, if he isn't interested, I mean, you know, I'll tell him he could make a lot of money through you guys, but, what if —"

"If he turns us down, we would consider it a declaration of war," snarled Jack.

"Oh," replied Slater softly. "I'll do my best."

"I'm sure you will. I'll come by your place at noon to see how you made out. And like I said before, we don't want anyone to know we are thinking of going in with the Mexicans. For now, I will be the only contact. We don't want word of this getting out."

"I won't tell a soul."

"Make sure you tell your Mexican contacts to keep their mouths shut and only deal through me, as well. At least for now."

Jack checked his watch as he drove home. He knew it was too late to be checking with the American authorities in El Paso to see if they had any recent unidentified female bodies.

And if they don't have any recent bodies from a motel ... then where is she?

chapter sixteen

Jack arrived home and checked on Mikey, who was asleep in his crib. He then stuck his head in his own bedroom.

"You're home," murmured Natasha, awakened by the door opening.

"Home, but not done. I've got a couple hours of notes to do. How is Mikey?"

"He's okay. I think he's better."

Jack took off his gun and put it on his dresser. He would have talked some more, but Natasha's breathing told him she had gone back to sleep. He went to the den and made notes about what he had learned.

Tomorrow morning he would call CC and meet with her and Wilson, but first there was something else he wanted to check.

Jack had heard for years about the hundreds of women who were disappearing or being found murdered around Ciudad Juarez, Mexico. He turned on his computer to search the Web.

It didn't take long to find a mass of material relating to the missing women. There had been hundreds. In a few instances there had been arrests, with a few bus drivers being implicated, but for the most part it was a war zone.

Armed cartel members kidnapped women in broad daylight without fear of repercussion. A few were unceremoniously dumped back on the street a day or two later, but many others were murdered and found in shallow graves or laying in drainage ditches outside the city. One woman was found with one breast cut off with a knife and the other bitten off.

Jack sighed and turned the computer off and went to bed. As he lay there, he thought about Slater and his admission that he told the Mexicans where Lily Rae was. He knew there was nothing he could legally do to Slater over what he had been told and the frustration burned inside him.

He did not want to think about what had happened to a naive young girl from Canada by the name of Lily Rae. He did not want to think about it ... but he did.

It was a long night.

Probably should have killed the bastard ...

Slater's night was worse. He went home and saw his girlfriend sitting on the sofa watching a movie.

"Where the fuck were you?" she yelled. "You couldn't even bother to call me?"

"I was busy. I forgot to phone you."

"You were too busy to take a minute and call me? What was her name?"

"I wasn't with a girl."

"Yeah, I just bet you ... fuck! Look at you! I can believe you weren't with a girl. Maybe a pig. You got dirt all over you. What were you doing?"

"Nothing."

"You were doing something. God, you stink, too. What was it?"

"I met some guy. We did a lot of talking."

"How did you get so dirty?"

"I fell in a hole. We were walking and I fell in."

"So you were stoned."

"No, it just happened."

"Well it sure as hell is too late to go to dinner now. Have you eaten?"

"No."

"Your voice sounds weird."

"What do you mean?"

"Monotone. You remind me of my grade eight history teacher."

"I'm tired."

"Me too. But I'm also fuckin' hungry."

"How about I make you an omelette?"

"Yeah, okay ... but shower first. You really reek of B-O."

Later, Slater went to the kitchen in his bathrobe and opened a carton of eggs.

"So who was this guy you spent all night talking to?" his girlfriend asked.

"Just somebody I met. It's business. I can't talk about it," replied Slater.

"That's what you always say when you don't want to explain what you've been up to. Hope you don't mind me saying this, but I really get the feeling you're shovelling me a load of crap."

Apparently Slater did mind. A hysterical cry emitted from his mouth and he repeatedly grabbed at the eggs with both hands, squeezing and crushing them as the broken bits of eggshell and yolk ran through his fingers.

chapter seventeen

It was nine o'clock Sunday morning when Connie Crane and Wilson arrived together at Jack's office.

"Well, we're here," said Connie. "When you called this morning, you woke me up. You did say Slater spilled his guts to you and we needed to talk. I heard right, didn't I? At first I thought I was dreaming."

"You weren't dreaming," replied Jack.

"Yeah? Well it better be good. Today would have been my first day off in two weeks."

"I don't know if it's good news," replied Jack, "but it's informative. Yesterday I met him through The Racquet Club and pretended to be a member of Satans Wrath. I said we had a business proposition for him."

"You told him you were with the club and he believed you?" asked Connie.

"I had him swing by the clubhouse after to meet me. I used Sammy from Drug Section in a quick UC to direct him down the street and park. I then sat in his car with him and he presumed I came out of the clubhouse."

"Pretty smooth," chuckled Wilson. "Better hope

Satans Wrath never finds out."

Jack nodded in agreement.

"So what did you say to him?" asked Connie.

"I offered him a chance to go into business together."

"With Satans Wrath?" exclaimed Wilson. "What if he goes to them looking for you?"

"I am a little concerned about that," admitted Jack. "When I used the ruse on him, I didn't expect it would turn into any long-term project. I was hoping a day or two would be all we needed to find Lily."

"So your cover story may not hold up for long," noted Wilson.

"For the short term I feel comfortable with it. I made a point of telling Slater to only deal with me. I've got a feeling he will do what I tell him."

"So then he opened up to you?" asked Connie, suspiciously. "He trusted you just like that?"

"Are you kidding? He was practically on his knees begging to work with me."

Connie stared at Jack, then opened her mouth to speak, but changed her mind.

"So, let me tell you what I learned," continued Jack.

Over the next half hour, Connie and Wilson each jotted down notes as Jack outlined what he had learned from Slater.

"I would never have believed he would open up so quickly upon meeting you," said Wilson. "You must have been pretty convincing."

"I guess he thought so."

"From what you have said, it sounded like the two of you had a really amiable conversation," said Connie, watching Jack closely. "Maybe we could use his admission against him as evidence."

"Uh …"

"Or when you said he was practically on his knees begging, should I take that literally?"

"Well, it was sort of literal," admitted Jack.

"Christ! I thought so! What did you do to the poor son of a bitch?"

"What do you mean the poor son of a bitch?" growled Jack. "He doesn't deserve any pity. He set up Porter to be killed ... which personally I am quite happy about, but he also set up Lily."

"But what did you —"

"Anything I did to him was strictly psychological," responded Jack, tersely. "I didn't hurt him physically. That's all you need to know."

"I think that's all I want to know," replied Connie, quietly.

"However you did it, your information is a huge lead," said Wilson. "I really appreciate it. With what we saw in the apartment security cameras it fits. I think Slater was being truthful to you."

"Oh, I'm sure he was," replied Jack. "He knows he'd be digging himself a hole he couldn't get out of if he was lying to Satans Wrath."

"And he thinks Tio sent a hit team up from Mexico, whacked Porter, and then skedaddled back to Mexico?" noted Wilson.

"That's what Slater believes. He says Tio does have Mexicans living here and distributing cocaine, but after Porter fled from the motel, one of Tio's men called and told him they were going to send a team up to Canada to take care of Porter. Also explains why the killers didn't worry about the security cameras. I bet they headed south the same day."

"We still have both of Porter's vehicles impounded," said Wilson. "I'll get the mechanics to take another look at his truck. See if it has a secondary deck in the back."

"Too bad you didn't know what motel Lily Rae was in at the time," said Connie. "Might have given us more of a lead if she was taken someplace else to be killed."

"Let's hope she hasn't been murdered," said Jack quietly.

"And from how these guys operate," said Wilson, "if they were going to kill her, I don't see them as the type to worry about hiding any bodies. At least, not driving a victim out to … how did Slater put it? A trailer?"

"Way to hell and gone out into the desert to some mobile trailer," said Jack.

"Exactly," said Connie. "If she's dead, the U.S. probably already has her body. I'll get on the horn today with the FBI and whatever other law enforcement agencies they have down there. Let's see if they have any unidentified victims who match Lily's description." She looked at Jack and added, "Not that I'm giving up hope. Just doing my job."

"I know," said Jack. "It's also Sunday morning. What do you think your chances are of finding out today?"

"Let's find out," said Connie.

Everyone was quiet as Connie started making phone calls, first to the FBI, then the state police, Texas Rangers, and finally the El Paso Police Department.

Her responses were much the same. Nobody was aware, offhand, of any victims fitting Lily's description, but each suggested it would be better to go through channels on Monday when the regular staff were on duty and could give a more informed answer.

It gave the Canadian investigators some sense of hope.

Over the next two hours, Jack, Connie, and Wilson completed reports, along with an operational plan to be approved by the brass. The basis for the plan rested on an attached report submitted by Jack that said while acting in an undercover capacity and portraying an image of an outlaw biker, he had befriended Clive Slater. His report then listed what Slater had told him.

Connie reviewed Jack's report and said, "You befriended him?"

"I've never met anyone who wanted so badly to be my friend," replied Jack.

"Yeah, I can only imagine. Would you mind if I added that Slater possibly might have felt intimidated by your role and the Crown would no doubt feel a conviction against him would be unlikely?"

"Knowing our justice system as I do, what you just said sounds most probable." Jack lowered his voice, cupped a hand to the side of his mouth and in a staged whisper added, "I did yell at him."

"Got a feeling that's not all you did," she replied, going back to work on the operational plan. When she was finished, the plan called for:

- Jack's undercover scenario to continue in the hope of identifying Tio and perhaps some of the men who worked for him in Canada. If Jack's undercover role led to the identification of Tio and his men, then his UC role would be finished unless circumstances indicated Jack might be successful in finding Lily Rae or her body.

- Permission for Jack to go to El Paso was requested should it be deemed necessary, along with a request the Americans be asked through the appropriate channels to provide assistance for his protection should that happen.

- That the Vancouver RCMP Drug Section work jointly on the project to take over the drug-trafficking aspect of the investigation.

- That Drug Section and Proceeds of Crime investigators would likely be required to travel to El Paso to gather evidence to support cocaine importation and money-laundering charges against the people in Canada. Should that be necessary, they would submit their own request in due course, while still bearing in mind their evidence might be needed to explain the motive behind Porter's murder at a trial in Canada. It was stressed the investigators from the different units would need to work closely together.

- It was further recommended that if the two suspects on the security camera in Porter's apartment were identified and arrested in El Paso, then permission was requested for Connie and Wilson to travel to El Paso to work with the American authorities and take part in any interrogations. Extradition proceeding would also be initiated.

- If it was learned that Lily Rae was murdered in El Paso, the United States would deal with it as it would be in their jurisdiction. In this case, Connie and Wilson would also work with the American investigators, as evidence obtained in Canada concerning Porter's murder might be needed in the United States or visa versa. The Canadian investigators would also look into the possibility that the U.S. judicial system might allow for Slater to be used as a probable hostile witness at criminal proceedings in the U.S.

It was noon when Jack went over to Slater's apartment and buzzed the intercom.

"Who is it?" asked a female voice.

"My name is Jack. I'm, uh, Clive's friend. Is he in?"

"You're his friend? Good, then come on up."

Minutes later, Jack was let into Slater's apartment by a young woman.

"Is he here?" asked Jack.

"Fuck, no."

"Do you —"

"I don't know where he is. He took off this morning. If you're his friend you can hang around and tell him it's over between us. I'm splitting," she said, stomping into the bedroom where she continued to throw clothes into a suitcase on the bed.

"Any idea when he might be back?" asked Jack.

"Nope and I don't care. The guy's a fuckin' nutcase."

"Why do you say that?"

"Well, for starters, he came home last night all covered in dirt and then had a meltdown."

"A meltdown?"

"Oh, yeah. A real doozie. He started smashing eggs and crying like a baby. I took him to the hospital and some shrink talked to him for an hour."

"Really? I wonder what that was all about? Did he say?"

"No, he wouldn't talk to the shrink … or to me. They gave him some pills to take, which he wouldn't, so I end up driving him back home at four o'clock this morning. Then at eight he tells me he's going out. 'It's Sunday morning,' I say. 'Where ya going?' Like that is too much to ask. He tells me it's none of my fucking business. Well, you can tell him it really ain't none of my fucking business because I'm done with him."

Seconds later, Jack watched as she dragged the suitcase off the bed and stormed out of the apartment, leaving Jack alone.

Jack quickly locked the apartment door and started

to search. He knew the search was illegal and anything he found would not be allowed as evidence, but decided as Slater already had a get-out-of-jail-free card, it really didn't matter.

A short time later, he hauled what seemed like an empty suitcase down off a shelf in the closet. In and outside pocket of the suitcase he found a hand-drawn map. On it were the initials *EP-W-CR14-12-U-L*. Above the initial *U* was a string of dotted lines coming up to a pile of small lines in a haphazard pattern with an *X* over one of them.

Jack recalled the house trailer out in the desert that Slater had mentioned to him and speculated the map was instructions on how to get to it. Slater had told him he didn't think the trailer was being used, but decided to copy it into his notebook, regardless. He had most of the pertinent details down when he heard the apartment door being unlocked.

Slater was startled to see Jack standing in the doorway to his kitchen.

"Your girlfriend let me in," he explained. "She said to tell you she's out of here. She packed a suitcase and just left. I'm surprised you didn't bump into her in the hallway."

"I couldn't care less about her," replied Slater.

"I was about to look and see if you had any coffee."

"Yeah, I'll get it," replied Slater, walking into the kitchen and opening a cupboard.

"I understand you lost it when you got home last night."

"Yeah, I guess. I'm okay now. I just, uh, never had that experience before."

His words sounded robotic and his face was without emotion. Jack knew it would be a long time, if ever, before Slater would be okay. "So how did you make out this morning?" he asked.

"I think you guys should be happy," replied Slater. "I met with my Canadian contact and told him what you told me to say. He made me wait while he emailed someone in a chat room who I guess then had to go to another computer and email someone else. Anyway, eventually the message was passed on to Tio. He had a couple of questions and we had to go through the whole process again, but in the end, he said he is willing to meet you in person."

"I thought he would be," replied Jack evenly, while controlling the excitement he felt. "What questions did he have?"

"He wanted to know how I met you, so ... well, you said not to tell anyone about last night. So I lied to them and said I've known you all my life. I told them you were my cousin. Is that all right?"

"Yeah ... it's perfect. You did really well." *They'll probably kill you for that later ...*

"He also wanted to know why I hadn't mentioned you before. I said I had never said anything to him or you because I was afraid you guys would look at each other as competition. Then I said when you invited me over to the clubhouse yesterday, you mentioned you guys were really unhappy with the Colombians. I said I told you I knew a guy in Mexico who could help and that one thing led to another and you wanted to meet him."

"Excellent. So when and where do I meet him?"

"He said you're to go to El Paso. One week from Wednesday."

"Ten days from now," noted Jack. "I wonder why then and not sooner?"

"I think because I'm supposed to make a delivery down there at the same time. He said for us to check in at a place called the Armadillo Motel and he would arrange for you to see him."

Arrange for me to see him? Tio doesn't plan on coming to the motel ... "Have you used that motel before?"

"Yes, it's the one we always stay at. It's where Earl was before he took off to another motel last time."

"Which you can't remember the name of."

"I think it had the word Sunset in it. Why is it important?"

"We want to make sure you're not bullshitting us on anything. The boys will be checking you out to make sure you're not trying to set us up for a rip or anything. I was told to get details. Any little details that don't jive ... "

"God, no! After last night ... man, I wouldn't lie to you about anything. I'm being totally straight with you."

"Good. Keep it that way."

"I will." Slater paused for a moment, unsure what to say.

"What's on your mind?" prodded Jack.

"About El Paso ... I guess we can drive down together. It's best to leave on the Sunday when there is lots of border traffic. Less chance of being checked."

"Fuck that. I'm not some flunky. I'll fly down and meet up with you."

"Oh ... yeah. I guess that would be better."

Jack took a deep breath and slowly exhaled. It was not good news that the motel was one picked by Tio. It could mean they knew the owner and the presence of anyone there to assist Jack could put the investigation ... and Jack, into jeopardy.

Let the games begin ...

chapter eighteen

Monday morning was busy for Connie Crane. Given the short time frame, she classified her operational plan a priority and had it approved regionally before it was forwarded to Ottawa. She also made calls to the FBI and the DEA in El Paso. Neither agency had any concrete leads to identify Tio. There were lots of "uncles."

The FBI said they would also check to see if any unidentified female bodies found in the area were a match to Lily Rae, as well as trying to locate the motel she had been taken from. Photos of the man who sneered at the apartment security camera were also transmitted to the FBI.

Wilson had news on two fronts. He said it took their mechanics five hours to figure it out, but by adjusting various knobs on the dash of Porter's truck, a hydraulic system raised the rear deck of the pickup truck to reveal a hiding spot that was shallow, but took in an area almost as large as the box of the pickup itself. Plenty of room to hide a lot of money.

The second piece of news from Wilson was that enhancement of the security camera images from Porter's apartment was not successful enough for positive identification of the second man, but it did show he was missing an earlobe.

Connie called Jack with the information and he quickly dubbed the second man *Lobulo,* after the Spanish word for lobe.

Connie sent an addendum to her operation plan, confirming the accuracy of the information Jack had received in regard to the hidden box on the truck, as well as forwarding Lobulo's photo to the FBI.

Before the day was over, Connie heard back from the FBI. They had located a motel on the outskirts of El Paso called The Cactus Sunset. The owner said a young couple had checked into a room twelve days ago on a Wednesday night, under the name of J. Roberts from Kelowna, Canada, and paid cash for the room. The owner of the motel said they left behind two suitcases. One full of men's clothes and the other woman's clothes. Neither suitcase had any identification. The motel did record the licence plate number when they checked in.

The FBI had already run the plate. It was registered to Earl Porter. The FBI would continue their search for possible witnesses, although said it was the type of place where couples often used false names.

The FBI also confirmed that Lily Rae did not match any unidentified bodies. Given the short time frame involved and her long, red hair, she would easily stand out. They had also checked with local hospitals in the event she had been admitted in an unconscious state, but were told she hadn't.

The FBI agent did note the Cactus Sunset Motel was located on the edge of a desert. Disposal of a body would be relatively easy and the wind would quickly cover any tire tracks.

At the RCMP headquarters in Ottawa, the prioritized

operational plan was accepted with little fanfare. Requests for Canadian investigators to travel to the United States were a matter of routine and the U.S. was always quick to give permission. Given the short time frame when travel would be necessary, a reply from the U.S. was expected either that afternoon or Tuesday morning.

This time was different. Approval did not come through regular channels, but a response came late Tuesday afternoon with a highly unusual request for a meeting between the U.S. ambassador in Ottawa and either the RCMP commissioner or a high-ranking officer if the commissioner was not available. A meeting was subsequently scheduled for eleven o'clock Wednesday morning when the commissioner would be available.

RCMP bureaucrats in Ottawa pondered over the situation. *What was different about this investigation that would call for a face-to-face meeting with the ambassador?*

In advance of the meeting, a team of bureaucratic RCMP officers did an analysis of the operational report submitted by Connie Crane. A name caught their eye. Jack Taggart had submitted a lot of reports over the years. Rumours and suspicions had percolated for ages about his methods and the deadly consequences of some of his investigations. Past investigative reports involving Taggart were scrutinized again.

Some of these reports had hand-written notations added by senior officers. Suspicions had been strongly aroused as to how he could so accurately predict in advance the organizational changes taking place in some organized crime families. His predictions about the future murders of some of the organized crime figures and who would replace them had also proven to be sur-prising accurate.

It was noted that Taggart had a knack for developing confidential informants who gave him inside information, but, that aside, if was generally felt there were far too many coincidences and Taggart's predictions were too accurate to accept that there was not an underlying complicity of criminal involvement on his part.

One chief superintendent questioned why so many criminal groups Taggart investigated seemed to self-destruct in a spree of murder and mayhem shortly after his investigations began, usually with the criminals apparently killing each other. The chief superintendent had even underlined the word *apparently* with a comment he had made to the Pacific regional commander, Assistant Commissioner Isaac, while discussing his concerns.

Hand-written notes that followed on the report noted that Isaac also had concerns about Taggart and agreed it appeared there were far too many coincidences to rationally believe the mayhem that befell the criminal organizations could all be coincidental to Taggart's seemingly innocent involvement.

That being said, Isaac did state there had never been any concrete evidence to prove that Taggart was a rogue officer. Isaac noted Taggart had been the subject of several Internal Affairs and Anti-Corruption investigations without any evidence of wrongdoing ever being uncovered.

It did not take the bureaucrats in Ottawa long to form an opinion.

Yes, the meeting with the U.S. ambassador must somehow involve Taggart. Did the U.S. somehow possess information about him to support the rumours? Perhaps even have evidence to lay a criminal charge? There was consensus that the Americans must have substantially solid evidence if they were going to accuse an officer in a foreign government of misconduct.

The scheduled meeting with the U.S. ambassador was immediately classified as on a need-to-know basis ... and it was decided nobody outside of a handful of bureaucrats in Ottawa needed to know.

Early Wednesday morning, when a routine telephone call from the officer in charge of the Integrated Homicide Investigation Team in British Columbia was received, wanting to confirm the approval of the operation plan, he was brushed off with an explanation the delay was because the U.S. counterpart who usually handled such requests was on holidays and someone new was temporarily filling in. The I-HIT officer was told the operational plan would likely be approved later that afternoon.

The meeting with the U.S. ambassador was held and the bureaucrats felt smug that they went armed with enough circumstantial evidence against Taggart to alleviate any embarrassment or inclination that they were not completely on top of the situation.

They were soon disappointed. It had nothing to do with Jack Taggart. The U.S. had their own special investigation going in El Paso involving a rogue agent of their own who was the primary suspect in a recent murder of a Mexican drug cartel member.

The ambassador said it was believed that the Canadian investigators would come in contact with the rogue officer in El Paso because he was apparently the most knowledgeable about the Mexican cartels in that area and also had a high-level confidential informant who supplied him with valuable information about the cartels.

He went on to say that their criminal profilers, armed with a psychological profile of their rogue agent, said the agent would be under a great deal of stress, which was evidenced by the sudden appearance of excessive drinking. It was predicted he would soon make an admission of guilt to someone, possibly as a psychological need for self-vindication.

The ambassador said he felt they were obliged to share the nature of the investigation with the Canadians so as not to ruffle any feathers and to alleviate any misunderstandings should the Canadian investigators accidentally be overheard in an ongoing wiretap investigation concerning their rogue agent. The possibility also existed that the Canadian investigators could become involved in future criminal proceedings to give evidence should the rogue agent make some comment or disclose something to help convict him.

The disappointment that the RCMP bureaucrats momentarily felt turned to elation. They explained that they, too, had a rogue officer who was involved in the intended investigation in El Paso. They suggested that with a little manipulation, they could not only assist the U.S. in their investigation, but perhaps kill two birds with one stone.

A flurry of phone calls ensued. The result was the U.S. special investigators and the district attorney assigned to the case were more than happy with the idea. The timing and the similar personality traits of the two men fit perfectly with what the criminal profilers said was needed for an ultimate admission of guilt. It was further predicted that an admission by one would generate an admission of wrongdoing by the other.

This joint U.S.–Canada investigation was given the code name of *Birds of a Feather*.

chapter nineteen

It was six-thirty Thursday morning and Jack was lying on his back, awake, when Natasha came out of the bathroom and slipped back under the sheets and cuddled up to him.

"You're a very dangerous man, Mr. Jack Taggart," she said, mischievously. "Do you know that?"

"A few people have suggested that," he replied suspiciously, as a half smile appeared at the corner of his mouth.

"Yup, armed and dangerous, I would say," she continued, as her hand gave a playful tug on his penis. "I think I should call you *Dead Eye Dick*."

"What are you talking about? You're not …?"

"Yes, indications are I am," she replied, giving a smile.

"It's only been a couple of weeks since we said we would try," said Jack, feeling dumbfounded. "How do you know already? I mean, is this for real or only hopeful thinking?"

"I just did a test."

"Did it come back blue, meaning it's going to be another boy?" joked Jack, while his brain still tried to process the moment.

Natasha smiled and said, "I think it's a good thing you never decided to enter the medical profession. I only know I'm pregnant. I figure we should be due around the middle of next April."

Jack felt at a momentary loss for words, so he hugged her and kissed her long and passionately on the lips and then on her neck, while holding her as close to him as he could. He felt her tears on his cheek. *Or are they mine?*

As Jack drove to work he glanced in the rear-view mirror. He saw he had a goofy grin on his face. It only made him smile more. As he got closer to his office, he wondered if Mikey would be getting a baby brother or a baby sister.

The thought of having a daughter made him think about Lily Rae and the joy he had been feeling disappeared. As a parent, he appreciated even more how much her mother must be hurting. He decided he would phone her when he got to the office. He would not risk endangering the secrecy of the investigation by telling her about El Paso, but he would make her a solemn promise to reassure her he would do everything he possibly could to find her daughter.

As he stopped for a traffic light, his mind went back to the hundreds of murdered and missing women out of Juarez ... and the thousands of loved ones who still must be grieving their loss. *How do they deal with the pain? Many of the bodies were never found. Some would never have closure ...*

As he sat waiting for the light to change, sadness was replaced by rage and his knuckles turned white as he gripped the steering wheel. *If someone ever came after my family ...*

Jack knew then he would do everything he could to find Lily Rae.

Including going into Mexico if need be ...

Assistant Commissioner Isaac received a call from Assistant Commissioner Franklin in Ottawa and Birds of a Feather was explained. He was told to ensure Corporal Taggart was sent alone to El Paso for a few days to work with Special Agent John Adams.

"Hopefully that will give the two of them a chance to bond without distractions from other investigators," Franklin said.

The muscles rippled across Isaac's clenched jaw. *Using Taggart like this is wrong. The fact that the commissioner didn't ever bother to talk to me about it is wrong ...* "You likely won't have to worry about Taggart bonding," sighed Isaac. "He's like a chameleon when it comes to fitting in and making friends. From the winos to the academia. People generally like him and go out of their way to accommodate him."

"You're probably right, there. The way he got Slater to trust him and open up so quickly was amazing."

"That's not an example I would use," replied Isaac.

"Oh, that's right. Corporal Crane made a notation Slater may have felt a little intimidated. But still, you agree this plan should work?"

"No, I didn't say that. Taggart is pretty sharp. Others might trust him, but he isn't one to put his trust in someone else or seek their approval."

"The psychological profile that the Americans have put together indicates there is a strong chance for success. These two have very similar personalities. The plan is fairly simple. All the psychologist says needs to be done is to isolate the two of them so they think they are on their own, while putting a little pressure on them to give them the feeling it is them against the world. It will help them bond."

"The Stockholm Syndrome," Isaac remarked.

"Basically. Our hostage negotiators do it all the time."

"And what pressure do they have in mind?" said Isaac bitterly. "I don't want anyone losing focus as to the primary reason why he would be going to El Paso."

"No, no. Of course not. They wouldn't do anything to really jeopardize the case they are working on. It would simply be bureaucracy, which often happens, anyway."

"Such as?"

"Taggart's history, as well as John Adams's, makes it abundantly clear they are both extremely dedicated to getting the job done."

"And is this the reason you came up with Corporal Taggart's name for this scheme? That he is extremely dedicated?" asked Isaac.

"Fanatical is more like it. Adams is apparently the same way. Look back on the investigations Taggart was involved in. Case after case where —"

"I am well aware of the cases he has worked on. In fact, I have made it my personal business to keep a close eye on him," said Isaac. "Quite frankly, I feel irked that I was left out of the decision-making concerning this project. He is, after all, under my command."

"Which is why I am calling you."

"Right," said Isaac, somewhat sarcastically, "after the big guy has already made the decision. So let's get back to the intended pressure that is to be put on these two men. What exactly is intended?"

"Simply holding back or delaying resources once in a while should do the trick. Bureaucratic-type stuff that would grate against their personalities. Neither of these two men have a reputation for following policy."

"Corporal Taggart is going to be working within a stone's throw of Ciudad Juarez, Mexico. I don't think

I need tell you how extremely dangerous that place is. It is also the home base of this Tio character. If you are cutting back or delaying resources, it better not be at the risk of anyone's life. Whether it is Taggart's, Adams's, or anyone else's."

"Of course not, but Texas is the only place Taggart is authorized to be. Mexico is strictly off-limits. If Taggart follows policy, then he should be safe enough."

"Safe enough? Every man, woman, cat, and dog owns a gun in Texas." Isaac snorted derisively. "We are already asking this man to risk his life in an undercover situation by sending him there. Think about it. He will be dealing with a Mexican cartel that has already sent a hit team to Canada to commit a murder. They'd kill him without batting an eyelash if they thought something was wrong. Safe enough my ass. Would you do it?"

"No, but like I said, he's a fanatic. We are well aware his assignment to El Paso is dangerous."

"Which should be stress enough without intentionally adding to it."

"I'm sure our American friends will be prudent. As far as his personal safety goes, he will be given whatever protection is possible in El Paso. If he is stupid enough to go into Mexico, he will be on his own. We can hardly ask our American counterparts to risk their lives by crossing that border also."

"Guess I can't argue with that logic." Isaac sighed.

"So you are in agreement?"

"Well, I really think whether I agree or not is a moot point. I am sure the decision by the man above us has already been made. He is not interested in my opinion … which is why he had you call me instead of him. You calling to ask for my concurrence is only a formality."

"You're right about that, but aren't you happy with the prospect of finding out if Taggart is dirty?"

"I would be, but let me go on record as saying I am opposed to Birds of a Feather for two reasons. The first being that Taggart is very sharp and I am not optimistic of success and —"

"The psychological experts would disagree with you," Franklin interrupted. "They think once one starts to talk, it will open up a floodgate of chatter. The U.S. is confident Adams will talk. Taggart might even be called to testify against him and vice versa. It will be a feather in our cap to help the Americans. No pun intended. I bet they'll be very grateful."

"And I was going to add that considering Taggart's intellect and his inherent ability to survive, all this brown-nosing you're doing to the Americans may backfire on you," said Isaac.

"Co-operation between countries is not brown-nosing, it's simply good police work. What is your second reason?" Franklin asked.

"I don't feel the basic concept of using a policeman from one country to catch a policeman from another country is a good idea. It won't build a trusting relationship for future investigations once word of it gets out."

"Listen ... are you sure you wish to go on record for being against it? Think about your career. I've heard rumours you could be the next commissioner. Disagreeing with anything the chief says could ... well, you know what he's like."

I must really be a candidate for the spot, otherwise he wouldn't be sucking up to me like this ... Isaac shook his head and replied, "I don't care, I want my opinion noted. And as far as being offered the top spot, I would refuse."

"You would?" replied Franklin incredulously.

"Being a political lackey for whatever government is in charge doesn't appeal to me. Neither does hanging out with him in Ottawa and sucking up to him every chance

I get, although I know you would disagree because you think brown-nosing is good police work."

A moment of cold silence was followed with, "Fine," came the crisp reply. "Your concerns will be duly noted. Now talk to Taggart's superior and clear the way for Birds of a Feather to proceed."

"I'm not done yet. You should know that if Taggart's life is put in jeopardy down there as a result of your Birds of a Feather, I won't remain quiet about it. International diplomacy be damned. Tell that to the commissioner!"

Staff Sergeant Rose Wood received a call from Isaac who said, "I'm letting you know Ottawa approved the operational plan submitted by I-HIT over the El Paso investigation, but with a few minor changes."

"Yes, sir ... and those changes would be?" asked Rose as she reached for her pen.

"Corporal Taggart has been approved as he will definitely be required due to his undercover role. He is to go to El Paso on his own for the first few days. With budget restrictions, Ottawa doesn't see any need for the other members to attend until there is something more concrete to investigate."

"I understand, sir," replied Rose, "but the investigation is barely getting underway. I'm sure within the next few days we'll identify Slater's contacts in Canada and then discover who they are contacting in the States. The complexity of the investigation, what with a murder, a missing Canadian girl, cocaine importation ... it will require a considerable amount of man hours and coordination."

"In regard to the manpower needed, we got lucky. The Americans currently have a secret task force of investigators in El Paso composed of FBI, DEA, Customs, and ATF, who are all working on the Mexican drug cartels. They have offered their services, including a Special Agent John Adams who will work directly with Corporal Taggart."

"Excellent."

"I am assured Corporal Taggart will be well-protected in the U.S., but under no circumstances is he to enter Mexico. Recent kidnappings, murder, and corruption have made it strictly off-limits. Is that clear?"

"Yes, sir."

"As Corporal Taggart is to be meeting the target next Wednesday, I would think it prudent he arrive in El Paso by Monday. It will give him a chance to meet who he will be working with and also do any preliminary investigative work needed to move this case ahead."

"Yes, sir."

"He is going into extremely dangerous territory. Parts of El Paso are basically like the suburbs of Juarez. The Americans will be in charge of his safety down there, but I want you to inform him that if something doesn't feel right, he should back out. Lily Rae may have been murdered down there, but I don't want Taggart becoming the next victim. Is that clear?"

"Yes, sir."

"Wish him good luck for me. I think he will need it."

chapter twenty

Late Friday morning, Adams walked into his office building. He stood for a moment and glanced at some of his co-workers. Few acknowledged his presence. He noticed Davidson sitting in Weber's office, drinking coffee. Weber looked over his cup, saw Adams, and said something to Davidson, who then turned and used his foot to kick the door shut.

Adams should have felt like a leper, but at the moment, he really didn't care. There was nobody, outside of Greg Patton, in the office he ever felt close with. He strode over to the board where the keys for the covert cars were hung. His favourite, a new metallic-silver Camaro with dark-tinted windows, was there and he snatched the keys. The drug trafficker it had been seized from was from New Orleans and had tried to use it to smuggle two kilos of cocaine back home.

An hour later, Adams was parked a block away from the same house Chico had used to sucker Patton into following him. A couple of the low-level hoods were still using the house, but with Chico's untimely death, Adams knew they would likely be feeling a little nervous and would be moving to a new location soon. He hoped he could follow one of them to find out where.

At noon, Adams received a call on his cellphone.

"Get back here," ordered Weber.

"Do I need to call a lawyer?"

"It's not about that," Weber replied and hung up.

Weber waved for Adams to enter his office and pointed to a chair across from his desk. Adams took a seat and quietly waited while Weber took his time to shuffle through some papers, pausing and pretending to read some of the daily bulletins, while casting the odd furtive glance at Adams.

Yeah, make me wait, asshole, just to let me know you're the boss. Does it make you feel important? Hoping to see me get pissed off? Well, two can play that game ...

A soft snore from Adams caught Weber's immediate attention and he saw Adams's chin resting on his chest.

"Adams! You son of a bitch! Wake up!"

Adams head jerked and he yawned, looking around.

"Are you drunk? You are, aren't you? I can smell it."

"Nope. Was up late last night on surveillance. Maybe spilled a beer on my pants when I got home. Did you call me in here to help you read those bulletins? There are some pretty tough words like *alias* and stuff."

"Fuck you, you degenerate bastard. If I wanted any lip from you I'd rattle my zipper."

"That's original," replied Adams, sarcastically.

"You're a real piece of work, do you know that? What you did ... you've gone against everything we stand for. Flushed our values down the drain."

"Do your values include the right to a fair trial? Or innocent until proven guilty? You're condemning me without —"

"Don't give me that bullshit," growled Weber. "You're just lucky you got away with it. What you did was totally wrong." He waved his hand in the direction of the general office and added, "There's not one guy out there who is willing to work with you now. What you did is totally against the values of what we stand for."

Adams glanced at the men in the outer office and said, "Maybe if the Mexicans started killing off their family members they'd think different. I'm hoping the head honchos in the cartel do think I killed Chico. It'll make them think twice about ever doing what they did again."

"Don't lay that crap on me. You're really fucked up."

"Is that why you called me off of a surveillance? To tell me that?"

"No," replied Weber, tapping a file on his desk with his index finger for emphasis. "I called you in here to let you know the Mounties in Canada are interested in some Mexicans who are running coke from here up to there."

"Wow," said Adams lamely. "I can just imagine the hell they must be going through up there. A bunch of coked-up Eskimos tossing their spears all around. At least it will give the seals half a chance."

"It's a little bigger than that. Some cartel from here sent a hit team up and whacked someone in Canada who was one of their runners."

"Which cartel? Guajardo or the Sinaloa?"

"They don't have a clue."

"Yeah, I'm sure they don't."

"They're trying to identify some Mexican who goes by Tio."

"You're joking, right?" replied Adams with a laugh.

"No. They're also looking for the guy's girlfriend who was snatched here in El Paso."

"Yeah, well you fly with the crows —"

"They're sending a Mountie down to investigate. His name is Jack Taggart and his flight arrives at the airport

Monday morning at 9:57. I want you to pick him up and babysit him for a few days."

"Fuck that! Get one of them to do it," replied Adams, gesturing with his thumb to two men in the outer office who were both reading the newspaper.

"They're busy."

"Yeah? Well, so am I. Greg and I have busted our asses on these cartels. The two of us have done more damage to them than everyone else in this office put together."

"So what?"

"So what? After what they did to Greg, it's all the more important that I don't back off. I don't need to have some hick cop from Canada slowing me down or fucking things up if I need to do something. What if I get some info from a CI and have to do immediate surveillance? I sure as hell don't need some jackass burning me."

"It's only for a few days. Find him a place to stay, too."

"But —"

"Forget the buts. You're not being asked to do this, you're being ordered."

"Well ain't that just lovely."

Weber pushed the file across the desk toward Adams and said, "Here are their reports. Read 'em and pay attention where it says Taggart has been ordered to stay out of Mexico."

"Good. Guess they're not completely clueless. The Mexicans would probably shoot him as soon as he crossed the bridge and sell his red jacket to the doorman at some whorehouse ten minutes later."

chapter twenty-one

On Saturday, Vancouver RCMP Drug Section conducted surveillance on Slater's apartment building and saw a Mexican arrive. The man parked his car — which was registered to a numbered company — out front and went inside. Moments later, he drove out of the underground parking lot in Slater's pickup truck.

The man was followed to an auto-body shop where the bay door was opened by another Mexican and the pickup was driven inside. Half an hour later, the truck was returned to Slater's apartment building.

Late Sunday morning, surveillance on Slater was terminated when he was seen driving through U.S. Customs in his pickup. It was decided not to risk jeopardizing the investigation by trying to follow him all the way to Texas.

A decision was also made to curtail surveillance of the Mexicans at the body shop in the event the Mexicans spotted it and blamed Jack for the sudden police interest.

Early Sunday evening, Jack caught a flight from Vancouver to Houston, Texas, where he had to overnight.

On Monday morning, he arrived on schedule at the airport in El Paso. He had been told that a John Adams would pick him up, but was also given a phone number to the general office if there was a problem.

The El Paso airport was relatively small compared to some, but several flights had arrived within minutes of each other and the crowd was shoulder to shoulder. Jack retrieved his two suitcases from the luggage carousel and glanced around. He spotted another man who was lanky in appearance, sporting about a week's worth of beard, and dressed in blue jeans and cowboy boots. He quickly breezed through the crowd while glancing around a couple of times and then made his way to the exit.

If this is who was sent to pick me up, he's not too keen about it ...

Jack caught up to him at the doors and said, "John?"

"Yeah," he replied somewhat suspiciously. "Who are you?"

"Jack Taggart from Canada."

"Oh!" replied Adams in surprise. "You, uh, don't look like a cop. At least, not what I was expecting."

Jack knew from Adams's quick trip through the airport that he wasn't happy about picking him up. It would take a little diplomacy to get him on board ... which was what was needed if they were to work together.

He sized Adams up quickly. *His eyes are red and it looks like he hasn't slept in weeks. His shirt is slightly stained with grease ... probably drippings from a hamburger. Good, the guy was probably working surveillance and downing food when he had the chance. Not the type who spends his days in the office sucking up to the bosses. Being sent to pick me up probably pissed him off ... he'd rather get back to whatever he was working on.*

"You breezed through the airport pretty quick," said Jack. "Looking for a guy in a red tunic, I take it?"

"Sort of, yeah."

"Don't have to wear it when I travel."

"I see," replied Adams seriously.

"Do you know where the general cargo area is at the airport? I have to go there."

"I'm not sure," replied Adams, looking around.

"Yeah, they had to fly my horse in on a FedEx plane."

"What?"

"Never mind. I was just messin' with your brain cell. I'm ready to go."

Adams looked taken back before muttering, "Okay. Good."

As they stepped out into the sunlight and walked toward a parking lot, Adams glanced at Jack and asked, "Did you already talk to Weber?"

"No. Who's he?"

"My boss."

"I tend to avoid bosses. Where I come from they can be counterproductive."

They took a few more steps and Adams glanced at Jack a couple of times before admitting, "They're the same here, but I was told to bring you in and meet with them. First, though, I'll take you to your hotel so you can check in."

"Fine, but after the protocol with your boss, I would like to get to work. I want to see a motel called the Cactus Sunset. A young woman from Canada was kidnapped out of it. Then, if we have time, I've got some rather cryptic directions on a hand-drawn map I'd like you to look at. I think it leads to a house trailer out in the desert someplace."

"What's there?"

"Nothing, I hope. Have you read our reports?"

"I skimmed through them the other day. Have been a little busy. I'll take a closer look at 'em when I introduce you to Weber and the others."

"I see," said Jack, feeling a little frustrated more interest had not been shown. "I'll fill you in some as you drive."

"I think you'll like the hotel I picked. They give the guests free drinks every day from four to six."

"Sounds good." Jack squinted up at the sun as they walked out of a shaded area. The heat felt like he was standing on the tarmac behind a jet engine and sweat immediately ran down the side of his head. He glanced at Adams and said, "Man, it's not even eleven o'clock in the morning and I can feel the heat burning through the soles of my shoes. Is it always this hot?"

"This is winter. You should try being here during our hot and dry season."

"Are you kidding?"

"Yeah," replied Adams, giving Jack a sideways glance. "I was just messin' with your brain cell."

Jack chuckled. "These free drinks at four ... seems like a long time to wait."

Adams smiled. "The bosses mentioned they want to come for lunch with you. I think I could find us a place where there's cold beer."

"Perfect."

"Just out of curiosity, how did you spot me in the airport?" asked Adams.

"You got a cop's bearing."

"What do you mean?"

"You exude self-confidence. You've also got a cop's eyes."

"Are you still just messin' —"

"No."

Adams frowned. He had always prided himself at blending in. *Who is this guy?*

As they approached the Camaro, Jack commented, "Nice wheels. Yours?"

"Company car. Used to belong to a dope dealer."

"It doesn't look like a police vehicle."

"It's the best one we have."

"Where I come from, the bosses scoop the best ones and leave the clunkers for the rest of us."

"Same here. I was lucky to find the keys on the board. You'll notice it has tinted windows all around so nobody can see my cops' eyes," replied Adams as he grinned at Jack.

Jack gave a lop-sided smile in response. He had a feeling he and Adams were going to get along fine.

An hour later, after checking into the hotel, Jack entered the office with Adams. He had barely taken two steps when Weber spotted him and came out to shake his hand. He was then invited back to Weber's office where he received warm handshakes from Davidson, as well as the two bosses who represented the DEA and ATF investigators.

Adams did not take part in the introductions and stood in the main office, watching quietly before going to his own desk.

Jack looked at the men in the main office. Adams was much younger and more physically fit than the rest. *Obviously the junior man ... the gofer assigned to pick me up.*

Jack also sensed Adams was treated with a certain degree of indifference by the others. *Perhaps like a young bull full of vitality and eager to go ... while the old bulls look upon him with a certain amount of contempt?*

Jack may have formed a different opinion had he known the real reason Adams was being ostracized.

Davidson told Jack that neither picture of the two killers taken from Porter's apartment security camera could be identified as anyone they knew, but they would keep their descriptions in mind for future reference.

All four bosses insisted on joining Jack for lunch so they walked into the main part of the office and Adams suggested a Mexican restaurant he knew. The bosses agreed to the choice and said they would follow in their own car.

As Jack and Adams walked out to their car, Adams said, "You mentioned you wanted to check out the Cactus Sunset and then some map you have after lunch."

"Yes."

"I didn't see the map mentioned in your reports."

"It, uh, is a little delicate how I obtained it. The fewer people who know, the better."

"I see," replied Adams. *Delicate? What kind of wussy word is that? A CI probably gave it to him … he should have said so.*

As they drove to the restaurant, Adams said, "I also checked out the Armadillo Motel while you were meeting with them," he said, gesturing with his thumb back to the four bosses in the car behind them. "We don't have anything on it, but that doesn't mean squat. The cartels have thousands of people in their pocket, so I don't recommend anyone approaching the management at the Armadillo on Wednesday when you check in."

"I agree with you there. It was Tio who told me to go there. I'm sure he has a reason."

"What kind of piece are you carrying?"

"I'm not armed. It's against policy for me to carry a gun in a foreign country."

"Are you fuckin' nuts?" replied Adams, incredulously. "I pack at least two all the time. One in an ankle holster and —"

"Of course you do, you're an American."

"What the hell is that supposed to mean?"

Jack hid his smile at the amount of weaponry the U.S. was famous for and shrugged in response.

"Well, for your information, you are in America," said Adams gruffly. "As soon as we stop for lunch I'll pop the trunk. Got lots for you to choose from. Anything from revolvers to pistols to fully autos."

"Thanks, but no. I don't usually carry one in Canada, either, if I am undercover. More often than not, I'm searched. If I had a gun the bad guys are liable to take it and use it on me."

Adams shook his head and said, "It's your funeral."

"Have you ever worked undercover?" asked Jack.

"Never. I've only done backup, so I expect you to take the lead when it comes to decisions in that regard. The Cactus Sunset is on the western edge of the city, about a block south of a main highway. The Armadillo Motel is on the main highway, but a few miles farther out. I'm not familiar with the Armadillo itself, but I know it is pretty barren out there."

"So a bunch of cops parked out on the road might look a little obvious."

"For sure ... and we can't approach the management to put guys in a room next to you, so what do you suggest?"

"Do you have a policewoman available? Maybe book someone in as a couple? Unless you want to pretend you're gay —"

"This is Texas! I'm not — I can get a policewoman," said Adams quickly, before seeing the grin on Jack's face. "Yeah, okay, wiseguy. I'll make sure I'm in one of the rooms myself, but depending upon what room I'm given, I may not be able to listen through the walls. Are you thinking of wearing a wire?"

"Definitely not. If I get caught with one of those, I'm dead. I've been scanned by dealers in the past with devices to check for transmitters ... and those guys weren't as high up the food chain as these guys. I don't want any bugs."

"Then how will I know if something is going wrong?"

"Listen for the sound of breaking glass. If I'm in trouble I'll toss something or someone out a window. If I'm really in trouble, I'll throw myself out."

"You are fucking nuts. Every undercover operator I've ever met is," he muttered seriously, before nodding toward a restaurant. "Okay, we're here."

Lunch consisted of tamales stuffed with shredded beef, roasted chillies, and an assortment of other fillings, which went well with a cold bottle of Lone Star beer. Everyone was exceedingly friendly with Jack and did what they could to make him feel welcome, including picking up his lunch tab.

"Seem like nice guys," said Jack, once he and Adams got back in the car.

"They're bosses. I guess they do what they're supposed to do," he added begrudgingly. "Now I'll take you to the Cactus Sunset."

The Cactus Sunset was appropriately named. It was a two-storey building with ten rooms on each level on the edge of the desert. Adams pulled into the parking lot and asked, "Do you want to talk to the manager?"

"No, the FBI have already done that, along with searching the room. I want to get out and walk around the back to see what's there."

Adams joined Jack and they strolled around to the back of the motel. There was nothing to see but sagebrush, cactus, and sand dunes.

Jack walked up the closest sand dune and looked. The view didn't change. "Okay, I've seen enough," he said, looking back at Adams, who had remained at the back of the motel, watching him. "Didn't know what I was hoping to find, anyway. I think I just wanted to get a feel for the place … and its surroundings."

They returned to the car and headed out on the highway toward the Armadillo Motel. They drove in silence for about a mile when Adams hit the brakes and pulled over to the side of the road.

Jack looked around and saw there were no other vehicles in sight. "What is it?" he asked.

Adams pointed far out into the desert.

Jack didn't see anything at first. Then some dots circling high in the air caught his attention and he felt his heart sink. *Vultures ...*

chapter twenty-two

For twenty-five minutes, Adams slowly drove and wound his way around clusters of cactus and small sand dunes. In a pickup truck, the trip could have been done rapidly, but the Camaro was built close to the ground and was not meant for off-road driving.

Eventually they came upon two sets of tire tracks from a pickup truck that had tandem rear tires. It appeared the truck had driven in the same direction as the vultures were and then had doubled back.

"Let's walk from here," suggested Adams. "This might be a crime scene. I don't want to drive over anything."

Jack nodded in agreement as two vultures swooped down from the sky and disappeared out of sight in front of them. He guessed they were only about a ten-minute walk farther ahead.

Both men walked beside the tracks until they came upon a deep ravine. Marks in the sand showed where the truck had turned around and backed up to the ravine.

Jack peered over the edge. Part way down the slope was a large flock of vultures jostling each other for space as they fought for room, while other vultures flew overhead or perched on nearby rocks to await their turn.

Jack saw a limb sticking out of the feeding frenzy. *Is it a leg or an arm?* He swallowed to try and keep his lunch down and watched as Adams picked up a rock and tossed it toward the vultures.

The vultures were not overly intimidated by the rock, but a few did leap away long enough for them to glimpse the carcass strewn open with its ribcage exposed.

"Just a cow or a steer," said Adams, as he turned and walked away.

Jack took a deep breath. He was relieved they hadn't found Lily Rae, but the sight of the vultures sickened him when he thought of what might have become of her. He looked around at the horizon and was glad he didn't see any other signs of vultures.

On their way back to the car, Adams asked, "Have you got that map you were talking about?"

Jack handed him his notebook with the roughly drawn map.

"EP-W-CR14-12-U-L," said Adams aloud as he looked at the map. "Then a bunch of dotted lines leading out to an X mark."

"There were more of a hodgepodge of other short lines near the one with the X," said Jack. "I didn't have time to copy them all down."

"You didn't have time?" questioned Adams. "I had presumed your … delicate situation meant you were protecting a CI."

"I strongly believe in protecting my informants," replied Jack, "but in this case, that is not what I meant. Do you have any ideas?"

"I would take a guess and say the EP means El Paso … and west of El Paso is an intersection to the start of county road number 14."

"We're west of El Paso. Is it close to here?"

"Not far. It's slightly south of the highway we're on. Incidentally, to get to Country Road 14 from El Paso you generally drive past a casino called the Sunland Park."

"Which means the casino wouldn't be all that far from the Cactus Sunset Motel where Porter moved before the Mexicans found him."

"Same general area. My guess is these directions mean twelve miles up Country Road 14. I don't know what the U-L is. Maybe the L is left. Let's take a look. It could be out along the border someplace. Maybe another trail into Mexico."

"Into Mexico?"

"Yeah, there are quite a few of them. Places are always popping up that the illegals use to enter into El Paso every day to work. Mind you, this seems a little far out for that. The other lines you mentioned ... it's hillier out there. Those could be hills or big sand dunes. Maybe the trailer is hidden amongst them."

"Okay to try and find it?"

"Yeah, can do. We're only fifteen minutes away from The Armadillo Motel. Want to swing past it first to see what it's like? Then head up Country Road 14?"

"Sounds good."

A few miles farther outside the city, a faded sign portraying the image of an armadillo hung in front of a single-storey row of motel rooms.

"Is that a rat or an armadillo?" asked Jack as they drove past.

"The one on the sign is an armadillo. The rats will be inside the place out of the heat."

Jack glanced around. There was not another building in sight and the land was flat. "I feel like I'm in Saskatchewan on the hottest day of the year," he said. "Except the wheat fields have been replaced by sand and cacti."

"You want the air turned up?"

"It's high enough. Air conditioners usually give me a cold."

"Know what ya mean. Normally I prefer to suck on a cold beer."

"Got one?"

"No, I figured you Mounties had a reputation for being goody-two-shoes type of guys. Never swear, never tell a lie ... follow the letter of the law."

"Yeah, that would be me."

Approximately five minutes down the road, they spotted a side road partially obscured by bushes.

"Could put a cover team in there," suggested Jack.

"Yeah, but it is still about five minutes away. A lot can happen to a guy in five minutes."

"I know, but I'll have you and a policewoman. That's more than I've had other times."

"Your funeral."

"I know," said Jack, quietly.

"Glad you know," said Adams abruptly. "Let's check out your map."

Twenty-five minutes later, Adams turned at a T-intersection where a sign indicated they were turning on to Country Road 14.

"I'll let you know when we're about twelve miles along," said Adams. "Keep your eye open for that *U* on the map."

At around twelve miles, Adams slowed the car down, but there was nothing to see except sand dunes or the odd shack. Adams drove for another two miles before turning around and driving back.

"That has to be it," said Jack, minutes later, pointing to a sun-bleached skull of a long-horned steer. It had been nailed to a fencepost from which a rusted gate hung open on one hinge. The nose of the skull had deteriorated in the sun and it was missing one horn.

"That skull is your *U* you think? How do you figure?"

"Bet it used to have two horns. Using your imagination ... it could be a *U*."

"Yeah ... maybe. Doesn't look like any recent vehicle tracks on the other side of the gate," noted Adams. "Still, with wind and sand, things disappear pretty quick. Okay, we'll take a look and see where it leads."

They drove through the desert as the trail wound in and around sand dunes and over hills. The Camaro periodically bottomed out in the sand and there were several occasions when both men feared the car would get stuck, but Adams was able to continue on.

"Christ, at this point I don't know if we're still in Texas or if we're in Mexico," said Adams with a worried look on his face as he glanced at Jack.

"I don't care. Let's keep going," replied Jack.

Moments later, they saw the roof of a mobile home sticking up from the far side of a sand dune.

"It's about time," breathed Adams with relief as he stepped on the throttle to give the car an extra boost along the trail leading over the dune.

The engine roared as the tires spun through the sand and the car burst over the top of the dune and slid down the other side.

"Oh, fuck," said Adams under his breath, while instinctively reaching for the gun in the holster on his belt.

chapter twenty-three

District Attorney White took the call and recognized Davidson's voice immediately.

"You wouldn't believe it," said Davidson with a chuckle.

"Believe what?"

"The Mountie from Canada arrived this morning. Adams picked him up and we all went for lunch and then left them alone. Talk about two peas in a pod! I'm on my other phone to one of our people doing the listening. They've only been alone together a couple of hours and sounds like they are already doing something they shouldn't be."

"What are they doing?"

"The Mountie had some map they were following."

"I don't remember reading about that ... just a minute," said White, reaching for a file folder.

"Don't bother looking. The Mountie didn't mention it in any report and said he didn't want people knowing about it. Hang on, I'm talking in two phones at once here. I've got the guy listening to the bug on my cellphone ...

He just told me it sounds like the two of them may have driven into Mexico."

"Christ, that didn't take long. Where in Mexico?"

"We're not tailing them. Adams would spot that pretty quick."

"I know. I meant a satellite tracker."

"We, uh, the four of us here talked about that. The only ones we have are being used on more important targets."

"I see," replied White. He thought of Davidson's comment after they first interviewed Adams. White wondered if the agency would move Adams in case the cartel would murder him. Davidson's reply had been, *'That would save everyone a lot of embarrassment.'*

"Anyway, this whole thing could be wrapped up in minutes," continued Davidson.

"They're talking?"

"No, I don't mean that. Something is going on. Adams's voice has gone up a couple of octaves. He's not a guy who gets scared easily. Hang on, my other phone ... sounds like they're in deep trouble. Maybe about to be grabbed ... not sure yet. Talk of guys pulling rifles on them. They're out of the car ... I better call you back."

Unaware that Adams was reaching for his pistol, Jack looked at the scene before them as their car slid to a stop in the sand. The collection of other short lines he had seen on Slater's map he now knew represented other house trailers. There were a dozen of them scattered like pick-up sticks around a small road paved with blacktop.

Half the trailers had trucks and SUVs parked beside them. There were no cars except the one he and Adams were in and it was attracting attention. Several men from different trailers had stepped out and were gesturing in their direction.

Jack could not see past some sand dunes to know where the blacktop road went, but it ended abruptly near where they had arrived.

"Look at all the skid marks at the end of the road," noted Jack. "Kids must be drag racing out here."

"Those aren't from kids," replied Adams tersely, holding his pistol in his lap. "It's from light aircraft landing. We just drove into the middle of a drug dropoff zone."

"Oh, shit," said Jack under his breath, feeling very stupid. It hadn't occurred to him a smuggler's drug dropoff site would be this big and include a paved runway.

To the right of their car and close to where the runway ended, sat a Mexican on a large cooler under a wooden lean-to. The man was fat, unshaven, and reminded Jack of a bad guy out of an old Mexican Western movie. The man's thick black eyebrows knotted together as he stared at them suspiciously.

"Damn it, the two guys over by that black pickup were hauling a table out of the trailer. Now they put it down and are grabbing rifles out of the cab," warned Adams, with a nod of his head in the opposite direction.

Jack looked past Adams out the driver's window and saw two men. Both had dark scowls on their faces and held their rifles at waist height as they started to approach. Jack estimated if the two men continued to walk, they would reach their car in about a minute.

"Take my gun while I try to drive us the fuck out of here!" said Adams.

"Keep it," replied Jack. "We'd never make it with what you're driving, anyway," he added as he opened the car door and stepped out.

"What are you doing? Get back in here!"

"Wait here. I'll be right back," he added, as he closed the door.

"What the fuck …" He glanced back at the two men approaching. *Using a pistol to go against two guys with rifles at this distance wouldn't be ruled an act of self defence, it would be classified as suicide ...*

Adams quickly got out of the car and said, "I'll cover you."

"No!" whispered Jack heatedly over the top of the car. "Smile and wave at the guy behind me in the lean-to. I'm going over to talk to him."

"Him? He's not the one with the rifles!"

"Ignore those two. Keep your back to them and act like you haven't seen them."

"What the fuck?" muttered Adams, feeling extremely vulnerable as he turned his back to the two men with the rifles. *Is Jack hoping to take these guys by surprise? Maybe yell and have me spin around and drop them both? This ain't fuckin' Hollywood ...*

Jack did his best to casually stride over to the lean-to as though he had done it many times, although a glance back at Adams, who was watching him over the roof of the car while clenching his pistol under his shirt, made it difficult to look relaxed.

The Mexican eyed him suspiciously as he approached, but remained seated.

"Buenos dias, amigo," said Jack.

The Mexican gave a slight grunt in response.

"Hace mucho calor hoy," said Jack, gesturing to the sun. *"Dos cervezas, por favor."*

"Si." The Mexican stood up, opened the cooler he was sitting on, and popped the tops off of two bottles of Corona and handed them to Jack.

"Muchas gracias," said Jack, as he paid him and then strolled back toward the car, stopping once to take a swig of beer. As he did, he noticed the two men with the rifles spoke briefly with each other and then walked back toward the trailer they had come from.

"Jesus Christ," said Adams as they got back inside the car. "How did you know that guy was selling beer?"

"My wife says I have a gift for finding cold beer," replied Jack, handing him a bottle, "but seeing a fat guy sitting on a cooler in the desert surrounded by dope runners ... well, it doesn't take much logic to know he wasn't selling salted nuts."

Adams breathed a sigh of relief and said, "Okay, let's see if they'll let us slowly drive away. The guys with the rifles are still staring at us."

"Not yet. Sit for a second and enjoy the beer. As you do, take a look around. My guess is the trailer marked with the X is that one straight ahead of us with the door facing the runway ... the one where the wind has made a small sand dune in the driveway. What do you think?"

Adams gulped down half his beer as his eyes scanned the different trailers. "Yeah, I think you're right."

"It looks abandoned. In fact, half the trailers do. I think they're clearing out. Let's take a look inside. It will also make it look like we belong here."

"Good point," replied Adams apprehensively, with a quick glance back to the two men who were now putting the rifles back in the cab of the truck.

Moments later, Adams parked beside the trailer. "We don't have a warrant, but if it's unlocked we can say it was abandoned and go in," he said.

Jack gave Adams a sideways glance. *A warrant? You really don't trust me ...*

They each got out of the car and Adams was the first to reach the door. "Shit, it's locked," he said, glancing nervously back.

Jack glanced around, as well. For the moment, nobody was staring at them.

"At least I don't smell a body," Adams noted.

Jack nodded, but didn't know whether to feel happy or nauseous at the comment.

"Hang on, I'm going around back to see if I can see in," said Adams.

Jack waited a moment before peeking behind the trailer. He saw Adams checking all the windows at the back of the trailer, hoping to find one that wasn't locked. Jack grinned to himself. *So he isn't averse to breaking in …*

Jack went back to the front door and took out his wallet. In it he kept a small set of lock picks. It took him less than ten seconds to unlock the door. He then opened it and said loudly, "What? Did you say come in?"

Adams scrambled around to the front of the trailer and his jaw dropped when he saw Jack holding the door open.

"I'm not sure," said Jack. "I think I heard someone say to come in."

Adams looked at Jack and then hurried past him into the trailer. Once they were both inside Adams turned to Jack and said, "It was locked. I know it was. There's nobody here …"

Jack flashed him the lock picks.

Adams stared at him for a moment and said, "So this is what you mean when you say you obtain something through a delicate situation."

"Sometimes," admitted Jack.

"It didn't take you long to pick," noted Adams. "Can you do that with all locks?"

"It depends on the locks. Trailer locks are easy. Most desk drawers I can do in about five seconds. Handcuffed behind my back, I can get out of it within a minute if I have a bobby pin."

"You could be a handy guy to have around sometimes."

"I'm not that good. Other locks, like deadbolts, are tougher. There are many I can't do."

"I wouldn't mind learning how."

"I'll teach you the basic concept sometime, but even when you do understand how locks work, you still have to practice regularly or you lose the ability."

A search of the trailer did not take long. It was completely empty. They got back in the car and nobody appeared to pay any attention to them as they drove away.

It was five o'clock when they arrived back in El Paso. While on their way to Jack's hotel, Adams received a short call from Weber.

"Looks like you're a celebrity," said Adams, when he hung up. "Davidson and Weber are coming over to join us and sponge some free drinks from the hotel for happy hour."

Jack and Adams were the first to arrive at the hotel and each ordered a Corona as they stood in the hospitality room.

"I've been wondering about Wednesday," said Adams.

"What about Wednesday?"

"When you meet Tio. What if he wants to meet you in Juarez?"

"Then I'll meet him there," said Jack firmly.

"That's what I was afraid of," sighed Adams.

"I'm telling you because I trust you not to tell anyone," said Jack. "You strike me as the type of guy who does what it takes to get the job done. So do I."

"I'm not worried about you ignoring orders. What concerns me is if I try to follow you in Juarez, I'll be spotted. There are too many places they could take you where a gringo like me would stand out."

"I don't want anyone following me. It would probably get me killed. Besides, no use in both of us getting in trouble with the bosses if something goes wrong. Just be forewarned that I may intentionally lose you and the cover team on Wednesday."

"I also don't think you appreciate how dangerous it is over there," said Adams. "That place we went to this afternoon ... I had never even heard so much as a whisper about it. And it was huge operation right under our noses." Adams took a swig of Corona and added, "Which to your credit, you led me to on your first day here."

"It was luck I found the map. It was you who deciphered it."

"Yeah, luck that you *delicately* obtained. Not to mention, it was you who figured out to turn at the skull. I'm going to check into it further, but right now I can tell you I've got some serious concerns about who is behind it."

"Who do you suspect?"

"It has to be either the Guajardo or the Sinaloa cartel, that part is obvious, but it is the level you're dealing with that concerns me."

"The level?"

"Whoever your Tio is, he's no Mickey Mouse player. For you to have a map of what we found today ... this isn't some chicken-shit low-end guy."

"Good."

"Yeah, good ... and dangerous. This guy will have a lot of protection and will be taking all the necessary precautions. You're going to be like an ant under a magnifying glass."

"Hope the sun doesn't come out."

"Yeah, well if it does, you better be prepared. First thing in the morning I'm going to show you different escape routes out of Mexico in case you do end up over there. If something goes wrong and you do manage to make a run for it, don't use any of the bridges."

"Thanks, I appreciate that."

"There's something else I'm going to do, as well ... and this is putting a lot of trust in you. Tomorrow I'm going to introduce you to someone. He's a commander of a police station in Juarez and has got the biggest set of balls of anyone I've ever met. The cartels would kill him immediately if they knew he was co-operating.

I'll introduce you to him. He might be the only guy in Mexico who could save your life."

"How will he feel about meeting me?"

"He's the type of guy who will help anyone he thinks is working for the right side. The first time I went to his office to meet him, he pretended to throw me out, but slipped me a piece of paper with a time and location to meet him later. We'll also show him the pictures of those two guys from the apartment security cameras who did the hit in Canada."

"I nicknamed the one guy El Burla for sneer and Lobulo for —"

"Hey, guys! How are you doing?" interrupted Weber as he and Davidson arrived.

"Doing great." Jack smiled.

"What did you do this afternoon?" asked Davidson casually.

"We checked out the Cactus Sunset and then the Armadillo Motel to see where I would be staying on Wednesday," replied Jack. "After that we went for a drive and had a cold beer."

"What do you think of our city?" asked Weber.

"I like it," replied Jack. He glanced at Adams and added, "Seems like there are some really good people around here."

Jack saw the trace of a smile of appreciation on Adams's face as they briefly stared at each other. What he didn't notice was the subtle wink Davidson gave Weber.

chapter twenty-four

Jack woke, had breakfast, and was waiting in the lobby at nine o'clock when he spotted the metallic-silver Camaro and went out to meet Adams.

"Hey there, two-gun gringo, how you doin'?" asked Jack.

"I don't have a hangover, so that's good."

"You only had two drinks last night."

"I don't like to drink much in front of Davidson and Weber. Besides, I had to drive. How long did you have to put up with them?" asked Adams.

"Not late," replied Jack. "They left shortly after you did. I was tired. I wanted to get a good night's sleep."

"Good. This morning when I dropped in to pick up the car, I told them I was taking you around to familiarize you with the various nightspots in El Paso. I said it might come in handy for you to know the area for when you do your undercover stuff."

"Good thinking."

"You have breakfast yet?"

"Already ate."

"Likewise. Let's get to work."

An hour later, Adams pulled up and parked near a small bridge southwest of the city. A U.S. Customs booth was on one end and a Mexican Customs booth was on the other.

"Get out and take a look," said Adams. "You probably won't believe it."

Jack got out of the car and walked up to the bridge. A small stream of Mexicans walked across the bridge and were stopping to be checked at U.S. Customs. Jack walked to the far side of the bridge, stopping short of the Mexican Customs. Below the bridge on one side was a clump of bushes. The growth on the opposite side the bank was sparse and he could see dozens of Mexicans walking across the small stream and clamouring up the far bank to enter the United States without clearing customs.

"You're right, I don't believe it," said Jack, getting back in the car.

"Only the honest ones clear customs," said Adams bitterly. "We don't have the manpower to rein in the thousands who cross illegally. Most work here during the day and go back the same way at night."

"That shallow stream they walk through ... I thought it was the Rio Grande that separated you from Mexico?"

"That is the Rio Grande. Most of the water has been run off for irrigation long before the river reaches here. Out here it is easy to cross, although there is talk of building a high wall as a barrier, so maybe that will change. I'll take you back to El Paso and show you other places in the city that aren't quite as easy as out here in the countryside."

As they approached El Paso, Adams turned up the volume on a police radio. It was a report of gunfire at the bridge where they had just been. The customs agents in the booth at the end of the bridge said someone was firing shots at them from the clump of bushes on the Mexican side.

"Are we heading back to help?" asked Jack.

Adams shook his head. "It would be over before we got there. They do it all the time. The good news is the Mexicans are lousy shots, except of course for the ones we trained and who were then hired by the cartels."

"Actually, I'm a crummy shot, too," admitted Jack. "What did you mean about that last comment? The ones you trained who joined the cartels?"

"It's not common knowledge and normally I wouldn't talk about it, but someone has already let the cat out of the bag on the Internet.

"Like toothpaste out of the tube. Hard to put it back in once it's out."

"Exactly. What happened was someone in Washington woke up and realized we were losing this so-called War on Drugs. Cartels are popping up everywhere in Mexico and a lot of them are at war with each other as they continue to expand and take over territory. Washington realized it would only be a matter of time before they firmly establish themselves in the U.S. and elsewhere."

"Like Canada."

"Yeah, so someone figured it would be a good idea to try and contain the bloodbath in Mexico. Our government trained an elite group of Mexican soldiers to be expert commandos and snipers. I don't think there would be anything on paper about it, but basically it was implied that the Mexican government could use these guys to selectively take out the heads of some of the cartels."

"Can't say as I feel real opposed to that idea," replied Jack.

"I feel the same way. Except it backfired. The cartels pay a lot more money than the military does. A lot of the commandos we trained were hired by the cartels ... and they can shoot the eye out of a scorpion up to a mile away."

"Something I should probably keep in mind," said Jack sombrely.

The next spot Adams took Jack was near the centre of El Paso. The Rio Grande basin had widened a little and a high chain-link fence acted as a barrier. Adams parked the car and said, "No use getting your feet wet. Sit and watch a moment."

Within a couple of minutes, Jack saw two Mexican men and a woman approach the fence from the Mexican side. They walked a short distance to a clump of bushes and suddenly appeared on the American side.

"The fence has been cut there," noted Adams. "Happens all the time. When we repair it, they cut it again someplace else."

"Sounds like that wall you said they're thinking of building is needed."

"It should help." Adams gestured to the Mexican side of the border. "I want you to take a good look at all the buildings so you can remember them in case you have to come through that way to escape. We're only about a mile upstream from the Bridge of the Americas, which is the biggest legal entry and exit point into Juarez. Don't under any circumstances think of trying to cross that bridge if you're on the run."

"The Mexican Customs are bought off?"

"Everyone is. The police, military, customs ... everyone."

"Dangerous country," replied Jack.

"I doubt you have any idea how dangerous. I stayed awake half the night last night wondering whether I should tell you some stuff."

"What sort of stuff?"

"I have special military training. Occasionally I'm still used for covert missions. There are some things I've learned that people wouldn't appreciate me talking about."

"Then don't tell me."

"A couple of things I think I should, just so you'll appreciate what goes on around here. The first thing I already told you."

"About the U.S. training assassins?"

"Exactly. Something else that happened is we Americans are getting blamed for something in Mexico we didn't do. There was a third powerful cartel in Juarez and all the kingpins of it were basically family members. They lived in five mansions on a mammoth estate out in the desert. They had their own runway, planes, helicopter crews ... and a small army guarding it. One night seven unmarked Huey choppers packed with commandos flew in and killed all the top guys and anyone else they thought was involved with the cartel. The choppers then flew away, apparently without suffering a casualty. Everybody was pointing their fingers at us ... but I know it wasn't us."

"Another cartel?"

"We thought that, until we found out that afterwards one of the choppers crashed on a mountaintop when they were low-flying at night to escape detection. Where it crashed was what caught our attention. It was on the southern border of Mexico going into Guatemala."

"Guatemala!"

"Exactly. It made us wonder, as well. Some locals reported a couple of men inside lost their lives, but another chopper stopped and retrieved the bodies. The only thing left behind was the wreckage ... which had no markings or identification to indicate where the chopper came from or who owned it. Then we learned another key piece of information that gave us a pretty good idea who was behind it."

"And it wasn't the CIA?"

"No. Turns out this particular cartel was supplying drugs to the Palestinians who were selling the dope to make money to buy weapons."

Jack took a deep breath and slowly exhaled. "That makes it rather obvious, doesn't it?"

"Yeah, I would say so. We're getting the heat for what the Israelis did."

"I had no idea how dangerous Mexico really is. You paint a different picture than the travel agencies do."

"What I told you is nothing. Right before you got here, I had a partner who went into Juarez. He got kidnapped and tortured for almost three hours by the police. They had him handcuffed to the bars and were dousing him with water and using a cattle prod on him. Luckily, four FBI agents found out where he was and rescued him."

"Jesus Christ," replied Jack in shock. "I had heard about the DEA agent who was kidnapped, tortured, and murdered. The one where the Mexican president's brother was implicated."

"You heard right. The guy they killed was Special Agent Enrique Camarena. A few key people were eventually arrested, but the president's brother and a couple of guys under him will never be charged."

"Did you know Camarena?"

"No ... but you know how it feels."

"It's like losing a brother, even if he did work in another country."

Adams nodded silently.

"Guess I was hoping the cartels wouldn't try it again."

"That kind of thinking could get you killed. They're becoming bolder every day. Greg had three years to pension, but he decided not to stay. He quit because of it."

"You're working these guys alone? Don't you have a new partner?"

"No. Just my cop friend in Juarez, but I can't be seen with him."

"So you are on your own."

Adams nodded. "Now that I've opened your eyes a little, are you still sure you want to go into Mexico?"

"I'm sure I don't want to … but I made someone a promise I would do my best to find Lily Rae. I keep my promises."

"Yeah, that's what I was afraid of."

chapter twenty-five

"Where to now?" Jack asked as Adams drove away from the border.

"This afternoon we'll go into Juarez. I'll show you another escape route. Then I'm going to introduce you to my friend over there, Jose Rubalcava. He might be the only guy who could help you out down there."

"How often do you go into Juarez?" asked Jack.

"A couple times a week, but I only meet Jose a couple times a month. His phones are likely tapped by the cartel, so we use a preset time and place. It's too risky for him to meet me any more often than that."

Jack was quiet as he thought of the gravity of the situation.

"We have some time to kill, so if you don't mind, I'd like to take a look at a house in El Paso," said Adams. "I think about a dozen couriers come and go from it. It was the one my partner was watching when they lured him into Mexico."

"They still using it?" asked Jack.

"Two days ago there were still some of their cars there."

"Two days ago?" said Jack. *He doesn't know about yesterday because he was busy driving me around. No wonder he was pissed off at having to pick me up at the airport.*

"Yeah. Lots of muscle cars. All with Mexican plates. I have no idea who they belong to. I'm thinking they'll be moving someplace else and would like to follow them. I know they work for the Guajardo cartel, but that's all I know."

"And you think the Mexican uncle I'm looking for is either with the Guajardo cartel or the Sinaloa cartel?"

"Yes. Jose might know which one, based on what we found yesterday in the desert."

A short time later they drove into a neighbourhood in El Paso with overgrown yards strewn with garbage and the odd partially dismantled or wrecked car.

"That's the house there," sighed Adams. "The red one in the middle of the block. Usually the driveway is full of cars. They must have moved out yesterday."

Jack grimaced as he thought of the frustration Adams must be feeling. "I'm sorry," he said. "If you hadn't been running me around you probably would have been here."

"I wouldn't call finding what we did yesterday a wasted day."

"Getting those who kidnapped your partner would outrank that in my book."

Adams paused as he looked at Jack and said, "Mine, too, but it's not your fault. Anyway, I'm going to take you home for lunch. Introduce you to my wife. After we'll head into Juarez."

"Hold it," said Jack, looking down the street. The largest, most muscular black man he had ever seen was walking along the sidewalk. He was in a postman's uniform and had a mailbag slung over his shoulder.

"You looking at the mailman?" asked Adams.

"Why not? Your targets know the house is hot so you've got nothing to lose. Why not ask him who lives there? Maybe he's got some mail for them and you could get some names."

"Are you kidding?" replied Adams, sounding exasperated. "We're not even allowed to say hello to a mailman, without going in front of a grand jury and getting a warrant."

"I'm not talking about opening the mail, just seeing the name on the envelope."

"I know what you're saying, but we have privacy laws here that are strictly enforced. Two years ago a postman showed a policeman a name on an envelope. Not only did the mailman lose his job, he was also sentenced to three months in jail."

Jack grimaced. The idea of an innocent person going to jail for helping the police sickened him. "But for this … can't you get a warrant?"

"No, I already tried. Despite what happened, having souped-up cars does not mean someone is a drug trafficker and I have no right to infringe on their civil rights."

"Bet the mailman would help if he thought the situation deserved it."

"Don't know what it's like in Canada, but take a look at that guy. Also take a look at this neighbourhood, which is likely where he lives. Do you really think he is police-friendly?"

"What if he showed me the mail and I passed it on to you. Could you list me as your CI in your application for a warrant and that way honestly deny that you received it from a postman?"

"Underhanded … but yeah, that would work, except he won't give it to you."

"Let's try."

Adams sighed. "Yeah, okay, I'll show you what it's like down here."

A moment later, Adams and Jack approached the mailman as he stopped in front of the house and retrieved a large handful of mail from his bag.

Adams flashed his badge and said, "I am hoping you can tell me who lives in this place. Any names on the —"

"You all got a warrant?" asked the mailman.

"No," admitted Adams.

The mailman's face darkened in anger as he clenched the wad of mail against his chest, purposely hiding the front of the envelopes from any prying eyes. "Then you all should know better than to be askin'," he snarled. "Get away from me! I don't even wanna be seen talkin' to you all."

Adams looked at Jack as if to say *I told you so*.

"That's okay, sir," said Jack. "We knew it was wrong to ask. It's my fault. I was hoping ... well, never mind. Have a nice day." Jack then turned as if to walk away and said to Adams, "I just feel so damn sorry for all those poor little black kids."

"What?" said the mailman. "What did you just say?"

Jack turned around and said, "Oh, uh ... I probably shouldn't be telling you, but what the hell, I think they're gone, anyway. Have you ever heard of snuff films? Where people are sexually tortured and killed so the film can be sold to perverts to watch and get their kicks?"

"Is that what they're doing in there?" roared the mailman.

Jack lowered his head and muttered, "I knew I shouldn't have told you, but we couldn't get a warrant."

"Here, take it," the mailman said, shoving the mail into Jack's hand.

"Are you sure? I don't want —"

"Take it!" he ordered.

Jack handed the mail to Adams, who took out his notebook and started writing.

"You all might like to know that three houses down the back alley from this house ... on the other side of the alley, there is a policeman living there," continued the mailman. "In case you need a place to watch it from or somethin'."

"Thanks," said Jack, "but we think the people in this house are moving someplace else, which is what we are hoping to find."

"If they leave a forwarding address, I'll give it to you all," said the mailman. "Just swing by in a day or two about this time and I'll be here."

"Appreciate that," replied Jack.

"I never would of thought," said the mailman, looking at the house.

"Yeah, people make you sick sometimes," said Jack. "We think they're also into dope."

"Oh yeah, for sure. I figured that, what with the cars they got."

"Here," said Adams holding out the mail. "Uh ..." he then handed the mail back to Jack.

"Keep it," said the mailman. "I don't care if I never see it again!"

Jack glanced at Adams, who shook his head. "I guess we have what we need," said Jack, handing the mail back.

The mailman reluctantly accepted it and Jack and Adams walked back to the car.

"God, that was something," said Adams. "I never would have believed it."

"I think most people are basically good," replied Jack. "Sometimes the law screws up what should be common sense. Make sure you always protect that mailman. I feel crappy for giving him a line like that."

"It worked."

"Yes, but if word of it ever leaked, sometime someone will be working on snuff films and they'll have a door slammed in their face. In this case I weighed what happened to your partner and decided that what I did was acceptable. Rotten, maybe, but acceptable enough for me to live with it."

When they got back in the car, Adams hesitated before putting it in drive and said, "I think you and I would be good partners. Wish we were."

"I've got a feeling we would be, too. Guess we are for a few days."

"Mind if we skip lunch? I'd like to go back to the office and check out some of these names. On the way I'll swing past a nightspot in El Paso that's popular with both Mexicans and gringos. I could see you ending up there."

"Good idea. Maybe grab a burger and eat as we drive."

A short time later, between popping French fries in his mouth, Adams pointed out the nightspot he had spoken about. It was a huge building and was appropriately named The Old Warehouse. Adams said inside was a massive dance floor with a high platform built on each of the four corners of the dance floor. At night, they played country music and dance instructors were on each platform showing people the moves. The outside of the dance floor was surrounded by tables for the patrons to drink.

Adams told him that on some nights women from Juarez would come over to compete in a beauty pageant. He said the place often attracted a couple of thousand people at night.

"Perfect," said Jack. "Let's get to your office." Jack liked The Old Warehouse. Not for being fun, although he was sure it would be, but if he had to use it as a ruse to lose a cover team it would be easy.

Adams and Jack entered the main office and Adams immediately went to his desk. Davidson was in his office talking to Weber and the other two bosses. He saw Jack and gave him a warm smile and waved him in. As Jack entered, Weber gave him a friendly pat on the back.

Conversation was light, with friendly bantering back and forth about the snow in Canada and what Jack must think of the spicy Mexican food.

When Jack noticed Adams stand up from his desk and give him a nod, he knew it was time to go.

"Anything you need, just ask," said Davidson as Jack left.

Once Jack and Adams left the office, Davidson received a telephone call. "It's the D.A," he said to the others. "Close the door."

Weber complied as Davidson talked to White.

"The profilers are hitting it right on," said Davidson. "An hour ago the two of them were wishing they could be permanent partners. Adams was also telling the Mountie about some military operations."

"Perfect," replied White.

"I've kept the profilers apprised. They say what Adams has told the Mountie so far is like foreplay for what he really wants to talk about. The Mountie couldn't have responded better than if he was working for us. They say Adams will definitely confess to him soon. Maybe even today."

"Make sure he does it where we want him to do it."

"We're on top of it. Adams is an experienced investigator. He'll do it when he feels there is nobody around but the two of them. Just like a Catholic going to confession."

"You said building stress was the key. Putting them in a situation where they feel it is them against the world type of thing. Have you done that yet?"

"Not yet, but if Adams doesn't spill his guts today, we can do it tomorrow when the Mountie goes undercover.

Mind you, it may not be necessary. They're putting enough stress on themselves by going into Mexico."

"Going into Mexico?"

"Adams is taking him there right now to meet a CI. I think they are already under enough stress, but if need be, we'll ramp up the pressure tomorrow. Delay allowing the Mountie to go to the Armadillo by saying we're busy and can't spare the backup team. Tell him he'll have to wait an extra hour or so. Not a big deal, but with their personalities it will increase their stress load. If it doesn't, we'll come up with something else."

"I wouldn't have thought they would have clicked as partners so soon."

"They really are birds of a feather. It will be a shame to break up their little partnership, but hey, they can become penpals," said Davidson with a smile.

chapter twenty-six

Adams drove Jack across The Bridge of the Americas and they stopped at the Mexican Customs booth.

"Taking my *amigo* to show him how to drink tequila," said Adams.

The customs officer grunted and waved them through.

It was quarter to three when Adams parked the car and the two of them cautiously made their way to an alley.

Jose Rubalcava arrived in the alley a moment later, approaching on foot from the other end. "I see you have brought a friend," he said.

"He can be trusted," said Adams.

"I know, otherwise you would not have brought him." Rubalcava smiled. "And how have you been, John? I have been worried about you, *amigo*."

Jack caught the subtle glance Rubalcava gave him when he spoke to Adams. *There is something Rubalcava does not want to speak about in front of me. His face looks like there is serious justification for his concern ...*

"I'm okay," Adams replied, giving Rubalcava a hard look. "Let me introduce you."

Introductions were made and Jack explained to Rubalcava why he had come to El Paso and told him he was in Mexico against orders.

"For you as a policeman to come to Mexico is extremely dangerous," said Rubalcava, "but for you to come here as an undercover agent ... I would not classify it as dangerous."

"You wouldn't?" asked Jack.

"No. I would classify it as suicidal. It is for good reason your government does not want you here."

"I know it is dangerous," sighed Jack, not wanting to dwell on the matter. "Do you have any thoughts or ideas on something I could do to entice Tio into the U.S.? Is there a popular attraction in El Paso I could offer to treat him to?"

"No, from what you say, I suspect Tio is wanted in the U.S., otherwise he would not hesitate to go there," said Rubalcava.

"That's what I'm afraid of," admitted Jack.

"We have photos of two men taken by the apartment security camera in Canada for you to see," said Adams, handing the photos to Rubalcava. "The picture of the guy sneering at the camera is good, but all we have of the other guy is that he is missing his left earlobe."

Rubalcava studied the pictures briefly. "I do not recognize the man who is sneering, but the man who is missing an earlobe might be Eduardo Cortez. He is an enforcer for the Guajardo cartel. A very dangerous man who was hired from the military. Several years ago, he got in a fight with his brother over a woman and his brother bit his earlobe off."

"Nice brother," said Jack.

Rubalcava shrugged. "Eduardo shot and killed him for it the next day." He handed the photos back to Adams.

"Our Canadian friend took me to an interesting place yesterday," said Adams, who then told Rubalcava about the place they had found in the desert.

"The area you were in indicates it is the Guajardo cartel you are dealing with," said Rubalcava. "The Sinaloa cartel does not operate in that vicinity. They also haven't been here long enough yet to have that sophisticated of an operation. Maybe in a few years they will, but not now."

"Sort of what I thought," replied Adams.

"You said it looked like they were clearing out?" asked Rubalcava.

"Half the trailers looked empty," said Adams. "I also saw men taking furniture out of one of the other trailers."

Rubalcava nodded thoughtfully. "Rumours have circulated the Guajardo cartel is creating a new smuggling route. A man, who had been drinking too much, bragged in a cantina about making a lot of money. He said he was put in the back of a truck he could not see out of, and that he, along with many other men, were taken to work building a tunnel. He was murdered an hour later, but the rumour is out."

"Any idea who murdered him?" asked Jack, wondering if it was the same men who murdered Porter.

"I think it was one of my men," replied Rubalcava, "but I cannot be sure which one."

Jack inwardly cringed at the comment and the danger Rubalcava endured, yet the man talked in a friendly tone like old friends talking about sports. Except this game was deadly.

"Jack, perhaps I could discover the tunnel if you could identify some of the mules being used?" continued Rubalcava.

"I'll do my best," replied Jack.

"What do you think the chances are of following Slater's truck once it is taken from the motel?" asked Adams. "Do you think they will use the tunnel, or rely on the hiding spot in the truck and cross the border normally?"

"I think they will cross the border normally," said Rubalcava. "They have much less to fear from our customs than they did when they entered the U.S. from Canada."

"I bet you're right," agreed Adams.

"I also have some business addresses in Juarez that Earl Porter and Clive Slater have invested with," said Jack, flipping through his notebook. "We asked our liaison officer in Mexico City to make inquiries and he passed it on to the *federales*. They said the addresses were legitimate companies. The one for Porter apparently makes tourist trinkets and the one for Slater is a fruit company." He showed Rubalcava his notebook. "Do you want to write them down?"

"I don't need to," Rubalcava replied. "I know it. The two streets are separated by the same building, which is owned by the Guajardo cartel. They do run a fruit company from the building, but I suspect for Porter and Slater it was only an excuse for them to explain their trips to Customs."

Adams's eyes picked up someone who peered at them from around a corner at the end of the alley. "Don't look now," he said. "It's probably nothing, but someone stuck their head out from around the corner at the end of the alley. Keep talking while I walk in the opposite direction and go around the block and come back on him."

Jack looked at Rubalcava. His eyes never even flickered and he maintained his friendly composure while taking to Jack. *One very cool guy ...*

"So ... Canada, there is lots of snow there, yes?" Rubalcava asked, as Adams walked away.

"Not at the moment," replied Jack. "It's a big country. Some places get very cold in the winter, but only the most northern places have snow this time of year."

"I have never been there. Last year my family and I were given a holiday to go to Israel. It was nice there."

"I see," said Jack. *Given a holiday? Guess that explains who helped the Israelis with the PLO's drugs- for-weapons initiative* ... "I think I know why you were treated so nicely by the Israelis," he added.

"Oh?"

"A small matter of five mansions in the desert?"

Rubalcava smiled and said, "I wondered how long it would take the Americans to figure it out. I wondered if John had told you."

"You hadn't told him?"

"It wasn't his business, but I am pleased they were smart enough to figure it out."

"Aren't you worried about the other cartels finding out?"

"They were happy to get rid of the competition. They think I did them a favour."

"Sounds like it worked out."

"Except the two remaining cartels will become even more powerful," brooded Rubalcava.

"Yes, but at the same time, with your limited resources, it gives you one less organization to focus on."

"True."

"Still, you really do put yourself at risk," said Jack. "Why do you do it?"

Rubalcava sighed and said, "This is not the Mexico it is supposed to be. Here in Juarez ... with the Guajardo cartel and the Sinaloa cartel, the greed and lust for power will mean the violence will only get worse."

"I've heard they are killing each other. Maybe not such a bad thing."

"It is not only each other," said Rubalcava. "Many innocent people are being murdered. The cartels have no reason to fear anyone. Many honest policemen, judges, and prosecutors have been murdered. And it's not just people connected to the judiciary. Our citizens are also being murdered. They often kidnap our women right off the street. Sometimes the drug couriers take them to a stash house and use them for several days to entertain themselves while they are waiting for deliveries. Some of the bodies that have been found were terribly mutilated."

"How can you stand living in Juarez?" asked Jack, watching as Adams turned the far corner in the alley before turning back to face Rubalcava.

"Because it is my country," replied Rubalcava, sounding indignant. "I am determined to stop men like Guajardo, or the jackals who work for him, like the Carrillo Fuentes brothers, from doing what they are doing. If they are not stopped, this plague will reach far beyond Juarez. You know yourself it has already touched Canada."

"You have to be the bravest man I've ever met," said Jack.

Rubalcava smiled and said, "I am not that brave. I am just afraid to break a promise to my wife. I promised her I would do my best to make Mexico a better place for our two sons. Someday I hope to see it."

"Meeting us here ... this might not be good," said Jack, with a slight movement of his head to indicate the alley behind him.

"Ah," said Rubalcava, as his eyes flickered to the end of the alley behind Jack. "John worries too much. I am sure it is nothing."

"But as a police commander being away from your office, does it not raise any questions?" asked Jack. "They might wonder where you are going."

"At this time of day it is okay. Every day I leave my office before three o'clock to pick my two sons up from school ... but you have reminded me of something." Rubalcava retrieved his business card and gave it to Jack and said, "John has a way of contacting me through his wife, but if she is not available, call me yourself if it is urgent. Please memorize the numbers. Do not get caught with this card tomorrow."

"Don't worry," replied Jack. "Tomorrow I will be travelling under a false surname and anything I have, like my real wallet or notebook, I will leave in John's office for safekeeping."

"That is good. So if you are in dire trouble, call me and say you were robbed by a policeman and got my number from your consulate. I will say you were probably robbed by someone pretending to be a policeman and hang up. Then I will come to this spot."

"Thank you," said Jack.

"I will also go through this alley every day at this time while you are working here, so you can meet me if you have something. I will also do it on my way to work, between eight-thirty and nine. If it is more urgent, then call me."

"Again, thank you. It is very much appreciated."

Rubalcava eyed Jack curiously for a moment and asked, "So tell me, Jack, why do you risk coming here? This is not your country."

Jack retrieved a picture of Lily Rae from his wallet and showed it to Rubalcava. "I promised her mother I would do everything I could to find her. You know how it is with promises. They are something that should not be made if you do not intend to keep them."

Rubalcava smiled. "That I understand, *amigo* ... that I understand." He glanced down the alley and added, "If John does not know the identities of the men Tio sends to meet you tomorrow, perhaps he can take their pictures. Maybe I will know them."

"Thank you. I am hoping I will learn much more when I meet Tio. I may act a bit like a tourist and bring my own camera. He might be willing to have his picture taken with me."

"He may feel safe enough to do that in Mexico," noted Rubalcava.

"Until I meet him, I do not know how long it will take to get what I want. It may take a few meetings with him to find out what happened to the girl."

Rubalcava stared at Jack a moment. "Out of curiosity, do you have children, too?"

"Yes, a baby boy and another baby on the way."

"Ah," replied Rubalcava as he reached out and grasped Jack's hand with both of his and shook it. "We have something in common, you and me … besides our work. It makes us even more like brothers."

Jack reflected on how much more dangerous Rubalcava's situation was. *I have been in some dangerous situations, but they pale in comparison. He is walking a very high tightrope without a net. How long can he stay before a gust of wind comes …*

Adams returned and said, "It was nothing. Only a street vendor."

Rubalcava smiled at Jack as if to say *I told you so.*

"Is this other thing still on for tonight?" asked Adams, speaking to Rubalcava.

"Yes, I have heard several policemen will be receiving extra pay tonight, but I do not know how large of a shipment it will be."

"Same place they used before?"

"Yes," replied Rubalcava.

"Good. Last time I found their tracks the next day where they crossed."

Adams looked at Jack and said, "The Sinaloa cartel is running a shipment of marijuana across the border tonight, a mile from the bridge I first showed you yesterday morning."

"Will you be there?" Rubalcava asked Adams.

"Only to watch and see who picks it up on my side of the border. Don't worry, I won't jeopardize you by doing anything."

"I know you won't, *amigo.*"

chapter twenty-seven

As Adams drove Jack back across the Bridge of the Americas, he said, "I forgot to mention to you, you're invited for dinner tonight."

"You don't need to do that."

"It's already done. Yolanda, wants to meet you. She's never met a real Mountie before."

"Is she expecting me to arrive on horseback?"

Adams chuckled and said, "No, I told her about you."

"Nothing bad, I hope," said Jack.

"From what I told her, she said you sounded like me ... except to say I'm not as genteel."

"Genteel? What the hell do you mean by that?"

"She meant at handling, what was your word ... yes, *delicate* situations. She suggested I could learn from you."

"I think we can learn from each other."

Jack was introduced to Yolanda. She was an attractive woman and her Mexican features suited her well. She was quick to smile and embraced Jack like he was a long-lost relative. The dinner she served consisted of numerous dishes, with Jack's favourite being a slow-cooked pulled pork. Conversation was light and Yolanda asked Jack about his family. When Jack told her Natasha was pregnant, he saw her give John a quick smile.

After dinner, as they sat at the table sipping white wine, Adams excused himself to go to the washroom.

Yolanda took the opportunity to look at Jack and say, "John speaks quite highly of you. He wishes you were his partner."

"I really like him, too. I guess for the moment we are partners."

"I'm slightly jealous of partners," said Yolanda. "I know they tell each other everything. More than they tell their wives. I never get all the real details."

Jack could see her eyes studying him. He had the feeling there was something bothering her in particular. "I think Natasha feels the same way, sometimes," said Jack. "Although she once told me she doesn't want to know anything secret, so she doesn't ever have to worry about slipping up."

"I guess there's that," replied Yolanda, frowning slightly.

Adams returned and suggested as Jack had a big day tomorrow, perhaps it was time to drive him back to his hotel.

"I thought you were working tonight?" said Jack.

"Going out around eleven. The shipments usually cross around one or two in the morning."

"Let me join you," said Jack. "I know I'm not here long, but I still feel like we're partners for the time we are together."

Adams smiled and said, "On one condition. Tonight you carry a piece."

"I told you I was a lousy shot ... but okay, just for tonight."

At midnight, Adams and Jack turned around at the same bridge southwest of El Paso where someone had previously fired shots at the U.S. Customs hut. Adams then backtracked about a mile and pulled off the highway and parked so the car was hidden by a few clumps of scrub brush.

Adams handed Jack a set of binoculars and said, "If you look left about a quarter-mile across the highway from where we came from, you'll see a slight ridge on the Mexican side of the border. Last time that is where they came over. All I want to do is try to identify the truck that picks it up on this side."

"You know it's a truck?"

"We're talking marijuana. They wouldn't be using the police to guard it if the shipment was small. Once they load, I'll belly-crawl to the road and take a look at the truck when it goes past. The guys guarding it over the border from Mexico should vamoose pretty quickly once the load is delivered. With luck, we'll wait about five minutes after it leaves and then pull out. We'll still have plenty of time to catch up to the truck before it reaches the city."

"Don't you have any of the other guys from the office to help?"

"I asked Weber and he said he doesn't want to pay for the overtime for anyone else. Pisses me off, but what else can I do?"

"Typical," replied Jack. "I often deal with the same problem in Canada."

"Well, as Weber said, it is no big deal to get a plate number and I should be able to follow a truck easy enough."

"How long do you think before the deal goes down?"

"You know how dope deals go."

"Never on time, that's for sure."

"Exactly, we could be waiting half the night."

Davidson and Weber sat in a car four miles away and smiled.

"What do you think?" asked Weber. "Turning up the pressure enough?"

"I would say so. If they sit there an hour or two waiting for the delivery, they're bound to talk about something."

"Hope so. I'm getting too old to be out this late," replied Weber.

"Good thing they're sitting in the car," noted Davidson.

It was after one o'clock and Adams was scanning the horizon with the binoculars when he blurted, "Fuck! They're here, but not where they crossed last time. Look," he said, passing the binoculars.

Jack focused the binoculars and looked to where Adams was pointing. He could make out the shapes of several men on the Mexican side of the border, but they were slightly to the right of them instead of the left as expected. "They came out practically on top of us," said Jack, handing the binoculars back.

"Yeah, except if the truck comes from El Paso it probably won't go past us," said Adams. "I'm going to have to sneak down the ditch about a hundred yards to get the plate. It could still be another hour or two."

"I'll come with you."

Ten minutes passed as Jack and Adams, both hunched over, crept along a ditch, stopping twice to lie down flat when a car and a truck passed. Eventually they could hear whispered conversation from the Mexicans guarding the drug shipment and knew they had gone far enough.

Adams tapped Jack's arm and pointed to a small knoll up from the ditch in the direction of the voices. There were a few clumps of dried grass to give them cover.

Jack nodded and they both crawled toward the top of the knoll to watch. As they went, he winced several times when sharp needles from small cactus plants found his elbows and his knees.

Once in place at the top of the knoll, Adams looked through the binoculars and then handed them over.

The binoculars were barely needed, but Jack used them to count about thirty men, many of whom were wearing Mexican police uniforms. Somewhere in the darkness behind the men, they could hear a truck idling.

"Must be a small shipment, maybe only one or two ton," whispered Adams. "For the really big ones the bad guys hire the military to protect the crossing. You'll see fifty to a hundred soldiers protecting it."

Jack felt his stomach knot as he thought of how dangerous Mexico really was for anyone who would dare to take on the cartels.

Another few minutes passed when the sound of a car racing up the highway from El Paso could be heard. It caught everyone's attention when the car came to a screeching stop a short distance down the road.

The whispers of the Mexican police officers became louder and more excited.

Seconds later, gunshots erupted from the car and bullets flew overhead.

Jack literally kissed the dirt as he stuck his face as deep as possible into a small indentation in the ground. Several of the Mexican police officers returned fire and the bullets whizzed like jet-propelled bees over Jack and Adams in the opposite direction. The truck that had been idling immediately sprang to life and seconds later all of the Mexicans ran back.

"What the hell happened?" asked Jack, as the car on the highway did a U-turn and sped away.

"The car had to be from the Guajardo cartel," replied Adams. "They must have found out at the last moment what the Sinaloa boys were up to and sent someone out here to fuck with them."

Adams and Jack both stood up and walked back to the car. On the way Adams asked, "Do you feel like going for a drink?"

"Normally I would jump at the chance, but I want to rent a car from the airport and be at the Armadillo around noon tomorrow. That may give the bad guys the impression I just arrived. I also don't know what tomorrow will bring, so I think I better take a rain check tonight and get some sleep."

"I understand. I'll pick you up in the morning around ten-thirty and drive you to the airport. I'll also arrange to get a policewoman and check into the motel before you do and put a backup team at that spot about five minutes down the road from the motel."

"Thanks."

"How are you going to handle it with my people if the bad guys want you to go to Juarez?"

"I'll say they want to meet me in the dance spot you showed me. The Old Warehouse. It's so big they'll have a hard time knowing if I'm there or not. I'll also tell the bad guys I want my own car, so I'll have some control."

"How will you communicate with me?"

"I'll tell the bad guys I have to call Damien and then call you on your cell."

"Who's Damien?"

"National president of Satans Wrath. He's the top boss in Canada and is who they will think I represent.

"And once you meet Tio?"

"Party hearty and try to gain his trust to find out what they did with Lily. Once I do that, I'll try to get anyone who was involved, including the two hit-men who killed Porter, back across the border into El Paso so they can be arrested."

"And how the hell will you manage that?" asked Adams as they arrived at the car and he unlocked the door.

Jack shrugged and said, "I don't know yet, I'll come up with something. It's what I do."

Adams stared silently at Jack over the roof of the car.

"Relax," said Jack. "What could possibly go wrong?" he added with a smile, trying to sound light-hearted.

"What can go wrong is you'll leave a pregnant widow and a son behind," said Adams tersely.

Jack quit smiling.

chapter twenty-eight

The following morning, Jack went to the hotel lobby with his laptop and only one of his suitcases. He had decided he would not check out of his room in the event he needed a safe haven later on.

In the lobby he used a pay phone to make a collect call to Natasha. He did not want to risk using the phone in his room in case a nosey hotel clerk listened in, nor did he want to use his cellphone in the event it fell into the wrong hands after and would have a record of his call home.

Natasha answered and Jack could hear Mikey banging a spoon on the tray of his high chair in the background.

"So where you been?" asked Natasha, sounding snippy. "Taking care of business?"

Jack smiled. Usually collect calls meant they could talk freely, but not always. Natasha always acted like a jilted woman until Jack gave her the clearance to talk. Even then, most details were left out.

"I called to tell you I love you," said Jack, "and Mikey, too."

"I love you, too," she said lovingly. "We miss you."

"I think the only thing Mikey misses is his food if it's a minute late," said Jack.

"No, he doesn't. You've seen his face light up when he sees you. Speaking of which?"

"Hope to have a business meeting today with this new partnership. With luck, I'll be back sometime this weekend."

"Call me as soon as you can."

"I will." Jack knew Natasha worried about him. They had made a pact that rather than have her worry needlessly, he would try to let her know when he was doing something risky and then call her as soon as it was over. In the long run, it was a bit easier on her that way.

Jack saw the Camaro pull up in front of the hotel lobby and knew he had to go. He quickly said goodbye and picked up his luggage and stepped outside.

Adams and an attractive young woman got out of the car as he approached.

"This is Sherry," said Adams. "My one night-stand," he added with a grin.

"Don't you wish," replied Sherry, rolling her eyes.

After arriving at the airport and giving his laptop to Adams to hold for safekeeping, Jack rented a car. He then went for breakfast to give Adams and Sherry time to ensure the cover team was in place and check into the Armadillo Motel before he arrived.

It was twelve-thirty when Jack arrived at the motel. He spotted the Camaro in front of a unit as well as five other vehicles parked in front of other units. Slater's truck was not one of them. The other vehicles made Jack feel a little more comfortable. The motel had enough business that the presence of Adams and Sherry should go unnoticed.

The motel manager turned out to be a skinny, nervous-looking man who constantly sniffled. Jack figured he either had a cold or a bad coke habit. *Probably the latter ...*

"Oh, you're the guy from Canada," said Sniffles, as he read the hotel registration sheet Jack filled out. "Got a message for ya," he said, reaching into a beehive of cubbyholes behind him and handing Jack a slip of paper.

The message was short. *Hit a deer and gotta wait for a new radiator. Will be there tomorrow afternoon. T's guys said they would be over to see you. Clive*

Jack didn't care if Slater was there. The important thing was to meet Tio. He got the key to his room and discovered it was a couple of units past where the Camaro was parked. He didn't look in the darkened room as he went past, but did notice the curtains were open a crack for someone to see out.

Jack hadn't slept much the night before and was hoping to get a few hours' shut-eye. He lay on the bed, but his adrenalin wouldn't allow him to sleep.

He was in the room less than an hour when he heard a vehicle pull up. He looked out the window and saw two Mexican men getting out of a white SUV. They both appeared to be in their mid-thirties.

The passenger was obese, with rolls of fat on the back of his neck like a walrus. He had a thick black moustache and his eyebrows met in the middle. His puffy cheeks gave the impression that his nose had sunken into his face and overall, he was one of the ugliest men Jack had ever seen.

Jack saw him hold up a hand to gesture for the second man to remain at the SUV while he waddled over to the door. Jack opened it as the man was about to knock.

"Señor Jack?"

"Jack will do. Who are you?"

"They call me El Pero," he said with a smile, extending his hand.

Jack shook the sweaty paw and discreetly wiped his hand on the sides of his cargo pants afterwards.

"*¿Habla usted español, Señor Jack?*"

"What's that?" replied Jack. "Are you asking me if I speak Spanish? Sorry, I only know a couple of words."

In fact, Jack knew enough to get by, but thought it might be in his best interests if the bad guys thought they could speak freely in front of him and believe they were not understood.

"El Pero in Spanish mean *The Dog,*" said El Pero. "It is what my *amigos* call me. You can call me by that name, too."

"Pleased to meet you, El Pero. Come on in."

El Pero entered and Jack glanced at the man standing by the SUV.

"He is okay," said El Pero. "He can wait."

Jack closed the door and gestured to one of two chairs in the room. After they sat, El Pero said, "I came by to welcome you and tell you that tonight I will take you to a party in Juarez."

"I was expecting Tio to be here," said Jack. "It may not be safe for me to go to Juarez."

"Tio?" asked El Pero. "Your uncle is coming?"

"Not my uncle. I'm talking about the man I came to meet. The man who told me to come to this motel," said Jack.

El Pero's triple chins shook as he wheezed out a laugh and said, "Now I understand. When I deal with Señor Slater he has heard me call my *tio*, which in Spanish means *uncle*. The man I report to is my uncle and that is who you were expecting to meet."

"Oh, I see … so what is your uncle's name?"

"Señor Alphonse Franco," replied El Pero.

Jack smiled. Finding out the uncle's name had been easy. Meeting him might not be as simple.

"Señor Alphonse Franco told me you had a concern

about going to Juarez," said El Pero. "You are not to worry. He has checked with the *federales* and the *policia*. They do not know you. Even if they did, it would be nothing we would not take care of."

"I see," said Jack, not overly surprised that the cartel had checked with the police.

"You will be Señor Alphonse Franco's guest tonight," said El Pero. "I will pick you up at seven o'clock and take you to meet with him for dinner. We have reserved an entire restaurant for the occasion."

"That sounds great, but I would prefer to drive myself there."

"I am sorry, but I must insist," said El Pero. "My uncle is always very careful that the Americans do not find him. He is afraid any car rented in America could have a satellite tracker installed in it by the authorities. The same rules apply for cellphones in the event the Americans triangulate the signal and locate our position. The only cellphones allowed are ones my uncle obtains through a special connection."

"Your uncle is a wise man," said Jack. "That is good. I do not like to do business with men who are stupid or careless."

"*Si*," replied El Pero with a smile. "I will tell him you are happy with the security measures being taken. Now you may wish to sleep. Tonight there will be a big fiesta in your honour."

Jack waited ten minutes after El Pero left before strolling to the motel office while tossing the key in his hand to announce his intention to leave. He dropped the key off with Sniffles for safekeeping and told him he was going into El Paso to look around. When he walked back toward his car he saw Adams standing in the doorway of his unit without his shirt on and yawning.

Jack pretended to ignore him as he walked past, but said, "Wait fifteen and then meet me at the first gas station you come to on the way back to town."

Thirty minutes later, Adams and Sherry pulled up beside Jack's rented car that was parked beside a garage where Jack was pretending to top off the air in his tires.

Adams unrolled the window to talk and Jack said, "Looks like we're delayed for a day or two. Got a message from Slater when I checked in that he hit a deer and damaged his radiator. I spoke to one of the two Mexicans who showed up and it looks like we'll have to wait until Slater gets here to get everyone together."

"Too bad," replied Adams as he looked at Jack and raised one eyebrow.

Jack gave a nod as though he was in agreement the delay was unfortunate.

"Typical," said Sherry. "Dopers never do anything on time. Guess we have to become lovebirds again, John."

"We did manage to snap a couple of photos of the guy who waited outside," said Adams, "but from the angle they parked, we never got to see the face of the guy you spoke with."

"That goof gave me the name for Tio. It's Alphonse Franco. Do you know him?"

"Big Al!" exclaimed Adams. "Damn rights we know him. He's one of the upper echelons. Only a rung or two down the ladder from the Carrillo Fuentes brothers. He definitely has the political standing to talk to Guajardo himself."

"Which he is probably doing if they think they will be doing business with Satans Wrath."

"Man, I didn't think you would reach this level so quickly," said Adams.

"Satans Wrath have a huge international reputation with a world-wide drug distribution network. It's a bit like GM approaching Nissan and suggesting they go into business together. It makes sense that they would send out their upper echelon to talk to me. Who knows, maybe Guajardo himself or the Carrillo Fuentes boys will show up."

Adams shook his head and said, "Not a chance. That I am sure of. Maybe if you were to really buy three or four ton off of them they might, but there is no way any of those guys would risk showing up yet. Big Al will have to vouch for you himself and oversee things to start with. As close as he is to the top guy, it would cost him his life if things went wrong."

"That's good to know. So why won't Big Al come into the U.S.?"

"We nailed his ass on a major cocaine beef four years ago. He'd be looking at a minimum of twenty-five years if we could get him deported. Unfortunately we can't. He's one of the untouchables over there. At the moment he's got his nephew running things for him in El Paso."

"El Pero?"

"Yes, that's his nickname. His real name is Pietro Franco."

"That's who spoke with me."

"I wondered if that was the fat fucker you were talking to. El Pero is halfway up the corporate ladder. Being Big Al's nephew, I'm certain the cartel has big plans for him."

"Sounds like everything is going good. We just have to wait. Which is fine by me for the moment. I'm running on empty when it comes to the sleep department. Think I'll go back to my room in the city and sleep for the next twenty-four hours. You can call the guys off and I'll give you a shout tomorrow morning when I wake up."

Adams rolled up his window and started to back up, then stopped and said to Sherry, "I'm going to invite him home for dinner in case he changes his mind about sleeping."

"I was thinking of asking him the same thing," said Sherry. "He's cute."

"Forget it. He's married," replied Adams as he got out the car.

"I know, but that is still no reason for him to be all alone. Besides, back at the motel you mentioned you had already had him over for dinner so —"

"Forget it. I know what you're thinking. He's very married."

"Very married?"

"You know what I mean," replied Adams, closing the door and walking over to Jack who was about to get in his rental.

"What's really happening?" whispered Adams.

"El Pero is picking me up tonight at seven to take me to meet Big Al. They've reserved an entire restaurant someplace in Juarez. I'm not allowed to take my rental or a cellphone. Big Al is paranoid you guys might use either one to try and trace him."

"I can't cover you over there. Our friend can't be seen, either."

"I know. I'll call you when I'm done."

"What if they want you to stay over? If you don't have a car or a phone —"

"I'll tell them I have to be at a certain gas station in El Paso in the morning to take a call from Damien. I'll use it as an excuse to have someone drive me back if the party goes on for too long. I'll call you as soon as I can."

"So, Juarez it is ..." said Adams sombrely.

"Yes."

The muscles rippled along Adams's jaw line as he clenched his teeth before turning on his heel and walking away. He knew he had made a mistake by befriending Jack. They were in a war ... and liking someone made it all the harder when that person became a casualty.

chapter twenty-nine

At seven o'clock, El Pero arrived at the Armadillo Motel. This time he had a different driver who came to the door, as well. Jack let them both in.

The driver was a husky man who stood as tall as Jack. His hair was short and his eyes darted around the room. His face had the scars of more than one battle, but it wasn't his face that spiked Jack's adrenalin. The excitement he felt was because the man was missing an earlobe. He knew it had to be Eduardo Cortez, the man Rubalcava had identified as being an enforcer for the Guajardo cartel.

Jack stuck his hand out and said, "I'm Jack."

Eduardo looked at El Pero who nodded, so he stood like he was at attention and shook Jack's hand and said, "I'm Eduardo. Pleased to meet you, sir."

Jack recalled Rubalcava's comment that Eduardo had received military training. Judging by the battle scars on his face, Jack suspected his training had frequently been put to use.

"Are you ready?" asked El Pero.

"Yes," replied Jack. "Is it okay if I take my camera? My boss would like to see who we are planning on doing business with."

"I do not see why not," replied El Pero, "but I will take your camera and ask permission when we arrive."

Jack handed him his camera and he gave Jack an apologetic look. "Señor Jack, I know it is unpleasant and I am sure unnecessary, but there is something we need to do."

Jack smiled and said, "I understand. My boss is the same way when he meets new people." With that comment, Jack turned and placed his hands on the wall and spread his feet so Eduardo could search him.

Forty-five minutes later, Jack was in the back of the SUV as it crossed the Bridge of the Americas and stopped at Mexican Customs. He found it slightly disconcerting when the immigration officer recognized El Pero and apologized to him for the inconvenience of stopping him, while hastily waving them through.

Soon after, Eduardo double-parked on the street in front of a restaurant and the three of them got out and walked to the front door. Jack counted four burly men loitering out front. Despite the heat, they all wore light jackets. Judging by the way they studied each approaching car and person, Jack concluded they had received training as V.I.P. bodyguards.

"Parking attendants?" said Jack to El Pero, with a nod of his head to one of the four men.

"If you are parked by them, Jack, you will never move again," replied El Pero with a grim smile.

The restaurant was large enough to hold sixty customers and had a bar at the far end. The only customers present were a group of fifteen men who were sitting at a few tables pushed together in the middle. They were all casually dressed and appeared to be enjoying themselves.

El Pero's uncle was easy to spot. Big Al was the biggest man at the table and when their eyes met, Jack could see his face looked like an older version of El Pero's ugly mug.

The men sitting on the same side of the table as Big Al scrambled to move their chairs out of his way as he rose and lumbered over to meet Jack. It was then that Jack noticed a huge difference between Big Al and El Pero. Big Al was muscular to the point that Jack suspected his physique was a result of weight-lifting and steroid use. Overall, he looked like he could have been a wrestler.

Jack smiled and accepted his firm handshake like they were already good friends and looked into the dark eyes studying him. *"Muchas gusto, señor,"* said Jack, intentionally stumbling over the words and mispronouncing them as he shook his hand.

Big Al smiled back, exposing a gold front tooth. "You speak Spanish."

"Sorry," said Jack, shaking his head. "It took me all day to learn to say that."

"Well … you said it very well." Big Al smiled. "I am Señor Alphonse Franco, but many of my gringo friends call me Big Al. It is a nickname I rather like. Come, I have saved you a seat beside me."

"Are we going to be talking business in front of all these men?" asked Jack.

"Business? No, no, no. First we eat and get to know each other. After, I have something planned to entertain ourselves. Everything is on me. If you see something …" Big Al smiled, nudging Jack with his elbow and added, "or perhaps *someone* you like, let me know. Tonight I want you to have fun. Business can come later."

Jack sat alongside Big Al and El Pero sat on the other side of him. Eduardo sat across from them. Next to Eduardo was a man whom Jack recognized. It was the same man who sneered into the apartment security camera. The man he had nicknamed as El Burla. *Tonight is turning out very well.*

Jack saw Big Al was drinking Taittinger champagne and requested the same. As soon as he was served, Big Al raised his glass and said first in Spanish and then in English, "Here is to the peoples of the world getting to know each other."

Jack clinked glasses with Big Al and took a sip. When Big Al continued to gulp the entire glass, Jack followed suit.

A waiter standing behind them immediately refilled both glasses. Jack raised his glass and said, "Water separates the people of the world, but wine unites us."

Big Al laughed and said, "Yes, water like the Rio Grande." He then translated in Spanish, which elicited a few smiles around the table.

"Señor Jack," said Big Al, "you have met my nephew ... he is handsome like his uncle, yes?"

"Exactly what I was thinking when I walked in," said Jack.

"We call him El Pero because he is like a dog. Isn't that right, El Pero?" laughed Big Al, while ruffling El Pero's hair.

El Pero beamed at the attention he received from his uncle. It was obviously an inside joke, but Jack smiled as if he understood.

The drinking continued, along with general conversation mixed with a few crude jokes while waitresses brought what seemed like a never-ending assortment of different dishes.

As the night progressed, Jack asked if he could have his camera back so he could take some pictures to show his boss how well he was being treated. Big Al readily agreed and had one of his men take a couple of pictures with Jack's camera.

"That is a good idea," said Big Al. "I also have some people who would like to know you are having a good time. Jack smiled and posed with drink in hand while several more photographs were taken with cellphone cameras.

Jack tried to act like he was really enjoying himself. A role he found difficult to do while some of the men, laughing with evil delight, groped terrified waitresses and yanked their blouses open to kiss their breasts. The liquor behind the bar was also freely ransacked.

Jack 's role of portraying a member of an outlaw motorcycle gang left him in a position where such behaviour was to appear acceptable to him, even applauded. The more he was forced to smile and laugh, the more his anger boiled inside him. As the night continued, he found himself frequently checking his watch, wishing the sickening spectacle was over.

It was midnight when Big Al mentioned it was time to leave and go to another place he had reserved.

"Another place?" asked Jack.

"A quieter place to drink and mingle with each other," he said. "I know some of my men wish to meet you. Your organization has gained a certain popularity it would seem."

Jack welcomed the chance to meet one of Big Al's men in particular. The man who sneered and thumbed his nose at the security camera before committing murder.

"Sounds great, but I shouldn't be too late," Jack said. "I have to be at a certain gas station in El Paso early tomorrow morning. It has been arranged that my boss will call me there."

"Ah, I see. That would be Señor Damien," said Big Al.

"You know him?" asked Jack, feeling his stomach knot.

"No, but his reputation is highly regarded."

"Yes, I certainly think the world of him. But of course, for now, it is Damien's idea you only deal through me. We do not want word of this meeting getting out until everything is running smoothly. We don't want it to cause problems with the people we have been dealing with. There are still some business transactions that haven't been concluded yet."

"I understand, *amigo*. We keep this secret. I only contact you and you speak for Señor Damien. Do not tomorrow ... worry in the morning," said Big Al, whose command of the English language had deteriorated slightly in accordance with the amount he had drank. "I will have my men take you back in time to call the gas station."

As the entourage walked out of the restaurant, Jack saw the owner of the restaurant thanking Big Al profusely for gracing his restaurant with his presence. A scene Jack found rather pathetic, considering nothing had been paid for.

Jack rode in the back of a silver SUV with Big Al and El Pero sat in the front with a bodyguard who was driving. The rest of Big Al's men piled into an assortment of other vehicles and formed small parade as they all drove away. Soon their driver decided it was too slow and quickly outdistanced the other vehicles.

As they drove, Jack saw the driver occasionally studying him through the rear-view mirror. Jack didn't know if it was the man's penetrating eyes, or how he professionally handled the SUV through the traffic, but his gut instinct told him the man was a police officer. When their eyes locked momentarily, Jack smiled and said hello.

The driver frowned and turned his attention back to the street in front of him.

"He doesn't speak English very well," explained Big Al.

Eventually they stopped on the street in front of a small boutique hotel. A minute later, the rest of the entourage arrived. Jack saw the four bodyguards — the

same ones who had been at the restaurant earlier —
bail out of another SUV and take up positions beside
the front door of the hotel. Two of the bodyguards held
MAC-10 mini-machine guns and strutted about looking
as menacing as they could.

The entire entourage remained parked, blocking
traffic, as the passengers casually got out. Nobody
waiting had the nerve to show their impatience by
blowing their horns.

"I have more men inside," smiled Big Al as his eyes
studied Jack's face for a response.

Jack nodded politely. He knew Big Al was putting on
a show for him. Had the bodyguards really been necessary, their driver would not have broken ranks with the
rest of the vehicles and the hotel would have already
been secured by bodyguards before they arrived.

Jack was pleased. *If he respects me enough to try
and impress me, he might be willing to answer a few
questions ...*

The hotel was a two-storey building with a flat roof
built in traditional Spanish architecture and had four
granite columns across the front. The entire building was
painted pink and set off from the rest of the buildings on
the street by a lane down each side leading to a parking
lot and back alley.

It was when Jack got out of the SUV he noticed the
sign on the roof. *El Toro Solitario*, which in English
meant The Lonely Bull.

Big Al slapped him on the back and said, "Remember,
tonight everything is my treat. I insist upon it."

Oh shit ... it's a brothel.

chapter thirty

The lobby floor of the brothel consisted of several clusters of sofas, chairs, and coffee tables. The room was open to the roof. A bar built of teak stretched along one side of the room and on the opposite side, a curved spiral staircase with teak railings led up to the second level where a horseshoe-shaped walkway led to the rooms. Jack counted seven rooms on each side and four rooms across the back. One large chandelier hung down from the centre.

The only patrons were the ones arriving in Big Al's entourage and it was obvious he had reserved the hotel. The attractive young women, who outnumbered the men two to one, were dressed in an assortment of low-cut dresses or blouses unbuttoned enough to reveal lots of cleavage. Several said hello to Señor Franco, who smiled and clutched Jack's arm, identifying Jack as his special friend.

Big Al took a seat on a sofa with each arm draped around a prostitute and gestured for Jack to sit on another sofa facing him. Jack remained standing and saw that several of the men were congregating at the bar, including Eduardo and El Burla.

"Big Al," said Jack, "you mentioned some of your men wanted to meet me. I would like to get to know them, as well. Maybe have a few drinks. Do any of them, besides El Pero and Eduardo, speak English?"

"*Si*, Jack. Several do." He looked toward El Pero, who was laughing while playfully pretending to bend a prostitute over the back of a chair. Deciding to leave him to his fun, Big Al then yelled in Spanish for Eduardo to look after Jack and introduce him to some of the men.

Eduardo smiled, waving his arm and said, "Come, Señor Jack. I will introduce you to some of the *hombres*."

The first man Jack met was El Burla, whose real name was Berto. Upon introduction, Berto was polite and his face showed nothing but respect as he offered a firm handshake. *Being Big Al's special friend may have its advantages*, thought Jack.

Berto then helped himself to a bottle of KAH Tequila Blanco from the bar and poured everyone a drink. The tequila bottle was in the shape of a human skull and Jack's thoughts returned to Lily again.

Over the next half hour, Jack drank with Eduardo and Berto, as well as several other men. The conversation was friendly, peppered with a few crude comments about some of the women. It was also evident Berto and Eduardo were good friends and Jack had the impression they had received military training together.

Jack noticed that El Pero seemed to be having trouble finding a prostitute. Unlike the other men who had prostitutes continually swarming around them, with El Pero they would either vanish as soon as he approached, or would disappear shortly after. Jack sensed it was more than just his ugliness that drove them away.

Later, Jack saw El Pero finally corner one young prostitute, who laughed and smiled politely, but then made an excuse to go to the washroom. Jack watched as she walked away, only to be approached and reprimanded by two other prostitutes. It was apparent from the gesturing that the young prostitute was afraid of El Pero and momentarily broke down in tears before being shoved back in his direction.

A prostitute in a Mexican whore house is upset with having to go with El Pero? He really must be one sick bastard ...

"Señor Jack," said Berto, interrupting his thoughts. "Eduardo and me, we think Canada is very cold ... yes?"

Jack caught the inquisitive look on Berto's face and knew he was wondering if Big Al had told Jack about who did the hit on Porter. He also caught the annoyed look Eduardo gave Berto and suspected it was not a subject he thought should be discussed. "Oh, so it was you two who went," replied Jack.

"I did not say we go ... I say we think it is very cold."

"That's okay," replied Jack with a smile. "I was told someone was sent, but I was not told who. You two must be highly regarded to be selected for such an important task. I am truly honoured to have met you."

Berto exchanged a quick smile with Eduardo at the compliment. "Thank you, Señor Jack. So you do know why we were sent?"

"Yes. You needed to teach somebody manners. That it's not polite to gamble with other people's money."

Berto laughed and said, "Yes, you are right, but he did not think it polite when I slit his throat, either."

Jack laughed along with Eduardo.

"What you talk about?" roared Big Al, placing a firm grip on Jack's shoulder.

Jack had not realized Big Al was behind him and felt his adrenalin kick in. *How much did he hear? Will he be upset that these two morons were talking in front of me?*

Jack turned and smiled. "We were talking about taking care of business."

"About our trip to Canada," said Berto, smiling as he ran his index finger across his throat.

"I do not want nobody talk business tonight," said Big Al, looking at Jack curiously. "Come," he said, steering Jack away by his shoulder. "Bring your drink. There are many *señoritas* here who wish to get to know you much better."

"Good, but I better switch to beer," said Jack.

"You no like tequila?" asked Big Al.

"I like it, but I am also familiar with that old expression."

"What expression?"

"One tequila, two tequila, three tequila, floor," replied Jack, accepting a Corona before moving away from the bar.

Big Al chuckled and as they wandered toward a sofa Jack stopped him and said, "Big Al, this is all great, but Damien is expecting me to have a couple of business details resolved when I speak to him tomorrow morning. I do not want to get in trouble. Please, I would like to talk about a couple of things."

Big Al sighed and said, "Okay, *amigo*. I do not want you to have any problems with your boss. I have bosses, too, so I understand. I was told to show you a good time."

"I am having a good time, I can assure you."

"Good. You know, before you come here, we were thinking you would look at us as enemy because we opened a new store in Canada."

"You mean you were worried we would look at you as competition?"

"Yes, that is what I say. So my bosses are very happy you have come to us. We want you to be happy and everybodies make *mucho dinero*."

"Exactly. We feel the same way. If we work together, everyone will be rich."

"So what business details does Señor Damien want to know about now?"

"We want to be cautious. Four or five ton a year is a lot of money."

"*Si*, but we will give you a good price."

"I'm sure you will, but at what price and where do we pick it up? If we have to come to Mexico —"

"No, no. We will bring it to you. Getting into Canada across the American border is easy. We drive trucks there every week."

"The border from Mexico into the U.S. is much more guarded. What if our shipment is taken down here?"

"Oh, here is no problem, especially now."

"Now?"

"Before we used planes to land in the desert where we had trailers for storage. But now that the Americans have increased security, we think it is no longer a good place." Big Al glanced around and smiled broadly before whispering, "Now we have *la Casa Blanca*. It took us two years to make."

"Casa Blanca? Like the movie? I don't understand."

"Movie? I don't know what movie. Our Casa Blanca is nicknamed for the colour of cocaine. Maybe the same as the American Casa Blanca." Big Al grinned.

"The American White House?"

"*Si, si*," laughed Big Al. "Maybe they build it with narco dollar, too."

"I still don't understand," said Jack.

"Our Casa Blanca … the house is not even white … but it has a hole in the ground to America. Two miles long."

"You have a stash house with a tunnel leading into the United States?"

"Yes," said Big Al proudly. "Outside of Juarez. It took two years to build and *mucho dinero* … but we do not need to worry about getting caught."

"Sounds great."

"Yes, so don't worry about your cocaine getting arrested ... no what you say?"

"Seized."

"Yes. But even if it was seized, it would not matter for you. Until we deliver it to you, it is not your problem. It is our problem."

"I see."

"So you can tell Señor Damien not to worry, okay?"

"Yes, I will tell him."

"But for the price you pay," continued Big Al, "I will still need talk to my bosses. How much you want, how often you want it ... it will all have to be worked out."

"That I can get back to you on, but there are still a couple of loose ends that have us worried."

"Loose ends?"

"Damien is a cautious man. He is worried because you murdered Earl Porter."

"Why? Señor Porter take our money ... we take his life. Very fair trade."

"We agree, but worry it could attract police attention to you. If they find out it was Mexicans who did the hit, the police will start looking at the Mexicans in Canada. Next time it would be better if you told me and we could take care of the problem for you."

Big Al nodded thoughtfully and said, "That maybe good. I will talk to my bosses about that."

"Great."

"So now we party, yes?"

"Uh, one more little thing to make sure there are no loose ends. We understand Earl Porter brought his girlfriend to El Paso. What happened to her?"

"Don't worry about her, *amigo*. El Pero took care of it."

"El Pero took care of it?"

"*Si*, El Pero and my driver," Big Al said with a shrug, with a nod toward the man who had driven them to the brothel. "They take care of his girl the same night he take our money. After that, Berto and Eduardo go to Canada and take care of him. You tell Señor Damien no *problema*."

Jack felt like someone had knocked the wind out of him. He'd known the odds of Lily being alive were remote, but he had still held out hope. For a brief instant he allowed himself the fantasy of grabbing a gun from a bodyguard and killing Big Al, El Pero, and the driver.

"You okay, Jack?"

"Yes," replied Jack, trying to sound upbeat, while in his heart he wondered how and when he should break the news to Lily's mom.

"Good," said Big Al. "Now it is time to be happy. *Señoritas!* I bring my special friend back."

Jack sat on an overstuffed leather chair while Big Al sat on a sofa beside him. Two prostitutes sat on either side of Big Al again, while a third sat on his lap. Within seconds, a young prostitute sat on Jack's lap.

"*Pura vida!* Yes, Jack?" said Big Al as he raised a glass of tequila, before pausing and saying, "Pure life!"

"Yes, pure video!" replied Jack, raising his bottle of Corona in response.

Big Al smiled over Jack's mispronunciation and took another gulp of tequila.

Jack's brain was still numbed over the discovery of Lily's murder and he took a long swallow of beer, but coughed when he felt the prostitute slowly run her hand up his thigh and lightly squeeze his penis.

"*Chile grande!*" she exclaimed, to the laughter of the other prostitutes.

Jack forced a smile and asked her if she would bring him another beer. When she got off his lap, he stared at Big Al. *So you're one of the untouchables ... safe here in Mexico. You have no idea how bad I would like to put a bullet between your wretched evil eyes ...*

"I think she likes you," said Big Al, looking at the young prostitute who went to get Jack a beer. "You like her, yes?" he added, with a nod of his head for Jack to take her upstairs.

"She's very pretty," replied Jack. *I hate you so much... Fuck it, quit fantasizing and do what I can to get the others ...*

Jack smiled and said, "There is one small favour I wanted to ask you."

"Anything, *amigo*."

"There is a bar in El Paso called The Old Warehouse. I have been told by one of my bosses I must go to it. He said it is a lot of fun. He said the place is huge. Apparently they teach country dancing and sometimes have beauty contests there."

"The Old Warehouse?" replied Big Al.

"The Old Warehouse," said the prostitute beside him. "I have been there. I did not win."

"I would offend my boss if I did not go," continued Jack, "but it would be no fun to go by myself. I was thinking about tomorrow night."

"I am sorry, Señor Jack. I cannot go to El Paso."

"No, I understand, but I thought perhaps a few of your men who speak English could come with me. I really like El Pero. He seems like a guy who likes to have fun. Also Berto and Eduardo look like they know how to have a good time. Maybe have your driver take us so we can all drink?"

"For El Pero, Berto, and Eduardo to go to El Paso is not a problem. I will tell them, but the driver, he is only for me. Eduardo does not drink much. He will be okay to drive."

Jack was happy enough to get the three he did and knew not to push it any further. He smiled. "Maybe they could meet me there around eight tomorrow night at the entrance."

"Yes, yes, I will tell them," said Big Al, looking toward the bar.

"I can tell them," said Jack, getting up quickly as the young woman returned. She handed him his beer and wrapped her arm around his waist as he walked over to El Pero.

El Pero was delighted he had been picked for another night of fun.

See how much fun it is tomorrow night when I find an excuse to get you alone and show me where her body is, you fat piece of shit....

El Pero called Berto and Eduardo over and told them they had also been picked by Señor Jack to party with him tomorrow night. Their smiles said they were looking forward to it.

Jack smiled with them and stood talking idly for a few minutes while the prostitute vied for his attention.

Jack's plan was to claim he was tired, feeling ill, and had to leave, but Big Al had other ideas.

"Señor Jack! Come!" ordered Big Al. "I have an idea. Everyone a picture. Everyone!" He pushed one prostitute away from him on the sofa and had Jack sit beside him. Except for a few people who were using the rooms on the second floor, everyone else crowded around to get in the picture.

Jack smiled and posed with Big Al, who gave a toast and said, "To new *amigos* and a golden future."

As Jack was about to clink to the toast, Big Al said, "Wait! Not yet." He yelled something in Spanish too fast for Jack to understand. The message became clear when most of the prostitutes exposed their breasts and leaned in to smile for the picture.

As soon as the photo was taken, Jack received permission to take a few pictures himself, making sure he included some of the bodyguards ... particularly the one who helped El Pero take care of Lily.

When Jack put his camera away, he told Big Al he was tired and needed to go.

"But you have not taken a *puta* yet," said Big Al, somewhat suspiciously.

"They're beautiful, but I have had very little sleep and am feeling a little sick," replied Jack, rubbing his stomach for emphasis.

"I paid much money for this," growled Big Al. It was obvious any façade of politeness had vanished with the number of drinks he had consumed. "You are a big, tough biker ... I think you should like to fuck women? At least one before you go," he added, menacingly.

"Put it this way," said Jack, "the last time I slept with a hooker, the condom broke. After that, my cock turned green and black. I thought it was going to fall off. The guys were calling me the rotten pickle. "

Big Al look surprised, but then laughed and said, "That is very funny. I am sorry for you, but it sounds funny."

"It is something I will not do again," said Jack, looking down at the crotch of his pants and shaking his head as if recalling the incident.

"These girls see a doctor. He says they are all clean," noted Big Al.

"That's what I was told last time."

In reality, Jack knew that, with the exception of AIDS, members of Satans Wrath looked at catching venereal disease like most people would look at catching the common cold. The look, however, on Big Al's face said his suspicions were somewhat alleviated.

"Okay, no problem I understand," said Big Al, getting up. "*Puta* not for you. We will go outside and I'll tell my men."

"Thanks, I appreciate it."

"No problem," said Big Al, with a sideways glance at Jack that left him feeling unsettled.

Big Al yelled to a couple of his men who joined them, along with El Pero, as they stepped outside. Big Al then went over and spoke to one of the bodyguards, who nodded.

Jack felt relieved, thinking Big Al was getting him a ride back to El Paso, but it was short-lived.

"That one is pretty, yes, Jack?" yelled Big Al, pointing at a young Mexican couple in a car creeping forward in a line of traffic.

Jack glanced at the young couple. They were talking and laughing about something. The woman had long black hair and flashed a beautiful smile ... until a look of terror engrossed her face.

Before Jack could respond, the bodyguards surrounded the car with their weapons pointing at the young man. He stopped the car and seconds later, El Pero dragged the screaming woman by her hair from the car. The terrified husband was told to drive or he would never see her alive again. He started to get out of the car when a bodyguard put a gun to his temple.

His wife screamed for him to leave. When he hesitated, she begged that it would be okay ... and said he needed to look after their baby.

"You go home and wait," he was told by a bodyguard. "Maybe then you will see her again."

Tears ran down her husband's face and he got back in the car and slowly drove ahead, stopping momentarily when he got to the end of the block, only to continue on.

"This one is not a *puta*," said Big Al, glowering at Jack.

El Pero gripped the woman by her arm and forced her through the doorway into the brothel, followed by Big Al. Jack felt both sickened and dazed as he stepped back inside.

"You take her now," ordered Big Al. "Then my men will drive you back to El Paso."

chapter thirty-one

Jack knew to embarrass Big Al in front of his men could have a deadly consequence, so he grabbed him by the arm, taking him aside before whispering, "This is bullshit!" The tone of his voice was venomous. "I can't believe you did this!" he hissed.

"You be careful how you talk to me!" warned Big Al, jerking his arm from Jack's grip as his face reddened in anger. "You no want *puta* ... okay. I get you a woman who is not a *puta*. Why don't you want her? I have heard many stories about Satans Wrath. Something does not seem right with you."

Jack shook his head and tried to sound apologetic as he said, "There is something I need to explain to you." He placed a hand on Big Al's shoulder, drawing him closer as if he was telling him a secret. "I was ordered by Damien to keep a low profile and not to draw any attention. It's not just the police we are worried about, but also the people we currently deal with. If they know we are coming to you, they might try to screw us on the final shipments. That's why I came alone so as not to

attract attention and why it is important you only deal
with me. My mission here is supposed to be secret."

"It is a secret. Only my men know who you are.
These *putas*," he said, with a wave of his arm toward
the prostitutes, "that woman," he added, with a nod
toward the terrified woman being clutched by El Pero,
"they only know you are a gringo. They do not know
who you really are."

Jack gestured to the street and said, "Perhaps, but for
you to go out on a busy street when I am with you and
snatch a woman ..." Jack shook his head in admonishment
and continued, "Let her go. Damien would be furious if
he found out. This could jeopardize everything."

Big Al paused for a moment to collect his thoughts.
He did not want to risk blowing a multimillion dollar
business relationship by angering Damien. His own
bosses would not forgive him ... a mistake he knew could
cost him his life. Still, he was not ready to relent yet. He
looked at Jack and said, "It is okay here. No *problema*.
The police will do nothing."

"You can't be sure."

"No, it is safe," replied Big Al. He pointed to two
bodyguards, including the men who had driven them to
the brothel and said, "They are *policia*, but they work for
me. Nobody will say anything. We do this all the time.
If the husband or anyone complains, we will kill them."

"Maybe you're right," replied Jack, "but I can't risk
it. If something was said, Damien would not understand
and blame me for screwing up. Especially on the first night
I meet you. I really like you, *amigo*. I think we have a lot
in common and I want to make sure I get to keep coming
back. I like your men, too. I'm looking forward to partying
with them tomorrow night. I am sure we will do a lot of
business together, but for now I must be extra careful."

"Okay," sighed Big Al. "If you are okay ... then I
am okay."

"I'm okay. This has all been great. A night I won't ever forget, but I am tired and need to get some rest."

Big Al nodded and said, "I will tell one of my men to drive you back to your motel."

"Thank you."

Big Al spoke to El Pero and said, "It is okay. Señor Jack does not want the woman. He is tired and will be leaving."

Jack was shaking Big Al's hand as a gesture of goodwill when he noticed an evil grin cross El Pero's face when he looked at the woman and said, "So, the gringo does not want you. Do not worry, I want you."

The woman cried and pleaded as El Pero shoved her onto the staircase, before grabbing her by the wrist. It made Jack want to retch. He knew he had to try and do something.

Jack looked at Big Al and gestured to the woman and said, "I hadn't realized how pretty she is. All dressed up for something ... she really is a beauty."

"Yes," agreed Big Al, looking at her bare legs thrashing out from under her skirt as she was dragged up the stairs.

"You fight me," yelled El Pero in Spanish, "and you will never see your family again!"

"I'm having second thoughts," said Jack. "You have already gone to so much trouble to get a woman for me ... it would be rude of me not to accept, yes?"

Big Al looked surprised, but then smiled and said, "Yes, it would be rude. Have you changed your mind?"

"Yes, but perhaps we do not ever need to mention it to Damien, okay?"

Big Al chuckled and put his finger to his lips and said, "It will be our secret, *amigo*."

"Thank you. I am sure you and I will have a long friendship," replied Jack.

El Pero was at a bedroom doorway at the back of the brothel when Big Al yelled to him that Señor Jack had changed his mind.

El Pero looked at the woman and spluttered something, while stomping his foot for emphasis. He was clearly upset, but turned to Big Al and nodded in compliance.

Jack hurried up the stairs and took the woman by the arm from El Pero.

"Call to me when you are finished," said El Pero. "I will have her next."

Jack nodded and roughly steered the woman into the room and closed the door.

"Please, *señor*," begged the woman.

"You speak English?" asked Jack.

"Yes … a little," she cried. "Please do not do this to me. Today my husband and I, we be married for two years. Tonight is the first time we go out … please, *señor*. I see this place has many beautiful women who want to please you. You don't need me."

"Listen," said Jack quietly. "Do not speak until I am finished. I am not going to rape you."

"Oh, *señor!* Thank —"

Jack slapped his hand over her mouth and tersely whispered, "Do not speak until I explain to you what will happen." He waited until she nodded before taking his hand from her mouth. "Even though I won't rape you, these other men downstairs will. I am going to try and help you escape. If you are caught, it will be very bad for the both of us. Do you understand?"

Her wide eyes stared back at him as her brain translated what he said. Finally she nodded and whispered, "Yes, I understand."

Jack quickly checked out the room. It was sparse, with a ceiling fan twirling over a double brass bed covered with a white sheet. A small, dark bathroom was near the door. At the back of the room, curtains partially hid a window overlooking the back alley and parking lot.

Jack looked out the window and did not see anyone. He pushed the window up with the heels of his hands and was relieved to discover that it slid open easily. He looked down and tried to gauge the distance to the ground. If a person hung from the window edge and dropped, they might not injure themselves.

A tap on his shoulder caused him to step aside as the woman peered out.

"It is not too high," whispered Jack.

She looked at him and said, "If it was ten rooms up it would not be too high. I would rather jump than have my husband see me every day and be reminded of the shame."

"The shame?"

"Shame he will feel for not protecting me. My shame for sleeping with another man."

"There should be no shame. You chose life over death. There was no other option."

"Gringos think different than Mexicans. There would be terrible shame." She pointed to the bed and suggested, "Maybe we could use a sheet to —"

"No, to use a sheet would take time. It has to look like you escaped quickly. If you climb out over the ledge, I will hold your hands and lean out and lower you as much as I can. We are only up one storey. I don't think you will hurt yourself. Once you are free, I will go out the door and say I am finished with you. Then I will yell as if you jumped out the window. *Comprende?*"

The woman nodded, but stared at him for a moment and asked, "Why are you doing this? Maybe they will kill you...." she added, glancing back at the door.

"Consider it an anniversary present. There is one more thing ... take this," said Jack as he handed her a hundred dollars in American money. "It's so you can call your husband or pay for a taxi to get you away from here."

"That is a lot of money, *señor*. Twenty dollars is enough for a taxi."

"Take the hundred," said Jack, forcing it into her hand.

She accepted the money and was about to stick it in her bosom, when she paused and looked at Jack. "They need to think you took me to bed."

"I know," said Jack, "I'll mess up the bed," he added, as he turned and ruffled up the sheet and tossed a pillow on the floor. When he looked back, he saw the woman had turned her back to him and was slipping off her panties from under her dress. She dropped her panties on the floor and a moment later, she tossed her bra on the bed, mussed up her hair, and ripped a couple of buttons off her blouse.

"Thank you," whispered Jack. "It looks more convincing."

El Pero was at the bar when Berto nudged him and pointed to Jack, who was leaning out over the railing above with his shirt unbuttoned. Jack waved and gave them the thumbs-up sign, before turning around and yelling, "Hey!" before running back into the room.

Seconds later, El Pero and Berto both burst into the room. They saw Jack leaning out the open window and cursing. El Pero stuck his head out the window, but the woman was gone.

"I am sorry, El Pero," said Jack. "I never thought she would jump out the window."

El Pero cursed and kicked her panties across the floor.

Jack breathed a sigh of relief and thought of an old undercover expression often used in response when asked about how an undercover operation went. *A few drinks, a few laughs … nobody got hurt.* He knew the young woman who escaped would never be laughing, but he felt giddy because she had escaped.

Jack only half listened as El Pero and Berto spoke to each other. His thoughts were elsewhere. *It's been a good night ... I've done all I can ... now get the hell out of here ...*

"Come on, El Pero," said Berto in Spanish, "don't be angry in front of this man. He feels bad already. Besides, tomorrow we have a delivery at Casa Blanca to look after."

"So?"

"Don't you still have that red-headed gringo bitch out there to play with? Or have you killed her already?"

Jack tried not to reveal his shock. *Did I really hear what I thought I did?* He knew some Spanish, but wasn't completely fluent. He held his breath, listening intently for El Pero to reply.

A rhythmic, pulsating sound from the ceiling fan overhead filled the room, sounding like you were inside a giant pumping heart as the seconds ticked past. Jack waited, resisting the urge to grab El Pero and shake the answer out of him.

El Pero did not respond as he stared at the floor. Slowly he bent over and picked up the panties and held them to his face and inhaled deeply. When he was done he slowly lowered them and looked at Jack and in English said, "I can smell her fear. It is like a good brandy with dessert. She was good to have, yes?"

"Yes," Jack replied, while fumbling with the buttons on his shirt, trying to look disinterested in whatever was being said.

El Pero turned back to Berto and continued in Spanish and said, "Yes, the red-headed one might still be alive, but I am tired with her. She acts like she is dead when I fuck her. Next time she will be."

"Do you not give her the choice like the other women? The cattle prod or you. She will be happy to please you."

"I have used the prod, but she has quit eating and is becoming too weak to please me. It is time to get a new one. I thought tonight we had."

Jack experienced intense emotions that seesawed back and forth between anger and joy. As he stepped out into the hall, a new plan formulated in his mind.

I'm far from being finished here tonight ...

chapter thirty-two

Jack saw Big Al, who was naked, peering out at him from behind a door from another room.

"What happened, *amigo?*" Big Al yelled to him. "I heard you yell. What is all the fuss?"

"When I was done with the woman, she jumped out the window before El Pero could have a turn," replied Jack.

Berto came out of the room twirling the woman's panties on his finger and then threw them over the railing at one of the men below. His aim was good and it landed on the man's head, bringing a few laughs.

Big Al smiled and said, "Do not worry, Jack. There are many women here for El Pero to choose from. I will get you a ride back to El Paso now."

"Thanks, but now I feel a little thirsty," replied Jack.

"Thirsty for another woman?" asked Big Al.

"No," replied Jack, faking a chuckle. "I think I will have another beer. I have also thought of something I should talk to you about in private before I go. There is no hurry. Maybe meet me at the bar when you are done."

Twenty minutes later, Big Al joined Jack and they moved to a quiet spot in the room.

"You have something to say to me?" asked Big Al, sounding sober again.

"Yes. You have treated me very well tonight. I know you are the guys to do business with and I am looking forward to many more trips down here to see you."

"That is good, Jack," smiled Big Al, slapping Jack on the shoulder.

"However," continued Jack, "I still have to convince Damien. As I see it, providing your prices are good —"

"They will be," assured Big Al. "My bosses will not risk losing Satans Wrath to anyone else. You and I will get to see much of each other."

"Good, but that is not the problem," said Jack.

"*Problema?* What *problema?*"

"All this seems like a fantastic dream. Your talk of taking two years to build a tunnel. Talk of the white house."

"Casa Blanca?"

"Yes. It all seems too good to be true."

"It is true," replied Big Al, sounding indignant.

"Don't get me wrong. I believe you, but I don't know if Damien will. He has heard stories of gringos coming here to buy cocaine and being murdered and robbed of their money."

"We do not plan to go to war with Satans Wrath."

"No, like I said, I believe you ... but I don't know if Damien will. It might take a few months for me to convince him you are telling the truth and that your organization really can handle the quantities we want. I have met you and trust you ... but convincing Damien we should simply believe what you have told me is another matter. It may take time and many more visits ... that is all I'm saying."

Big Al thought a moment before smiling. "What if you saw the tunnel with your own eyes?"

"If I saw the tunnel?" said Jack, while trying to appear thoughtful as he scratched his chin. "Wow ... yeah, that would work. If it is as you say, it would easily prove your organization is who we should deal with. Of course, I would have to see Casa Blanca, as well, otherwise Damien might think you took me to a mine shaft."

"When would you like to see it?" asked Big Al.

"As soon as possible. I guarantee once I see it, we will be going into business with you immediately."

Big Al nodded and said, "For this, I need to speak to my boss." He glanced at his watch and said, "It is two-thirty. I will check with his security. If he sleeping, I will call him in the morning. If not, maybe I can take you to Casa Blanca tonight."

Jack waited while Big Al strode to the far end of the bar and made a call. When he returned, he was all smiles.

"Good news, *amigo*. Not only is my boss awake, but he was on his way home and is not far away. He will be here in about twenty minutes."

"Great, I'd like to meet him," replied Jack, wondering if either Guajardo himself would show up, or one of the Carrillo Fuentes brothers.

Big Al frowned and said, "I am sorry, but I was told to meet him outside. I do not think he is ready to meet you yet. Maybe after we are in business for a year or two he would agree to meet you. I hope this does not offend you or Señor Damien, but —"

"I understand," replied Jack. "We are in a business where we must be careful. To me it shows your boss is not careless. That is good. We would not want to do business with someone who was careless."

"Then you are not angry," replied Big Al. "And Señor Damien will not be offended?"

"Of course not."

Big Al and Jack talked idly for the next twenty minutes before a screeching of tires out front and a wave from a bodyguard told them the boss had arrived.

"Please, wait here," instructed Big Al, as he hurried outside.

Jack casually strode to the front door and looked out through the glass. Parked in the middle of the street were a row of four black SUVs. Bodyguards had stepped out of some of the SUVs and were watching everyone and every vehicle. Big Al had gone around to the far side of an SUV that was the third one down the line.

Moments later, the bodyguards leaped back in their vehicles and all four SUVs roared off.

Big Al smiled as he returned to talk to Jack inside the brothel.

"Yes, I am allowed to take you," said Big Al, "but not when it is dark."

"Not when it is dark?"

"My boss is concerned about ... well, that is his orders."

"Tomorrow then?" asked Jack.

"Yes. At twelve o'clock my men will pick you up at your motel and bring you to Juarez. Then you are to be blindfolded for the trip to and from Casa Blanca."

"I understand, but Damien will be expecting to talk to me as soon as I see it. How long will it take?"

"Oh ... maybe an hour and twenty minutes each way, perhaps twenty minutes to show you Casa Blanca and then return. I think three hours will be enough. I am sorry we need to pick you up so early, but a delivery is being made later in the afternoon and I was told to have you away from Casa Blanca before then." Big Al paused and said, "Again I must apologize. It is not me who does not trust you. It is my boss who is —"

"It's okay," replied Jack. "Somebody else's coke does not interest me. I do need to arrange a time with Damien to be able to tell him I have seen it with my own eyes. As soon as that happens, we'll be in business."

"Good, *amigo*. I will have you back in El Paso by three, so you can make whatever arrangements you wish after that."

After Jack left, Big Al could hardly contain his glee. He believed he had orchestrated what would surely be one of the largest business opportunities the cartel ever had. Jack had guaranteed him that all he needed to convince Damien was to see Casa Blanca. That would take place in a matter of hours.

Big Al smiled to himself at what a shrewd business-man he was. He had impressed Jack ... and now that business was guaranteed, it was time to impress Señor Damien. What better way to impress him than to give him a photo of Jack and himself surrounded by topless young women ... along with the gift of a diamond-and-gold-encrusted Rolex?

Big Al glanced at his own watch. The time differ-ence in Vancouver was an hour earlier. If he hurried, perhaps his men in Vancouver could purchase the watch first thing in the morning and deliver it to Señor Damien by noon ...

chapter thirty-three

It was four o'clock in the morning when Jack was dropped off at the Armadillo Motel by one of Big Al's men. Jack showered, changed his clothes, and then drove into El Paso. After driving down a few darkened alleys to assure himself that he was not being followed, he went to the hotel room Adams had originally booked for him to write his notes.

Verbal evidence given to an undercover operative, particularly if it could be quoted word for word, was vital when it came to court. Jack had a lot of quotes he had been memorizing and was anxious to jot them down before his memory faded. First he knew he needed to call Adams.

It was five o'clock and still dark when he called Adams at home. The phone was answered on the first ring.

"You okay? How did it go?" asked Adams.

"I think Lily's alive!" said Jack excitedly.

"You found her?" gasped Adams.

"Not yet, but I will. El Pero and one of Big Al's bodyguards kidnapped her and took her some place to use as a sex slave. I don't have time to talk now. I'm at the safe house and I've got a ton of notes to write. I want to meet your friend this morning and show him a picture. He said he would check the alley every morning between eight-thirty and nine."

"No problem, I'll take you. A picture of who?"

"A bunch of Big Al's guys, including the one who was with El Pero when they kidnapped Lily. The guy is a cop. I also got an admission from the two men who murdered Earl Porter. Those two, along with El Pero, are meeting me at the The Old Warehouse tonight. Hopefully we'll be able to arrest them. Before then, I hope to find where Lily is."

"Fantastic! Man, this is great!"

"Give me until seven-thirty to write my notes, then pick me up and I'll fill you in on the details. Also grab my laptop from your office and I'll download some pictures to show your friend."

Jack finished his notes shortly after seven and decided to go down to the hotel coffee shop for breakfast. He found Adams already there.

"I've already had two cups of coffee," said Adams. "I was waiting until seven-thirty like you asked."

"I could use about a quart myself," replied Jack. "Also breakfast … is there time?"

"If you make it quick. Traffic coming this way on the bridge in the morning is heavy. Going in should be light. I've got your laptop in the car, so you can download the pictures as I drive."

Jack ordered breakfast and filled Adams in on all the details as he ate. When he finished talking, Adams leaned back in his chair and said, "I gotta tell you something. I was really pissed off when I was first told I had to work with you."

"I noticed."

"Yeah ... sorry about that. But you have done one hell of a great job. I wish you and I could be partners permanently."

"Thanks. I feel the same way."

"I'm not trying to get mushy or anything, but I would really feel bad if something happened to you."

"Not as bad as I'd feel."

"Good point," chuckled Adams, "but what I am trying to say is we could use some more manpower. Maybe it's time for you to phone your boss and get permission to go to Mexico. Then I could go to my office for help."

"Forget that. If Ottawa did give permission, our policy states it would only be after Mexico gave their permission, along with approval from various police agencies."

"Do that and you may as well phone Guajardo himself and tell him who you are."

"Exactly."

"But if I ask my bosses for help, they will contact your people about it and then refuse because you weren't given permission."

"Of course. That's what bureaucracy is all about."

"The thing is, as it stands now, if you do find her, you'll be in shit for going into Mexico."

"I've been in shit before."

Adams brooded silently as he twirled a spoon around inside his already-stirred coffee. When he looked up he said, "Actually, I'm in deep shit myself right now."

"Oh?"

Adams twirled the spoon again, then let out a deep sigh and said, "I'll tell you about it another day. Let's focus on what we're doing."

"I do need to do that. I haven't been to bed since the night before last."

"Runnin' on adrenalin."

"Mixed in with a little alcohol and caffeine. Hell of a combination, but as far as me being in shit goes, I'm willing to take my chances. One way of getting me off the hook would be if I find her ... and we can pinpoint her location, how about you going to your bosses and saying a CI told you where she is? Leave me out of it. Ottawa wouldn't need to know."

"I could do that," Adams agreed.

"And as far as arranging to arrest the guys at The Old Warehouse tonight, tell your bosses I went back to the Armadillo last night to see if Slater had shown up and ended up running into Big Al's men. Say we had a few beer and El Pero told me he kidnapped Lily and Berto and Eduardo told me they did the hit on Porter in Canada. If they ask you where I was drinking with them say you presume it was in my room. If we're lucky, by then we will have found Lily and make it look like your friend told you."

"What will you say if it goes to court?"

"The truth. I will never lie on the stand ... maybe refuse to answer to protect a source, but I will never lie. Court's not a worry. Except for whether or not someone was convicted, my bosses never bother to find out the details. They'll presume I stayed on this side of the border ... unless someone from here tells them otherwise."

"My bosses would never bother hanging around a courtroom either, although I don't know if the D.A. handling the case would blab. It would depend upon who we got."

"That's a chance I'm willing to take."

"You don't mind taking chances, do you?" replied Adams, looking thoughtful.

"The important thing is to rescue Lily."

"Yeah ... and keep you alive," replied Adams sombrely.

At eight-thirty that morning Davidson was having a terse meeting with Weber in his office.

"So the fucking Mountie called him at five o'clock this morning?" repeated Weber. "I thought the son of a bitch said he was taking the night off to sleep."

"He didn't. Everyone thought he had gone to bed, but then the bug picked him up entering the room about five this morning. He called Adams shortly after to tell him the girl is still alive and is being held someplace as a sex slave."

"And he got an admission from the two hitters who went to Canada," noted Weber. "You gotta admit, the guy is good."

"You've said the same thing before about Adams. We all could be if we broke the law or ignored policy."

"That's true."

"Besides, I wouldn't give them too much credit. Once the arrests take place tonight, there is no way any of the bad guys will talk. The Mountie did okay getting these guys to meet him tonight, but when you think about it, what he is really doing is signing the girl's death warrant. For her sake, I hope it is quick," said Davidson.

"Yeah ... I agree with you there."

"Another scenario I envision tonight is seeing them grabbing El Pero prior to the arrests and taking him for a ride out in the desert to make him tell them where the girl is. If Adams is true to form, he might kill him after and claim he escaped or something."

"We could get them both on conspiracy to commit murder."

"If we get there in time to rescue him. Otherwise it could be murder."

"There's always that," replied Weber. "So what was Adams up to all night?"

"He did spend the night at home," replied Davidson. "Then came in first thing this morning, grabbed the car, and split before anyone arrived."

"So where are they?"

"Meeting one of Adams's CIs," replied Davidson. "They just got out of the car."

"Did they talk in the car?"

"Nothing of interest."

"What about what the Mountie did last night? He must have talked about that?"

"He left his room shortly after seven. Adams was out of his car at six-forty so I think they might have bumped into each other in the hotel lobby or coffee shop."

"What if —"

"Not to worry. With whatever happened last night, it didn't give them much time to talk about anything else. Besides, we would have heard something about it when they got back in the car."

"It sounds like things are really coming down to the crunch," said Weber.

"For sure. I spoke with the profilers this morning. They say once El Pero and the two hitters come into El Paso tonight and get arrested, it should do the trick. Adams and Taggart will feel a kinship with each other. Once the arrests are made, Adams knows Taggart will be heading back to Canada. They are confident Adams will spill his guts to him before he goes. Once that floodgate opens, it will make them more inclined to talk about other things they've done, as well."

Jack and Adams stood in an alcove in the alley. It wasn't long before Rubalcava arrived and Jack quickly filled him in on what had happened the previous night.

Rubalcava listened intently and his voice became grave when Jack mentioned the parade of four black SUVs that arrived when Big Al went to talk to his boss. "My friend," he said, putting his hand on Jack's shoulder, "this is very serious. It tells me who you are dealing with."

"Guajardo himself?" asked Jack.

"No, his protection is even bigger. But what you have described fits the men who are directly below him. They are extremely dangerous and would kill their own mother for a peso. You must be very, very careful, *amigo*."

Jack nodded solemnly.

"Now, you have some pictures to show me?" said Rubalcava.

Jack turned on the laptop and brought up the pictures. Jack expected a little good-natured ribbing when the pictures from inside the brothel were displayed, but there was none.

Rubalcava's dark eyes flashed out from beneath his furrowed brow as he looked. "I know three of these men," he said bitterly. "They are sworn to uphold the law, not break it. This piece of shit here," he said, pointing at the screen with his finger, "is a detective who works out of my office. His name is Sanchez."

"That is who drove Big Al last night from the restaurant to the brothel. He is also the one who went with El Pero when they grabbed Lily Rae."

Rubalcava stared at Jack for a moment as his thoughts went back to the day Greg Patton had been kidnapped. "Lily Rae ... do you know if she wore a necklace?"

"Yes. Apparently she wore a pendant that was —"

"A small frog," said Rubalcava.

"Yes. How did —"

"Sanchez gave it to a secretary in my office the same morning Greg Patton was kidnapped." Rubalcava spat on the ground and uttered a string of profanities in Spanish.

"My original plan was to have El Pero, Berto, and Eduardo arrested tonight in El Paso," said Jack, "but only if we could rescue Lily first ... if she's still alive."

"If you are blindfolded, it may be difficult to find out where she is," said Adams.

"Big Al said it was outside of Juarez and they would have me back at the motel three hours later. Between driving through El Paso, clearing customs, and driving through Juarez ... then the return trip, I figure it can't be more than a thirty-minute drive outside of Juarez."

"That covers a big area," said Rubalcava. "The place will be heavily guarded. Other houses in the area will be owned by the cartel. For something as important as this, they won't have guards who are asleep or drinking tequila under a tree. They will be professionals." He glanced at Adams and said, "Perhaps even trained by your government."

"I told Jack about the commandos we trained who were then bought out by the cartels," said Adams ruefully.

Rubalcava looked at Jack and said, "So you realize how dangerous it will be. They will have a lot of security to ensure they are not being followed once you are picked up. With city traffic it would not take them long to spot us. Even if we succeeded, once they left the city ... well, to follow you into a rural area would be a one-way trip. None of us would return."

"Big Al was told not to take me there when it was dark," noted Jack. "They don't entirely trust me and are going to blindfold me ... you'd think they would take me when it was dark. It would be even easier to see if someone was following."

Adams looked at Jack and said, "You're thinking of lights?"

"Exactly. Maybe an airport beacon or something. Perhaps a sign on a hotel roof in the distance. Something they don't want me to see that could help pinpoint the location."

Both Jack and Adams looked at Rubalcava. "I am sorry," he said. "I can't think of anything like that outside the ... no, wait." Rubalcava's brow furrowed as he thought. "I just remembered. West of here is a radio tower that is only a few miles south of the border. The area has many hills, so perhaps the tower would be difficult to pick out against the background in the day, but at night is has a light on it to warn aircraft."

"That gives us a direction," said Jack.

"Possible direction," corrected Adams.

"If we are able to locate Casa Blanca and Lily is still alive, how do we rescue her?" asked Jack, looking at Rubalcava. "Are there people you would trust to go in and do the job?"

"With what we are talking about, there is nobody I can really trust," replied Rubalcava.

"If we arrest El Pero, Berto, and Eduardo tonight, maybe a trade could be negotiated?" suggested Jack.

Rubalcava sighed and said, "If we locate the tunnel, there will be no trade. For making such a mistake, the only reason the cartel would take them back would be to kill them."

"Not such a bad thing," said Jack, noticing a nod of agreement from Adams.

"There would also be no reason for the cartel to let Lily live," noted Rubalcava. "In fact, her death may be long and painful out of revenge."

"I take it they wouldn't have to worry about being arrested if they did that," said Jack bitterly.

"No. If political pressure was put on our government for her murder, then someone else would be framed and arrested for the crime. Perhaps someone who wasn't even a criminal."

"So what do we do?" asked Jack, aware that his feelings of optimism at what he thought he had accomplished had turned to frustration and despair. *Peaks and valleys … always peaks and valleys …*

"If we find the tunnel and you approach the Mexican authorities for help, there is a very real possibility someone involved in her rescue will have been bought off."

"If we locate the tunnel, what about using it to conduct a raid from your side of the border?" asked Jack, looking at Adams.

"I was thinking the same thing myself," replied Adams. "I think under the circumstances that might be the safest route to take."

"That is a better idea," said Rubalcava, "although I am sure the American end of the tunnel will be heavily guarded, as well. To get there in time to save her may be difficult, but it might still be the safer way to do it."

"We have people trained for such matters," replied Adams. "Although recon could take a day or two. It will have to be done properly so as not to alert the men at Casa Blanca before we reach it."

Rubalcava smiled. "Of course you have men trained for these matters. The same ones who taught the commandos hired by the cartel. They might even know each other."

"Don't rub it in." Adams scowled.

"So we won't be doing any arrests at The Old Warehouse tonight," noted Jack.

"Guess it depends on what you find out this afternoon," said Adams. "There are thousands of bad guys — the important thing is to rescue the girl."

"Definitely," agreed Jack. "Besides, with luck I should be able to convince them to join me at The Old Warehouse a second time and make it coincide with when the raid does take place."

Rubalcava glanced at his watch. "I should get to the office." He looked at Adams and said, "Can you have your wife call me before lunch? Perhaps with the time needed, you should tell her that she wants to rendezvous with me for the whole afternoon." Rubalcava grinned when he saw Jack give him a sideways glance and said, "It is not what it seems, I assure you."

"Somehow, you two didn't strike me as the type to be into wife-swapping," replied Jack, giving a lopsided grin.

Rubalcava's face became serious as he turned his attention back to Adams. "I will then join you and perhaps we can set up on the highway west of the city." He looked at Jack and added, almost apologetically, "If we see Big Al's SUV it may give us a general location of where you are going, but I know we will not be able to follow if he turns off the main highway. In that area there is a maze of dirt roads. There would be little traffic and the dust would announce the presence of any vehicle."

"I understand," replied Jack. "Big Al's SUV is silver and El Pero's is white. I suspect I will be riding with Big Al. If you do see us turn off, what with the time I have been given, I don't think I should be gone much more than half an hour. If the roads are dusty, you may even have a general direction of where I am being taken."

"Even if we do know where you're at," noted Adams, "I doubt we could ever get to you in time, even if we did know you were in trouble."

"I'm aware of that," replied Jack.

Adams and Rubalcava looked at each other and grimaced. The idea of standing by and not being able to save an officer in trouble would be a gut-wrenching experience.

chapter thirty-four

Despite the light rain in Vancouver, Jarvis was proud of the colours he had recently earned, making him a full member of Satans Wrath. He wanted everyone to see he was now sporting the full club logo on his back. As he pulled out of the compound of the west-side chapter clubhouse, his bare muscular arms, black with tattoos, gunned the engine of his Harley Davidson as he roared out on to the street.

Minutes later, a car with two men pulled alongside him and the passenger rolled down his window and gestured for him to pull over.

Jarvis pulled to the curb, but kept his bike running as the car double-parked beside him.

"Who the fuck are you two guys? Cops?" asked Jarvis.

"No," said the passenger. "I'm Miguel and this is Ramiro. We need to talk to Señor Damien."

"What are ya? Fuckin' reporters? Talk to our media guy."

"We're not reporters. We have a very valuable gift for Señor Damien. It's business. We need to meet him, but were warned the police could be watching your clubhouse."

"If you're in business with Damien, why don't you call him yourself?" asked Jarvis as he looked around, wondering if the club was trying to test his response.

"We've never met him. We don't have his number. We want you to call him."

Jarvis hesitated about what to do. Although he had earned his full patch, he was not senior enough to ever be allowed to talk to the National President directly. "Tell ya what," he replied. "I'll take you to an alley where it is safe to talk. You wait there and I'll go talk to someone."

Lance Morgan, president of the west-side chapter of Satan's Wrath, went to the clubhouse and listened to what Jarvis had to say. When Jarvis was finished talking, Lance called Damien and spoke briefly.

"Damien doesn't know either of these guys," said Lance when he hung up. "Maybe they're trying to set him up for a hit. Take the boys over and check them out."

Twenty minutes later, Miguel and Ramiro had guns shoved in their faces by six members of Satans Wrath. They were both jerked out of their car and slammed up against a garbage dumpster and roughly searched. Lance was watching from a distance and waited until Jarvis gave him a wave before walking up to them.

"No weapons," said Jarvis. "They do have a new Rolex watch in their car though. It's still in the box."

"Are you Señor Damien?" asked Miguel meekly. "It is for you. A gift from Big Al. There is also a picture in a brown envelope."

Jarvis retrieved the items from the car and handed the watch to Lance.

Lance nodded appreciatively as he examined the jewel-encrusted watch. Jarvis then handed him the picture.

"That is Big Al," said Miguel helpfully, pointing to the picture. "Many beautiful ladies, yes? I think your man is having a good time."

Lance's jaw gaped open as he looked at the picture. "My man?" he spluttered.

"You do not know him?" asked Miguel, looking shocked.

"Fuckin' rights I know him," replied Lance hotly, before turning to Jarvis and saying, "Hold these two until I get back with Damien."

In Juarez, Jack and Adams walked down the alley to return to their car.

"What are you going to do now?" asked Jack, with a final glance at Rubalcava, who was walking away in the opposite direction.

"After I drop you off at the hotel, I'll go to the office and feed the bosses the scenario you told me," replied Adams.

"I'm so groggy from lack of sleep, do you mind running it past me? What did I suggest?" asked Jack.

"Fuck, I always heard you Canadians were polite. What you're really wanting to know is if I have it right … right?"

Jack grinned in response.

"Okay," continued Adams. "I'll tell the bosses you met some of the bad guys last night and give them the news about what you learned, except for the part of you being taken to Casa Blanca. I'll tell them I'm contacting my CIs to ask about a possible location for Casa Blanca and also line up a potential arrest scenario for everyone to be in place at The Old Warehouse."

"Which, by the sounds of it, we'll have to postpone."

"Yeah, but hopefully by then we'll know where Casa Blanca is. How long we postpone it may depend on what you find out. If she's already dead …"

"I know." Jack sighed. "That would change everything. Will your people expect to cover me at the Armadillo? They might expect me to go there to see if Slater is around."

"I'll tell them it's not needed. I'll say if he is there, that you're only swinging by to invite him to The Old Warehouse, as well."

"Sounds like we have our ducks in a row."

"Then I'll split from the office and be waiting for you with my friend on the highway."

"They pick me up at twelve and I should be back to the Armadillo by three. I figure we should be going by you around one."

"Yeah," said Adams glumly. "*If* we are on the right highway and *if* you are in the right vehicle so we can spot you."

"Don't worry if you don't. If it isn't near the radio tower, I'll figure out some way to find the place again, even if I have to crawl up on the roof and mark it with a big *X*."

"It was finding you I was thinking of ... before you're *X*'d. *C-X*'d that is."

Jack normally would have smiled. *C-X* was a term used in target-practising to indicate the kill zone of the heart or lung vicinity. At the moment, Adams's comment didn't seem all that funny. He glanced at Adams and sombrely replied, "Like you said before, there is nothing you can do, regardless."

They drove back across the Bridge of the Americas to Jack's hotel in El Paso in utter silence. Both men were quietly wondering what the next few hours would bring. When Adams pulled up to the front of the hotel, he leaned over and shook Jack's hand.

"Good luck," Adams said.

"Thanks. See you for a beer later," replied Jack as he got out.

Adams remained parked for a moment as he watched Jack walk away.

I wonder if I will ever see him alive again ...

chapter thirty-five

It was eleven o'clock when Jack arrived back at the Armadillo Motel and saw Slater's pickup truck parked in front of a unit. Seconds later, Slater let him into his room.

"When did you get in?" asked Jack, flopping down into a chair.

"About ten minutes ago. I've been on the road since four o'clock this morning."

"You poor guy," said Jack, somewhat sarcastically.

"Yeah, I'm pooped. I was about to call my contact and let him know I'm here. Have you met any of the guys yet?"

"Last night. They took me out on the town. I met the uncle."

"Everything okay?" Slater asked.

"Couldn't be better. You may as well hold off on contacting them. They're picking me up within the hour to show me some of their operation."

"Will I be coming with you?"

"Definitely not," Jack intoned.

"Good, then depending on what they want me to do with the money, I might be able to get some sleep."

Promptly at twelve o'clock, Berto and Eduardo arrived in El Pero's white SUV. After a brief conversation, it was decided Jack would travel with Berto in the SUV and Eduardo would ride with Slater in his pickup truck to show him where to deliver the money.

"The place where we are taking Señor Slater is also where we are meeting Big Al and El Pero, explained Berto. "Señor Slater will stay there while the rest of us continue on. Once you have seen *Casa Blanca*, El Pero, Eduardo and me will take you back to El Paso. We can maybe have a few drinks, go out for dinner and then go to The Old Warehouse tonight."

"Sounds great. Too bad Big Al couldn't join us."

"Yes, that is unfortunate. Now, I am sorry but I must —"

Jack turned away and leaned spread-eagled against the wall. Neither Berto or Eduardo had their shirts tucked in and by the telltale bulges, Jack knew they were both armed. *Too bad they wouldn't accommodate me, too ...*

Fifty minutes later, the four men pulled up to an auto body shop in Juarez. Berto parked out front while Slater was told to park inside the shop. Jack was then directed to Big Al's silver SUV, which was parked farther down the street.

As Jack walked over, Big Al and El Pero got out to greet him. He and Big Al then sat in the back while El Pero got in the front. Sanchez stared at Jack from where he was sitting behind the wheel and Jack smiled at him. The smile was not returned.

Jack had not seen any telltale signs to indicate if Big Al or El Pero were armed, but there was no doubt in his mind Sanchez was.

Eduardo left Slater at the body shop and rejoined Berto, who then pulled up behind them in the white SUV. Jack felt slightly relieved. Not only were the vehicles known to Adams, but two SUVs travelling down a highway would be easy to spot. The windows were too tinted for anyone to see for sure which one he was in, but it didn't matter as long as both SUVs stayed together.

"Now I must do this," smiled Big Al apologetically as he held up a black cloth bag with a drawstring.

"It's okay. I need some sleep, anyway. Nudge me if I snore."

Big Al smiled as he placed the bag over Jack's head and tied it shut.

Jack purposely avoided conversation as they drove. He tried to keep track of turns, stops, and any noises, but with the air conditioner running, along with the radio on and idle conversation, he quickly lost track. He also had the distinct feeling they had driven in circles a couple of times to make sure they weren't being followed.

Adams and Rubalcava were sitting parked in Adams's car at a gas station on the outskirts of Juarez when they saw the silver SUV drive past, followed by the white.

"Bingo." Adams smiled and pulled out to follow them. It was a paved road, but traffic was light, with only about one or two vehicles every minute. Adams stayed far back and tried to keep two cars between him and the SUVs.

After driving for about ten minutes, Rubalcava said, "We are getting close."

"How do you know?" asked Adams, concentrating on the vehicles in front of him.

"We passed an old farmhouse on the right. There were two tan coloured SUVs parked under a shed. A poor farmer could never afford vehicles that nice."

Adams glanced in his rear-view mirror and nodded.

Half a mile further, the two SUVs slowed and turned right on to a dirt road.

"The road we are on basically faces west in the direction we are going," said Rubalcava. "Where they turned, if they keep going north, they are only about four miles from the border."

As they drove past, they saw that both SUVs had stopped to check in with someone parked in a crew-cab truck behind an empty fruit stand. Adams continued driving and watched in the rear-view mirror as the dust billowed up when the two cars continued north. Moments later, they disappeared from sight.

"Now what?" asked Adams, checking his watch. "From the times we were given, Jack should be on his way back out within thirty minutes."

"Look, you can see the top of the tower from here," said Rubalcava, pointing to the left. "It might be the closest vantage point we can find, unless these guys are also using it. The turnoff to it must be just up ahead."

Adams glanced at the tower. "In this heat, a guy wouldn't last long up there. My guess is anybody out here on security will be sticking close to the air conditioners. If someone is there, I'll get out and make it look like I pulled off the highway to take a piss and then leave."

A few minutes later, Adams parked beside the radio tower and was relieved to see no other vehicles present. At the base, scrub brush and a small cement building blocked their view of the main road from the sandy trail they had come in on. The facility itself was surrounded with a chain-link fence, topped with two strands of rusty barbed wire.

Adams parked the car beside the fence and went to the trunk and retrieved an old set of gloves, which he intended more for climbing the tower than getting over the fence. Touching metal exposed to the hot sun would be like putting your hand on a stove element.

Adams then hung a set of binoculars around his neck and used the hood of the car to help him climb over the fence. There was a ladder on the tower, but it faced the road and he was afraid to use it in case he was spotted. Instead, he climbed up the back of the tower where natural rungs in the girders accommodated his hands and feet. The mass of girders also gave him some cover. A couple of minutes later he climbed high enough to get a view.

"See anything?" asked Rubalcava from the where he stood beside the car.

Adams adjusted his binoculars and said, "I got an eyeball on the fruit stand that the truck is parked behind. Also the farmhouse we passed with the two tan coloured SUVs. The dust trail made by the two SUVs we were following disappears over a couple of hills in the distance. I should see them coming when they return to the main road."

"I think we are in the best spot to watch then."

"Jack is going to owe me a cold beer for this," muttered Adams. Although he was fairly well-concealed, he was still cognizant of the truck behind the fruit stand. He knew the power of a sniper's scope and tried to remain motionless as he clung to the tower, sweat trickling into his eyes, down his armpits, and soaking into his shirt.

He remained on his perch for fifteen minutes when he heard the sound of gunfire coming from the direction of where he was looking. His muscles automatically tensed, ready to spring into action and his mouth gaped open as he strained to listen. *Two shots ...*

"You hear something?" asked Rubalcava.

"Gunshots!" replied Adams. The sound of two more shots was heard, then a flicker of movement caught his eye and he adjusted his binoculars. "There's another tan-coloured SUV hidden amongst some bushes on top of a sand dune about a half-mile northwest of the fruit stand," he said quickly. "I hadn't spotted it until now. Two guys are getting out of it … one guy with binoculars … and the other guy just laid a sniper rifle laid over the hood," he yelled excitedly.

"I don't understand! Is it the sniper that is shooting?"

"Not yet! I think the sniper is sighting in on where the gunshots came from," yelled Adams.

A fifth shot was heard in the distance, followed almost immediately by a louder explosive clap from the sniper's rifle. Adams watched in horror as the man with the rifle received a high-five slap of congratulations from the second man.

chapter thirty-six

"We have arrived," said Big Al, as Sanchez came to a stop. Big Al took the bag off Jack's head and he rubbed his eyes.

"Welcome to Casa Blanca," added El Pero.

All four men stepped out of the SUV and Jack glanced around. He was standing under an open shed where the SUV had parked. Berto and Eduardo were parked beside them. Jack saw a modest ranch-style home in front of him partially shaded by a large tree in the front yard.

Lily Rae ... are you in there?

As they walked toward the house, Jack discreetly took in as many visual details as he could. The home was built in a hollow, making it difficult to see far, but there were no other buildings within sight. He tried to memorize the layout of the land while trying to imagine what it would look like if he flew over it in a plane.

Near to the house, a plot of land was being used in a crude attempt to grow corn, but the stalks were few and the ones that had managed to grow were parched and only knee-high.

Big Al saw what he was looking at and laughed. "That used to be a gully," he explained. "We used it to get rid of the dirt from the tunnel. From the air it will look like a garden. Good idea, yes?"

"Yes, replied Jack, wondering what else had been disposed of in the ravine.

They entered the house and were greeted by two men standing in the kitchen. Both had close-cropped hair, M-16A2 automatic rifles slung over their shoulders and each wore drab green military singlet T-shirts, sand-coloured camouflage pants, and army boots. Their skin was a darker brown than the others, leaving Jack to speculate they spent considerable time outside the house, as well.

They each gave a respectful hello in Spanish to Big Al, who nodded curtly in reply. The two men then smiled and gave a friendly nod to Berto and Eduardo. There was no doubt they had all been soldiers, or perhaps the two with the M-16A2s still were, thought Jack, as he recalled Adams comments that sometimes soldiers were used to protect large drug shipments.

Big Al interrupted his thoughts. "You are standing beside the entrance to the tunnel," he said, smiling.

"Can you find it, Jack?" challenged El Pero.

"The entrance is in the kitchen?" replied Jack, looking around. The floor was made from yellow ceramic square pieces of tile. The grouting was a light brown and Jack looked to see if there was an area where the grouting was missing. It all looked in order.

The kitchen table, cluttered with empty beer bottles and a deck of cards was light-weight and easy to see underneath. The countertops were also cluttered with empty beer bottles, a few dishes, and men's magazines. Nothing seemed particularly out of place.

Jack glanced at the fridge and stove, then looked at Big Al and raised his eyebrows.

"It is not under the fridge or the stove," replied Big Al smugly.

"Is it okay if I search the rest of the house?" asked Jack, desperately wondering if Lily Rae was nearby.

"No, the entrance is in this room," said Big Al.

"Then I give up."

Big Al smiled and went over to a counter. On the wall behind it was an eye-hook from which a key-rack hung. He turned the hook sideways and Jack heard a small click. As this happened, Big Al grabbed the end of the counter and swung it away from the wall. One section of the counter was on hinges, attached to another section of the counter. Big Al then let go of the spring-loaded switch and the hook returned to its upright position.

Jack stepped forward and looked at the shaft that led into the ground from where the counter had hidden it. A ladder on the side of the shaft descended out of sight.

Big Al leaned in the hole and flicked a light switch. "Go ahead, climb down. Berto will show you."

Jack climbed down the ladder after Berto. The ladder descended about one storey underground. When he reached the bottom, he came to a tunnel about twice the width of his shoulders. Periodic overhead lighting stretched for as far as he could see, given the darkened conditions.

"Wow! This is really something," said Jack.

"And much cooler down here away from the sun," replied Berto.

"Speaking of cooler," said Jack, fishing to see if he would learn any further security details, "the two men upstairs with the automatic rifles are fairly dark. They must spend a lot of time outside in the sun, as well."

"No, no," replied Berto. "They are darker because they are not Mexican. They are mercenaries who have come here from South America. There are other teams who supply perimeter security. The house is never left empty."

"I see. You and Eduardo seemed like friends when you greeted them, so I thought perhaps you were in the military together."

"We have had similar training, which is what makes us friends," replied Berto.

"It looks amazing," said Jack, gesturing with his hand down the tunnel. "I have seen enough to know you are capable of moving a lot of dope."

"You can walk along it if you like."

"That's okay," replied Jack. "I should be getting back."

"We have a special cart we use for moving big loads," said Berto, as they were climbing back up the ladder. "But I think we need two carts. With one, it always seems to be at the wrong side."

"Then you would have two at the wrong side," replied Jack.

"You're probably right," chuckled Berto.

"So what do you think?" Big Al smiled when Jack reappeared into the kitchen.

"It's fantastic. What about the other end? Is it well-protected?"

"Yes, much like here," replied Big Al.

"Absolutely incredible. Your organization is exactly who we want to do business with."

"That is great, *amigo*. I will have my men drive you back to your motel now. Señor Damien will be pleased, yes?"

"Yes, but first, is there a bathroom I can use?"

"Around the corner and down at the end of the hall," gestured Big Al with his thumb.

Jack headed down the hallway. The first room held a laundry tub, under which was a thick lead pipe fastened close to the wall and used as a drain. A pail and bottles of cleaning fluid were in the corner, along with a dirty mop that had bloodstains on it.

Jack grimaced and continued on. The next room was a bedroom and the door was open. He glanced in and saw two mattresses on the floor and a cheap dresser.

The next room down the hall was padlocked shut.

Bingo ... Jack nervously looked back to make sure nobody was watching and then held his breath and put his ear to the door and listened. He did not hear anything. *Come on Lily ... please be alive ... We'll get you out of here ...*

The sound of movement in the kitchen caught his attention so he quickly continued down to the washroom. He waited a moment, flushed the toilet and returned to the kitchen.

"I see you've got a bedroom door padlocked shut," said Jack. "What's in there?"

"Oh ... that's the men's entertainment room," said Big Al.

"Entertainment?" asked Jack.

"They get bored, so they keep women in there."

"With the padlock, I take it they are not *putas*," said Jack, smiling.

"No, we would not risk such a person knowing about Casa Blanca," replied Big Al. "The women in there don't come back. Whores make money. To kill them would not be good for business and would make some of our colleagues angry."

"A bedroom does not seem very secure," noted Jack. "Have you ever had anyone escape?"

"No. A woman cannot get out of there," said El Pero. "At least not alive."

"Would you mind if I see for myself?" asked Jack.

Big Al shrugged and said, "Why not."

"I'll show you," offered El Pero, removing a key from the rack over the counter.

Jack, Big Al, and Eduardo followed El Pero down the hall. Jack watched in anticipation as El Pero fumbled with the padlock and opened the door.

Jack took a deep breath and stepped inside the room. He looked at the naked young woman who was curled up with her back to them on a bare mattress on the floor. Her long red hair told him he had found Lily Rae.

The mattress was so stained and dirty that the original colour was unknown. Jack didn't know if he wanted to cry out in anguish at her suffering or feel elation because he had found her. He tried to look disinterested in Lily as he looked around the room.

The room was empty of any other furniture and stunk of urine and feces. A plate of beans and rice was beside the mattress, but the beans had gone mouldy. Beside the plate was a plastic bottle full of water.

The only window in the room was covered with a thick sheet of plywood fastened to the wall with a multitude of screws.

Big Al spoke in Spanish to El Pero as Jack walked over to the closet. It was evident Big Al had not realized Lily was there and was still alive.

Jack slid one of two bi-fold closet doors open to reveal a plastic pail that explained the odour. The pail was the toilet. He pushed the door shut and tried not to let his rage show.

Lily had not moved and remained with her back to everyone. He stared at her to see if he could tell if she was breathing. Bruises covered her back and legs, but they were turning yellow and were obviously not fresh. Whatever fight she once had in her was gone.

"I am sorry, Jack," said Big Al. "This is the girlfriend of the hombre who robbed us. I did not know she was still alive. I will have my men deal with her at once so you can assure Señor Damien that there are no … what you say … loose ends."

"There's no need to kill her," replied Jack. "I can see there is no escape."

At the sound of Jack's voice, Lily turned her head to face the men. Her eyes fixed on Jack and he could see the new hope flash across her face at the sight of seeing a gringo. She half-rose from the bed and extended her hand toward him. "Please," her mouth tried to say, but her throat was dry and only her lips mouthed the word. She swallowed several times and finally croaked out an audible plea. "Help me. You are English. Please …"

Jack's face hardened at the role he knew he must play. He grabbed her face with his hand and shoved her backwards onto the mattress. "Fuck off, bitch!"

Jack then turned to Big Al and said, "I have to admit, she is very pretty. It would be a shame to rob your men of their entertainment … and I know Damien would feel bad about doing so simply to appease him. The important thing is I know she will never leave here alive."

Jack glanced down at Lily. She lay on her back with her eyes staring blankly at the ceiling like she was in a trance. Her final bit of hope was gone. Her body relaxed and a calm settled over her emotions as her brain accepted she was going to die and there was nothing she could do to save herself. *Perhaps*, thought Jack, *at this point she even welcomes death*.

"She most certainly won't leave here alive. Still, I am sure you would feel better if you knew she was dead," he added, with a nod toward Berto, who reached for his pistol.

"Please, not now," said Jack. "There really is no rush and Damien would be upset if he knew I was implicated in a murder. As a favour, I would appreciate it if you made sure I was away from here for at least a day or two. That way it could never be said I was somehow involved or responsible."

"You never would be held accountable," Big Al assured him.

"I know, but as I said, Damien has not met you and may not understand. He would be angry with me. He expects this first meeting to go without incident."

"As you wish," replied Big Al. He spoke in Spanish to Berto and told him to take care of her later. Berto replied that one of the men had told him she had not eaten or drank any water for several days. He expected her to die soon regardless.

Big Al shrugged in response.

Berto's comment caused Jack to worry. *Going without food isn't a problem. Going without water in this heat will kill you in a matter of days. What if the operational plan to save her gets delayed for a day or two? Reconnaissance could take that long ... will she still be alive then?*

Jack knew to say something to give her the will to live could have disastrous consequence. It could be like trying to save a drowning person who panics and takes you with them.

As the men were walking out of the room, Jack decided to follow what his heart told him to do.

"Just a sec," he said, giving an evil grin. "I've never tasted a redhead and there's something I've always wondered." With that comment, he returned to Lily and in full view of the men, slowly licked his lips, bent over, and made a show of nibbling on her ear and pretending to stick his tongue in as he shifted his body to block their view.

"Do not speak," he whispered in her ear. "Things are not what they seem. I promised your friend that I would bring her little froggy home. Hang in there. Help is on the way."

Lily did not move as Jack stood up. She stared at him silently as her brain, fuzzy from dehydration, tried to digest if what she heard was real or if she had dreamed it.

Jack smiled as he walked toward the men watching him from the doorway and said, "It is true. Redheads do taste spicier."

The men laughed and El Pero slapped Jack on the back and said, "If you think redheads are spicy, *amigo*, you should taste a *señorita*," a giggle shook his chubby belly and he wiped a tear from his eyes with the back of his hand before continuing, "with a *habanera chile* inside her. But be careful your own *chile grande* does not touch it!"

Jack forced a laugh to join the others and then smiled at El Pero and patted him on the shoulder. He hoped his smile hid his true thoughts.

I am going to kill you ... I don't know how ... but I will ...

Jack did not risk glancing back at Lily as El Pero closed the door. He was too afraid she might say something.

Lily stared at the door and heard the padlock click shut. *A promise to bring little froggy home? Only Marcie calls me froggy ...*

Then it hit her and her body trembled as fear and hope washed over her at the same time.

That was the Uncle Jack that Marcie told me about!

She crawled over to the door and sat, wrapping her arms around her knees and trying to stifle her sobs as she listened, hoping to hear more of Jack's voice. When it sounded like he had left, she crawled back to the bottle of water and drank.

chapter thirty-seven

When Jack and the men returned to the kitchen, El Pero was about to hang the key back on the rack, but before he could, something outside the window caught his eye. He swore in Spanish and ran outside.

"He saw the iguana again," explained Big Al, shaking his head while pointing out the window to a big lizard clinging to the trunk of the tree. "It has become a matter of pride for him. Any of the other men here could easily kill it in a single shot ... even if they were drunk. Unfortunately, El Pero has not had their training. He thinks the iguana knows this and is laughing at him."

Jack watched as El Pero ran to his SUV and retrieved an H&R .32-calibre, six-shot, long-barrelled revolver from the glove box.

"He has replaced his pistol with a new gun," observed Big Al. "Before his gun had a shorter barrel. Maybe now his aim will be better."

El Pero rested the barrel on one arm and aimed, before firing two shots at the iguana. Neither shot came close enough for the iguana to even flinch.

"No, he is still a terrible shot," muttered Big Al.

"Is there a danger someone might hear the shots?" asked Jack, concerned Adams or Rubalcava would hear the shots and come barraging in to try and rescue him.

"No," replied Big Al. "The men often target-practise out here. The only people who could hear are security men."

"I haven't even seen any security," said Jack, "other than these two," he said, with a nod toward the two mercenaries.

"Oh, there at many others out there," Big Al assured him. "And much better shots than El Pero," he added, "who will be lucky if he does not shoot himself in his foot."

As if to emphasize the point, El Pero fired two more shots and the iguana safely crawled higher into the tree, more perhaps, to escape El Pero's string of profanity than from the bullets.

"This has gone on long enough," said Big Al, sounding frustrated. "I will demonstrate to you that we do have security. Step outside and you will see something."

With that comment, Big Al made a brief telephone call while Jack went outside and watched as El Pero fired another errant shot up into the tree.

The iguana was barely visible, as it had sought refuge amongst some leafy branches. A second later, the sound of a single rifle retort from off in the distance was followed by the iguana tumbling to the ground with the top of its head missing.

Jack looked from where the shot came and could barely make out two figures near an SUV on a far hill. He turned back toward the house and saw Big Al standing on the porch smiling at him.

"Your example of security has been well illustrated," said Jack, respectfully. "You have a hell of a good sharpshooter out there."

"There are many such men out there," replied Big Al, with a wave of his hands toward the surrounding hills. "Now, unfortunately we must go," he added. "There is a delivery being made soon and some more men will be arriving to look after it. I was told you must not be here then."

"I understand. Besides, I do not want to be late to call Damien."

"Okay, we — excuse me." Big Al stopped to answer his cellphone. When he did, he smiled at Jack and held up two fingers. "Wait here, I will be right back," he said, before stepping back inside the house to continue his call.

There was something about Big Al's smile Jack didn't feel comfortable about. *Were Adams and Rubalcava in the area? Did they hear the gunfire and think I need help?*

Jack walked over and pretended to look at the dead iguana. In reality he was considering grabbing the revolver from El Pero if Adams responded to the gunfire. As he kicked the iguana carcass with his foot, he glanced around. The lone SUV parked on the far hill remained where it was. There did not appear to be any reason for alarm. *Good, considering El Pero only has one bullet left in his revolver …*

Jack glanced at El Pero, who cursed some more and shook his fist in the direction of the sharpshooter. When El Pero turned to face him, Jack shook his head in apparent sympathy while looking at the hills around them. *Good, no sign of any rescue attempt …*

Jack turned back toward the house as the sound of footsteps clumped across the porch. It was Big Al, Sanchez, Berto, Eduardo, and the two mercenaries … who were both aiming their M-16A2 automatic rifles at him.

Jack stared silently at Big Al who walked up to face him. "I have some news that concerns you," said Big Al, practically spitting the words out.

"Concerns me?" said Jack innocently. He knew he couldn't successfully disarm these men and it was up to his wits and his tongue to get him out of the situation.

"Yes," replied Big Al. "My men in Canada have spoken with Señor Damien."

Oh, fuck ... I'm dead ...

"Señor Damien says you are a very dangerous man, Corporal Jack Taggart," continued Big Al. "He says we should kill you immediately."

Jack was only partially aware that one of the mercenaries had moved in behind him. He did see Big Al look past him toward the mercenary and give a slight nod of permission.

Jack started to turn around as the mercenary raised his weapon, but he was much too late.

Big Al stepped back as a spray of blood splattered his shirt as Jack's bloody body collapsed to the ground.

chapter thirty-eight

Adams half-slid and half-climbed down the tower, cursing openly at Jack and the risks he took.

"What happened?" Rubalcava yelled up to him. "What did you see?"

"They got 'im," replied Adams tears of rage filling his eyes while he continued to climb down. "A fucking sniper took him out!"

"Are you sure? Did you see —"

"That fucking asshole," cried Adams. "I told him he was taking a big risk. Did the fucking hillbilly cop listen to me? Fuck no! Now I gotta go in there and probably get fucking killed, too."

"Did you see Jack fall? Are you sure he's dead?"

"I didn't see Jack, but I saw the fucking snipers congratulating each other," replied Adams, gesturing toward where the tan SUV was parked. He expected the SUV would be driving to the kill scene, but it was still parked. He stared at it, then used his binoculars again.

"What is it?" asked Rubalcava.

"They haven't moved," replied Adams. "The snipers in the SUV are still parked in the same spot."

"If they had killed Jack, wouldn't they be driving over to look?"

"You would think so ... unless they are waiting to see who else shows up."

"Or fired their weapons as a test to see if someone would respond."

"Maybe."

"Or perhaps were only target-practising at a tin can or something."

"Christ," muttered Adams. "I better climb back up and wait."

Inside the laundry room at Casa Blanca, Big Al looked down at Jack's naked body where he lay sprawled on his back with his head caked in blood and sand. Big Al then spit on him, before nudging him in the stomach with his foot.

"Wake up, you piece of shit!" yelled Big Al.

Jack emitted a low moan and pink bubbles of froth foamed from his mouth.

Jack heard Big Al's words as though they were spoken down a long tube. He opened his eyes and saw blurred images of men standing over him. *What happened? I was looking at the iguana ... what happened?*

Typical of concussions, Jack was suffering from retrograde amnesia and had momentarily lost his memory from the time he had walked over to look at the dead iguana.

"Good, you are still alive," said Big Al, leering down at him. "Although you will discover that being alive will be most unfortunate for you," he added, kicking Jack hard in the stomach.

Jack tried to roll away, but discovered his hands were handcuffed together with one cuff having been slipped behind the lead pipe below the sink in the laundry room. His vision was clouded and what he did see appeared in multiple images. Pain wracked his skull and nausea took over. *What the hell happened?*

The rifle butt he had received to his head had done more than split open his scalp. He had also bitten his tongue. He tried to spit the blood out of his mouth, but only succeeded in having it run down his chin.

"Why are you doing this?" he asked, slurring his words like he was drunk. "Why do you have me like this?"

"Why are we doing this?" roared Big Al. "Why the fuck do you think we dragged you in here?"

I don't know, but I'm pretty sure it's not to enjoy myself ...

An image came closer to him and he tried to focus. It was El Pero holding an electric cattle prod. The reason Jack was naked was about to be made painfully clear. He automatically tried to move back, but any movement he had was limited to the short distance his hands could move along the straight piece of pipe between the base of the sink and a wide strip of metal holding the pipe in place halfway up from the floor.

Upon contact with the cattle prod, Jack lurched up and backwards on the heels of his feet, hitting his head on the bottom of the sink. His scrotum felt like it had been whacked with a club barbed with needles. He gagged a couple of times before vomiting and slipping back into unconsciousness.

Moments later, he was awakened to the taste of bleach being poured on his face. The closet sized room was like an oven in the heat and one of Big Al's men used the bleach to dilute the gagging smell of the vomit.

Big Al leaned forward and said, "I think Señor Damien must be a pussy cat. You do not look very dangerous to me." He gave a hearty laugh and looked at his men who respectfully laughed in response.

Damien ... Jack's memory of the event leading up to being clubbed with a rifle butt came back to him. *Never did like that guy ...*

"Now ... I have some good news for you," continued Big Al. "Unfortunately, I also have some bad news. The good news is I am going to go bring a doctor back to look after you." He paused and stared at Jack for a response.

Jack blinked his eyes, trying to bring the room into focus as he looked up at the ceiling. His thoughts were becoming less muddled, despite fighting waves of nausea.

"The bad news," continued Big Al, "is that the doctor will only be used to keep you alive and awake while you are tortured."

"Small minds do petty and inhumane things," sputtered Jack as a fresh supply of blood trickled down his face from hitting his head on the sink.

"The torture is not without purpose," replied Big Al. "Besides finding out what you know, it will also be a warning to others who try to interfere with our livelihood."

"It will only make other police officers more angry and vengeful," replied Jack. "They will come for you."

"Yes ... we have learned that men are often willing to take risks and even sacrifice themselves for a cause. Perhaps you are like one of these men. A man who will endure a lot of pain ... before telling us what we wish to know. But you will tell us ... that I can assure you. Everyone does."

"I will save you the trouble. It is hardly a secret why I am here. I'm a cop from Canada looking for a missing Canadian girl. I fooled Slater into thinking I was a gangster. I received permission to go to El Paso to conduct inquiries because that was where she was last known to be. I did not have permission to enter Mexico, but thought I could sneak across the border for a couple of hours in the hope of figuring out where this place is. Then I was going to go back to the Americans and ask for their help to rescue the girl."

"I figured you came here without permission," replied Big Al. "Otherwise I would have been notified."

"That is why I came alone," replied Jack.

"Where is your partner?"

"My partner is on holidays, so I have been working alone. That is why Slater has never met anyone else but me."

"Perhaps you did come alone ... or perhaps you didn't. We took precautions to make sure we were not being followed, but even if someone did slip through our net, you should know that my men have arranged a welcoming committee. If anyone comes close to Casa Blanca, they will either be killed or join you in this room. So do not hold out any hope of rescue."

"I have no hope of rescue because nobody knows I am here. So now that I have told you everything," said Jack bitterly, "kill me and get it over with."

"Everything? I think not. We have many questions to ask you. Perhaps Señor Damien will also have questions he would like asked. Now that you have introduced us, the possibility does exist that we will go into business with him. I should thank you for that!"

Jack felt too sickened to reply.

"As a matter of fact, I am sure Señor Damien will find this interesting," said Big Al, taking out his cell-phone to take a picture. "Say cheese."

Jack momentarily wondered if he shouldn't say something glib, or perhaps flip his middle finger up for the picture ... but instead he hung his head. *I'm not some tough guy in a movie ... I'm just me ... and I'm so scared I feel numb.*

"We need more information than the reason you came here, if we are to convince others from becoming martyrs."

"Something more?" asked Jack.

"Some men are willing to die for what they believe in ... but are they also willing to sacrifice their families?

Mother and father, brothers and sisters ... perhaps a wife and children?"

Jack tried unsuccessfully to hide the sheer terror he felt.

"Ah, I see that last comment got a reaction."

"I will not tell you a thing," replied Jack, adamantly, as he resolved to replace his fear with determination.

"Yes, yes. I know what you think. Many have made the same promise. I have not had one man yet who kept it. I will tell you how it will work. First we will start off slow. Perhaps it will take seconds, perhaps minutes ... perhaps hours ... but the pain will cause you to talk about people you think we already know about, or could easily find out about. Organizational structures. People you work with. You will eventually start to talk."

"What makes you think I will tell the truth?"

Big Al smiled as though talking down to a child. "My men in Canada will easily verify what you tell us. Lies will be punished by more people being killed. Once you do start to talk, it will become easier for you. Next you will give us the names of the family members of the people you work with. Soon, other names and addresses will cross your lips. Your wife's name ... your children. You know," added Big Al, looking reflective, "I think that is when you truly become dead inside."

"I am not married and do not have children," replied Jack. "You will be wasting your time. Names of my colleagues can be found out easily by calling the office."

"When you are dead, we will dump your body in the trunk of a car and park it on the Bridge of the Americas. We will let the Americans deliver you to Canada. I am certain there will be much publicity. If you do have a wife and family, I am sure there will be a big funeral they will attend. My men will be there, as well." Big Al's tone turned to admonishment when he added, "Did you not hear me when I said more people will die if you lie to me?"

Jack looked around the room. Depression seeped through his brain like it was acid and for the first time, genuine thoughts of how he could commit suicide crossed his mind. His brain began to swim in a fog of nausea and he willed himself to wake up from what he hoped was a nightmare.

"Nothing to say, Corporal Taggart?" asked Big Al. "Don't worry, I am sure you will have lots to say when I return with a doctor. Then, as you say, it will be time to let the games begin.

Jack's only response was to retch again before slipping into the abyss of unconsciousness.

chapter thirty-nine

Before leaving Casa Blanca, Big Al gave explicit orders to the other men in the house. The cocaine delivery was expected soon and he told Berto to call the men who usually unloaded the drugs and tell them there was a delay and not to come.

He made it clear he did not want anyone else to know that they had captured a Canadian policeman until they were completely finished with him. He was not risking any chance of a rescue and told them to unload the truck and stash the cocaine in the tunnel themselves.

El Pero quickly suggested that Jack should be guarded continuously and volunteered for the job. Big Al agreed.

Sanchez rolled his eyes at the other men. He knew El Pero was using Jack as an excuse to get out of the physical labour involving the drug delivery. *Being Big Al's favourite nephew has its privileges ...*

From his perch on the tower, Adams saw a coordinated flurry of activity. "Something is going on," he yelled down to Rubalcava. "The two tan-coloured SUVs from the farmhouse joined the crew-cab pickup at the fruit stand. In total I count six … no, eight, guys getting out and having a confab with each other. The SUV with the snipers has also moved closer and is perched on another hill facing the fruit stand."

"What do you make of it?" asked Rubalcava.

"I don't know … hang on, some of the guys at the fruit stand are getting back in their vehicles again."

"Maybe a shift change or something?"

"Yeah, maybe that's — fuck that! They're setting up a textbook military ambush for a crossfire situation!"

"I'm a policeman, not a soldier. What are they doing?"

"Son of a bitch, Jack!" cried Adams aloud. "Why the hell did I ever let you go in there?"

"Tell me what you see!"

"I'll tell you what I see," said Adams glumly. "I see professionals preparing to take someone out. They've driven the crew-cab truck a short distance down from the fruit stand and parked it sideways over a hill to block the road. They've also hidden guys with weapons on each side of the road leading up to the truck. If anyone comes along, the guys in the ditch open up on both sides, as well as from behind. If the person manages to survive and steps on the gas, they'll be finished off when they reach the truck, where they'll also be shot at from the front."

"Is the ambush designed for someone heading south to the main road?"

"No … I wish it was. It would give me hope Jack is still alive. The ambush is for someone who would be heading north off the main road."

"You think Jack —"

"Yeah, I think he was burned. Now they're setting up an ambush in case someone tries to find him."

"Those shots we heard …"

"I know," replied Adams. "I don't think they were shooting at tin cans. At this point I'm thinking he's dead. Christ, we don't even know what's over those hills. Could be several houses."

"I know these back roads a little. Maybe there is another spot we could use to try and confirm where Casa Blanca really is."

Adams agreed and descended the tower. They both drove in silence until they returned to the main highway.

"Which way," asked Adams harshly, angry with himself that he hadn't somehow stopped Jack.

"Go west away from the fruit stand. I think farther down there is another road that goes north toward the border."

"I'm sure they'll have it guarded, as well."

"Perhaps, but maybe we will find another hill in the vicinity to give us a different view."

Adams was pulling out onto the highway when he slammed on the brakes. Off in the distance, a telltale cloud of dust told of a vehicle racing toward the area of the fruit stand.

"That looks like it is coming from the same road they took Jack down," said Adams. "I'm going to drive past and take a look."

Adams drove slowly and was rewarded when they passed the fruit stand and saw Big Al's SUV approaching the highway.

"Maybe he is still alive," said Adams, excitedly. "Big Al might be returning him. What do you think?"

"I don't know," replied Rubalcava. "Perhaps everything is okay. Maybe the ambush is only a precaution because they brought Jack to Casa Blanca."

"You would have thought they would have had it set up to begin with," noted Adams.

"Perhaps it was an afterthought."

"Jack mentioned a delivery was to be made this afternoon. Maybe they do it to make sure nobody is following whoever does the delivery. It might have nothing to do with Jack."

"Possible. That makes more sense. Let's hope you're right."

"I'll drive slow. If Jack is in Big Al's SUV, they should be passing us on the way back to Juarez any minute."

A short time later, both Adams and Rubalcava breathed a partial sigh of relief as Big Al's silver SUV went racing past them.

Damien and Lance Morgan sat beside each other at a picnic bench in Vancouver's Kitsilano Beach Park overlooking English Bay. Across from them sat Miguel and Ramiro, who had requested they meet again in the afternoon after their first initial encounter that morning.

Both Miguel and Ramiro were each sipping on a bottle of cola, after assuring Damien they would be receiving an important message any minute in regard to Jack Taggart.

That there were numerous members of Satans Wrath in the area providing security did little to impress Miguel and Ramiro. Where they came from, such security was common to protect the top drug lords. What they did find amusing were the counter-surveillance teams put in place to ensure they were not being followed by the police. In Mexico, they used the police as their own bodyguards.

Damien, along with other members of Satans Wrath, were frequently watched and photographed by the police. For Damien it did not particularly bother him much, but with the advice he had given to murder Jack Taggart, he did not want to risk that his potentially new business partners might say something that could be

picked up by the police through parabolic microphones
or any other listening devices.

Damien was also curious as to whether the police
knew about Miguel and Ramiro. The fact they were
not being followed did not necessarily indicate the
police didn't know them. He had correctly theorized
the police might not be conducting surveillance for fear
of jeopardizing Taggart's undercover role. If the police
surveillance was discovered by Miguel and Ramiro, the
timing of the sudden police interest with the arrival of
Taggart into their midst would be too coincidental.

Miguel excused himself to look at a message he
received on his BlackBerry. When he did, he smiled and
held the device out for Damien and Lance to see a picture.

"I have been told to ask you if you think this man is
still dangerous," said Miguel.

Damien and Lance looked at Jack's naked body lying
on a floor and scrutinized his face.

"Is it him?" asked Lance. "With all that blood and
shit, it's —"

"It's Taggart," said Damien. "I saw him in court last
month. There's no doubt."

"Looks like they did a real number on him first,"
added Lance.

"Yeah, he doesn't exactly look his best, that's for
sure." Damien looked at Miguel and smiled. "You can
let Big Al know that I no longer think he is dangerous."

"Good," replied Miguel, looking pleased. "I am
also to find out if you would like any questions asked
of him?"

"What do you mean," asked Damien, glancing at
the picture again. "Isn't he dead?"

"No, not yet. We will torture him for a few days to
find out everything he knows before we allow him to die."

"How can you be sure he will tell you the truth?"
asked Lance.

"We can be very persuasive." Miguel gave a smug smile. "Besides, he is not that strong. I was told when my boss touched him with a cattle prod only once, he passed out."

"Big Al nailed him with a cattle prod?" replied Damien, now understanding why Jack was naked in the picture.

"Actually it was my boss," replied Miguel. "He is called El Pero and works for Big Al, who is the one who asks the questions."

"It looks like they beat his head in," noted Lance.

"Yes, but he will survive to tell us what we wish to know. I am told he will receive a doctor's care to keep him alive for as long as we want. Very few men die without telling us what we wish to know."

"I know this guy," said Damien. "He won't break easily. If he does talk, I am sure it will be a combination of lies to distort the truth. Something to disrupt our organizations and send us on wild goose chases. I think you should kill him immediately. Same for the girl you told me about. What if they are rescued? I am sure someone knows he was picked up by Big Al or El Pero or whoever."

"We are certain nobody knows where he is. Even if they did, Taggart and the girl would be killed immediately if there was any sign of a rescue attempt. He is handcuffed to a pipe and being guarded in a house in the middle of a desert with many armed men, including trained commandos. Outside of the house are more professional soldiers hired for security. There is no chance he could be rescued. Also, Big Al and El Pero are well-protected in Mexico. They would never be arrested for killing anyone," said Miguel.

"That's good to hear, but as far as questioning him about my club, like I said, I am sure he will simply tell a pack of lies."

"You may be right, but it is not only questions about what he knows about us we will be asking. We wish to make an example of him to prevent other police officers from interfering,"

"By killing him I can guarantee there will be a lot of police attention," said Damien. "Although, under the circumstances, I can see you have no choice."

"The police will not be so eager when we kill a few people who are close to them," said Miguel.

"People close to them?" asked Damien.

"Yes. We do it in my country all the time. Killing policemen is nothing significant, but killing their families is. Those are the type of questions we will be asking him."

"Questions about his family?" said Lance.

"Yes. We will also be asking him the names of wives and children belonging to the people he works with. Big Al has already asked him if he has a wife or children. He has told Big Al he does not, but we will find out. Perhaps you know if —"

"Messing with a cop's family is a bad idea," said Damien. "Asking questions in that regard is like digging your own grave."

"What do you mean?" asked Miguel.

"Have you ever been to a bullfight?" asked Damien.

"Yes, many times," replied Miguel. "In Mexico it —"

"Then you should know if you play with the bull, you get the horns. All it takes is one rogue cop to seek revenge ... and I am not talking about legal revenge."

"Our people are well-protected in Mexico," interjected Ramiro. "We have done this many times. It is not a problem."

"You do not think it will be a problem?" replied Damien, looking at Lance and raising his eyebrows.

"Not at all," said Miguel. "So with that in mind, do you know if this man is married or if he has children?"

"I only know that he works for the RCMP Intelligence Section in Vancouver," replied Damien.

"I see. Well, perhaps we should meet again tomorrow. Then I will tell you what we have learned so far and perhaps you will think of something you would like us to find out from him."

Damien nodded in agreement and said, "Stay here and somebody will explain what steps you need to take to set up tomorrow's meeting."

As Lance and Damien walked away, Lance said, "I take it you had a reason for not telling them Taggart's wife's name is Natasha and she's a doctor?"

"Hell, yes, I have a reason. There is no way I want any of that to come back on us. I meant it when I said they would be digging their own graves."

"I agree with you there. These guys have a lot to learn about the cops in this country."

"No shit. They don't seem to appreciate how much they're crossing the line. How many other cops out there have Taggart's mentality? I'm not afraid to face our court system or some cop who follows the rules, but I sure as hell wouldn't want someone like Taggart coming after me if I fucked with his family."

"Still thinking about going into business with them?" asked Lance, with a jerk of his thumb back toward Miguel and Ramiro.

"That's the dilemma. We have a great opportunity to make a lot of cash, but at the same time, killing Taggart could generate a lot of heat."

"A hell of a lot if they start knocking off wives and kids."

"If they do, we'll immediately sever all ties. I need to think about this. Maybe convince them to wait a while after they kill Taggart and see what comes of it. I was thinking if they killed him down there, it might not cause too much heat up here. There is huge potential for financial growth with these guys, but they need to be educated."

"Sounds to me like you just tried. I don't think they were listening. If they do start killing cops' families ... what do you think will come of it?"

"Something those two clowns could probably never imagine."

chapter forty

Jack stirred as a blinding pain in his skull brought him back to reality. He opened his eyes and saw El Pero sitting on a kitchen chair facing him from the hallway outside the laundry room. The long-barrelled revolver was shoved in his belt and he was skimming the pages of a *Playboy* magazine before pausing to hold up the centrefold.

El Pero saw Jack watching him and turned the picture around for Jack to see. "No more of this, for you, gringo!"

Jack did not respond, but El Pero laughed and shouted down the hallway in Spanish. Jack's brain was too numb to follow the conversation, but a couple of men in the kitchen also laughed and yelled back.

El Pero went back to looking at more pictures and Jack tried to focus. If he turned his head slowly, images no longer appeared like multiple overlaps of themselves. He stared at El Pero while carefully cupping the pipe with his hands. His muscles strained, but he was unable to turn the pipe from where it was attached to the laundry tub.

A rubber drain plug dangling over the side of the tub gave him an idea. He could use the small spring steel loop attaching the chain to the drain plug to pick the handcuffs ... given enough time and privacy.

Jack brooded about how to get El Pero to close the door. The room already reeked and he toyed with the idea that if he defecated, it might cause El Pero to close the door. *But then what? Open the door and try to grab his gun? Even if I succeeded, the guys in the kitchen would gun me down ... not to mention the snipers outside.*

He looked at the other items in the room. The containers of bleach and ammonia sitting next to a mop, broom, and dustpan in the corner gave him another idea.

A combination of bleach and ammonia together produce a deadly chlorine gas. If I do get El Pero to close the door and get free, I could use the dust pan to pour them slowly out under the crack of the door. Maybe El Pero will die. I could sneak out and take his gun and ... what the hell am I thinking? Great idea for a movie or a book. Not so good in real life ... there has to be another way ...

Big Al's conversation about what they would learn from his torture came back to haunt him. He thought of Natasha and Mikey. For a moment, a small, half-smile formed on his lips as he recalled the moment.

Michael Edward Taggart ... you're our little boy. Michael Edward Taggart, you're our pride and joy. Michael Edward Taggart, you're such a little clown. Michael Edward Taggart, you're fun to have around!

Jack's smile disappeared as he reached a decision. The fear that had been overwhelming him was replaced with sadness. He truly understood how Lily felt when she believed there was no hope.

I can't risk being taken alive. If I can get El Pero to close the door, I need to dump the bleach and ammonia in the tub and kill myself before Big Al comes back ...

The sound of a truck arriving outside told Jack the expected delivery was being made. Someone in the kitchen hollered to El Pero to come and help. He hollered back that Big Al had told him to guard the gringo. The others would have to unload the truck themselves.

The sound of the men going outside caused Jack to hastily go over his plan again. He did not know how much time he had before the men outside returned, but for the moment, it was only El Pero he had to contend with. He eyed the bottles of bleach and ammonia once more, but was distracted when he noticed El Pero giving a few furtive glances down the hall toward the kitchen … and then back at Jack.

What is he up to? Jack let his head slump to his chest and closed his eyes. He heard the grate of the kitchen chair as El Pero stood up and dropped the magazine on the chair. Next he heard El Pero shuffling down the hall and opening the padlock to Lily's room.

For Jack, it gave him hope. Thoughts of suicide were replaced with hope of survival. He knew he only had a matter of minutes to get free and turned to the drain plug, using his teeth to bite the plug and pull it free from the chain. When he did, he was able put the plug in his hands and extract the wire ring.

Normally he could have picked the lock in a few seconds. Today was not normal. The circulation had been cut from his hands because the cuffs were on too tight. His fingers were like sausages and the exertion caused his scalp to start bleeding again, causing a mixture of sweat and blood to seep into his eyes as he frantically picked at the lock.

A couple of minutes ticked past and from the painful moans emitted by Lily from down the hall, he knew he had little time left. Finally one cuff opened and he slipped it past the pipe, not bothering to take the time to try and pick the other cuff.

He crept to the doorway and looked down the hall. There was nobody in sight so he hurried to Lily's room, leaving a trail of blood droplets along the way. The door was partially open and he looked in.

Lily was on her hands and knees on the mattress facing away from him. So was El Pero, who was mounting her anally from behind, supporting part of his weight with one hand on the mattress while clenching Lily's hair with the other hand. Between grunts he cussed at her and his fat buttocks shook as his strokes increased in tempo. His shirt was still on, but his pants and the .32-calibre long barrelled revolver were beside the door.

It was what Jack had hoped to find. He picked up the revolver and glanced at the cylinder to see the lead ends of the bullets sticking out. There was only one. *The bastard didn't reload ... one will have to do.*

Jack knew the use of deadly force was restricted to imminent life-threatening situations to either the public or himself. Despite what El Pero was doing, he was unarmed. To shoot him would qualify as murder.

In theory, as Jack did not have the authority to work in Mexico, he should make a citizen's arrest and perhaps attempt to take El Pero hostage until he could turn him over to the proper authorities.

Yeah, to murder him would be wrong ... but somehow, it feels so right ...

Outside, the sounds of the men unpacking the truck could clearly be heard, but he knew they would not hear the shot. *I wonder if El Pero has even heard of an Italian silencer ...*

El Pero's body went rigid and he belched in pain, letting go of Lily's hair and looking back over his shoulder. Jack had rammed the pistol so hard, that his own knuckles were between El Pero's fat buttocks.

"You like things up the ass, fatso?" asked Jack.

El Pero's eyes went wide with fright, his buttocks automatically clenching tighter as he gasped and his lips floundered as his brain searched for what to say.

"You have the right to remain silent," said Jack, as he pulled the trigger.

The muffled explosion that followed caused El Pero's body to immediately go limp when the bullet travelled from his rectum, up through his intestines, stomach, and heart before stopping at his shoulder blade.

"Come on, we've got to get out of here," said Jack, grabbing El Pero by the arm and rolling his body off of Lily, who lay collapsed under his weight. "Are you able to walk?"

Lily half-rolled on her side and stared up at Jack in shock, but didn't respond.

"Did you hear me?" asked Jack. "We don't have much time. Are you able to walk?"

"Why aren't you wearing any clothes?" Lily asked tearfully.

"Christ, I'm not here to —" Jack paused, shocked that Lily would even think what she was thinking. He sighed and said, "I'm not wearing any clothes because they took them from me. They were torturing me, too. Come on, I came to take you back to Canada."

"Oh," replied Lily in shock. She blinked her eyes a couple of times and looked at Jack as he grabbed her arm and said, "Your head ... you're bleeding really bad! You'll never be able to save —"

"Keep your voice down. Head wounds tend to look worse than they are. I've cut myself shaving worse than this. We don't have time to talk. There are men outside unloading a truck. We only have a couple of minutes. Come on, let's see if you can stand."

Lily slowly pushed herself back up on one knee as Jack held her arm and helped her to her feet. She stood wobbling for a moment.

"You're doing good," said Jack, trying to sound encouraging. "Can you walk on your own?"

"I think I can," she replied and Jack cautiously let go. She took one step and stumbled, but Jack caught her before she collapsed and lowered her back to a sitting position on the mattress.

"I can't," she said, her voice becoming louder as panic overcame her shock.

"Shhh! Don't worry. I thought you might not be able to walk so I have a plan. Wait here and try to catch your breath. I'll be back in a minute."

Jack didn't wait for a reply. Still holding the empty revolver, he grabbed El Pero's pants and ran back to the laundry room, checking the pants pockets on the way. They were empty. *What? You leave your cellphone in the SUV ... probably along with your spare bullets ... You fat bastard ... wish you hadn't died so fast ...*

Jack knew El Pero's pants were far too big for him, so he grabbed his own pants and shirt from the laundry room, but did not take the time to put them on as he padded barefoot out to the kitchen and peeked out the window.

The men had unloaded boxes from a cube van that had a tomato logo on the side of it. A few boxes had been piled to one side and the men were putting the other boxes back in the truck. Jack knew he only had a minute or two left before they would be back in the house.

chapter forty-one

Berto was the first to enter the kitchen as the truck drove away. He grunted as he set a box down on the floor, then turned and wiped his brow and looked at Sanchez and Eduardo who had entered behind him, each carrying a box. He saw Sanchez's face pale as he stood clutching the box while staring at the floor.

Berto looked to see what the problem was … and then saw the bright red drops of blood leading across the yellow-tiled floor to the counter, which was partially open.

The two mercenaries outside heard the frantic yelling of the men inside. In unison, they dropped the boxes they were carrying and with weapons in hand, burst into the kitchen.

Eduardo pointed to a bloody hand mark on the wall beside the key rack as Sanchez ran down the hall.

Seconds later, Sanchez hollered to confirm that Jack had escaped. He emitted a much louder yell when he screamed that the girl was gone and El Pero was dead.

Eduardo and Berto left the mercenaries to guard the tunnel and ran to the bedroom and stood beside Sanchez as they stared at El Pero's body. A feeling of dread engulfed them as the realization sunk in that Big Al's favourite nephew had been murdered ... on their watch.

Moments later, the men huddled over the entrance to the tunnel. Berto bent down and flicked on the light switch, but the tunnel remained in darkness. An indentation in the wood revealed where Jack had used the barrel of the revolver to pry a wire lose from the switch.

Berto immediately called the men on the American side of the tunnel. They had not seen or heard anything yet, but would wait with their weapons poised should Jack and the girl attempt to break out at their end. When Berto hung up, he stared at Sanchez.

Sanchez swallowed nervously.

"You do it," ordered Berto.

Sanchez nodded and used his cellphone to call Big Al.

Adams and Rubalcava were entering the outskirts of Juarez when they saw Big Al's SUV speeding past in the opposite direction.

"What the hell? Now what?" questioned Adams.

"He couldn't have been that far ahead of us," noted Rubalcava. "I don't think he would have had time to drop Jack off yet."

"Maybe they forgot something," suggested Adams. He looked back at the SUV and added, "Christ, whoever is driving is going like a bat out of hell."

"Jack said they wanted him out of Casa Blanca before a delivery came. Maybe that is why the big hurry."

Adams didn't respond as he spun the wheel hard to turn around and follow.

Big Al's SUV continued to drive at high speed. Adams attempted to keep up for a few minutes, but knew at the speed they were going it would make it too obvious, so he dropped farther back in traffic. They were close enough, however, that when they passed the fruit stand they were able to see a cloud of dust billow over the small hill and know it was Big Al's vehicle pulling away from the vicinity of where the crew-cab truck was blocking the road.

"Back to the tower?" suggested Rubalcava.

Minutes later, Adams hollered down from the tower. "Little change except the SUV with the two snipers has moved back to its original position on the far hill. The ambush past the fruit stand is still in place like before."

"Maybe in a few minutes we'll see Big Al's SUV returning."

"Yeah, maybe."

Big Al pulled up to the doorstep and ran into the house. "Where is he?" he asked.

"They're in the tunnel," replied Berto.

"Not that piece of shit gringo! My nephew! Where —"

"He was shot in the bedroom," said Sanchez. "I'll show you."

Big Al, Sanchez, Berto, and Eduardo went back down the hall while the two mercenaries stayed to cover the entrance to the tunnel.

Big Al walked into the room and saw his nephew lying on his back on the mattress with his legs over the side. He was naked from the waist down and blood and bodily fluids had oozed out from his buttocks. His lifeless eyes, already dry from evaporation, stared dully up at the ceiling. His fat face was even more grotesquely distorted, like a rubber mask.

"And nobody heard the shot?" yelled Big Al.

"He was shot here," said Sanchez, holding his hand like a pistol and pointing toward his own buttocks. "It muffled the sound. We were outside and did not hear it."

Big Al dropped to one knee beside the bed and held El Pero's hand. He made a solemn promise the gringo would pay dearly for what he had done. Then he folded El Pero's hands across his chest, interlocking the fingers to keep them in place before gently using his fingertips to close El Pero's eyes. Next he slowly got to his feet and mumbled a prayer, which he followed by using his finger to make the sacred sign of a cross on his own body.

Sanchez, Berto, and Eduardo politely went to make the same sign on their own bodies, but were interrupted when Big Al yelled at them to find something to cover his body.

"We have no sheets," replied Eduardo, meekly.

"There is a towel in the bathroom. I will get it," Sanchez said and then scurried off.

Big Al strode back to the kitchen and stood over the tunnel entrance and screamed in rage.

"Jack Taggart! I make this vow!" he yelled in English. "You murdered my nephew ... so now everyone in your family will die! Not just you! Everyone! Their skin will be burned from their bodies while they scream and plead for their lives!"

Big Al stood, panting heavily for a moment, then yelled at his men in Spanish. "What are you waiting for? Go get him! Bring him to me alive, if you can."

Before his men could respond, Big Al received a call on his cellphone. It was his boss and he gestured for his men to be quiet as he stepped back from the tunnel. He was not surprised to be called, he had already informed his boss about Jack's real identity.

"Why have you not picked up the doctor yet?"

"There, uh, has been a big problem," replied Big Al. "The gringo managed to grab El Pero's gun and shoot him with it. Then he ran into the tunnel."

"Your nephew is dead?"

"Yes. I found out about it a few minutes ago and returned to Casa Blanca."

"And the gringo?"

"My men will drag him back out of the tunnel in a few minutes."

"If he escapes …"

"There is no chance of that. He is like a rat trapped in a hole. I can have him plucked out very easily. When I do, we will use the doctor for a very long time."

Jack squatted in the dark as Lily sat in front of him with her back huddled up to the front of his chest. She was only wearing Jack's T-shirt, which acted like a short dress on her. Jack was barefoot and only wearing his pants.

He held her with one arm wrapped high around her chest and shoulders, while his other hand caressed her hair. She was going through periodic episodes where her body would shake uncontrollably, but seemed to take some comfort in his touch. What she didn't know was Jack had positioned himself to put her in a sleeper-hold if she uttered a sound.

Jack pondered on what his next move would be. He knew when the time came, he would have to leave her alone to use the element of surprise. *Would she be quiet then?*

A second problem crossed his mind. *I have no bullets … if I aim the gun directly at someone, they might see the cylinder is empty. If I don't point it at them, they will realize something is wrong …*

Jack came up with what he thought was an alternative. *If I get a chance, point it at the back of their head … otherwise point it at their balls and see if they want to risk losing those. Bluffing is our only chance until I get a gun with bullets …*

Big Al tucked his phone back in his pocket and looked into the tunnel opening. Berto had retrieved a flashlight from a kitchen drawer and shone it down the hole. Big

Al peered in while his two soldiers aimed their weapons down the opening.

"Why do you not turn on the lights?" asked Big Al.

"The gringo broke it with El Pero's gun," replied Sanchez, "but it will be easy to fix."

For a moment, the two mercenaries, along with Berto and Eduardo, debated whether to fix the lights. They had the option of calling out to the SUVs on the outer perimeter to bring in the night-vision goggles that they were equipped with. In that way, they would be able to see while the gringo would be in total darkness.

"I do not care what you do, just do it!" snarled Big Al.

"I will assure you," replied one of the mercenaries, "we will take his head off ... just like the iguana that fell from the tree." He nodded toward the window. "Then we will drag him out by his feet."

"I want him alive, if possible. Shoot him in the legs if need be but —" Big Al stopped talking and looked out the window at the carcass of the dead iguana lying in the dirt. "Did any of you see El Pero reload?" he asked.

The men looked at each other and after a short conversation it was realized the spare box of ammunition for the revolver was in the glove box of El Pero's SUV. After Jack had been hit in the head with the rifle butt, El Pero did not return to the truck to reload, but walked with them as they dragged Jack back inside the house.

"He kept the gun ... so he either does not know it is empty or is hoping to bluff us," said Big Al, giving a grim smile.

"I'll fix the light switch," said Berto. "Night vision will not be necessary. Even if he is at the far end of the tunnel, we will have him on his knees in less than fifteen minutes."

"Remember, I do not want you to kill him unless absolutely necessary," said Big Al.

"The four of us have had training in these matters," said Berto, with a nod toward Eduardo and the two mercenaries. "Our training included going up against men armed with machine-guns in barricaded rooms. We can bring him out whichever way you wish."

Big Al thought for a moment and said, "Shoot off his kneecaps and make him crawl out."

"As soon as we see him, his kneecaps are gone," noted Eduardo.

"After that we will ask him to surrender," added Berto, with a sneer.

chapter forty-two

Jack heard the murmur of voices and the commotion at the entrance to the tunnel as the men descended the ladder.

"Stay here. I'll be back for you," he whispered in Lily's ear.

"But if you don't —"

"If that happens, others will come and find you. Do what you must to stay alive."

In his heart, Jack knew if he didn't succeed, Lily would be immediately killed, too, but he wanted her to remain quiet and still. He had decided she was traumatized enough without telling her the truth.

"Marcie has talked about you," she said quickly, in a subconscious desire to have him stay with her a little longer.

"She's still your friend," he said, picking up the revolver beside him and standing up. Lily reached up and clung to his wrist. "I have to go," he said.

Lily slowly let go and wrapped her arms around her knees, drawing them tight to her chest. "I hope you kill them all," she whispered bitterly.

Jack had not told her the revolver was empty. "I'll do my best," he said, wondering how many men were being sent down the tunnel after him.

Eduardo handed his pistol to Berto and then descended the ladder first, but paused on a rung of the ladder above where the roof of the tunnel started. The possibility existed that Jack could be hiding in the tunnel near the shaft, outside the view from above and attempt to grab the gun of the first person who descended the ladder.

Eduardo glanced up at the two mercenaries who were aiming their weapons down the shaft and gave a slight nod before jumping the remaining distance. He landed in a crouched position with his back against the end of the tunnel wall.

Eduardo's smile and a wave of his hand told the others it was clear. Big Al and Sanchez peered down the shaft as the two mercenaries and Berto made their way down the ladder.

Big Al tapped Sanchez on the shoulder and said, "Go with them. Stay out of their way, but use your phone to give me a running update. After they shoot his kneecaps off, go to him and hold the phone near his ear. I will have a message for him."

"A message?" asked Sanchez.

"Yes. That I am here waiting for him and the amount of time it takes him to crawl back will be the amount of time his family will be tortured before they die. I want to hear him scream in pain and in sorrow every time he grabs a handful of dirt to pull himself toward me."

Jack quietly opened the bi-fold door and gingerly stepped around the plastic pail used as a toilet. He glanced at El

Pero's corpse and had a fleeting feeling of satisfaction as he headed for the hallway.

He was relieved when he saw only Big Al sitting on a kitchen chair beside the entrance to the tunnel. Big Al was at a right angle to him, but Jack still hoped he could sneak across the floor undetected and put the barrel of the gun to the back of his head.

Jack was halfway across the floor and felt a little less relieved when he realized Big Al was talking on his cellphone to someone in the tunnel. Jack was about to take another step closer when Big Al saw him.

Jack pointed the revolver at him and whispered, "Quietly hang up the phone and put your hands on your head. Make any noise, or try to warn anyone and I'll blow your balls off."

Big Al didn't move as he stared back in amazement. His eyes flickered toward the hallway as he put it all together.

"Hurry up," ordered Jack. "You're driving us both out of here. If anyone tries to stop us, you'll be the first to get it."

"The gringo is with me in the house!" screamed Big Al in Spanish over his cellphone as he leaped to his feet. He glared at Jack and slowly and deliberately placed his open cellphone on the counter. "You will die for what you have done!" he said evenly.

Jack made one last attempt to bluff him by crouching in a combat position and holding the revolver with both hands as he pointed it at Big Al's crotch.

"We all know the gun is empty," roared Big Al, grabbing the chair and charging at Jack like an enraged bull.

"Oh, shit," was the only thing Jack had time to utter as he turned sideways to keep from having his ribs punctured with the bottoms of the metal chair legs.

The forced hurled him across the kitchen like he was stuck on the front of a freight train, before coming to a sudden stop when he was rammed against the wall.

One of Jack's arms was pinned close to his body, but the other hand holding the revolver was free. Jack tried to smash the gun butt against Big Al's face, but he saw it coming and pulled his head back.

Jack's next assault on Big Al's hand loosened his grip and Jack pushed the chair aside, only to be tackled to the floor by Big Al, who wrapped his arms around him like a grizzly bear as they rolled across the floor.

Big Al had the advantage of weight and soon came to rest on top, crushing Jack with his arms and his immense weight. Jack tried to knee him in the groin, but Big Al simply moved his lower body to one side without letting go.

They were face to face as Jack tried in vain to wriggle free. Eventually he stopped struggling.

"Giving up so easily, my little gringo?" smiled Big Al, as sweat dripped off his face onto Jack's.

Jack lunged his head forward, biting and twisting as his teeth ripped and tore through the end of Big Al's nose like a starving pit bull tearing into a steak.

Big Al screamed, pushing Jack on the chest in a frantic bid to get away. When he did get to his feet and break free, Jack spit out the end of his nose and delivered a swift punch to his solar plexis.

The wind exploded out of Big Al's lungs like a popped balloon and he gasped for air. Another grunt and expulsion of air followed when Jack savagely kicked him in the groin, followed by a punch to his throat and a final kick to his knee that sent him sprawling face-down on the floor.

Big Al had no strength to resist when Jack sat on his back and used a scissor-like grip with his arms around Big Al's neck to strangle the flow of blood his carotid artery supplied to his brain. Given enough time the hold would kill, but the sound of yelling from the tunnel told Jack he didn't have the time.

As soon as Big Al lost consciousness, Jack rolled him over on his back and took the keys from his pocket.

He knew he should call for Lily, but as he looked at Big Al, the memory of the questions Big Al had asked him were still vivid.

What the hell ... if they get me for killing El Pero, they may as well get me for killing you too ...

Jack leaped high in the air, drawing his feet under him before landing with his heels on each of Big Al's collar bones. They both snapped like kindling.

Big Al awoke with a scream and tried to move, before realizing his arms didn't work and any movement brought severe pain.

Sanchez was running full tilt and nearing the bottom of the ladder when he heard Big Al screaming for help and yelling that Jack had broken both his arms. Unfortunately for Big Al, he had his head tilted back toward the tunnel when he was yelling and didn't see Jack's next move, which was to jump again, landing on his rib cage, breaking more bones.

Big Al cried out and closed his eyes in pain. Jack jumped once more, only this time he kept his legs tucked under and landed with his knees on the ribcage, driving the broken ribs into Big Al's lungs.

Another voice yelled in Spanish and Sanchez realized it was Jack yelling at Big Al.

"You got any more questions to ask me about my family? Eh? Do you?"

The last sound Sanchez heard from Big Al was a loud, gurgling scream as he plunged headfirst down the shaft.

Jack tore the mended wire from the light switch, plunging the tunnel into darkness. He was shoving the counter back into position when he heard Sanchez screaming from the bottom of the ladder that the gringo had killed Big Al.

It gave Jack a sense of satisfaction to hear the panic in Sanchez's voice. *That's right, you bastard. The big boss died on your watch ...*

Jack hollered for Lily and grabbed Big Al's cellphone off the counter, before running to the hallway where he met Lily who stumbled and hysterically crawled in a frenzy toward him.

chapter forty-three

Jack wrapped an arm around Lily and helped her to the door and peered outside. Big Al's SUV was parked at the bottom of the steps leading up to the porch. He could also see the other SUV with the snipers parked at the spot from where they had killed the iguana.

With the sun setting in the west, he knew he was facing south. From having been in the yard earlier, he also knew the only road he had seen came from the south, ending at Casa Blanca. Leaving on the road would take them closer to the snipers, who were to the southwest.

He hoped there was another way.

"There are bad guys on that far hill," said Jack, as he pointed. "I've got the keys to the car at the bottom of the steps. We'll keep low and make a dash down the steps. The SUV has tinted windows, so if they don't see us, once I start to drive they might think it's their own guys leaving."

"Where are the rest of the guys?" she cried, looking around in panic.

"I don't have time to talk. We gotta go."

Jack crouched, not letting go of Lily's waist as they scrambled down the stairs. Once there, the vehicle blocked them from the view of the snipers.

So far, so good, thought Jack. He saw his own sandals near the bottom of the steps where they had fallen off earlier. He put them on before opening the driver's door and pushing Lily inside. "Sit on the floor and stay below the dash," he ordered.

Jack started the engine and pulled away. As he drove, he sat low in the seat and leaned toward the middle of the vehicle. He hoped if the snipers tried to take him out that they would aim for the windshield directly in front of the steering wheel. It left him in an awkward position, but he was still able to grip the steering wheel with both hands while eyeing the snipers' SUV on the far hill.

When no shots came after about half a minute, he handed Big Al's cellphone to Lily and gave her the number to call Adams. "When he answers, tell him who you are and that you're with me," he said tersely. "If they start shooting at us I'm going to need both hands to drive."

In the tunnel, the loss of lights was only temporary. Berto still had the flashlight he had taken from the kitchen drawer earlier. While he and Sanchez examined Big Al and believed he had died of a broken neck, the two mercenaries were each using their own cellphones to alert the security teams outside. The teams on the American side were also called to cover the border in the event Jack tried to drive cross-country.

As Jack told Lily the numbers to dial, he saw a figure emerge from the SUV on the hill and hustle around to the other side of the vehicle to join the other man who was looking out over the hood of the vehicle. He knew they were likely using the SUV to steady their aim. *They know ...*

"It's ringing," said Lily. "Is he near here?"

"How the hell ..." Jack stopped, trying to control the panic he felt and said, "I don't know. Maybe."

"Where should I tell him we are?" she asked, bringing her head above the dash to look around.

"Stay down!" yelled Jack.

Jack didn't want to tell Lily he didn't know where they were. Her body was shaking uncontrollably and her voice was shrill with panic. He wanted her to keep it together in the event they ended up ditching the vehicle and making a run for it.

"I'm sorry," she cried, ducking back down.

"It's okay. I shouldn't have yelled. Tell him we're driving southbound toward a paved highway from Casa Blanca."

"It's ringing, but nobody is answering," cried Lily.

Damn it, John! Where are you? Answer!

Seconds later, Jack drove out of the hollow where Casa Blanca was situated and it gave him a better view as he scanned the area. His first thought was to turn around and drive over the rough terrain to the border. He knew it had to be close as he had been told that the tunnel was two miles long, but also remembered Big Al saying there was as much security on that side.

Jack realized that not only would the men on the American side know the layout of the land, but by the time he tried to drive the distance over rough land, they would have a reception waiting for him, while the men on the Mexican side closed in behind.

He tried to remember when he was blindfolded as to what happened when they turned off the highway. He remembered the vehicle stopping almost immediately as Sanchez spoke to someone who was obviously providing security. *Was it the same guys who are on the*

*hill looking down at us? It wasn't long after when we
reached* Casa Blanca ...

He looked to the east. The land was rugged and he did
not see any roads, but a reflection from the sun on a far-off
hill told him there was likely a security vehicle there.

Jack clenched his jaw and continued to drive south
while keeping a watchful eye on the snipers. They didn't
move and slipped from his vision for a few seconds
periodically when the dirt road dipped in and out over a
few small knolls.

"It's rung, like, twenty times ... he's not answering!"
said Lily.

Jack grabbed the phone, hung up, and pressed redial.
Why haven't they opened up on us yet? He saw that Lily
had dialled the number wrong and quickly punched in
the correct digits.

As the phone rang, he came over a small hill and
saw another road branching off to the right. It looked
less travelled and would take him directly in front of
where the snipers were. *Is this why they haven't shot yet?
Hoping I'll turn off and drive by in front of them?*

He thought it was an easy decision to stay on the road
he was on. It also looked hillier up ahead and offered a
few more hidden spots where he would temporarily be
out of sight of the snipers ... if he could make it that far.

As he approached the intersection, he grabbed the rear-
view mirror, twisting it down and using it to see the road
ahead while looking up from below the dash. He expected
the windshield to explode with bullets any second.

His driving slowed, but he still accidentally hit the
ditch, causing his vehicle to slide sideways. He sat up
in panic and regained control of the SUV, but decided
against trying to use the mirror to drive.

Adams clung to the tower, occasionally wiping the sweat

from his eyes as he used his binoculars. "We got some activity," he reported down to Rubalcava. "The guys at the ambush area beyond the fruit stand are out on the road talking. Looks like the truck that was blocking the road is pulling out. Probably coming back to pick them up."

"Good. Maybe Jack is finished and on his way out."

"Yeah, hope so," replied Adams, refocusing the binoculars to look at the snipers on the far hill. "Fuck! What the hell is going on? The two snipers are out of their vehicle again. One has a sniper rifle laid across the hood and the other is spotting with binos."

"Aiming where they did before?"

"Yeah ... hang on, my cellphone is ringing." Adams fumbled with the binoculars, not wanting to put them down as he watched the snipers. Eventually he looped one arm through girder and was able to use that hand to hold the binoculars while fishing in his pocket for his phone.

"Am I glad to hear your voice," said Jack when Adams answered the call.

"Where the hell are you?" Adams's voice was sharp with relief.

"I was hoping you would know. I've been burned. They know who I really am. I've got Lily. We stole Big Al's SUV and we're southbound from Casa Blanca on some dirt road."

"There's a sniper on a hill lining up on you right now!"

"I know. I see them. They're to the southwest of me. I'm surprised they haven't shot at me yet. Maybe they don't think I see them and are waiting for me to get closer. Where are you?"

"Watching from a radio tower south of you."

"I can't see any tower."

"I can't see you, either," replied Adams, swinging around to take another look toward the fruit stand. The group of men were setting up the ambush again, only this time in the opposite direction.

"I'm leaving a lot of dust behind," continued Jack. "You should see something soon. If the sniper doesn't pop me in another minute or two, I'll be out of his sight."

"Don't come south!" screamed Adams. "A bunch of guys have set up an ambush. There is no way you could survive it."

"Explains why the assholes on the hill haven't shot at me yet."

"You gotta turn off. Don't come this way!"

"There's a small hill up ahead. I'll be out of the sniper's sight. Guess our only hope is to try and drive overland to the east, but I know there is someone there, as well."

"There's a farmhouse to the east where the bad guys were. Also a road leading south from it. They'll have a lot of guys there waiting for you long before you reach it."

"Leaves us to try and sneak out on foot," said Jack, as he glanced at Lily. The ground was splattered with small cactus plants and the ground was extremely hot. Lily was barefoot and he thought of shredding the T-shirt she was wearing and using it to wrap her feet, but he knew in her condition he would still end up carrying her.

"Christ, I'm coming in," said Adams. "You two will never make it on foot on your own. Maybe I can distract their fire or something."

"Not yet. You're my eyes right now …" Jack glanced toward the snipers and saw that a hill was blocking his sight. "I'm out of sight of the snipers," he reported. "Don't know for how long."

"I can see dust!" said Adams excitedly.

"Mine or someone else's?"

"I hope yours. Coming from the same direction they took you down."

So close, yet so far, thought Jack.

"Wait! The snipers on the hill are mobile!" yelled Adams.

"Where? Which direction?"

"Give me a minute … okay, I think they are moving east toward another hill where they were earlier. It will give them a view of the ambush."

"How long will it take them to get there?"

"Five or ten minutes."

"I'm going back. There was another road that went to the west," said Jack. "I didn't take it earlier because it would have passed right in front of the snipers."

"They'll see your dust. They'll know you turned around."

"It's not like I have a choice. Here, meet Lily. I've got some driving to do," said Jack as he handed the phone to Lily who was crouched under the dash.

Jack spun the vehicle around and drove back from where he came. The SUV bounced over the potholes as Jack wrestled with the steering wheel to keep it on the road. Twice it became airborne over small dips in the road. The first time it caused Lily to bang her head on the dash and drop the phone, but she didn't complain, scrambling to pick it up again while wedging her body tighter between the seat and under the dash.

From the conversation Jack heard, he knew Adams was trying to soothe her.

When Jack approached the intersection, he saw another cloud of dust approaching from Casa Blanca. The men were obviously out of the tunnel.

Jack cranked the wheel and headed west, trying to keep his eyes on the road while taking occasional glances at the hilltop where the snipers had been parked moments ago.

"Tell him we're westbound, but I have no idea where the road will take us," said Jack, trying to keep his voice even so he would at least sound like he was in control of the situation. He estimated about three minutes passed before the white SUV from Casa Blanca sent up a wave of stone and dust as it turned on to the same road to follow him in hot pursuit.

Lily relayed back and said, "He says he can't see your dust trail anymore. He is going to come down off the tower and head west on the highway and see if he can join up with us."

"Good idea. Right now we've only got one vehicle chasing us. It would be nice to know what to expect farther up —"

A *click* sound came from the door panelling behind him and he swore to himself, realizing that the snipers had returned to the hilltop. Most people would presume being in a vehicle struck with a bullet would sound like you were in a tin can being beaten by somebody with a ball-peen hammer. In reality, a high-powered bullet, providing it doesn't hit a cross-bar, passes through the tin on door panelling like it was made of paper and sounds more like somebody flicking their fingernail against metal.

Jack also knew the same was true for the human body. If hit, the head or body is not flung back like action sequences in a movie. The bullet passes through at such a high velocity, that for a person sitting hunched on the floor like Lily, the first indication she may have been hit could be her silence.

"Are you okay?" asked Jack anxiously.

"No! I'm scared," she replied, turning to look up at him.

"Good," uttered Jack, feeling relieved.

"Good? What do ya mean, *good?*"

"If you weren't scared it would mean you were a moron," replied Jack.

Lily screamed as the rear passenger-side window behind Jack exploded and the bullet passed through the front passenger side of the windshield, making a large, spider-webbed hole.

"Well I must be a fuckin' genius, 'cause I'm really scared now!" Lily cried.

Jack didn't know if she was intentionally being funny or if it was something she blurted out in panic, but he had no time to respond as he crested another rise in the road and saw it swerve sharply to the north. It gave him some relief as the dust trailing out from behind would act as cover. Some, but not completely. He heard another *click* in the roof above his head.

Seconds later, the road came to an abrupt end and Jack came to a sliding stop as the dust overtook and billowed around him. They were at what had once been someone's home, but all that was left was a cement pad and a few concrete blocks from where the floor had been.

Behind the ruins was a gully zigzagging its way down from the hills and Jack had abruptly driven up to it. He estimated the gully to be about twice the depth of the SUV and about as wide as the length of an Olympic swimming pool. There was a dried creek bed in the bottom, but the gully was far too steep for him to drive in and out of. Even if he made it to the bottom of the creek bed, there were too many boulders, rocky outcrops, clumps of brush, and collapsed creek banks for him to attempt to drive along it.

Jack glanced to his left and right. To go overland would make them like slow moving ducks at a carnival … only with trained sharpshooters who could pick off their body parts as they pleased.

The gully itself contained enough hiding spots that it would take four or five men to form a line to clear it. *But then what? Once we're discovered …*

The dust was settling around him and he knew the SUV from Casa Blanca would soon be upon them. A bullet took out his side mirror, prompting his next move. "Hang on!" he yelled, while stepping on the gas and driving nose-first into the gully.

The vehicle slid down the bank and came to rest with the undercarriage hung up on a boulder. It hadn't quit rocking yet when Jack was out and helping Lily climb out.

"I'm okay. I think I can walk," she said, still gripping the cellphone.

Jack considered telling her that walking was not really an option, but the sound of Adams yelling into the cellphone changed his mind. He grabbed the phone and said, "John, I ditched the wheels and am in a gully. Give me a sec."

Jack figured he had about three minutes before the men from Casa Blanca arrived. *I left these guys a false trail before … will they be tricked again?*

"Head that way," ordered Jack, pointing to the south.

If a person was careful, they could thread their way along the stones in the dried creek bed without leaving much of a trail. He was also hoping their pursuers would think they would want to head north to the border.

As Lily scrambled away, Jack followed her and purposefully dislodged a few fist-sized stones while speaking on the phone with John.

"You still there?" asked Jack.

"Yeah, I'm coming. I'll find the gully and come and get you. I'll bring you a piece and we can shoot our way out."

Jack knew that anything but a small army would lose against the number of professionals they were up against. He glanced up at the sides of the gully. *Talk about shooting fish in a rain barrel … but up above would be worse.*

Jack grimaced as he stared at the cellphone. He knew John would risk his life for them without question.

"Did you hear me?" asked John.

"What the fuck is it with you Americans and guns?" said Jack, hoping his voice sounded angry and not scared like he really was. "Stay the hell away until I need you. I gotta shut the phone off or the bad guys will hear. I'll call you when I need you."

"What the fuck! If you don't need me now, when the hell will you need me?"

"When I call you back. Until then, wait on the highway someplace to the south of me," said Jack, before hanging up.

When Jack came to the first bend in the gully, he came upon a waist-high cactus plant. He ripped his back pocket off and was sticking it on the spines of the cactus when he heard the men from Casa Blanca arrive.

Jack saw that it was too far to make it undetected to the next turn in the gully. He grabbed Lily and took cover under a clump of dried brown reeds that hung over the creek embankment. It was only a couple of steps past the cactus plant from which his pants pocket hung, but it was the best spot he could find in the time he had available.

He jammed Lily in a prone position tight to the bank and crouched over her and tried to arrange the reeds to cover them. He knew it would only stand for a cursory glance before he was seen. These men were professionals. His hiding spot might remain undetected from above, but for anyone approaching from below, once they walked alongside them, they would be clearly visible.

If he attacked, he knew he would be shot, but if he succeeded in crushing the skull of even one of them, it would give him some satisfaction. He wrapped his fingers around a rock and waited.

Besides, being shot is better than being taken alive ...

chapter forty-four

Adams climbed down from the tower and clamoured over the fence to his car where he updated Rubalcava on the situation as he drove. Moments later, they turned onto the highway and headed west. Several minutes later, Adams spotted a large culvert that ran under the highway. "Ya think this is it?" asked Adams.

"I don't know," replied Rubalcava. "Not what I would call a gully. Let's drive farther."

A ways down the road, they came to a dip in the highway that crossed a bridge over a more promising gully.

"This has to be it," muttered Adams as they drove past and scanned the gully below.

"He wants us to wait in the car?"

"The asshole is trying to protect me. I'll park and go in and find them. You better stay in the car. They don't know me, but they sure as hell know you and your family."

Rubalcava sighed and said, "No, wait. I remember a bridge on this highway, but I don't think this is it. A little farther ahead there is a bigger bridge. Also, there are more gullies after that."

"Christ."

Two minutes down the road, Adams discovered that Rubalcava was right.

"What do we do?" asked Rubalcava.

"I don't know. I guess we wait until we hear from him," replied Adams bitterly. He found a place to park, opened the windows and shut the car off to listen.

Jack listened to the voices of the men as they looked down over the edge of the gully. He was hoping they would sound excited. Excited people make mistakes, but these men sounded calm. He heard one of the mercenaries give an order. Berto, Eduardo, and the second mercenary scrambled into the gully and he heard them yell back that the vehicle was empty.

Jack did not hear Sanchez and presumed he had been left to guard Casa Blanca. *That leaves me with four trained professional killers ... and more on the way.*

Soon Berto yelled, "This way!" and the three men fanned out and started to move south along the gully toward their hiding place, while the mercenary up above moved along the edge of the gully with them.

Berto was the first man Jack saw come into view, quickly followed by one of the mercenaries. Berto pointed to the piece of cloth on the cactus and the two men approached to look at it. Jack only had a profile view of the mercenary, but Berto faced him directly and he stared into his scowling face.

Jack held his breath and was conscious of Lily doing the same. Berto was close enough that he could see the beads of sweat on his forehead.

The mercenary pulled the piece of cloth off the cactus as Berto took another step closer as his eyes scanned the creek embankment. Jack gripped the rock and tensed his leg muscles, ready to spring forth.

"It's his back pocket," said the mercenary. "The turned rocks … this … he has given us a false trail," he said. He turned and yelled to the other men, "The other way. He has gone north, toward the border!"

Jack waited a full minute after they left before leaving the hiding spot. Any noise, a slip, or stones moving beneath their feet would bring them back. He helped Lily to her feet where she swayed and grabbed a clump of reeds for support.

"I'll piggy-back you," he whispered.

"I think I can walk," she whispered back. "Just give me a minute."

"In your condition you won't be able to walk without making noise. Also you'd burn your feet. I'll piggy-back you. In the meantime, no talking."

Twenty-five minutes later, Jack lowered Lily to the ground and held his finger to his lips as he gestured to her to be quiet. "I need to rest," he whispered, while listening intently to see if they were being followed. He did not hear the sound of anyone trailing them, but was rewarded by the sound of a truck passing by somewhere ahead of them.

Adams answered his phone on the first ring.

"We're close," said Jack, "and I don't think we have any company. The problem is we've come to a fork in the gully. Tap your horn twice, will you?"

Adams did as requested and asked, "Did you hear it?"

"Yup. Sounds like I need to take the right fork. Shouldn't be long."

"I'm parked at the end of a bridge, pretending to change a tire. Hope it's over the same gully."

"Guess we'll find out. I'm hanging up, but give me ten minutes and tap again."

A few minutes later Jack called again. "Don't bother to honk, we see you."

"I'll be right down," replied Adams, when he spotted Jack waving at him in the distance.

"Think you should stay there. If we need covering fire you'll be in a better position. Of course, I'm Canadian, what the hell do I know about gun fights ..." Jack knew that humour was a good way to relieve stress and right now he could use a truckload of it.

As soon as he hung up, Lily asked, "Is it okay to talk now?"

"Yeah, I hope so. I think we've made it." Jack knew it was a mistake as soon as he said it. Lily was able to keep her emotions in check when the stress was still on her because she knew she had to. Now she thought she was safe and let her emotions erupt by bursting into tears and sobbing. Jack lowered her and held her in his arms to comfort her.

"Can I phone my mom, now?" she pleaded.

"Sorry, not on this phone. It belongs to a bad guy. I don't want them knowing your mom's phone number. Wait until we get to the car and use John's phone."

Lily released her embrace and said, "And my boyfriend, Earl. He's gotta be going out of his mind with worry," she added, looking closely at Jack's face.

Jack sighed and said, "Actually, John's phone isn't a good idea, either. We'll need to keep it available. You'll have to wait until we get you to the hospital."

Lily stared silently at Jack.

"What is it?" asked Jack.

"He left me, didn't he?"

"Did who leave you?"

"Please, what I have been through ... what we have been through. Tell me the truth. One of the men who raped me said Earl took their dope money and split. He said they killed him a few days later. Is that true?"

Jack sighed and said, "Yes, it's true."

"So he was into dealing drugs, just like Marcie warned me," said Lily, tearfully.

"He was a mule. Running money back to the cartel."

"Did he even report me missing?"

"No. Your mom did that and Marcie told me about it. I'm really sorry."

"Don't be," replied Lily bitterly, as her sorrow was replaced with anger. "I've had a lot of time to think about it. Marcie was sure right about the guy. Wish I had listened."

Jack looked up and saw two vultures circling overhead. It gave him an uneasy feeling and he said, "We better get going. You can use John's phone to call your mom," added Jack, as he turned around and squatted to piggyback her again.

"I want so bad to talk to her," said Lily, as she climbed on Jack's back.

"I'm sure," replied Jack, as he stumbled forward. "I've met your mom. She seems like a really nice lady."

"She's the best mom there is. I haven't exactly always been an easy kid to get along with."

"I don't know. You seem like a good kid to me. I know you're a hard worker."

"Yeah? What makes you say that?"

"I've seen how you look after the yard. Looks great. A lot of kids wouldn't make the effort you put into it."

"Are you kidding? Mom makes me do yard work as punishment. I'm always out in the yard weeding or doing something."

Jack chuckled, despite still being worried about their safety.

"I never thanked you for what you did," said Lily.

"It's okay."

"You saved my life and, and ... killing that guy who was ... thank you."

Oh yeah ... that. "I need to put you down for a moment," said Jack. Once he faced her he said, "Killed what guy?"

"You know … the guy who was … who was … you know, on me when you came in the room."

"To shoot an unarmed man like that would be murder."

"But —"

"Please listen to me. You're suffering from deep shock. Your brain has blocked out certain things. What happened was I was there in an undercover capacity. They found out who I was and handcuffed me to a pipe in the laundry room."

"I know. I heard them … and you, once, when you screamed."

"Yeah, well, after that they left me alone. Then I heard a couple of the bad guys arguing about whose turn it was to rape you. First I saw a guy named El Pero walk past the laundry room and minutes later, another guy I don't know went by with a revolver. It must have been him who killed El Pero. I picked the lock on my handcuffs when he returned to the kitchen and went into the bedroom to get you."

Lily stared at him and Jack knew she wasn't believing a word he'd said.

"But you had the gun in your hand. I saw it," she said.

"It was empty. No bullets. Guess that is why the guy left it. I didn't know until after I picked it up."

"You're trying to tell me you didn't shoot him?" she said, incredulous.

"Under the circumstances, not only would I not have been allowed to shoot him, if I actually did shoot him, I might be returned to Mexico to face charges for murder. You would be called as a witness, as well."

"Oh my God … for real?"

"Yes, a damned good chance of it."

"But the other men who were there — what will they say?"

"They're not going to come forward and say anything. It would be admitting their part in the smuggling operation as well as kidnapping and assaulting you. Besides, they're bad guys. Who could believe anything they say? The basis of truth will rest upon the statements you and I give … providing you never give a different account of anything to anyone else."

Lily nodded and said, "Now I understand, but, like, for a statement … I want to make sure I say the right thing."

"I want you to say the right thing, as well."

"So after some guy shot El Pero and left, you came in the room and told me to wait and went back to where they were?"

"Yeah, well, first I heard the man who did the shooting get in a big fight in the kitchen with a guy named Big Al."

"If you say so."

"I do say so."

"Okay, it's coming back to me now."

"Good. Then a truck showed up to unload cocaine and I snuck into the kitchen and stole a set of keys off the counter when the men were down the tunnel hauling the dope away."

"Then you came back and got me and we ran out of the house."

"Exactly."

"Okay, I think I've got it now."

"Good."

"So, to clarify everything, you and I weren't hiding in the closet when some guy was praying over the body in the room and later was screaming he was going to kill you because you killed his nephew?"

"Nope. I never hid in any closet … let alone kill anyone."

"Okay. I guess I didn't hide in a closet, either."

"Good." Jack gave her a sideways glance and added, "It must have been two other people who were hiding in the closet."

"Yeah, it must have been," smiled Lily. It was the first time she had smiled in twenty-one days and nineteen hours.

chapter forty-five

As soon as Jack and Lily scrambled into the back seat, Adams quickly drove away. Under Rubalcava's direction, Adams headed west on the highway and turned on another road going south. This road intersected with yet another road that would see them back in Juarez half an hour later.

Rubalcava, Adams, and Jack were all seasoned veterans. One would expect them to have become as emotionally tough as one could imagine, but all three men had tears spilling out of their eyes as Lily, sitting with Jack's arm around her, called her mom to say she was alive.

When Adams stopped in an alley in Juarez to let Rubalcava out, Jack also got out to say a quick goodbye.

"I just realized it is dinnertime," said Jack. "What about your two sons at school? You weren't there to pick them up."

"My wife took care of it. I was a little busy this afternoon."

Jack smiled and said, "Having an affair, according to the rumours."

Rubalcava grinned. "Of course, but I do recall getting some work done this afternoon, as well."

"For that, I want to thank you. I really owe you one."

"No, *amigo*, it is my country that owes you a debt. Perhaps someday it will be safe for you to bring your wife and children here to meet my family. It would be an honour to have you stay with us."

"I would really like that. Be safe, my friend," added Jack, as they gave each other a hug.

Twenty minutes later, Adams drove across The Bridge of the Americas with Jack and Lily both crammed into the trunk. It was an extra precaution that was not needed, as the trip was made without incident.

Once in El Paso, Adams drove Jack and Lily to a hospital for examination. Jack was immediately taken for a CAT scan while Lily was admitted to a different examining room.

Jack lay momentarily unattended on a gurney while waiting for the results of the scan and Adams took the opportunity to talk to him. It was the first time they had been alone together since morning.

"I should call Weber and tell him what happened," said Adams.

"He's your boss. You better call him."

"What did happen?"

"Don't get yourself in trouble. Tell them the truth. I heard the bad guys last night saying Lily was still alive, but that they were going to kill her soon. I made a decision to go to Mexico on my own as I believed there wasn't time to save her if I had gone through channels. You and your friend helped me. I found Lily, grabbed her, and stole a vehicle and ... well, you know the rest."

"Yeah, but ..."

"But what?"

"You make it sound so simple. They found out who you were and busted your skull open. These guys were armed to the teeth and you had nothing. How the hell did you escape? What happened in there?"

"They handcuffed me to a pipe. I simply picked the handcuffs, stole a set of keys, grabbed Lily, and bolted. There's nothing more to say."

"What about El Pero?"

"What about him?"

"He was Big Al's nephew for Christ's sake. I don't believe one of the guys shot him."

"I was shocked, too, but you can ask Lily. Must have been someone higher up the ladder than Big Al's nephew. Maybe the guy who killed him was related to Guajardo himself, or one of the Carrillo Fuentes brothers."

"Big Al would go ape-shit if that happened."

"I did hear Big Al fighting with someone later in the kitchen."

"Yeah, that's what you said. Then you said they all went outside to unload a truck. Sounds to me like Big Al got over the death of his nephew pretty easy. Then everyone heads down the tunnel with the dope and you grab some keys and escape with Lily."

Jack nodded.

"That's another thing. I don't see Big Al doing a peon's job of going down the tunnel. He would have stayed in the house."

"Maybe that's who it was," said Jack, thoughtfully.

"What are you talking about?"

"Did I mention I thought there was someone using the bathroom when we left?"

Adams stared silently at Jack.

"Listen," said Jack, "I've been beat on the head, tortured, still having vision problems, and I'm exhausted. I'm sure some details will come up that need further explaining, but now is not the time."

"You do know I'm your friend, right?"

"Without a doubt. I'm just really tired. Try to imagine how I feel. A lot of things are going through my mind right now."

"I bet I know exactly how you feel. Tired, scared … and feeling alone and wondering if you did the right thing."

This time it was Jack who stared silently in response. *Feeling alone and wondering if I did the right thing? Few people know about that, unless …*

"Anyway," replied Adams, "I'll give you some time to think about it. In the meantime, I'll call Weber."

Jack remained on the gurney, but watched as Adams walked down the corridor while calling Weber on his cellphone. When he returned, Jack asked, "What did he have to say?"

"He was astounded," replied Adams. "He wanted to come right over and congratulate you and meet Lily, but I convinced him you both needed your rest tonight."

"I appreciate that. Did he give you any flak about me going to Mexico?"

"He doesn't care about that. He's not your boss and as far as I go, he knows I sneak across quite often to meet my CIs. He said he wasn't surprised we went. He said he could tell you and I were two of a kind from the first day we met."

Their conversation was interrupted by a neurologist and a hospital psychologist who both arrived to talk to Jack.

Jack was told he had a hairline fracture in his skull, but there was no sign of bleeding under the skull. It was, however, recommended he stay overnight for observation.

Lily was suffering from dehydration, but her physical injuries were relatively minor compared to the psychological damage and it was recommended she also stay overnight, but be returned to her home environment as soon as possible. Jack said he would try to arrange for their trip tomorrow.

"I don't believe the psychological damage will ever completely heal," said the psychologist, "but in time she will think about it less and less."

"She is going to have nightmares for years to come," said Jack.

"Sadly, I would agree with you," replied the psychologist. "Do the media know about it?"

"Not that I am aware of," replied Jack. "In Canada it was being investigated as a missing person. We didn't find out until today that she had actually been kidnapped."

"Her recovery will go a lot smoother if she is not being hounded," said the psychologist.

"Only a few people know," said Jack. "I don't see anyone calling the media."

After a short discussion, Adams made some calls and Jack and Lily were admitted to the hospital under fictitious names. They were both put in the same room where they were to be placed under armed guard for the night. Adams stayed in the room with them while waiting for the security detail to arrive.

As soon as the orderlies left the room, Jack looked at Adams and asked, "Did you talk to Weber about the tunnel?"

"Oh, yeah. I think he was dancing on his desk he was so happy," replied Adams. "Speaking of which, do you think you're up for a quick airplane ride tomorrow morning to do a little recon?"

"If my head doesn't explode, I will be. I'm sure I'll be okay."

"Good. All the troops will be out first thing in the morning. As soon as we locate Casa Blanca and figure out where the tunnel comes up on our side, they'll be going in. Davidson is arranging things on the Mexican side."

"We know how that will go with the Mexicans. There won't be anyone there," said Jack.

"Yeah, but it's not like the bad guys don't know we're coming, anyway."

"Think there will be an attempt at retribution?"

"Against you or your family ... possibly, if Big Al has his way," Adams noted.

"You think there's a chance he won't have his way?" Jack kept his expression neutral, masking his knowledge that Big Al wouldn't be getting his way ever again.

"He was responsible for letting you escape ... along with everyone else in that house. I wouldn't want to be in any of their shoes right now."

"Think they'll get spanked?"

"There's a good chance of it, although Big Al is high enough up he might be able to deflect the heat off onto the others. We'll have to wait and see what happens. Maybe our friend will hear something. In the meantime, when you get back to Canada you may want to think about packing a gun with you on a permanent basis."

"Just one?"

"What are you trying to do? Become an American?"

Jack chuckled and was relieved the rest of their conversation was light-hearted. Two men arrived for the security detail and after Adams made a quick introduction, one of them handed Adams two cellphones. He gave one each to Jack and Lily and said, "Make as many calls as you want on these tonight. Courtesy of the U.S. government."

Lily immediately called her mom and while she was on the phone, Adams looked at Jack and said, "I should stay with you tonight."

"It's almost six ... I haven't slept in forty hours," complained Jack, "and I have the worst headache I've ever had in my life. What do you want to do? Keep me awake bullshitting all night?"

"Well … yeah," grinned Adams. "I thought we could talk about what kind of gun you should carry. I could explain the different calibres to you and what type goes best if you're wearing a bathing suit. That sort of thing."

"Please, no jokes. Laughing makes my head hurt worse. Go home to Yolanda. We've got work to do in the morning and I've still got my notes to write tonight."

Adams nodded and said, "Get some sleep. You, too, Lily! I'll see you in the morning."

As soon as Adams left, Jack called Natasha. With the one-hour time difference it was five o'clock in the evening in Vancouver.

"Hi, babe! It's free to talk," said Jack.

"Good. Where are you?"

"Still in El Paso, but the mission is accomplished. We found Lily. She's with me right now talking to her mom on another phone."

"I know. Lily also called her mom about an hour ago. Her mom called Marcie and she called me. That's wonderful. I'm so happy."

"Me, too."

"So everything went okay?"

"A few drinks, a few laughs, nobody got hurt. Well, I picked up a small cut on the top of my head. Nothing serious."

"Your voice doesn't sound quite right. You sure everything is okay?"

"Actually it was hell, but I'm okay. I'll tell you about it when I get home. Right now, I'm exhausted and … uh …."

"And what?"

"It's been one of those days where the importance of family really hits home. I love you so much."

"I love you, too."

"I've got a favour to ask. Is Mikey awake?"

"It's five o'clock. What do you think? He's propped up in his highchair with Pablum all over his face. Do you want to say hi?"

"Yes, but first I wonder if I could get you to sing to him. There's something I would like to hear."

"Sing to him? Okay ... do you want me to sing the Dr. Hook song, *Freakin' at the Freaker's Ball?*"

"No, not that one. Your song about him being our little boy, our pride and joy."

"I can do that."

Jack listened to Natasha sing the song and didn't care if someone saw the tears streaming down his face.

"How was that?" asked Natasha.

"Probably the most beautiful thing I've ever heard. Let me say hi to the little fart."

Jack unsuccessfully tried to get Mikey to talk, but eventually Natasha cut in and said, "Well, you got him to smile and spit Pablum all over the mouthpiece."

"I heard him."

"So when are you coming home?"

"Tomorrow is Friday ... we have a mop-up operation to do in the morning. A couple of houses to search. I also have to arrange for Lily to get proper travel documents, not to mention clothes. Everything she had was stolen. Still, with luck, there is a flight out of here tomorrow around four in the afternoon and it arrives in Vancouver just before ten at night. I'll call you later to confirm it."

"So tomorrow won't be dangerous?"

"No. The bad guys know we're coming so they won't even be there."

Jack was right about the fact that he didn't have to worry about the bad guys. It was the good guys who were still after him.

chapter forty-six

Just before dawn, Adams arrived at the hospital and handed a bag full of clothes to Lily.

"You're a little smaller than my wife," he said, "but at least it will give you something until you get home."

After Lily thanked him, Adams looked at Jack and said, "So? Are you ready to go for a ride?"

"I feel good. Let's do it."

After promising Lily he would be back to pick her up before noon, Jack left with Adams.

On their way to the airport, Adams said, "Slater never returned to our side of the border yesterday."

"I'm not surprised. I don't think the cartel would have taken too kindly to him saying I was his cousin and he has known me all his life."

"Maybe we could send a request over to Detective Sanchez to investigate his disappearance," chuckled Adams.

Jack smiled. "I'm sure Sanchez knows the right people."

Minutes later, Jack and Adams taxied onto the runway in a U.S. Customs plane. By first light, they were flying along the border within easy sight of the radio tower on the Mexican side.

"You owe me a beer for making me hang and bake on that son of a bitch," said Adams.

"I'm surprised you could climb it with all the guns you carry."

It didn't take long before Jack spotted Casa Blanca. There were no vehicles visible in the yard or on the surrounding hills.

The plane circled over three potential houses on the American side of the border. Two of the houses had vehicles in the yard. The third house didn't.

Jack and Adams looked at each other and silently nodded in agreement.

The plane was taxiing back up to the private hangar when Adams received word that entry teams were preparing to hit the houses on each side of the border simultaneously. Each team also had a representative from the opposite country.

"We've been invited to watch," said Adams. "You're the guest of honour. They want you there to give the signal for the teams to go in."

"Uh, thanks for the honour, but tell them not to wait for me," said Jack. "The places will be empty." *Well ... except for maybe two bodies at Casa Blanca ...*

"They know, but it will take them that long to get the warrant. They'll wait for you, regardless. Everyone thinks you're a hero. Go out and act like one. You're in my country, it's the American thing to do."

"Will I be expected to shoot a gun off or something?"

"Hell, yeah! Did you bring your camera? Maybe we could even stage a car chase."

"Had enough of that yesterday."

Their one-hour drive out to the American side of the tunnel was strangely quiet. Both men knew it would be the last day they would work together and each dealt with the sadness quietly.

When they arrived, Jack was taken inside the back of a SWAT command-post truck where he was handed the police microphone and given the nod. Jack grinned at Adams as he squeezed the button and said, "Teams ready?"

"Team one ready," drawled a voice in response.

"Team two are ready," came a second voice.

"Go, go, go!" yelled Jack.

The initial results on the American side were as expected. The house had been cleaned out, but a tunnel entrance was located under a kitchen counter like the one in Casa Blanca.

Casa Blanca itself was a different story and the SWAT commander relayed the information as he received it over his headset.

"They've got six bodies over there," said the commander.

"Six?" replied Jack.

"Five in the kitchen were lined up against a wall and taken out with one or more automatic weapons. Another body is in a back bedroom."

"Have they identified them?" asked Adams.

The commander nodded and said, "Just getting to that. Of the five in the kitchen, three were known members of the Guajardo cartel. Sanchez … who they say was a cop, Eduardo Cortez, and a guy they call Berto. The other two are unidentified."

"There were two mercenaries hired to work as security," replied Jack. "Berto told me they were from South America, but I never got their names. Bet it's them."

"You gotta be kidding," exclaimed the commander into his microphone. He looked at Adams and Jack and said, "The body in the bedroom is another cartel member by the name of Pietro Franco who goes by the nickname of El Pero. He was found half naked and someone literally put a round up his ass. No powder burns so it must have been real up close and personal."

"Yeah, Jack said someone was shot in a bedroom," replied Adams, while staring at Jack. "I just didn't hear the part about it was up his ass."

"Hang on, there's another one," continued the commander. "They found a seventh body at the bottom of the ladder in the tunnel. They say it looks like someone chewed the guy's nose off and threw him headfirst down the shaft. Probably has a broken neck."

"Let me guess," said Adams. "Was it Alphonse Franco? More commonly known as Big Al?"

"Yup. How did you know?"

"Just a lucky guess," replied Adams, looking at Jack.

"Hang on, someone else has something," said the commander.

As they waited a moment, Adams leaned over and whispered in Jack's ear. "Hope you used dental floss after."

Jack looked surprised at the comment, then a look of concern came over his face, and he shook his head in denial.

"Okay," said the commander. "Doesn't look like we can give you guys a tour of the tunnel. The bastards have it booby-trapped with plastic. We'll probably blow it up ourselves rather than risk anyone's life by trying to dismantle it."

Both Jack and Adams voiced their agreement and stepped out of the command vehicle.

"Looks like the Guajardo cartel didn't appreciate some of their guys letting you escape yesterday," said Adams.

"Looks that way."

"You want to hang around and see them blow the tunnel?"

"Not really. I'm hoping to catch an afternoon flight."

"I'm still supposed to take you back to the office. The bosses want to shake your hand and congratulate you before you go."

"Politics."

"You got it."

Adams unlocked the Camaro and seconds later, they started the one-hour trip back to El Paso.

"Guess you'll be glad to get home," noted Adams.

"You wouldn't believe how bad," said Jack sombrely. "I want to go home and give my wife and kid the biggest hug I ever have. I didn't have time to get into all the details with you yesterday, but after Big Al handcuffed me to a pipe, he had El Pero give me a shot with a cattle prod while asking me some personal questions."

"Like the names of the guys you work with? Their home addresses, names of their relatives … and your wife and kid's names?"

"Exactly," said Jack in surprise. "How did you know?"

"Those are some of the same questions they asked my last partner when they grabbed and tortured him. I told you about him. He ended up quitting because of it."

"You told me he was tortured. I didn't know they were going after his family."

"Yeah, well … they were."

"That's … that's … I mean, you can't let them get away with that!" said Jack vehemently. "Once that starts happening we've all lost. No cop will do their job."

"Tell that to our friend across the border."

"Okay. Very few cops will do their job. But you must know what I mean? You're a street cop. Front line. Not some desk jockey who doesn't understand."

"Oh, I understand alright. Believe me, I understand," said Adams.

Jack looked at Adams's face. Earlier he had thought his friend was simply tired. But there was more to it. His face was haggard and dark sacks of skin hung from eyes which were now twitching. Something more than lack of sleep was troubling him and Jack could see he was trying to decide whether to tell him something.

Jack remained silent, not wanting to press him. *If he wants to tell me something, he will. If not, that's his choice ...*

And then Adams talked. The words started to spill out of him, picking up speed as he went. "Remember when we had coffee at your hotel the morning after you went to the whore house with Big Al? When I told you I was in deep shit?"

"Yes, but you said you didn't want to talk about it because we needed to focus on what we were doing."

Adams took a deep breath and let out a long sigh and said, "Well, I'll tell you about it now. You know Rafael Guajardo heads the cartel?"

"Yes ... and below him are the Carrillo Fuentes brothers."

"Right, but below them comes three lower bosses, who also happen to be brothers. One of them, a guy by the name of Chico, took part in my partner's kidnapping."

Something about the tone of Adams's voice gave Jack an indication about where the conversation was going.

Jack suddenly understood something. Something that floated in the back of his mind from the first day he met Adams.

This car ... Adams is the junior guy, but he always gets the best car ...

"I grabbed Chico outside a bar in El Paso and —"

"Man, this is a great car!" exclaimed Jack. "Stereo, air conditioning —"

"I'm trying to tell you something," said Adams, looking hurt that Jack would interrupt him when he was talking about something so serious.

Jack gestured to his mouth with his fingers and pointed at the air vents on the dash.

Adams frowned and continued, "So I grabbed him and took him about fifty miles out into the desert and —"

"I always wondered why you got the nice car," said Jack loudly.

"Jack," pleaded Adams, "I'm trying to —"

"Remember when I commented on it? I know where I come from the bosses scoop the best cars, but you always end up with this one. Wow," added Jack sarcastically, "you sure are a lucky guy. The bosses must think you're pretty special."

Adams stared at Jack as his mind processed the conversation.

Jack made the gesture again of putting his fingers to his lips, as though he was pulling the words out and tossing them into the air vents on the dash.

A look of absolute shock came over Adams' face when he realized what Jack was telling him.

"Sorry to interrupt," said Jack, "but I have to take a leak. Mind pulling over?"

Adams looked dumbfounded, but nodded and mumbled, "Me, too," as he pulled over to the side of the highway.

Once Jack and Adams took a short stroll away from the car, Jack said, "The problem with being a good cop is learning to live with your conscience … especially doing our type of work. You're always questioning whether or not you're doing the right thing."

"Yeah, I agree with you there," mumbled Adams, still looking dazed.

"Maybe that's what differentiates a good cop from a bad one. Sometimes we make mistakes and have to learn to live with what we did. That's the problem with being human."

"What are you really trying to tell me?" asked Adams.

"Well, to start with, I'm telling you I think you are a hell of a good cop. I'm really going to miss working with you."

"Thanks," mumbled Adams, glancing back at the car, wondering if Jack's fear was simply paranoia.

"You and me think … and act much alike," continued Jack. "Our job is also filled with secrets. Some secrets if known could get someone killed … or sent to jail. I have done things I felt were morally right, but a court of law would not agree."

"Like yesterday?"

"Maybe, maybe not."

"That pisses me off."

"What does?" Jack asked.

"Okay, I know five of the bodies they found in Casa Blanca were knocked off by the cartel because they fucked up. Probably means good news for you, because they took the retribution out on them."

"I'm happy with that. So what's your point?"

"My point is I thought you and I were friends," said Adams.

"I think we are."

"Friends trust each other … but you obviously don't trust me."

"Why would you say that?"

"You didn't see the look we both gave you yesterday in the car when you said some guy killed El Pero?"

"No … guess I was busy consoling Lily," said Jack, frowning.

"There is no goddamned way any of the cartel guys at Casa Blanca, with the exception of Big Al, would have ever picked a fight with El Pero."

"We spoke about that last night. Maybe it was someone else's relative."

"Bullshit. El Pero was too high up. Even Big Al wouldn't give him shit in front of the guys. So for you to say somebody argued with El Pero about whose turn it was to rape Lily is absolute crap. Then to say the guy went in and shot him after is ludicrous. At first I was thinking you didn't want Lily to know … and that makes sense. I presume she didn't see you or had her eyes closed or something?"

"Do your bosses think its bullshit?" asked Jack, avoiding Adams's question.

"They're desk jockeys. They don't know squat. That's not the point. Let me finish. Now I learn Big Al was found at the bottom of the shaft with a broken neck and his nose bitten off ... there is no fucking way his guys would do that."

"You sound pissed off about it."

"Yeah, I'm pissed off!" said Adams. "Not over him being dead. I'm pissed off at you. With everything we have been through, I thought you would trust me enough to tell me the truth."

"Listen ... I'd trust you with my life ... but that doesn't mean I'm going to tell you something you don't need to know just to try and ease my conscience. Sure, sometimes I would like to confide in someone. Maybe get their assurance that whatever I did was the right thing."

"So why don't you? I was about to do that with you."

"And look what might have happened. Does it really matter if someone else agrees or not?" said Jack. "You have your own conscience and have to live with what you did. Confiding in someone might give you temporary relief, but it's the rest of your life you have to deal with. In the long run, having told someone else will give you one more thing to worry about. It is also a burden for the person you told. Keep in mind what Al Capone once said: 'Two can keep a secret if one is dead.'"

Adams looked up at the sky, then sighed and looked around at the landscape, avoiding Jack's intense stare as he thought about what had been said. He then focused his gaze on the Camaro and his face darkened. Without warning, he scooped up a rock and threw it as hard as he could and swore as the rock bounced off the car fender.

"Feel better?" asked Jack.

"No, I should have shot it," replied Adams.

"It would be the American thing to do."

Adams stared hard at Jack a moment, then grinned. "Don't give me that shit. If you had a gun you would probably put a slug up the muffler and then chew off the radiator hose and push it over a cliff."

Jack smiled in response and said, "We each have our own style."

Adams put his hand on Jack's shoulder and said, "Guess I'm not pissed at you. What you say makes sense. I think I'm pissed off at the world we live in. Don't know who the good guys are anymore."

"In my books, I'm talking to one of the good guys," replied Jack.

"Thanks, buddy."

"Let me give you a hug ... or are you afraid that will ruin your two-gun-packing macho image?"

"Only if you keep your underwear on and promise not to tell anyone. Otherwise I'll be forced to shoot ya."

"You wouldn't be the first," replied Jack.

Adams followed Jack into the main office and saw the open door into Davidson's office. Inside, District Attorney White was standing and talking to Davidson, who was sitting behind his desk.

What's he doing here again? Am I being arrested?

Then Adams saw Weber and the other two bosses were also in the office talking. By the looks on their faces, he knew they were angry.

Jack also saw them and as he approached, Davidson spotted him and gestured at him with his hand. The others turned and looked at Jack and their faces displayed a combination of anger and pure hatred. As Jack neared, Weber stepped forward and slammed the door in his face.

Jack shrugged and returned to where Adams stood. "I suddenly feel like I'm persona non grata right now. Gee, I wonder why?"

Adams didn't reply, but stared at the closed door with his mouth gaped open. Seconds later, his body trembled as he gazed around the office. Up until this moment, he still had some doubts that his car had been bugged. He didn't want to believe he was really considered a bad guy. Now he had no doubt.

As he looked at his colleagues sitting at their desks, he felt like he was in no man's land, with enemies on both sides. Family was the only thing he had left and all he wanted to do was go home and hug his wife.

"I thought I felt alone before," mumbled Adams, "but it was nothing compared to how I feel now. Are you done? I want to get the hell away from these guys."

"I'm done."

As they were heading for the door, three men were sitting in the general office talking in hushed tones to each other. One looked up at them and said, "Hang on a sec." He gave a furtive glance toward Davidson's office, before rushing into Weber's empty office, only to return a moment later and hand Jack a desk ornament. It was a small U.S. Customs and Immigration flag attached to a small plastic pole and stand.

"The guys … me …" the man started to say to Jack, but glanced at Adams and mumbled apologetically, "We didn't know, uh, until a few minutes ago that they," he nodded toward Davidson's office and continued, "uh, that they were doing what they were doing." He looked at Jack. "We wanted to give you something," he added solemnly, before turning on his heel and returning to the others.

When Jack and Adams stepped outside, Jack waved the flag in front of Adams's face and said, "Looks to me like you might not be alone as much as you think."

chapter forty-seven

It was Friday afternoon in Vancouver when Miguel and Ramiro parked their car beside a car wash. They were immediately met by two members of Satans Wrath, who directed them into the public washroom. Neither Miguel nor Ramiro protested when they were then searched for weapons and any electronic listening devices. After that, they were taken for a ride in a van being driven by one of the bikers.

Lance strolled with Damien through Stanley Park and each man was enjoying an ice-cream cone when Lance received a message on his BlackBerry.

"Seems our two Mexicans have picked up heat today," said Lance.

"Which means the police knew them all along," said Damien.

"Also means Taggart is probably dead and the cops don't give a shit if we see them or not," replied Lance.

"Looks that way."

"What do you want to do?"

"Tell them to bring the two taco boys over. We'll have to take some precautions, but I want to hear what they've got to say. We're also going to have to prepare them for the amount of heat that will be coming down on them. Make sure they don't do anything stupid like popping off wives and kids."

Twenty-five minutes later, Miguel and Ramiro met with Damien and Lance on the beach at Stanley Park. Their backs were to a seawall that rose above head level and they stood amongst a cluster of sun-bleached driftwood logs strewn on the beach.

Several members of Satans Wrath patrolled nearby to ensure none of the police who had been following would be in a position to monitor any conversation.

Damien was not a man who was shocked easily, but even his mouth hung open in stunned silence as he listened to what Miguel had to say.

"You mean to tell me you let him escape?" he said, flabbergasted.

"Not me," Miguel hastened to say. "The men in the house."

"Let me get this right," said Damien. "You beat him unconscious, strip him naked, handcuff him to a pipe, torture him, threaten his family, and then ..." Damien paused, rolling his eyes at Lance, before turning back to Miguel, "and then you let him *escape?*"

"Yes, that is what happened."

Damien glanced at Lance who shook his head and muttered, "I can't believe it."

Damien turned his attention back to Miguel. "Do you just think he might have been a little pissed off?"

"A little pissed off?"

"Do you recall me telling you Taggart was ... make

that is, a very dangerous man and to kill him immediately?"

"Yes, but —"

"But what?" snarled Damien.

"That was not my decision. It was Big Al who made that decision."

"And this house ... let me get this correct," said Damien facetiously, "you said was out in the desert, surrounded by professional soldiers with trained commandos inside."

"Yes."

"And not only did he escape, but first he shoved a gun up El Pero's ass and shot him, then bit Big Al's nose off, broke his arms, threw him down a shaft, and broke his neck?"

"Yes ... it is very sad about Big Al. They even said from the blood Big Al coughed up, it looked like his ribs had been broken, which punctured his lungs, as well."

"Yeah, it sounds to me like Taggart was a little pissed off," said Lance.

Miguel saw the sarcastic look on Damien's face and squirmed his back against the protruding end of a driftwood log before adding, "But I have a new boss, so everything is okay now. We are still interested in doing business with you."

"Do you believe me now that Taggart is a dangerous man?" asked Damien.

"Yes, of course."

"Think about what he did to El Pero and Big Al for asking questions about his family."

"What do you mean?" asked Miguel.

"Could you imagine what someone like Taggart would do if you had actually harmed his family?"

"Well ... I —"

"Then you brought a parade of policemen with you when you went to meet my guys at the car wash. Did it occur to you the police might wonder what part I had in

Taggart being tortured and the questions asked?"

"Yes, that is unfortunate," replied Miguel looking around, "but I am sure the police cannot hear us."

"I don't think you're hearing me."

"No, it is windy ... and these birds are very noisy, but it is okay, I can still hear you."

Damien looked at Lance, who shook his head in disbelief.

"So what can I tell my new boss?" asked Miguel. "Are you interested in going into business with us?"

Damien glanced at the seagulls squawking around them and smiled and said, "I'll tell you what, wait here and I will confer with my colleague for a minute before giving you an answer."

As soon as Lance and Damien walked up the stairs to the top of the seawall, Damien said, "Find out where the closest cops are."

Lance walked over to another member of Satans Wrath and returned a moment later and said, "The young couple who are sitting on the park bench down from us."

"The ones holding hands, looking like they're on their honeymoon?"

"Yup. They were both in a white Ford Taurus and followed the guys all the way from the car wash to here. At least two other cars were involved, as well."

Constables Helen Fraser and Darcy Cummings both sat on the park bench. It was Helen who first suspected their little charade wasn't working.

"Crap, I think we've been burned," she said. "Damien is pointing right at us and it looks like he's coming over."

"Be cool," cautioned Darcy. "He's probably only guessing and trying to see what our response is."

"Hello, officers," said Damien with a smile as he approached. "Make any busts under the Controlled Drugs and Substances Act yet today?"

"I'm sorry," said Darcy, looking confused. "I don't understand what you're talking about."

"Then let me explain it more clearly and help you out," replied Damien. "The two Mexicans you were following this morning in your white Ford Taurus ... you know, the two guys who led you to Wet Willy's Car wash?"

Neither Helen nor Darcy answered.

"Well as it turns out," continued Damien, "they wanted to see me. I had met them for the first time yesterday when they came uninvited to one of our clubhouses. They say they want to go into business with me."

"Uh, we don't, uh know what you're —"

"Forget it, Darcy, he knows," interjected Helen.

"Thank you," said Damien. "Now, they are both waiting for my answer as to whether we should go into business together."

"And what business would that be?" asked Helen.

"There is some confusion on that issue. All I know is it was a business agreement that Corporal Jack Taggart of your Intelligence Unit was trying to arrange. You can ask him about it."

"I see," replied Helen, "but as things stand, do you think you might be going into business with them?"

Damien glanced back at the seawall and saw where Lance was standing watching him. Lance gave him a nod and Damien turned back to Helen and Darcy and said, "You'll find the answer to that on the other side of that wall."

"We will?" asked Helen.

As Damien turned to walk away he said, "Oh, one more thing. Tell Taggart if he wishes to remain above ground, not to pretend he belongs to our club ever again."

Helen and Darcy looked at each other a moment, then hurried over to the seawall and looked down.

"Oh, Christ," muttered Helen. "Call an ambulance."

chapter forty-eight

The flight Jack and Lily took back to Vancouver went as scheduled and Jack used the time to prepare his report. They cleared customs at the Vancouver International Airport Friday night.

Jack was acutely aware of the psychologist's recommendation about keeping Lily's ordeal away from the media. He knew the reunification between Lily and her mom would be an emotionally charged event that could draw unwanted attention, so he had made arrangements to drive her directly home to her mother instead.

Jack and Lily were greeted at the airport by Natasha and Mikey. After a quick introduction and hugs, they drove Lily home.

Upon arrival at the house, Jack saw the tree in the front yard was adorned with a large yellow ribbon. He had not yet shut the engine off when Lily burst from the car and ran to hug her mom, who appeared on the porch in her wheelchair. Marcie, standing under a "welcome home" banner strung over the door, anxiously waited for her own hug.

Jack was right in his prediction about it being an emotionally charged moment. The only one who didn't have tears in their eyes was Mikey, who remained asleep in his car seat.

Monday morning saw Jack back at the office. He gave a copy of his undercover notes to his boss, Staff Sergeant Rose Wood, along with his report. She read them carefully while he sat across from her desk.

"Basically what you said when you called me Friday afternoon," she said, leaning back in her chair and nodding at the report.

"That's about all there is to say," said Jack, gesturing to the report.

"All there is to say? I think not," she said firmly.

"Oh?"

"It goes without saying I'm pleased everything turned out okay, but why the hell didn't you call me before Friday? You went into Mexico totally on your own, without authorization and without so much as even a phone call to me or anyone else to get permission."

"Three reasons," replied Jack. "First of all, there wasn't time to sit and wait for Ottawa to make a decision ... and even if they did make it in time and give authorization, policy dictates the police in Mexico would have to be informed. That would have jeopardized both Lily's life and my own."

"You might be right, but Ottawa will still be furious. You could be facing disciplinary action."

"I feel what I did was right."

"There is no moral servitude in Ottawa. They dance to what the politicians want, no matter the cost. If they think you upset some Mexican politician they'll land on you with both feet."

"I'm aware of that, but nothing they could do to me would take away how good I felt Saturday night when I brought Lily home. Let them take their best shot — it was worth it."

"What were your other two reasons for not seeking permission?"

"If I called you and gave you the details, you would have come to the same conclusion about Ottawa as I did, leaving you with two choices. Tell me I couldn't go, knowing Lily would die because of it, or give me permission to go on your own and risk both Lily and myself being murdered ... which really would have put you in hot water."

"I would have given you permission. I know you would have gone anyway," said Rose.

"I know. That was the third reason. You would have been in trouble from Ottawa for something I was going to do, anyway."

Rose drummed her fingers on her desk for a moment. "I don't need you to judge what is in my best interest. Should something like this ever occur again, let me make that call."

"Will do. Is that all?"

"No, it is not all. Besides the fact you went into Mexico without authorization, I have no idea what Ottawa or Isaac will think of all this," she said, gesturing to Jack's notes and his report. "You're basically saying you went down there, found the girl, and escaped with her when the bad guys were fighting amongst themselves."

"Timing was fortunate," replied Jack, being careful not to use the word *coincidence*, which had been used all too often in his past investigations.

"Then the next day the police discover there are a total of seven bodies. Was that all good timing ... what the hell ... a coincidence, too?"

"No, that was not a coincidence. Five of those men were killed by the cartel for letting me escape."

"I see. So it is only two out of seven who died coincidentally with you being there?"

"Uh, yes, I guess you could say that, although I understand Clive Slater is missing. I am sure he was killed, as well."

Rose sighed and flipped through Jack's notes again before looking up. "You said you were clubbed over the head, stripped naked, handcuffed ... and Big Al was going to ask you questions about colleagues and ... family," she noted, putting the emphasis on the last word.

"Correct."

"You were then poked with a cattle prod by El Pero and passed out."

"Correct."

"And when you regained consciousness and were picking the lock on the handcuffs, El Pero was actually in the act of raping Lily."

"I believe so. That's when I saw another guy going —"

Rose's face hardened. "Stop it right there!" she snapped. "Don't you ever —" She paused, and after letting out a deep breath and regaining her composure, she said, "I think I've got a clear enough picture of what happened, despite my belief there are certain omissions in your report and your notes." She stared hard at Jack. "What? No acting surprised? No look of concern followed by denials?"

"I had the distinct feeling you didn't want me to lie to you."

"Good. I hope we understand each other. Who knows, maybe someday you will trust me enough to tell me exactly what those omissions were."

"I should put you in touch with Special Agent Adams on that issue."

"Oh? Would he be more forthcoming?"

"On the contrary. He almost got in trouble for telling a friend something."

"I see," replied Wood with a frown. "Well at least I know you had nothing to do with Miguel and Ramiro."

"Who are they?"

"Two Mexicans from the auto body shop here in Vancouver. The same shop where they took Slater's truck, just before you left to go to El Paso. On Friday, the narcs followed them to Stanley Park and saw them meet Damien."

"When I was being tortured, Big Al said, thanks to me, they were thinking of going into business with Satans Wrath."

"Guess the business proposal the Mexicans offered wasn't accepted. After the bikers left, the narcs found both Miguel and Ramiro in bad need of medical attention. They're both still in hospital."

"Did the Mexicans identify who did it?"

"No, they're not that stupid."

"Guess I should thank Damien."

"He had a message for you, too. He said if you want to stay above ground, never to use his club like that again."

"Yes, I figured he was irritated when he told Big Al to kill me."

"I want you to go home for a couple of days. I'll have the secretary type up your UC notes and forward them with the report. Ottawa won't be happy you didn't get permission, but I'll do what I can to support you."

"Thank you," replied Jack, getting up.

"There is one more thing," said Rose, "about your torture ... the cattle prod ... were you prodded where I suspect they would have prodded you?"

"Yes."

"Explains why you passed out."

"I'm glad I did."

"Any long-term bad effects?"

Jack grinned and said, "The boys seemed to work fine last night. The only thing I wonder about is if I father another child, will it have really curly hair?"

chapter forty-nine

On Wednesday morning, Assistant Commissioner Isaac received a call from the commissioner in Ottawa, who skipped any pleasantries and immediately asked, "What are you doing about Taggart?"

"In what way?" asked Isaac.

"In what way? That is the question. I'd like him charged with a criminal offence."

"A criminal offence? Are you questioning the validity of his report in regards to the seven bodies found at the house in Mexico?"

"No, not that, but I appreciate your thinking. I've already looked into it. Our liaison officer in Mexico City was contacted by a police commander in Juarez. One of his own detectives was one of the seven bodies they found. The commander wanted to thank us for the work we did in identifying the corrupt officer and also for finding the tunnel."

"He wasn't upset to find out a Canadian policeman had gone there without authorization?"

"Apparently not. The commander said he understood

341 Birds of a Feather

there were some tight time restraints and a life was at risk. Anyway, our L.O. asked him about the victim who was shot anally and the other victim who died of multiple injuries. The commander said it happens all the time where these guys get drunk and fight amongst themselves. Also the retribution on the other five men was predictable, considering the damage done to the cartel's smuggling route."

"So what criminal offence are you talking about in regard to Corporal Taggart?" asked the commissioner.

"Birds of a Feather. Taggart deliberately told the subject of a wiretap investigation there was a bug in the car. That is an offence. At lease it is in Canada. I'm sure it is in the U.S., as well."

"Corporal Taggart was also targeted."

"It doesn't matter. Even if a criminal trips over a bug in his own house, it is a criminal offence for him to tell anyone else about it."

"I don't have any transcripts of the conversation that took place in regards to Birds of a Feather. Did Corporal Taggart actually tell Special Agent Adams there was an electronic eavesdropping device in the car?"

"Not in those words, but it was obvious he changed the conversation when Adams was about to tell him what he did."

"That would hardly hold up in court."

"That's the problem. I said I would like him charged with a criminal offence, I didn't say we could. You know Taggart ... do you think we could get him to crack under interrogation or at least say something incriminatory?"

"I'm certain he wouldn't. Look how it went with Birds of a Feather ... and that was when he should have felt safe to talk openly."

"This is really embarrassing. A national disgrace."

"A national disgrace?"

"We sent Taggart down there for the purpose of

helping the Americans catch their rogue agent. This was supposed to make us look good. Instead, this happens. They're absolutely furious down there."

"I thought the primary objective was to find the girl. Corporal Taggart did that," Isaac said.

"That's incidental. We didn't even get any press on it. Right now the issue is Taggart. If we can't charge him criminally, then at the very least, I sure as hell expect you to give him an official reprimand for his personnel file."

"As you wish, but we still shouldn't overlook that he did do an admirable job down there under extreme risk of his own personal safety."

"Admirable job? What are you talking about? He went down there without authorization!"

"I don't think Lily or her mother cares about that."

"Who? Oh, them. That's not the point. Besides, as far as rescuing the girl, Taggart simply got lucky."

"Lucky?"

"It was a lucky coincidence for him that the Mexicans started fighting each other when he was rescuing the girl, or things might have turned out much differently. His overall stupidity and complete disregard for policy could have gotten them both killed."

"There's no doubt he placed himself at extreme risk."

"You're damn right he did. It was totally unacceptable. I have to go, but I want you to send me a copy of the official reprimand you put on his file."

"Yes, sir."

After Isaac hung up, he muttered, "Lucky coincidence?" and shook his head. His next telephone call was to Staff Sergeant Rose Wood, telling her he expected to see Corporal Taggart in his office first thing the following morning.

At eight-thirty Thursday morning, Jack entered Isaac's

secretary's office and was told to go directly in.

Isaac sat behind his desk and with an angry nod, gestured to a chair across from his desk. After Jack sat down, Isaac said, "You went into Mexico without authorization ... even after it was made totally clear in the operational plan that you were not to do so."

"Yes, sir, I did."

"Did you even try to call anyone to gain permission?"

"No, sir, I did not."

"Your behaviour was cavalier, irresponsible, and reckless. You not only risked your life, but the potential lives of other policemen who may have tried to save you because of the stunt you pulled."

"Yes, sir."

"What I am telling you is documented in writing before me. Sign it as acknowledgement you have read it, after which it will be placed on your personnel file."

"Yes, sir," replied Jack, taking the document and reading what he had been told verbally. He signed the bottom of the page and handed it back.

"That is all," said Isaac. "Get out!"

As Jack was leaving the secretary's outer office, her phone rang and she answered, then said, "Corporal Taggart, please wait a moment." She spoke into the phone briefly and when she hung up she said, "The assistant commissioner wants you to go back in."

Jack sighed and went back into the office as the secretary closed the door behind him.

Isaac immediately approached him with his hand extended and said, "Jack! Good to see you! I wanted to tell you I think you did a fantastic job down in Mexico," he said, smiling.

Jack accepted the handshake as he tried to figure out what was happening.

"I was so pleased to find out you were able to rescue Lily Rae."

"It made me happy as well, sir."

"At immense personal risk to yourself, I might add. As a member of the force, I have to say … what you did makes me feel proud."

"Thank you, sir."

Isaac handed Jack a document off his desk and said, "I have written a letter expressing my views for the purpose of placing it on your personnel file."

Jack read the letter and saw it was filled with accolades.

"Thank you, sir. I don't know what to say."

The smile disappeared from Isaac's face and he lowered his voice and said, "I would suggest you say nothing … ever. There is one more thing I want you to know … and it is to be kept strictly between us."

"Sir?"

"It was not my idea to send you to El Paso. That decision was made in Ottawa."

Jack felt stunned. Up until this moment he had thought it was only a coincidence he had been paired up with Adams. *This was no coincidence … they were after me, too …*

"You look surprised," noted Isaac. "Did you think it was a coincidence you were assigned with Special Agent Adams?"

"Yes, sir, I did."

"You, of all people, shouldn't believe in coincidences. I know I don't."

epilogue

On April 10th, Jack and Natasha announced the birth of their second son, Steven Thomas.

Drug lord Rafael Aguilar Guajardo was assassinated by his under-boss, Amado Carrillo Fuentes, two years after the author worked on assignment in Ciudad Juarez.

Amado Carrillo Fuentes then died under mysterious circumstances while undergoing plastic surgery four years after taking power. His brother, Vicente Carrillo Fuentes, took over as head of the cartel.

Three years after the author met with Jose Refugio Rubalcava in a back alley in Ciudad Juarez, U.S authorities checked an abandoned car parked on the Bridge of the Americas. In the trunk they discovered the bodies of Rubalcava and his two sons. The cartel left the bodies on the bridge as a sign they believed Rubalcava had been talking to the Americans too much.

Vicente Carrillo Fuentes has been charged with the murders, but despite a $5-million reward posted for his capture by the FBI and a $2-million award posted by the Mexican authorities, he remains a free man.

At the time of this book's printing, Vicente Carrillo Fuentes continues to remain in charge of one of two major cartels locked in a vicious battle for control of the drug market in the region.

Within the last couple of years, the murder toll in Ciudad Juarez alone has surpassed six thousand. With the increasing appetite of Canadian and American cocaine users, financial support for the cartels is growing ... as is the ever-increasing greed of the cartels.

The continued acts of violence and murder involving innocent citizens are also expanding geographically. Recently in the United States, it was discovered Mexican cartels have been paying teenagers on retainer to commit murders, including the assassination of U.S. law enforcement officers.

The cartels are currently viewing Canada like a beach hawker views a new tourist.

Anyone interested in further information concerning the murders of the Rubalcava family, Vicente Carrillo Fuentes, or the impact the cartels are having on Canada, can find it at the following websites:

Amarillo Globe News: http://amarillo.com/stories/2000/ 09/15/tex_cartel.shtml

Corpus Christi Caller-Times: http://www.caller2.com/ 2000/september/15/today/texas_me/4249.html

Denver Post: http://blogs.denverpost.com/captured/2011 /12/21/in-focus-mexico-drug-war-five-years- later/5151/

Toronto Star: www.thestar.com/article/642966

Wikipedia: http://wapedia.mobi/en/Vicente_Carrillo_ Fuentes

more jack taggart mysteries

Loose Ends
A Jack Taggart Mystery
978-1550025651
$11.99

Jack Taggart, an undercover Mountie, lives in a world where the good guys and the bad guys change places in a heartbeat. Taggart is very good at what he does. Too good to be playing by the rules. The brass decide to assign a new partner to spy on him. Taggart's new partner discovers a society dependent upon unwritten rules. To break these rules is to lose respect. To lose respect is to lose one's life. *Loose Ends* is terrifying. It is a tale of violence, corruption, and retribution, but it is also a story of honour and respect.

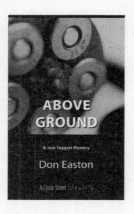

Above Ground
A Jack Taggart Mystery
978-1550026818
$11.99

For RCMP undercover operative Jack Taggart, the consequences of his actions in *Loose Ends* linger. His deal with
Damien, leader of the Satans Wrath motorcycle gang,
has put him in a bind and has jeopardized an informant
in the gang. Meanwhile, other members of the gang, led
by a mysterious figure known only as "The Boss," have
been working to eliminate Taggart by destroying the
lives of anyone with connections to him. And if the bad
guys aren't enough of an obstacle, there are problems to
be found on the force itself. With Jack's life and career on
the line, *Above Ground* is a tough and gritty follow-up
that will more than satisfy readers who were pulled into
the dark Vancouver underworld by *Loose Ends*.

Angel in the Full Moon
A Jack Taggart Mystery
978-1550028133
$11.99

In this sequel to *Loose Ends* and *Above Ground*, Jack Taggart continues as an undercover Mountie whose quest for justice takes him from the sunny, tourist-laden beaches of Cuba to the ghettos of Hanoi. His targets deal in human flesh, smuggling unwitting victims for the sex trade. Jack's personal vendetta for justice is questioned by his partner, until he reveals the secret behind his motivation, exposing the very essence of his soul. This is the world of the undercover operative: a world of lies, treachery, and deception. A world where violence erupts without warning, like a ticking time bomb on a crowded bus. It isn't a matter of if that bomb will go off — it is a matter of how close you are to it when it does.

Samurai Code
A Jack Taggart Mystery
978-1554886975
$11.99

In the fourth Jack Taggart Mystery, the implacable Mountie goes undercover to follow the trail of a cheap Saturday-night special found at the scene of a murder. He traces the gun until the trail leads him to a suspected heroin importer. Taggart poses as an Irish gangster and penetrates the criminal organization, only to discover that the real crime boss is a mysterious figure out of Asia. When Taggart and his partner find themselves alone and without backup in the lair of one of the largest yakuza organized crime families in Japan, the clash of culture explodes into violence when their real identities are discovered.